UNDERWORLD

UNDERWORLD

Novelization by Greg Cox
Based on the screenplay by Danny McBride
Story by Kevin Grevioux and
Len Wiseman & Danny McBride

POCKET STAR BOOKS
New York   London   Toronto   Sydney

This book is a work of fiction. Names, characters, places and incidents are products of the author's imagination or are used fictitiously. Any resemblance to actual events or locales or persons, living or dead, is entirely coincidental.

An *Original* Publication of POCKET BOOKS

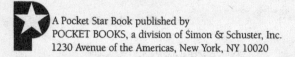

A Pocket Star Book published by
POCKET BOOKS, a division of Simon & Schuster, Inc.
1230 Avenue of the Americas, New York, NY 10020

Copyright © 2003 by Lakeshore Entertainment Group LLC
Motion Picture Photography © 2003 Lakeshore Entertainment Group LLC
Motion Picture Artwork © 2003 Screen Gems, Inc.
All rights reserved.

ISBN: 0-7434-8071-6

First Pocket Books paperback edition September 2003

10 9 8 7 6 5 4

POCKET STAR BOOKS and colophon are registered
trademarks of Simon & Schuster, Inc.

Manufactured in the United States of America

For information regarding special discounts for bulk purchases,
please contact Simon & Schuster Special Sales at 1-800-456-6798
or business@simonandschuster.com

UNDERWORLD

Chapter One

Budapest was no stranger to war. Over the long, bloody centuries, the Hungarian capital had been captured and fought over by a succession of conquerors—Huns, Goths, Magyars, Turks, Hapsburgs, Nazis, and Soviets—before finally reclaiming its independence in the concluding decade of the twentieth century. But all these merely human conflicts were fleeting in comparison with the shadowy, ageless war now being fought in the moonlit streets and alleys of the ancient city.

A war that, at long last, might be nearing its end.

Driving rain pelted the rooftops, while the howling autumn wind carried a hint of winter's bite. A grotesque stone gargoyle, oily black and slick with rain, perched on the crumbling ledge of the historic Klotild Palace, an imposing, five-story apartment block adorned by elaborate Spanish-Baroque stonework. The one-hundred-year-old edifice, whose ground floor now housed an art gallery, a café, and various stylish boutiques, overlooked Ferenciek Square, a busy hub of pedestrian and auto traffic located near the heart of central Pest. Buses, trolleys, and taxis zipped along the cobblestone streets below, braving the torrential downpour.

Another figure crouched beside the petrified gargoyle, very nearly as still and silent: a beautiful woman, clad in lustrous black leather, with long, dark brown hair and alabaster skin. Heedless of both the storm and her own precarious roost upon the narrow ledge, she gazed grimly from the rooftop. Her striking chestnut eyes were fixed on the teeming streets beneath her, even as her somber thoughts looked back upon centuries of unremitting warfare.

Could it truly be, Selene reflected, *that the war is almost over?* Her elegant face, as pale and lovely as the moon goddess after whom she was named, was a mask of cold-blooded concentration, betraying no sign of the restless anxieties troubling her mind. *It seems unthinkable, and yet . . .*

The enemy had been losing ground for nearly six centuries, ever since its crushing defeat back in 1409, when a daring assault team had penetrated the opposition's hidden fortress in Moldavia. Lucian, the most feared and ruthless leader ever to rule the lycan horde, had been killed at last, his men scattered to the wind in a single evening of purifying flame and retribution. Yet the ancient blood feud had proved unwilling to follow Lucian to the grave. Though the lycans were fewer in number, the war had become even more perilous—for the moon no longer held her sway. Older, more powerful lycans were now able to change form at will, posing an even greater threat to Selene and her fellow Death Dealers. For close to six hundred years, the Dealers, an elite squad of vampire warriors, had pursued the surviving man-beasts, the weapons changing but never the tactics: hunt the lycans down, and kill them off, one by one. A most successful campaign.

Perhaps too successful, she mused ruefully. The tail of her glossy black trench coat flapped in the wind as she leaned forward over the edge of the rooftop, defying gravity. A five-story plunge beckoned precipitously, but Selene's mind still dwelt on the war and its potential aftermath. According to all their intel, obtained at great cost by undercover agents and paid human informants, the lycans were scattered and in disarray, their numbers scant and diminishing. After countless generations of brutal combat, it appeared the loathsome beasts finally had become an endangered species, a thought that filled Selene with profoundly mixed feelings.

On one hand, she eagerly looked forward to exterminating the lycans once and for all; this was, after all, what she had lived for all these years. The world would be a better place when the carcass of the last savage man-beast was left rotting in the sun. And yet . . . Selene couldn't help feeling a tremor of apprehension at the prospect of an end to her long crusade. For such as she, the final extinction of the lycans would signal the close of an era. Soon, like the discarded weapons of the previous centuries, she, too, would become obsolete.

A pity, she thought, her tongue tracing the polished contours of her fangs. Tracking and killing lycans had been her only pleasure for ages, and she had come to love it dearly. *What will I do when the war is over?* the shapely vampire fretted, facing an eternity without purpose. *What am I if not a Death Dealer?*

The icy rain sluiced down her face and form, forming sooty puddles on the ornate rooftop. The smoggy night air smelled of ozone, presaging thunderbolts to come. Selene ignored the fierce wind and rain, maintaining her stakeout upon the ledge. She searched intently for her prey, craving action to dispel the melancholy doubts haunting her mind. She glanced impatiently at the clock tower of the Klotild's sister building, on the other side of busy Szabadsajto Avenue. It was a quarter to nine, the sun had been down for hours, so where the hell were those goddamn lycanthropes?

The crowded sidewalks below were choked with umbrellas, obscuring her view of the pedestrians scurrying about in the rain, defying the storm from beneath their concealing bumbershoots. Selene clenched her fists in frustration, her sharpened nails digging into her ivory palms. Surveillance teams had reported definite lycan activity in this district, but she had yet to spot a single target. *Where are you hiding, you bloody animals?* she thought irritably.

She began to fear that their prey had eluded them, that the wolf pack had decamped under the cover of daylight, seeking a more secluded lair elsewhere. Sadly, it would not be the first time a mangy pack of lycanthropes managed to relocate before the Death Dealers caught up with them.

She shivered beneath her leathers, the inclement weather beginning to get to her despite her snug attire and intense resolve. It was tempting to give up and call it a night, but no, that was not an option. A look of stubborn determination came over her face as she shrugged off her momentary weakness. There were lycans abroad tonight, she knew it, and she wasn't about to let them get away, even if it meant crouching in the rain until nearly sunrise.

Her keen eyes searched the hectic streets below. At first, she spotted nothing suspicious. Then—*wait! Over there!* Her eyes narrowed as they zeroed in on two unsavory-looking individuals making their way down a crowded sidewalk. Eschewing umbrellas, the two men roughly weaved through the ambulatory throng, using jabbing elbows and surly glares to clear a path for themselves amidst the myriad other pedestrians abroad in the storm. Scuffed leather jackets protected the men from the worst of the wind and rain.

An angry hiss escaped Selene's pale red lips. Even in

4

human form, the roving lycans filled her veins with hatred and revulsion. Their present shape could not deceive her; she knew full well that the two ruffians were not really people at all, just filthy animals masquerading as men.

She recognized them at once from her intel briefings. The larger lycanthrope, some one-hundred-plus kilos of barely contained murderous intent, was known as Raze. Some of the analysts back at the mansion maintained that the muscular black lycan was now the alpha-male of the central European pack, while others speculated that some other lycan, as yet unidentified, outranked even Raze. Either way, the bald-headed bruiser struck Selene as a formidable opponent; she looked forward to filling him full of silver.

His companion, a smaller lycan maybe eighty kilos in weight, was obviously a lesser specimen. He was Caucasian in appearance, with nervous, ratlike features and a head of untidy brown hair. Selene watched as Raze rudely shoved the other lycan, whose name was reputedly Trix, out of his way as the bullying lycan hurried down the congested sidewalk, intent on the Elders only knew what sort of barbaric mischief.

Looking past the two lycans, trying to anticipate their destination, she found her eyes briefly snared by a good-looking young man trekking through the rain about half a block ahead of Raze and Trix. Ruggedly handsome, with light brown hair and a disarmingly scruffy fringe of whiskers, he was dressed casually in a windbreaker, dark pants, and sneakers. No umbrella shielded his slender person from the storm, and he hurried east with his hands cupped above his head. Something about his manner and bearing suggested to Selene that the attractive youth was an American. She felt a twinge of regret that she couldn't get a closer look at his eyes.

Never mind that! she scolded herself harshly, appalled that she had allowed the human to distract her from her mission, however momentarily. This was no time for boy watching, even if there were room in her life for romance, which there most certainly was not. She was a soldier, not a dreamy-eyed maiden or wanton seducer; her immortality had been given over to the crusade against the lycans, and killing werewolves was the only passion she indulged.

And after the war? Once again, her misgivings about the future intruded upon her consciousness, mixed with the tantalizing possibilities of a brand-new existence. *What then?* But first, she reminded herself, there were still battles to be won—and lycans to be slain.

Turning her attention back to Raze and Trix, Selene looked up to see if her fellow warriors had detected the two lycans as well. A smile of satisfaction lifted her lips as she saw that, atop a neo-Gothic office building on the other side of a dingy alley, Rigel already had his digital camera out and was busily taking snapshots of the unsuspecting pair below them. *I should have known better than to doubt his alertness,* she thought, pleased by the dashing vampire's skill and professionalism. Rigel's serene, angelic expression belied his effectiveness as a Death Dealer. He had killed more lycans personally than Selene readily could recall.

Like her, the other vampire was perched like a gargoyle above the streets. The yowling wind made it impossible for Selene to hear Rigel's camera at work, but she had no doubt that the expensive digital device was clicking away as Rigel took advantage of his lofty vantage point to capture several candid photos of their foes. Examining the photos afterward would help Selene confirm tonight's kills.

Assuming the hunt went well, of course. She knew better than to underestimate their lycan prey.

Rigel lowered his camera, his surveillance work complete. Selene glimpsed his turquoise eyes shimmering in the moonlight. His slicked-backed hair and refined Slavic features lent him an (entirely unintentional) resemblance to a young Bela Lugosi, back when the legendary movie Dracula was still a matinee idol on the Hungarian stage. Rigel cocked his head like a bird of prey and peered across the lonely alley separating the two buildings, awaiting Selene's signal to proceed.

She didn't even bother to check on Nathaniel, confident that the third vampire was equally ready, just as a Death Dealer should be. Turning her gaze downward, she watched in silence as the two lycans passed directly beneath her roost. They moved with deliberate purpose, seemingly unaware of the vampires' presence. Selene wondered in passing what foul errand had drawn Raze and Trix from their hidden den.

No matter, she concluded, tracking the disguised manbeasts with hate-filled eyes. The very sight of the vile creatures made her deathless heart beat faster, provoking an instinctive urge to wipe the voracious beasts off the face of the earth. Long-dead images flashed before her mind's eye.

Twin girls, no more than six years old, screaming in mortal terror. An older girl, on the verge of womanhood, her throat savagely torn open. A silver-haired man in antiquated attire, his skull cracked open to reveal the pulped gray matter of his brain. A cozy parlor, its sheltering walls liberally splattered with gore. Mutilated bodies and limbs, once belonging to deeply cherished souls, ripped asunder and cast aside like crimson flower petals . . .

Unhealed wounds bled afresh deep within Selene's core. Her fingers rested on the cold metal grips of the twin automatic pistols holstered beneath her trench coat, and she glared in silent fury at Raze and his skulking accomplice. The lycans' intentions were of no consequence tonight, she resolved. Their plans were about to be canceled—permanently.

More than twenty meters below, Selene's quarry loped down the block. They splashed carelessly through greasy puddles as they elbowed their way east onto Ferenciek Square. Holding her breath in anticipation, she waited a beat, then flashed a silent hand signal to her waiting comrades in arms. Without a moment's qualm, she stepped confidently off the ledge.

Like a leather-clad specter, she plummeted a full five stories toward the stony, unyielding floor of the alley. The death-defying fall almost certainly would have killed a mortal woman, or at the very least left her broken and bleeding upon the pavement, yet Selene landed with the nimble elegance of a jaguar, so inhumanly smooth and graceful that she appeared to be striding briskly away before her black leather boots even touched down upon the rain-swept cobblestones.

She was thankful that the punishing weather had cleared this particular side street of humanity, unlike the busier thoroughfares nearby. No startled eyes, human or otherwise, witnessed Selene's preternatural descent or heard the stealthy rustle of wet leather that heralded Rigel's appearance from around the corner. Selene acknowledged the other vampire's presence with the merest nod of her head, then looked up as Nathaniel—a pale-skinned apparition with a mane of flowing black hair—dropped onto the cobblestones from above, falling in behind the other two Death Dealers.

A trio of steely-eyed killers, more superlatively lethal than any merely human assassins, Selene and her deadly comrades melted into the crowd on Szabadsajto Avenue. Remaining far less conspicuous than their more ill-mannered prey, they expertly shadowed the two lycans, neither of whom displayed any sign that he was aware of their pursuers. *Just as it should be,* Selene thought, smiling in expectation of the slaughter to come. The comforting weight of her 9-mm Beretta pistols rested securely against her hips.

The bustling city square, packed with innocent human bystanders, was obviously no place to stage an ambush, but she felt positive that an ideal opportunity would present itself if they just followed the lycans long enough. *With any luck, they'll be dead before they even know they're under attack!*

Downtown Pest, as opposed to palatial Buda on the other side of the Danube, was a thriving urban center equipped with all the amenities of modern life. Smoky espresso bars and Internet cafés looked out onto Ferenciek Square, named after an eighteenth-century Transylvanian prince. Bright yellow boxes, housing state-of-the-art computer terminals, squatted on the street corners, providing automated information and directions for both tourists and residents alike. The high-tech guides coexisted with red public post boxes and closely monitored parking meters.

Selene saw Raze furtively glance back over his shoulder and ducked behind the welcome cover of a tall green telephone box. Luckily, the wary lycan did not seem to have spotted her and promptly continued on his way.

A lighted sign, flaunting a large blue M against a white background, caught her eye. From the looks of it, Raze and Trix were navigating toward the sign, which indicated an entrance to a Metro station beneath the square. *Of course,* she realized; the prowling lycans were doubtless heading for the Underground, to catch the M3 line to parts unknown.

This did not concern her overmuch. Having finally

sighted two promising targets, she was hardly going to let them elude her so easily. Selene signaled her companions, pointing out the Metro station's assorted entrances and exits, and the three vampires dispersed noiselessly, blending into the churning sea of umbrellas like ethereal beings composed of nothing but insubstantial shadows and rain . . .

Chapter Two

Shit! Michael Corvin thought as he dashed for the Metro entrance, holding his hands above his head in a futile effort to keep from being soaked entirely by the nocturnal deluge. The young American kicked himself mentally for forgetting his umbrella back at his tiny apartment. *Just my luck we had to get the storm of the century,* he thought, shaking his head in good-natured bemusement. His light brown hair was plastered to his scalp, and a trickle of cold rainwater leaked beneath the collar of his nylon windbreaker to send an ice-cold shiver down the entire length of his spine. *The night's already off to a bad start, and I haven't even made it to work yet!*

He glanced at his *(thank God!)* waterproof wristwatch. If he hurried, he could still make it to the hospital in time for his nine o'clock shift, assuming the subways were running on schedule. Then he only had to survive nine-plus hours in the ER before venturing out into the open again. *Probably still be raining then, too,* he figured.

A gibbous moon peeked through the massed black storm clouds overhead. Michael grimaced at the sight of the moon—and the thought of the long hours ahead. He wasn't looking forward to tonight's shift; the casualty ward always got crazier as the full moon approached, and the swollen yellow disk in the sky was only a sliver away from full.

Times like this, he couldn't help wondering if moving to Hungary had been such a good idea . . .

His sneakers overflowing with water, he sloshed over to the steps leading to the subway station. *"Bejarat,"* read the metal sign posted above the stairs, much to Michael's relief. "Entrance" and "Exit" (*"Kijarat"*) were two of the first words he had learned upon arriving in Budapest months ago, along with the Hungarian equivalents of "Do you speak English?" (*"Beszel angolul?"*) and "I don't understand" (*"Nem ertem"*).

He was thankful his Hungarian had improved since then.

To his frustration, the concrete archway at the bottom of the steps was clotted by a swarm of damp Hungarians fumbling with their umbrellas, which forced him to spend several more seconds in the pouring rain. By the time he finally reached the shelter of the station itself, he looked and felt like a drowned rat. *Oh, well,* he thought, trying to maintain a sense of humor about the whole situation. *If I wanted to be dry all the time, I should have looked for a residency in the Sahara!*

Although Budapest had boasted the first underground Metro system on the Continent, constructed in 1894, the blue M3 line had been in operation only since the 1970s. As a result, the Ferenciek Square Station was sleek and modern looking, with spotless tile floors and pristine, graffiti-free walls. Michael fished a pale blue ticket (good for thirty days) out of his pocket and franked it in the machine in front of the nearest turnstile. A puddle formed beneath him as gravity did its best to dry him.

Sopping wet, he slicked his hair back as he rode an escalator down to the platform, which was jammed with milling commuters. A good sign, he realized; the large crowd meant that he hadn't just missed an uptown train.

Idly scanning the soggy assemblage, he caught his breath in his throat as his gaze fell on an amazing-looking woman standing on the platform below, leaning back against a kiosk. A startling and spectacular vision, she was clad in glistening black leather from her neck down to her knee-high boots. A long black trench coat, belted at her waist, failed to conceal her lithe, athletic figure, while her porcelain features bore a timeless beauty and glamour. A jagged crop of dark brown hair gave her a sexy electricity that made Michael's pulse speed up. She looked out of place amidst the everyday hustle and bustle of the Metro station: an exotic apparition, wild, mysterious, enticing . . .

Everything I'm not, he thought wryly. Absolutely riveted by this astonishing eyeful, he was unable to look away, even when she raised her head to stare right back at him!

For an endless moment, their eyes met. Michael found himself drowning in enigmatic chestnut-colored pools that seemed to hold unfathomable depths far beyond his ability to probe or comprehend. The mystery woman returned his gaze, her eyes seeming to penetrate all the way to the back of his skull. Her frozen, neutral expression divulged little clue to what was going on behind that perfect face. Michael found himself wishing that he wasn't looking quite so bedraggled at the moment.

The chestnut orbs examined him frankly, and just for a split second, Michael thought he saw a glimmer of interest, mixed with perhaps a trace of ineffable sorrow and regret. Then, to both his relief and his disappointment, she looked away, choosing to glance up and down the length of the platform instead. *Who are you?* Michael wondered, consumed by something more than mere curiosity. *Where did you come from? What are you looking for?*

The escalator carried him downward, closer to the woman by the kiosk. Michael swallowed hard, debating whether he had the nerve to say something to her. *Excuse me, miss,* he rehearsed mentally, *but I couldn't help gawking at you . . .*

Just as the moving stairs reached the bottom, however, and Michael started to step onto the platform, a bright blue train came roaring into the station, accompanied by a gust of cool air and a deafening blast of noise. The train's sudden arrival startled Michael, momentarily shattering the spell the bewitching stranger had cast over him, and when he turned to look again for the lady in question, he discovered that she had vanished from sight completely.

"Damn," he muttered under his breath. The subway doors hissed open, and the impatient commuters surged toward the waiting train. Michael expended a few more seconds searching for a glimpse of the leather-clad enchantress, then reluctantly headed for the train as well.

Probably just as well, he thought, utterly failing to convince himself. An amplified voice spoke over the station's loudspeakers, instructing the people on the platform to step aside and let the arriving passengers exit the train. *I'm running late for work as it is.*

Hidden in the shadows beneath the escalator, Selene watched the wide-eyed American youth turn toward the sleek blue train. For the second time in less than ten minutes, she chastised herself for letting the nameless human's striking good looks divert her from the mission. Still, she had to admit that her undead heart had skipped a beat when she saw him coming down the escalator, even as her

14

fascinated gaze had lingered on his chiseled countenance much longer than it should have. *I must be getting feeble-minded and girlish in my old age,* she thought archly, unable to shake the memory of the American's pale brown eyes.

Raze and Trix came down the escalator a few moments after the unlikely object of her attention. The odious sight and smell of the lycanthropes brought her back to business. She watched intently as the uncouth pair joined the horde descending on the newly arrived train. Farther down the platform, artfully concealed amidst the station's murkier nooks and crannies, Rigel assiduously kept his eyes on the lycans as well. He and Selene exchanged a glance, then simultaneously slipped from their hiding places to trail after their detestable quarry.

Selene was grateful for the backup when the two lycans split up, spreading out through the advancing throng like timber wolves converging on an unsuspecting deer. She signaled Rigel to take Raze, who was heading roughly in the other vampire's direction, while she stayed close to Trix. Nathaniel, she knew, was still aboveground, keeping watch over the station's entrances just in case any lycan reinforcements showed up unexpectedly.

So far, so good, she thought, maintaining a discreet distance from both lycans. The motion of the crowd carried them toward the open doors of the subway train, and Selene wondered curiously where the clueless lycans were leading them. Perhaps all the way to the creatures' latest lair?

She glanced over at Raze, who was standing outside the train, about midway down the platform. To her concern, he suddenly halted in his tracks and sniffed the pungent air of the station. *Hell,* she thought, instantly on guard. *I don't like the looks of this.*

Her hands crept toward the matching Berettas hidden

15

under her trench coat, even as Raze spun about suddenly, catching a glimpse of Rigel. Panic flooded his dark mahogany face, and he reached beneath his own jacket and whipped out a modified Uzi. "BLOOOOODS!" he shouted in a deep, *basso profundo* voice. Gunfire erupted from the muzzle of his submachine gun, turning the crowded Metro platform into a scene of utter panic.

The Uzi's harsh report echoed cacophonously within the subterranean confines of the subway station, all but drowning out the frightened shrieks of the terrified human commuters. Frantic men and women hit the deck or else stampeded for the nearest exit. Selene and Rigel dived for cover, taking refuge behind adjacent concrete support columns as they swiftly drew their own firearms. Rigel was equipped with an MP5 submachine gun, while Selene relied on her trusty Berettas.

Ignoring the fear-crazed humans, Raze swept the platform with a blistering hail of automatic weapons fire. Peering out from behind the concrete column, as the relentless fusillade chipped away at the white enamel tiles covering the support pillar, Selene observed that the lycan's chattering Uzi was firing a type of ammo she had never encountered before. The cascading bullets literally glowed with their own built-in illumination, shining so brightly that it actually hurt her eyes to look at them.

What in the Elders' name . . . ? she thought in confusion. Her fingers squeezed the triggers of her Berettas, returning the lycan's fire with a barrage of silver bullets.

Nathaniel paced back and forth in front of the Metro entrance, beneath the protective awning of a bistro across the street from the station. *They also serve who only stand and wait,* he mused, recalling the immortal words of Milton.

16

Nathaniel had met the great poet once, in London in 1645, while tracking down a band of renegade lycans amidst the chaos and bloodshed of the English Civil War. *A shame that we never tried to make him an immortal . . .*

The leather-clad vampire maintained a lookout over the streets and sidewalks surrounding the station, lest his comrades be surprised by another pack of lycans on the prowl. It distressed Nathaniel that Selene and Rigel most likely would have to follow the two lycans onto a departing train, leaving him behind, but he trusted his fellow Death Dealers to contact him once they reached their destination. If the fates were kind, Nathaniel would not miss out on all the action.

The unmistakable clatter of gunfire upset the night, coming from the subway tunnels below the square. Nathaniel sprang into action, racing across the street toward the entrance to the station. Horns honked angrily behind him as he took the stairs several steps at a time. Terrified commuters, fleeing the alarming din of the unleashed firearms, came rushing up the steps, impeding his progress, but the impassioned vampire tossed the frightened men and women aside like rag dolls.

Hold on! he thought urgently as he landed deftly upon the mud-tracked floor of the subway. He was only too aware that Selene and Rigel faced an equal number of bloodthirsty lycans. A Walther P-88 pistol in each hand, he tore down the tunnel toward the turnstile, anxious to lend the other Death Dealers a much-needed numerical advantage. The continuing blare of the gunfight added fuel to his haste. It sounded as though his embattled comrades were holding their own, but for how much longer?

The soles of his boots smacked loudly against the tiled floor. Traumatized humans, pale-faced and gasping, threw themselves against the tunnel walls to avoid the gun-wielding, black-clad figure rushing insanely toward the clamorous din of the underground combat. Nathaniel paid no attention to the agitated mortals, intent on rejoining Selene and Rigel.

Stand fast! he silently entreated them. *I'm on my way!*

The incandescent rounds ricocheted wildly about the underground platform. Glowing bullets took out many of the overhead lights, which exploded like pyrotechnic amusements, showering sparks onto the cement floor below. The remaining lights flickered fitfully, casting creeping shadows over the besieged station.

What the hell? Michael thought, suddenly finding himself stuck in the middle of a full-scale firefight. Along with several other fearful bystanders, he huddled behind an automated ticketing kiosk while the echoing explosions pounded against his eardrums, overpowering even the strident screams of the hysterical commuters. The acrid smell of cordite assailed his nostrils.

He couldn't believe what was happening. One minute, he was trudging toward the waiting subway, still half-looking for that breathtaking woman in the black leather, when unknown parties abruptly started shooting up the crowded platform. Doing his best to keep his head down, Michael couldn't get a good look at who was doing the shooting, but his overwrought brain desperately tried to make sense of the situation.

Some kind of Russian mob thing? he speculated. Downtown Pest wasn't exactly Hell's Kitchen, but organized crime had been thriving in the former Warsaw Pact nations ever since the fall of the Berlin Wall. Maybe this was a turf war between rival mobsters.

A teenage girl, maybe seventeen years old, made a break for the up escalator. She almost made it—before getting caught in a vicious cross fire. High-powered blasts tore into her upper leg, and she dropped to the floor like a brightly painted marionette whose strings had just been slashed by a razor. Blood spurted from beneath her miniskirt as she stared in shock at her perforated leg. From the bright red color of the blood, Michael knew that the bullets had opened her femoral artery. He couldn't hear her gasping over the roar of the gunfire, but he saw her chest heaving erratically as all the color drained from her face.

Screw it! Michael thought. With no other choice, he bit down on his lip and darted out from behind the ticketing machines. Crouching as low as he could, he scurried through the line of fire like an army field medic. Bizarrely glowing bullets whizzed past his head, creating dancing blue spots at the periphery of his vision, but he kept on going until he reached the wounded teen, who was lying sprawled on the platform in a swiftly spreading puddle of her own blood.

He dropped to his knees beside her and began feverishly applying pressure to the injured limb. Hot blood soaked through the knees of his pants, dispelling some of the chill left behind by the autumnal weather outside. Adrenaline coursed through his veins, giving him the energy he needed to help this girl.

"You're going to be all right," he assured her, raising his voice to be heard over the reverberating screams and gunfire. He struggled to make eye contact with the girl even as he kept pressing down on the wound with both hands. Sticky arterial blood seeped between his fingers.

To his dismay, the teen's violet eyes were already glazed and unfocused. Her face was pale, with a slight bluish tint, and her skin felt cool and clammy. *I'm losing her,* he realized, recognizing the telltale symptoms of hypovolemic shock. "No, no, no!" he blurted at her. "Don't close your eyes. Stay with me now." Her eyelids drooped alarmingly, and he thrust his face at hers. "Stay with—"

Another burst of automatic weapons fire rocked the platform, interrupting Michael's desperate attempt to rouse the half-conscious girl. Heavily mascaraed eyelashes fluttered weakly, then snapped awake at the booming sound of the guns. *That's it!* Michael thought, shielding the girl's ashen face with his own body. Every fresh blast made him cringe, expecting to feel bullets slam into him at any minute.

Was it just his imagination, or had he actually succeeded in slowing the girl's rapid blood loss? For a split second, he was mentally transported back to a lonely roadside in New Haven, watching another young woman slowly die right before his eyes. *Not again!* he thought, feeling a familiar pain stab him sharply in the heart. *Hang in there,* he urged the Hungarian girl, forcing the thought of that other woman out of his mind. *I'm not going to let you die.*

Even if it kills me . . .

Chapter Three

*A*cross the platform, Selene winced as Raze's gunfire chipped away at the concrete column protecting her. Bits of powdered stone pelted her face as another unnaturally radiant bullet missed her by centimeters. She angrily wiped the grit from her cheek with the back of her hand before firing around the corner of the pillar with a blazing Beretta.

She glanced to her left and saw Rigel similarly pinned behind another column farther down the platform. A sturdy advertising kiosk loomed midway between them. Selene tipped her head toward the adjacent structure and nodded at Rigel. He nodded back, understanding.

Firing continuously with both hands, she dived for the rear of the kiosk, as did Rigel, who met up with her behind a mounted poster for the Hungarian Ballet. All around them, luminous steel rounds slammed into the walls and ceiling of the Metro station, turning the polished tiles into an explosion of broken splinters and shards.

Selene and Rigel hid behind the colorful kiosk, their backs pressed up against each other. "Whatever kind of ammo they're using," she exclaimed, her heated observation sounding like a whisper amidst the thunderous racket of the gun battle, "I've never seen it before!"

"Likewise," Rigel replied. Concern creased the smooth planes of his perpetually youthful features. As if ordinary ammo wasn't dangerous enough to their kind!

Selene slammed a fresh magazine into her right-hand Beretta and risked a peek around the edge of the kiosk. To her surprise, she saw that same handsome American youth tending to an injured human girl right in the middle of the platform. She raised an attentive eyebrow, impressed by the young man's courage if not by his sense of self-preservation. *I've known vampires,* she thought, *who were not so brave amidst gunfire.*

The tangy scent of the girl's spilled blood reached Selene's nose, causing her mouth to water automatically. *None of that now,* she told herself firmly; the drinking of innocent blood had been strictly banned for centuries.

Her eyes widened in alarm as she spotted the smaller lycan, apparently overcome with blood lust, charging at the kneeling mortal from behind. Although Trix had not been reckless enough to shed his human form in so public a venue, his bestial nature was betrayed by his blood-streaked cobalt eyes, sharpened incisors, and clawlike fingernails. A white froth foamed at the corners of his mouth as he lunged for the human with outstretched claws!

Intent on his wounded charge, the compassionate American appeared oblivious to the berserk lycanthrope closing upon him. *Forget it,* Selene thought emphatically, unwilling to see the courageous youth butchered by the likes of Trix. She quickly took aim at the oncoming lycan and squeezed the trigger. *Eat silver, you stinking cur!*

BLAM! An argent bullet ripped into Trix's shoulder, sending him crashing to the ground. Selene smiled coldly, even as the engrossed American youth remained unaware of his near brush with death and mutilation.

The doors of the parked subway train had remained open throughout the frenzied melee, perhaps in hopes of giving the endangered commuters on the platform an avenue of escape. Rebounding from his bullet-propelled fall, Trix took advantage of an open door to scramble onto the train itself, clutching his wounded shoulder.

The floor of the train exploded beneath his feet as Selene's nonstop fire chased him. He dashed across the width of the subway car, barreling into the sealed door at the opposite side of the corridor. Powerful fingers dug into the rubber-lined seam between the closed pneumatic doors, and he grunted in exertion as his superhuman sinews struggled to pry the doors open.

Selene kept on firing, her unleashed bullets eating up the floor behind him. The train's unlucky passengers cowered beneath their seats, but Selene squeezed tightly on the triggers of her Berettas, confident in her ability to hit only the hated target she was gunning for. She had no intention of letting the injured lycan escape with his life.

Growling savagely, Trix made one last ferocious effort, and the closed metal doors came apart with a *whoosh* of pressurized air. The lycan hurriedly threw himself through the gap, dropping onto the subway tracks on the other side of the train.

Damnation! Selene cursed, irked by her quarry's last-minute escape. She moved to go after him, only to see Raze charging toward her from the northern end of the platform. His Uzi blazed volcanically, drawing her fire.

She ducked back behind the corner of the kiosk, unable to chase the smaller lycan as she would have preferred. *Very well*, she thought. Her upraised pistol was only centimeters from her face, filling her lungs with the intoxicating smell of gunpowder and hot metal. Adrenaline spiked the undead ichor in her veins. *I'll settle for the big dog instead.*

"Shit. Shit. Shit."

Trix slumped against the wheels of the stalled train. His right shoulder burned where the vampire bitch had nailed him with her silver. Grimacing in agony, he thrust his fingers into the gaping wound, a task made all the more difficult by the fact that he was right-handed in his human form. The smell of his own blood enraged him as it streamed down his chest to puddle at his feet.

Good-for-nothing bloods! He longed to transform, to revert to a more primal and powerful state, but that was impossible; only the oldest and most powerful of lycans could transform after being wounded by a silver weapon. Thanks to the bullet in his shoulder, Trix was trapped in human form until the metallic poison dissipated from his blood, which could take hours—or even days.

His fingers burrowed painfully into the shredded meat and gristle, finally locating the bloodied remains of a single silver bullet. The flattened slug was slick and difficult to hold onto, and the hated metal burned his fingertips, but Trix gritted his teeth and violently wrenched the bullet from his shoulder. Steam rose from the fleshy pads of his fingers as they hissed and sizzled from contact with the silver. Snarling at the back of his throat, he hurled the captured slug as far away as possible, hearing it clatter upon the metal tracks several meters down the line.

"Son of a bitch!" he growled. Now he was pissed!

Trix licked his scorched fingers, then slammed a fresh magazine into his own gun, a .44 Magnum Desert Eagle. He popped up behind the gap in the subway doors and fired through the train at the platform beyond.

His feral heart beat in exultation as he saw that, to the right side of the platform, Raze was already strafing the vampire's kiosk with automatic fury.

Friggin' bloods! he raged, enthusiastically adding his own luminescent fire to Raze's. Aboard the train, lily-livered humans trembled and pissed themselves, but Trix reserved the entirety of his seething contempt for the vampires themselves. *We'll teach those arrogant leeches to mess with our clan!*

In a moment of prudence, some unseen human had turned off the escalators leading to and from the platform. *No matter,* Nathaniel thought, racing down the motionless steps at blinding speed. His long black hair whipped behind him as he ran. The platform below rang with the sound of frenetic gunfire. *And to think I was afraid of missing all the action!*

The lycans' guns assaulted the kiosk at right angles to each other, backing Selene and Rigel into a single narrow corner behind the targeted structure, which was rapidly being ripped to shreds by the lycans' ceaseless fire. Their situation, she realized, was swiftly becoming untenable.

Despite her own dire predicament, though, she couldn't help worrying about the safety of the heroic American. Was he still unharmed, or had both he and the injured girl already perished in the hostilities? *A pity our war had to endanger innocent humans,* she thought with sincere regret.

Just in time, a vigorous volley of fresh gunfire targeted Raze, forcing the larger lycan to turn tail and seek the shelter of a nearby subway car. Selene looked back over her shoulder to see Nathaniel descending the escalator, his trademark Walther pistols spitting out an unrelenting stream of silver bullets.

Well done! she thought proudly, grateful for the timely intervention of the valiant Death Dealer. Nathaniel's fortuitous arrival was just what they needed to turn the tables on these revolting animals. *We have them outnumbered now!*

She and Rigel seized the opportunity to abandon the bullet-riddled kiosk, bolting across the platform to a less pulverized concrete pillar. She looked with concern for the handsome good Samaritan and his injured charge, who were still dangerously out in the open. Amazingly, they were both still alive.

But although Raze had been driven off, his subhuman accomplice still lurked on the other side of the beleaguered train. The muzzle of his handgun flared repeatedly—*BLAM, BLAM, BLAM!*—and a burst of incandescent ammunition caught Rigel across the chest.

The reeling vampire stumbled and lurched sideways into a wall. The glowing bullets sliced through the strap of his camera, causing the compact digital device to go skittering across the concrete floor of the platform. Rigel staggered clumsily, fighting to stay on his feet. His once-seraphic countenance contorted with indescribable pain and suffering. As Selene looked on in horror, rays of searing light erupted from his wounds, blazing forth from the jagged tears in his dark leather attire. The blinding effulgence burned through the vampire's transfixed body, incinerating him from the inside out!

Selene felt the excruciating heat of the light upon her own ivory features. Aghast and astounded by what was happening to her friend, she tried to keep on watching, if only to be able to report back to her superiors on what she was witnessing, but the actinic glare grew so bright that she had to look away, crimson tears leaking from the corners of her eyes.

The sickening smell of burning flesh filled the underground station as the unnatural light flared up like a supernova before finally dying out.

Selene opened her eyes just in time to see Rigel's carbonized corpse hit the floor. Smoky fumes rose from the vampire's body, which was burned and blackened beyond recognition. The charred remains looked as though Rigel had been left out in the sunlight to die.

No! Selene thought in stunned disbelief. *This can't be happening!* She had known and fought beside Rigel for years and years, yet the smoldering ruin before her eyes left no doubt that her ageless comrade had been eliminated forever.

An all-consuming wrath possessed her. She whirled around, her anguished heart screaming for retribution, and opened fire on Trix, who took another silver bullet in the shoulder, not two centimeters from where she had shot him the last time. *Does that hurt, you bastard?* Selene thought vindictively, savoring the agonized expression on the lycan's face. *I hope it burns like hell!*

If only silver acted as quickly as the lycan's obscene new ammunition!

The craven lycan had clearly had enough. Relinquishing his position on the other side of the metallic blue subway car, he turned and galloped down the underground Metro tunnel. Selene sneered at the lycan's cowardice; such craven behavior was more like a jackal than a wolf.

Run while you can, she taunted him silently. Despite the overwhelming thirst for vengeance engulfing her soul, Selene retained the presence of mind to snatch up Rigel's fallen camera and quickly ejected its memory disk. Pocketing the disk, she discarded the camera before racing into the train after Trix. She charged down the center aisle of the car, running parallel to the lycan fleeing alongside the train.

Through the windows to her right, she could see Trix making a break for the dimly lit tunnel ahead. She was tempted to fire at him through the transparent glass window but feared that a stray ricochet might kill or maim one of the train's human passengers. Mortals were strictly noncombatants in the war she fought, and Selene had always striven to avoid undue collateral damage. Not that she intended to show any such mercy to the despicable lycanthrope outside the train.

The memory of Rigel's smoking remains added wings to her heels as she sped through one car after another, sprinting like leather-clad lightning past the shell-shocked humans cowering in their seats. She squeezed the grip of her Beretta so tightly that her fingers sank into the handle, leaving impressions in its high-impact polymer frame.

She reached the end of the rear car and bared her fangs as Trix came zipping around the back of the train and took off down the center of the tracks. Perhaps he thought he could elude Selene amidst the stygian recesses of the murky tunnel?

Fat chance. Selene didn't even slow down before diving headfirst through the train's rear window. Glass exploded onto the tracks as she came soaring out of the subway car, the back of her jet-black trench coat flaring out behind her like the wings of some enormous vampire bat.

She hit the ground like an Olympic-class acrobat, executing a flawless diving roll before springing up onto her feet. Gun in hand, she pursued the lycan with all her preternatural strength and speed, plunging into the forbidding blackness of the tunnel without a second's hesitation.

I'll get you, you murdering animal, if I have to follow you all the way to Perdition!

Back on the platform, near the middle of the train, Nathaniel was running low on ammo. He lurked under the cover of the escalator as he and Raze vehemently exchanged fire. The barbaric lycan had taken refuge in a crowded subway car, from which he vainly sought to nail Nathaniel with one of his phosphorescent rounds. The combat-savvy vampire carefully kept his head; having seen what the glowing bullets had done to Rigel, he was in no hurry to experience their incendiary effect himself.

I still can't believe that Rigel is actually gone, he brooded darkly. *It happened so fast!*

Whistling silver and radiant particles of light zipped past each other, carving out a no-man's land between the escalator and the stalled subway car. Raze fired his Uzi around the door of the car, until the spewing muzzle of his gun suddenly fell silent. Nathaniel saw the lycan scowl angrily at his weapon and realized that the Uzi must have exhausted its ammunition.

And none too soon, the vampire thought appreciatively. His own pistols were out of ammo as well. He groped in the pockets of his trench coat for another magazine, only to come up empty. "Bugger!" he swore under his breath, even as he spied Raze fleeing toward the back of the train.

Lacking either the time or the ability to reload, Nathaniel tossed his pistol aside and ran toward the next car down, hoping to cut Raze off. *These lycans will pay for what they did to Rigel,* he vowed. *I swear it upon my eternal life!*

The snarling lycan rushed past the petrified passengers huddled together on the floor. He yanked open the door between the cars and threw himself across the gap above the coupling, provoking ear-splitting screams from the startled humans in the next car, who suddenly found themselves confronted with a wild-eyed thug brandishing a smoking submachine gun.

Racing diagonally across the platform, Nathaniel glimpsed Raze through the windows of the train. There was no way that he could beat the lycan to the next open doorway, so, instead, raising his arms to protect his head, he hurled himself through one of the car's side windows. Glass shattered with a stupendous crash as the vampire came zooming like a meteor into the car, tackling Raze. His headlong momentum threw the lycan into the opposite window, cracking the heavy glass.

Nathaniel's surprise attack infuriated the ambushed lycan, eating away at his flimsy pretense at humanity. Shaking off the bone-numbing impact, Raze glared at the Death Dealer with inhuman, cobalt-blue eyes. He bared his fangs, exposing a mouthful of serrated canines and incisors. An atavistic growl escaped his lips.

The semitransformed lycanthrope grabbed Nathaniel with both hands and flung the vampire down the aisle toward the front of the train. Against his will, Nathaniel found himself sliding backward across the floor, but he quickly halted his supine retreat and sprang back onto his feet. The colored irises of his eyes disappeared, leaving only the whites and pupils. His own fangs snapped together angrily, and his outstretched fingers sported razor-sharp nails.

He was more than ready to engage Raze hand-to-hand if necessary, but the lycan had other ideas; turning his back on Nathaniel, Raze made a breakneck dash for the rear of the train.

Not so fast, the vampire thought, giving chase. Pouring on the steam, he pursued the lycan through car after car, slowly gaining on the fleeing gunman. Nathaniel's legs were a blur of superhuman speed, hurling him after his considerably less than human quarry.

Within seconds, they had reached the final car, where Nathaniel observed the telltale signs of some earlier struggle. Bullet holes riddled the floor, and the window at the far end of the car, mounted halfway up the painted steel exit, had been smashed to pieces. Nathaniel briefly wondered what had become of Selene and the other lycan, only to see Raze closing fast on the exit in question, less than forty meters ahead of him.

Tapping hidden reserves of speed and energy, the determined vampire leaped forward and tackled Raze once more. His talons grabbed on tightly to the lycan scum as they slammed into the rear exit, their combined momentum blowing the heavy steel door off its hinges.

Locked together in a death grip, Raze and Nathaniel came flying out of the train. They crashed down onto the tracks, skidding across the rusty iron rails. The hard landing broke them apart, and they rolled away from each other before scrambling back onto their feet.

Vampire and lycan faced off at the edge of a darkened tunnel. Flickering fluorescent lights created a strobe effect that only added to the bizarre, nightmarish ambience of the hellish drama playing out behind the ravaged subway train. Predator versus predator, the two deadly night creatures circled each other warily, flaunting demonic fangs and claws. The vampire's eerie white eyes blazed with inhuman malice, while Raze glowered back at him with eyes as cold and impenetrable as a shark's—or a wolf's.

Nathaniel suddenly felt terribly exposed and vulnerable. A tremor of apprehension shook his ageless bones as, in the pulsating glare of the erratic lights, his lycan adversary began to *change*.

31

The grotesque transformation was visible only in quick, fragmentary glimpses.

Wiry black hairs sprouting from Raze's face, scalp, and hands.

A lupine snout protruding from a flat human countenance.

Gaping jaws packed with gleaming yellow fangs.

Foam dripping from an immense, hungry maw.

Thatches of bristling gray-black fur jutting through torn and shredded clothing.

Jagged claws tearing free of leather boots.

Human ears growing tufted and pointed at the tips.

Cobalt eyes peering down as the inhuman shape-shifter grew a full half meter in height, his massive shoulders expanding as well.

Upraised claws the size of steak knives . . .

Nathaniel swallowed hard, his mouth suddenly as dry as the Valley of the Kings, where he had once dabbled in archaeology beside Howard Carter and Lord Carnarvon. He promptly realized that he had committed a grave tactical error in confronting the desperate lycan away from the inhibiting gaze of the mortals. As long as Raze had remained in his human form, Nathaniel had been more than a match for the lycan where hand-to-hand combat was concerned, but only the most powerful of vampire Elders could hope to survive unarmed against a fully transformed werewolf.

Six centuries of immortality passed before his eyes as he backed away from the towering beast. Another snatch of Milton raced through his mind:

Of Cerberus and blackest Midnight born,
In Stygian cave forlorn,
'Mongst horrid shapes, and shrieks, and sights unholy—
Growling horrifically, the werewolf fell upon Nathaniel

like some ravening prehistoric monster. Jagged claws sliced through his leather garb as though it were tissue paper, rending the undead flesh beneath. The doomed vampire struggled helplessly against the huge, voracious creature, but the hell-beast was too big, too strong. Powerful jaws closed on Nathaniel's throat, crushing the vampire's neck between rows of ivory fangs. A horrendous scream rang out, and cool vampiric blood gushed upon the tracks.

In his last instants, Nathaniel prayed that Selene would not meet the same awful fate.

Chapter Four

Run all you can! Selene thought fiercely as she chased Trix through the winding subway tunnel, taking care to avoid the electrified third rail. The dim lighting posed little difficulty—vampires have excellent night vision—yet the determined Death Dealer would have charged headlong into utter blackness if necessary. *You're not getting away from me!*

Rigel's fiery death still burned brightly in her memory, stoking her ever-smoldering hatred of the lycan breed to an even more consuming blaze. She held on tightly to her Beretta, aching for a chance to strafe her comrade's killer with red-hot silver.

The fleeing lycan disappeared around a bend in the track, but Selene was only a few seconds behind him. Rounding the curve herself, she was surprised to discover that Trix had seemingly vanished into thin air. *What?* she wondered in confusion, slowing to a halt between the iron rails. *Where in hell . . . ?*

Vampire eyes searched the floor of the tunnel, swiftly discerning a trail of muddy bootprints and scattered droplets of blood leading to a shallow alcove on the right-hand side of the underground tube. Undaunted by the thickly gathered shadows filling the inauspicious nook, she stepped toward the empty recess, her gaze glued to the ground in search of further evidence of Trix's present whereabouts. *He can't have gone far,* she assured herself, determined to see the lycanthrope dead by dawn.

A gust of hot air, accompanied by a distant roar, interrupted her search. *What the devil?* Selene whirled around toward the sudden noise, then cautiously peeked around a bend in the tunnel. Her eyes widened in alarm as she saw the northbound train, hightailing it out of the battle-scarred station, whip around the corner. Glaring headlights blinded her like malevolent sunbeams.

Move! her brain shouted at her. *Now!*

She jumped backward into the concrete alcove, flattening herself against the inner wall of the niche. She turned her face away from the oncoming train, just as the Metro carrier zoomed by her, its metallic epidermis passing only centimeters away from her exposed white cheek. The booming thunder of the cars riding madly over the rails drowned out the world, while a violent surge of wind caused her trench coat to flap wildly. Flickering lights strobed from the speeding cars; looking down, Selene saw the inconstant glare reflected by the glistening blood and bootprints next to a rusty drainage grate. *Aha!* she thought, despite the clamorous passage of the train. *Heading downward, are we?*

The blue M3 train took forever to traverse this particular stretch of track, but Selene finally watched its luminous red taillights recede into the distance, heading north. Letting out a sigh of relief, she dropped to her knees beside the metal grating, which was wet and slimy with mold. She yanked up the grate with both hands, then paused momentarily to peer down into the uncovered pit.

The floor of the drainage tunnel, running beneath the

Metro line, was hidden by vigorously coursing rainwater, but Selene judged that it was hardly deep enough to conceal Trix in his entirety or to have carried him away to a watery doom. *If he can brave the flood, so can I*, she resolved, thankful that, contrary to myth, vampires had no genuine aversion to running water.

She dropped down into the dark, crumbling tunnel, landing ankle-deep in the turbid stream. Any muddy bootprints had been washed away by the rain, so she hesitated, uncertain which way to turn. She sniffed the air, catching a whiff of freshly spilled blood to her right; Trix's wounded shoulder, she surmised, unhealed thanks to the toxic presence of her silver bullet.

Her nose wrinkled in disgust. Unlike human blood, which invariably attracted her despite her best intentions, the unclean blood of a lycan held no allure; indeed, it was considered anathema to her kind even to think of partaking of a lycan's tainted essence. Despite the fangs projecting from her gums, she fully intended to slay Trix the proper way: with cleansing fire and silver.

Her gun raised and ready, she ventured cautiously in the direction of the blood scent, only to be greeted by the flare of a gun muzzle and the clattering report of a semi-automatic pistol. Like enraged fireflies, three incandescent bullets punched through her coat, barely missing her leather-corseted ribs.

Careful, she cautioned herself. *Don't let your anger at Rigel's death make you careless. He wouldn't want that.*

She caught a glimpse of Trix at the far end of the drainage tunnel and dive-rolled out of his line of fire, blasting away with her own gun even as she smoothly tumbled head over heels. The blare of the weapons echoed thunderously in the cramped confines of the narrow tunnel.

Trix missed.

She didn't.

The lycan toppled over, splashing down onto the submerged floor of the tunnel. His right hand still wrapped around the cold steel grip of his pistol, he flopped spasmodically upon his back like a fish out of water. Hot steam rose from the bullet holes sprouted across his chest.

Selene wasted no time finishing him off. Hissing like an incensed panther, she drove her boot down onto the supine lycan's neck and mercilessly emptied the remainder of her silver ammo into his chest. The faces of the little girls, the old man, and the butchered maiden once again flashed across her mind, this time joined by the searing image of Rigel bleeding shafts of deadly light. *Die!* she thought passionately, as she always did when she had a lycan at her mercy. *Die, you bloodthirsty animal!*

Trix's body rocked beneath the explosive force of the gunshots, not going limp until Selene's Beretta clicked upon an empty cartridge. She stepped back, contemplating the lycan's devastated corpse with cold satisfaction. Her gaze fell on the modified Desert Eagle still locked in the dead lycan's grip. *Kahn will want to inspect this new weapon,* she realized.

Thrusting the Beretta back into its holster, she bent and pried the pistol from Trix's stiffening hand. The painful radiance of the lambent rounds forced her to wince and look away as she methodically ejected the ammo clip.

An eerie silence fell over the lonely tunnel, broken only by the sibilant gurgle of the draining water. Then a deafening roar came from the subway tracks above. Another speeding train, Selene wondered anxiously, or something far more dangerous?

No longer trapped in the puny shape of a man, Raze exulted in his regained strength and speed. There were certain advantages to a human form, granted, such as an opposable thumb and the ability to blend undetected amidst the gullible mortal herd, but when he became a wolf, he became his truer, more primeval self. Guns and knives were all very well and good, but nothing equaled the sheer unbridled exhilaration of tearing apart a foe with your own teeth and claws!

The blood of his latest prey still stained his matted black fur, while bits of undead flesh and gristle lodged between his serrated yellow fangs. The flesh of the male vampire had only whetted his appetite, though; he wanted the female, too. *Two down,* he thought, eagerly recalling how the first vamp had been burned alive by Trix's ultraviolet ammo. *One more to go.*

His lupine snout sniffed the air, readily determining which way Trix and the vampire bitch had gone. He hoped that his fellow lycan had not already killed the bloodsucking leech on his own; he was looking forward to rending the flesh from her shapely body, then cracking her bones and eating the marrow.

At the back of Raze's mind, his human half remembered that he still had a vital mission to complete, one interrupted by the vampires' unwanted appearance on the scene, but the wolf was in ascendance now, and long-term plans would have to wait. He had tasted blood and wanted more.

I'll find that miserable human later, he promised himself, before bounding down the tunnel after his prey.

His muzzle twitched in anticipation of fresh meat as he quickly located the open grate and dropped down into the waiting drainage tunnel. Stalking forward on two legs, the transformed werewolf stooped beneath the low ceiling of the moldering conduit, his tufted ears brushing against the crumbling brickwork.

Gunshots blared loudly ahead of him, then abruptly fell silent. The acrid stench of gunpowder reached his canine nose. Had Trix eliminated the she-vampire, he wondered, or the other way around? Wading through the turbid water, he advanced toward the sound of the fleeting battle, his knife-edged claws extended before him.

The fact that he smelled only hot lycan blood, not the tepid red ichor that flowed through a vampire's veins, gave him cause for concern, which was promptly validated by the sight of the female vampire bending low over the fallen remains of his fellow lycanthrope. Tainted by the vampire's cursed silver, Trix had died in his human form, unable to change shape as Raze had.

The crouching vampire had her back to Raze, apparently unaware of his approach. Fleshy black lips peeled back hungrily, exposing the werewolf's bloodstained incisors as he crept forward, eager to avenge the death of his pack member. Sinewy muscles tensed in expectation, and saliva dripped from the corners of his mouth. The vampire was easy prey . . .

With a ferocious roar, he pounced at the vampire, who surprised him by twisting around at superhuman speed and hurling four coinlike silver disks at the charging werewolf. Razor-sharp blades snapped out of the disks, turning them into deadly silver throwing stars.

Shards of jagged pain mixed with feral rage as the flying *shuriken* sliced into the werewolf's massive torso. He reared backward, growling in fury, his claws slashing fruitlessly at the air. *Goddamn blood!* he howled inside, the angry curse emerging as an inarticulate snarl. *You'll pay for that, you sneaky bitch!*

But the vampire was already gone.

*   *   *

Her perforated trench coat flapped behind her as Selene ran like hell away from the injured werewolf. She had no illusions that a handful of throwing stars would be enough to bring down a fully transformed alpha-male like Raze. With the last of her ammunition buried deeply in the corpse of the smaller lycan, discretion was clearly the better part of valor.

Killing Raze would have to wait for another night. *At least I avenged Rigel,* she thought, her boots splashing through the muddy rainwater. She only hoped that Nathaniel had survived as well.

Selene ran for her life, undead veins surging with adrenaline. Listening carefully for any signs of pursuit, she was surprised to hear a burst of frenzied growls and wild human cheers coming from somewhere nearby. *What in the world?* she thought.

Darting around a corner, she spotted rays of filtered light shining up through a rusted metal grate, not unlike the one she had used to enter the decaying drainage system. The boisterous roars and shouts seemed to be coming from the same direction as the unknown light.

Curious despite her present jeopardy, Selene warily stepped toward the grate, trying to peer downward through the moldy iron slats. Before she could see anything, however, she heard heavy paws tramping noisily through the tunnel behind her, accompanied by a rumbling growl that was growing louder and more inescapable by the second.

Raze, getting closer.

Damn, she thought, realizing that there was no time to investigate whatever was creating all that commotion on the other side of the metal grating. Escaping Raze had to be her first and only priority.

But I'll be back, she vowed, running like mad away from the oncoming werewolf. Monstrous claws scraped against the floor of the tunnel behind her as she searched for the quickest available route back to the surface. *I'm going to find out everything that's hiding down here, assuming I ever get out of these tunnels alive!*

Chapter Five

The abandoned tunnel was packed with lycans, both male and female. Hooting and hollering, they crowded the underground ruins, which were lit by the erratic light of crude torches wedged here and there into the crumbling brick walls. Water dripped from the ceiling, and the musky air was pungent with the smell of smoke, sweat, pheromones, and blood. The greasy, unwashed clothing of the lycans added to the general stench. Anthropomorphic shadows danced wildly on the cobweb-covered walls, and gnawed white bones, human and otherwise, littered the rocky floor. Rats scuttled around the edges of the tunnel, feeding on the lycans' grisly leavings. Empty bottles of beer and Tokay clinked loudly as they rolled between the revelers' feet. The entire scene had the riotous, unruly frenzy of a Hell's Angels rally or perhaps an eighteenth-century pirate bacchanal.

Animalistic growls and snarls came from the center of the commotion, as the riled lycans clustered in a ring around an irresistible entertainment, rudely jostling each other for a better view.

Two gigantic male werewolves were locked in fierce

combat, snapping and clawing as they circled each other like enraged pit bulls. Tufts of gray-black fur went flying as the frothing beasts traded gouging slashes and bites, lunging savagely at each other, to the tumultuous delight of the crowd. Fresh blood splattered the thrilled faces of the lycan spectators, who were dwarfed by the seven-foot-tall werewolves. The fur-crested skulls of the creatures towered above the heads of the mostly humanoid audience.

"Go get 'im!" a jubilant lycan shouted, although it was unclear which monstrous man-beast she was cheering for. "Tear 'im apart!"

"That's it!" another onlooker called out loudly, stomping his boots on the floor. A plump black rat scurried for safety. "Don't back off! Go for his throat!"

Disgraceful, Lucian thought, observing the sorry spectacle. With a weary sigh, he raised his shotgun.

BLAM! The resounding blast of the rifle cut through the echoing yells and growls like a silver blade slicing through a werewolf's heart. The obstreperous mob fell silent, and even the two battling lycanthropes halted their brutal clash. Startled eyes, both human and lupine, turned toward the solitary figure standing at the rear of the dilapidated tunnel.

Although deceptively slight in appearance, Lucian carried himself with the carriage and bearing of a true leader. The unquestioned master of the lycan horde, he had an air of polished cultivation that his uncouth subjects sorely lacked. His expressive gray eyes, long black hair, and neatly trimmed beard and mustache gave him the look of a somewhat urbane Jesus. His hair was combed back in a widow's peak, exposing a lofty brow of Shakespearean proportions. He looked to be in his early thirties, although his true origins were lost in the impenetrable mists of history. He was also very much alive, despite his supposed death nearly six centuries ago.

His dark brown attire was also significantly more expensive and stylish than the cheap, thrift-store wear that draped his subjects. The tail of his oiled leather coat flapped behind him like a monarch's robes. His gloves and boots were equally slick and polished. A crest-shaped pendant hung from a chain around his neck. The gleaming medallion reflected the torchlight, throwing dazzling beams about the dimly lit catacomb.

Cowed lycans edged nervously from his path as he strode confidently into the crowd, a smoking shotgun resting lightly upon his shoulder. His disapproving eyes raked across the faces of his gathered minions, who shrank back in apprehension. They bowed their heads in submission to their leader.

"You're acting like a pack of rabid hounds," he said disdainfully, speaking Hungarian with a crisp British accent. "And that, gentlemen, simply will not do. Not if you expect to defeat the vampires on their own ground. Not if you expect to survive at all." He looked over the drooping heads of the blood-spattered spectators to where the two mighty hell-beasts had been contending. "Pierce! Taylor!"

The crowd parted entirely to reveal two human gladiators, their naked bodies slick with blood and perspiration. Nasty cuts and scratches marred their heaving chests as they panted in exhaustion. Both men looked as though they had just run a marathon through a field of thorny rose bushes, but their eyes still glowed with feral glee and rapacity.

They should save their predatory zeal for our foes, Lucian thought, appalled at such a pointless waste of blood and energy. And the truly sad thing was, these were two of his more reliable lieutenants.

Cold gray eyes regarded the brawling pair with open contempt. Pierce, the taller of the two, was a brawny Caucasian whose uncombed, shoulder-length black hair made him look like a comic-book barbarian. Taylor, his partner, was also white, with reddish-brown hair and whiskers. They stood stiffly at attention, their heads hunched below their shoulders and their arms and fingers extended at their sides, as though their hands still sported dagger-sized talons.

Lucian shook his head. *You can take the man out of the wolf,* he thought philosophically, *but you can't take the wolf out of the man.* "Put some clothes on, will you?"

The Ferenciek Square subway station, recently the site of so much gunfire and bloodshed, was now swarming with Hungarian police officers and forensic examiners. Like their American counterparts, the local cops wore navy-blue uniforms and stony, hard-boiled expressions. Michael watched a pair of forensic assistants examine the charred remains of what looked like a burn victim. *Funny,* he thought, blinking in confusion, *I don't remember a fire breaking out . . .*

Pale-faced and shaken, Michael leaned against a chipped and bullet-riddled support column as a chunky police officer, who had identified himself as Sergeant Hunyadi, took his statement. The dazed young American's pants and T-shirt were still soaked through with blood. Amazingly, none of it was his own.

"Tattoos, scars, any other identifying marks?" the cop asked, hoping for a description of the assailants.

Michael shook his head. "No, like I said, it happened too fast." His gaze drifted over the officer's shoulder, to where a couple of paramedics were strapping the injured Hungarian girl to a gurney. The unlucky teen had lost a lot of blood, but it looked as though she was probably going to make it. He breathed a sigh of relief, grateful that he had managed to keep the girl alive until help could get to her. *No wonder I can't remember what the shooters looked like,* he thought. *I was too busy dealing with a severed artery!*

Hunyadi nodded, jotting something down in his notebook. Behind him, the medics started wheeling the girl toward the handicapped elevator. "Doctor!" one of the EMTs called out to Michael. "If you want a ride, you better hurry!"

The cop glanced down at the hospital ID badge pinned to the young American's jacket. "Sorry," Michael said with a shrug. "Gotta run."

Thank God! he thought, anxious to leave the violated subway station. He shouted back over his shoulder as he hurried after the medics. "I'll give you a call if I remember anything useful!"

As if there was any way he could ever make sense of what had happened here tonight.

The mansion, long known as Ordoghaz ("Devil's House"), was located about an hour north of downtown Budapest, outside the picturesque little town of Szentendre on the western bank of the Danube. Pounding rain still streamed down the tinted windshield of Selene's Jaguar XJR as she neared the intimidating cast-iron gates of Viktor's vast estate. Mounted security cameras scoped her out thoroughly before the spike-crowned gates swung open automatically.

Despite the slippery conditions, the Jag raced down the long paved driveway as quickly as its driver dared. Kahn and the others needed to know what had transpired in the city as soon as possible, although Selene was not looking forward to returning without either Rigel, whose blackened corpse she had been forced to leave behind, or Nathaniel, who was missing and presumed dead as well. *Two Death Dealers laid low in a single night,* she pondered in dismay. *Kraven will have to take this seriously . . . I hope.*

Ordoghaz loomed before her, a sprawling Gothic edifice dating back to the days when feudal warlords ruled Hungary with fists of iron. Jagged spires and battlements rose atop its looming stone walls, while majestic columns and pointed arches adorned its brooding façade. The lambent glow of candlelight could be glimpsed through the mansion's narrow lancet windows, suggesting that Ordoghaz's lively nocturnal activities were still going strong. A circular fountain, situated across the drive from the wide arched doorway, sprayed a plume of churning white water into the cold night air.

Home sweet home, Selene thought without much enthusiasm.

Parking right outside the main entrance, she stormed up the marble steps and through the heavy oaken doors. Fledgling vampires, waiting at the door, offered to take her coat and gear, but she brushed past them, intent on getting the word to those who mattered. The disk from Rigel's camera rested securely in her pocket, holding vital photographic evidence of his killers.

The foyer was as impressive as the mansion's exterior. Priceless tapestries and oil paintings hung upon lustrous oak-paneled walls. Marble tiles stretched across the floor to where the sweeping main stairway rose majestically toward the upper reaches of Ordoghaz. An immense crystal chandelier glittered above the stately entry hall, welcoming Selene in from the night.

Brushing aside a hanging tapestry, she stepped briskly into the grand salon, which was decorated in tastefully subdued tones of black and red and rich walnut brown. Lighted candelabras were mounted along the wall and hanging from the ceiling, shining down on a rose-colored wool carpet bearing a floral design. Ornamental brass lamps with opaque black shades rested upon antique mahogany end tables, beneath the elaborately carved wooden moldings running along the borders of the ceiling. Heavy velvet curtains of deepest burgundy were draped over the windows, keeping out any prying eyes whose owners might have made it past the gates outside.

A flock of well-dressed vampires loitered in these luxurious surroundings, lounging indolently on plush velvet divans or mingling in the corners, exchanging carefree giggles and gossip. The trill of high-pitched laughter mixed with the gentle clink of crystal goblets filled with an enticingly crimson beverage. Pearly-white fangs peeked from the jaded smiles of elegant vampire men and women, wearing the latest fashions from Chanel and Armani.

Selene's face hardened. She had little patience with such as these. Although vampires to be sure, these preening sybarites were no Death Dealers, merely undead socialites and libertines, more interested in their own epicurean pleasures than in the never-ending battle against the hated lycanthropes. *Don't they know there's a war on?* she thought for maybe the millionth time.

The decadent atmosphere was redolent of expensive perfume and steaming plasma, but, despite the numerous bodies crowded into the salon, the temperature remained pleasantly cool; vampires were cold-blooded by nature.

Her sudden arrival attracted little notice. A few curious heads swung toward her, examining the drenched Death Dealer through bored and disinterested eyes, before returning to more engaging amusements. She barely caused a ripple in the flow of sophisticated chitchat and witty repartee working its way around the lavishly appointed chamber.

No matter, Selene thought. These were not the vampires she needed to speak to. Her eyes scanned the room, hoping to locate Kraven himself, but the manor's surrogate master was nowhere to be seen.

A bitter smile reached her lips. If Kraven was not here, presiding over the salon's festivities, then she knew where he had to be . . .

Not for the first time, Kraven thanked the dark gods below that, contrary to myth and folklore, vampires were perfectly capable of admiring their reflections in the mirror.

He posed bare-chested before the trifold mirror in his sumptuous private suite, which had once belonged to Viktor himself. The dressing room itself was the size of a small apartment and was lavishly furnished in showy pieces of superlative quality and design. An armoire of gargantuan proportions held the regent's considerable wardrobe, while an intricate Persian rug cushioned his neatly pedicured feet. A custom-made Tiffany lamp shone overhead, allowing him a surfeit of light in which to admire himself.

The standing mirror offered three equally flattering views of the vampire lord's Adonis-like physique. A mane of shoulder-length black locks gave him the romantic dash of Heathcliff or Byron, while his well-built chest and biceps were impressive even by vampiric standards. Piercing black eyes looked back at him from the center mirror, liking what they saw. Only the ruddy tint of his flesh, pinker than was normal for a vampire, hinted at centuries of overindulgence.

Not bad for seven hundred plus, he noted with approval. Kraven had been a gentleman of leisure since at least the Renaissance . . .

Two attractive vampire women, each less than a mortal lifetime old and hence little more than servant wenches, attended to him diligently, seemingly just as enthralled by his physical perfection and considerable manliness as he. They knelt beside him as they gently eased a pair of tailored silk trousers over first one foot, then the other. Their cool, eager fingers traced the rippling contours of his sculpted musculature as they raised the trousers up his legs, then proceeded slowly to button the front of the pants from the bottom up, one delicious centimeter at a time. Trading a glance, they giggled like naughty schoolgirls.

Kraven basked in the servant girls' adoration. *Let them have their fun,* he thought magnanimously. Why shouldn't they feel privileged to wait upon the person of the lord of the manor? Was he not the preeminent vampire on the Continent?

And soon to be so much more.

The double doors of his suite banged open, jarring him out of his blissful reverie. He turned to see Selene, of all people, barging into the privacy of his chambers. The Death Dealer's dark brown hair was soaked in a most unflattering manner; nevertheless, Kraven felt a surge of lust at the sight of the striking female vampire. Too bad that, judging from her severe expression, Selene's mood tonight was something less than amorous.

So what else is new? he thought sourly.

The servant girls backed away instinctively as Selene strode across the room. Dripping water onto his imported Persian carpet, she reached beneath her coat and slammed a heavy object down onto the lacquered top of Kraven's antique walnut desk. He observed, with some distaste, that the metallic item was a firearm of some sort. Kraven didn't see anything particularly noteworthy about the gun, but Selene evidently felt otherwise.

Intense brown eyes locked onto his. "We have a serious problem," she stated.

The dojo was located on the top floor of the mansion, in a converted attic loft. Unlike the opulent decor found elsewhere in Ordoghaz, the training area was Spartan in appearance, dedicated exclusively to the art of war. Sparring mats, along with a soundproofed firing range, occupied most of the spacious garret, while the dense stone walls supported rack after rack of exotic stabbing weapons and firearms. Silver glinted from every lethal edge and surface.

Besides her own private quarters, the well-armed attic was one of the few places within the mansion where Selene felt truly comfortable. It was a place for warriors.

"I'll definitely have to run a few tests," Kahn stated, holding up a glowing bullet with a pair of forceps. Tinted safety glasses allowed him to examine the luminous projectile close up. "But it's definitely an irradiated fluid of some sort."

Concern and curiosity alike registered on the sharp, intelligent features of the Death Dealers' daunting commander and weapons master. An imposing vampire of African descent, Kahn was dressed entirely in black. His leather fighting gear matched Selene's, minus the streaks of blood and muck. He spoke English with a thick Cockney accent that he had acquired during a long stint as a slave on a merchant vessel.

Kahn was centuries old, his origins shrouded in mystery. Some said that he had once fought beside the great Shaka himself, while others speculated that the enigmatic Death Dealer had been trained as an adept in the martial arts be-

51

fore being initiated into vampirism. All Selene knew for sure—all she *needed* to know—was that Kahn's commitment to the war was as unshakable as her own. Unlike the immortal dilettantes Selene had encountered downstairs in the salon, Kahn was all business.

He set the bullet down on his workbench, next to the disassembled pieces of Trix's pistol. The overhead lights glinted off the ebony surface of Kahn's shaved skull.

Selene raised a hand to shield her eyes from the stinging radiance of the captured bullet. "Ultraviolet ammunition," she marveled aloud.

"Daylight, harnessed as a weapon," Kahn concurred, removing his tinted glasses. "And from what you've described, extremely effective."

Selene winced inwardly at the thought of Rigel's fiery demise. She still could see the corrosive beams of light exploding from his ravaged body. *At least he didn't suffer long,* she thought by way of bitter solace. *He perished within seconds.*

Kraven, on the other hand, could not have been less interested or impressed. "You expect me to believe that a mangy animal came up with a bullet specifically engineered to kill vampires?"

Looking distinctly bored, he stood alongside the workbench with Kahn and Selene. He wore a dark cotton tunic with a brocade collar beneath a smart black jacket. Polished gemstones flashed from the silver settings of his rings. As usual, his blasé attitude dismayed Selene. She had long suspected that Kraven had once served as a Death Dealer, only to advance his own position within the coven; in a hierarchy based largely on seniority, a reputation as a war hero provided an efficient shortcut to the upper echelons of vampire society. Slaying the infamous

Lucian had made Kraven's name, and, at least as far as Selene was concerned, he had been coasting on that triumph ever since. To her perpetual dismay, the vampire regent had zero patience for anything that interfered with his hedonistic amusements, which clearly included this impromptu gathering.

A few meters away, lounging against an antique weapons cabinet packed with silver daggers and scimitars, two of Kraven's nubile handmaidens dutifully tittered at his remarks. The servant girls' presence at the debriefing irked Selene; she had nothing against the frivolous *filles de chambre*, who could hardly be blamed for their immaturity, but they had no business at a serious war conference. Surely Kraven could have done without his worshipers for at least the length of the meeting?

"No, I'm betting it's military," Kahn replied, addressing Kraven's sarcastic query. He nodded at the glowing UV projectile. "Some kind of high-tech tracer round."

Selene found herself growing increasingly impatient. "I don't care where they got these things," she declared, not wanting to lose sight of the larger issue. "Rigel is dead, and Nathaniel could still be out there. We should gather the Death Dealers and head back down there in force."

It wasn't even midnight yet, she observed. There were still plenty of hours before sunrise.

"Out of the question," Kraven said bluntly. "Not now. Not for a random incursion." He shook his head at the sheer absurdity of the notion. "The Awakening is only a few days off, and this house is in a state of unrest as it is."

Selene couldn't believe her ears. "Random? They opened fire on us in full view of the public." That alone, she reflected, violated the unspoken rules governing the long

53

twilight struggle between the vampires and the lycans. "And from the commotion I heard down in that tunnel there—"

"You said yourself that you didn't actually see anything," Kraven interrupted her. He crossed his arms over his chest, challenging her to contradict him.

Selene took a deep breath, making an effort to hold onto her temper. Like it or not, Viktor had placed Kraven in charge of the coven, on the basis of his historic victory in the mountains of Moldavia; this was no time for them to squabble like rival siblings.

"I know what I heard," she insisted coolly, "and I know what my gut tells me. And I'm warning you that there could be dozens of lycans down there in the subway tunnels. Who knows, maybe even hundreds."

A hush fell over the attic at Selene's ominous pronouncement. Even the two giggling servant girls shut up and paid attention, appalled at the very notion of a lycan horde dwelling practically underneath their noses. Kraven shifted uncomfortably for a moment, before assuming a look of amused disbelief.

"We've hunted them to the brink of extinction," he stated flatly. A condescending grin slid across his face.

Even Kahn seemed to doubt Selene's claims. "Kraven's right," he assured her. "There hasn't been a den of that magnitude for centuries . . . not since the days of Lucian."

Or so we've always believed, Selene thought gloomily. "I know that, Kahn." She couldn't fault him for his skepticism. "But I'd rather have you prove me wrong by checking it out."

Kahn nodded, seeing her point. He turned to Kraven, seeking the other vampire's okay.

Kraven, in turn, glanced impatiently at his watch. He heaved a weary sigh. "Very well," he conceded. "Have your men tighten up security around here. I'll have Soren assemble a search team."

Soren was Kraven's personal pit bull, reporting directly to him. Selene had always considered Soren more of a thug than a soldier, lacking the discipline and commitment of a true Death Dealer. The simmering rivalry between the Dealers and Soren's goon squad had endured almost as long as the war itself. "I want to lead the team myself," she declared.

"Absolutely not," Kraven said. "Soren will handle it."

Selene looked to Kahn, hoping that the seasoned commander would insist that a Death Dealer take charge of the investigation, but the African vampire declined to challenge Kraven's decree. *He must think this not worth fighting over,* she realized, disappointed by Kahn's apparent lack of faith in her instincts.

Perhaps emboldened by Kahn's silence, Kraven couldn't resist gloating a bit. "Hundreds, really," he scoffed, shaking his head in his most patronizing manner.

Selene stood her ground. "*Viktor* would have believed me," she announced icily, before turning her back on Kraven and storming out the door. *If only Viktor were truly among us once more!* she thought anxiously, her fixed expression concealing a growing sense of apprehension. *How can it be that our safety and future depend on an insufferable egotist like Kraven?*

The target of her contempt was rendered speechless by Selene's brazen impertinence. *How dare she walk out on me like this?* Kraven thought, seething with indignation. *And to invoke the name of Viktor, no less! I am the lord of the manor now, not our slumbering sire!*

His face flushed with blood not his own, Kraven glared at

Selene's retreating form. Kahn diplomatically refrained from commenting on the female Death Dealer's abrupt departure; nonetheless, Kraven felt both slighted and humiliated. His brain searched frantically for some withering witticism to help him save face.

To his surprise, one of the hovering servant girls came slinking up to him, laying a hand gently on his arm. "I would never dream of treating you like that," she cooed seductively, brushing a finger up and down his arm, an obvious invitation for anything he might desire.

Kraven glanced down at the clinging vampiress. In fact, he had all but forgotten about the two underlings' presence, but now he took a closer look at the simpering maidservant at his side. She was a slim, blond thing, with violet eyes and a sylphlike figure that was scarcely hidden by her sequined black frock and long black gloves. A lacy black choker encircled her neck, offering veiled glimpses of her jugular.

What is her name again? Kraven pondered absently; he had dim memories of initiating her at a nightclub in Piccadilly less than thirty years ago. *Ah, yes . . . Erika.*

She pressed her tender form against him, basking in his attention. Her adoring eyes promised him absolute devotion and obedience, in both body and soul.

"Of course you wouldn't," he informed her bluntly, his dismissive tone striking the lovestruck vampiress like a slap across her face. *To think that she has the audacity to offer me the blind allegiance that is already mine by right!* His wounded pride took some comfort in the crushed and chastened expression on the silly tart's face. *At least I can still put someone in her place around here,* he thought bitterly.

He coolly detached her arm from his. "Now, run along

and make sure that Selene is dressed and ready for the arrival of our very important guests."

Erika crept away meekly, choking back a heartbroken sob. Kraven watched her slip submissively down the stairs, accompanied by her less presumptuous sister in servitude. *If only Selene could be so obliging,* he thought wistfully.

In every respect.

Chapter Six

*H*idden away several stories below the dojo, in the mansion's deepest subbasement, the viewing room was, appropriately enough, quiet as a tomb. Marble benches lined the narrow chamber, facing what appeared to be a blank stone wall. A single large mirror adorned the polished granite. The high vaulted ceiling gave the room the feel of some somber Gothic cathedral.

Selene shivered as she entered the chamber. By design, the air-conditioned viewing room was kept at a temperature uncomfortably cool even for the undead. Her footsteps echoed hollowly in the sepulchral hush as she strolled up to the mirror and stared pensively at her reflection. Her expressionless face belied the turbulent thoughts and anxieties roiling inside her.

Everything is happening too fast, she worried. *Two vampires dead, on the very eve of the Awakening . . .*

An electronic buzz greeted her arrival, and the seemingly opaque mirror instantly turned transparent, revealing a security booth on the other side of the glass. A single vampire, whose name was Duncan, manned the booth. He raised a quizzical eyebrow, and Selene nodded in assent.

Knowing why she was there, Duncan hit a button on his control panel. The remainder of the "stone" wall split in half, sliding away to expose a thick plexiglass window underneath. Selene stepped forward and peered through the glass at the shadowy chamber beyond.

Darkly lit and cavernous, the crypt was the slowly beating heart of Ordoghaz. Polished granite steps led down into a sunken area that was easily visible from the viewing room. At the center of this lower tier, housed within a concentric pattern of interwoven Celtic circles, were three shining bronze hatches embedded in the floor. Each circular hatch had been ornately engraved with a single letter: A for *Amelia,* M for *Marcus,* V for *Viktor.*

Selene stared at the latter hatch with anguished eyes. She leaned against the plexiglass barrier separating her from her sire's tomb. Her cool breath steamed the even more frigid glass.

How I wish I could awaken you, my lord, she thought forlornly. *I am much in need of your strength and wisdom.*

We all are.

The lengthy corridor was lined with marble busts, commemorating many of the coven's greatest warriors and leaders. This effort to immortalize the great and near great was a tad superfluous, given that the individuals being honored were already blessed with eternal life, but even vampires can have egos.

And hurt feelings.

Erika stormed down the empty hallway, biting down on her lower lip so hard that she tasted blood. The other servant girl, Dominique, had scurried away on another errand, but Erika barely noticed her associate's departure. Her bruised heart still ached from Kraven's casual disregard. His harsh, indifferent tone rang in her ears.

How could he just dismiss me like that? she agonized. *Doesn't he know that I would do anything for him?*

If she were honest with herself, Erika would have to admit that her attraction to Kraven was only partly inspired by the aristocratic vampire's undeniable good looks and charisma. His lofty position in the coven appealed to her just as much as his irresistible physique and features. As a relative newcomer to the coven, less than a mortal lifetime old, Erika was stuck at the bottom of the vampiric pecking order, and she could think of no faster way to climb the ladder than by attaching herself to the most powerful *nosferatu* in all of Europe. Although born human, unlike the pure-blooded Elders, Kraven was still a vampire to be reckoned with, and Erika had spent many a long day, sequestered away from the sun in the modest servants' quarters she shared with four or five other vampire newbies, fantasizing about reigning over the manor as Kraven's royal consort.

But all he cares about is that coldhearted killing machine, Selene!

A bust of Kraven caught her eye, his regal profile captured in chiseled stone. She swerved purposely to one side, knocking the bust off its pedestal. The sculpted head crashed to the floor, exploding into a zillion pieces. Snow-white shards of broken marble went skittering everywhere.

Not so handsome now, are you, my lord?

A moment of vindictive glee gave way to alarm as she realized exactly what she had done. She stopped in her tracks and looked back at the frightful mess on the floor. In a panic, she scampered back and dropped to her knees beside the remains of the bust. Looking about her furtively, she hastily began sweeping the incriminating fragments behind the concealing folds of a large hanging tapestry.

Crimson tears leaked from her eyes as her anguished soul

rebelled at the cruel injustice of it all. *Why Selene?* she wondered bitterly, torn between despair and indignation.

Why not me?

Selene was still gazing sadly at Viktor's tomb when Erika slipped into the viewing room behind her. *One of Kraven's adoring acolytes,* the older vampiress noted distantly. She didn't bother turning around.

"It's a waste of time, you know," the servant girl said a few moments later, after waiting in vain for Selene to acknowledge her presence.

"What is?" Selene asked. She remained facing the crypt, her back to the lissome blond vampiress, whose name was Erika if she recalled correctly.

Summoning up her nerve, Erika crept up next to the preoccupied warrior woman. She motioned casually at the metal hatch marking Viktor's secluded resting place. "I seriously doubt Viktor wants you freezing your ass in here, staring at his tomb for hours on end."

For the first time, Selene turned to look directly at the other woman. "No," she agreed vehemently. "He'd want the Death Dealers out there right now, scouring every square centimeter of this city." She clenched her fists at her sides, giving vent to her frustrations. "Damn Kraven! He's a bureaucrat, not a warrior."

"What's the difference?" Erika asked cheekily. "He'd still be a prick."

The girl's flippancy caught Selene by surprise, forcing her to take a closer look at this puzzling baby vampire. *Perhaps she has a bit more brains and independence than I first assumed?*

"But then again," Erika said, flashing a wicked grin as she leaned languidly against the thick plexiglass window, "he is quite the devilishly handsome prick."

There's no accounting for taste, Selene thought, mentally lowering her estimation of Erika by a notch. "Trust me," she said drily. "He's all yours."

A pained expression passed over the blond vampire's face, indicating that Selene had touched a sore spot, but Erika quickly managed a forced smile. "Come on," she said lightly, "we need to get you ready."

Selene blinked in confusion. She had absolutely no idea what Erika was referring to. "For what?"

The petite maidservant rolled her eyes, as if she didn't believe Selene could be so clueless. "The party. Amelia's envoy will be here any time now."

Oh, that, Selene thought without much enthusiasm. Her gaze drifted to the bronze hatch marking Amelia's tomb, which was unoccupied. In theory, the female Elder would take her place in the crypt upon Marcus's Awakening, but Selene would have preferred a very different transition of power. *If only we could skip ahead a hundred years and wake up Viktor instead!*

Rats and spiders scurried away from the cooling body, frightened by the alarming sound of something large and powerful advancing through the moldy drainage tunnel. Although the rain momentarily had ceased falling on the city streets above, oily puddles remained scattered around the sewer as evidence of the deluge. Massive paws splashed through the stagnant pools of rainwater, mixed with the sound of bony claws scraping against the brick-lined floor of the tunnel. Trickles of light filtered down through rusty grates in the ceiling, throwing the shadow of an enormous beast upon rough, uneven ground.

Bones snapped and twisted noisily, further disturbing the

verminous denizens of the sewers, as a grotesque metamorphosis took place in the murky shadows. Dense fur rustled scratchily as it receded into an almost hairless brown hide. Feral snarls evolved into recognizably human grunts and moans.

Man-shaped once more, Raze staggered through the dank and decaying tunnel. His naked body was streaked with blood, and four jagged silver throwing stars were lodged painfully in his chest, sending searing jolts through his body with every step he took. He reached instinctively to remove the stars, only to yank back his hand as the cursed metal singed his fingertips. *Damn silver!* he fumed silently, licking his scalded fingers. *Vein-sucking vampire bitch!*

Newly human eyes adjusted to the gloom. Raze panted loudly like a dog, exhausted by both his injuries and the awful strain of his transformation. He had tried to catch up with the slinky blood who had killed Trix, but her fucking *shuriken* had slowed him down, allowing the bloodsucking tramp to escape. Now there was nothing left to do but collect Trix's body and report back to Lucian, who was not going to be happy to hear that the bloods had interfered with the mission.

For a second, Raze worried about the larger implications of the vampires' surprise appearance tonight. Just another random hunting expedition, or did the goddamn bloods know about Lucian's interest in that mortal, Michael Corvin?

No, he decided quickly. *That's impossible. The bloods have no idea what we're about. Our mole would have told us if they did.*

Confident that tonight's confrontation was just an inconvenient setback and not any sort of preemptive strike on the part of the vampires, Raze felt more positive about the future. There would be time enough to track down Corvin again. Right now, he had another chore to do.

He lurched down the tunnel, occasionally reaching out with his hands to steady himself. Slime coated his palms and oozed down his arms as he returned to the blood-spattered stretch of tunnel where he had found the despicable vampiress bending over the lifeless form of his fallen pack brother.

Trix was right where Raze had left him, lying sprawled on his back in a puddle of gory muck, his human face frozen in agony. A trail of bloody entrance wounds stretched across Trix's chest, leaving little doubt about his cause of death. The lycan's own gun was missing, Raze noticed glumly.

He threw back his head and howled in rage and lamentation. Trix was only the latest pack member to fall prey to the bloods and their filthy silver. Raze couldn't wait to catch up with that dark-haired she-vamp again—and make her pay for Trix's untimely demise. He stared down at the bullet-riddled corpse with blood in his eyes.

Could be worse, he consoled himself. Blood oozing from his chest, the silver-scarred lycanthrope bent over and, grunting in pain, hefted the dead man up into his arms. *At least we killed two of the bloods tonight, twice the number of wolves claimed by the vampire bitch.* He could still taste the tangy meat of that careless male blood between his jaws, while their new ultraviolet ammunition had performed exactly as promised, roasting the other male vamp from the inside out. *Two of them to one of us,* he reflected savagely. *Not a bad outcome.*

He just hoped Lucian felt the same way.

Struggling under the weight of his doleful burden, Raze retraced his steps through the ancient sewer system.

Heading deeper.

Selene's room at the mansion was almost as Spartan as the dojo upstairs. Although her elevated status in the coven entitled her to a roomy suite of her own, complete with a balcony looking out over the front lawn, the actual furnishings were on the sparse side. A modern-looking steel desk gave her a place to work, while a richly upholstered divan allowed her to rest her head when she felt like taking a break. A portrait of a human family, consisting of a mother and father, two daughters, and a pair of twin girls, occupied a position of honor upon the desk. The framed photo served as both keepsake and inspiration, reminding Selene of why she hated the werewolves in the first place.

As if she could ever forget.

Moonlight entered her office through the balcony window, casting pale blue shadows onto the stark white carpet covering the floor. The ceaseless rain spattered against the window panes. Selene sat at her desk, staring intently at the illuminated screen of her laptop, which now held the disk from Rigel's digital camera. Still clad in her fighting leathers, she clicked rapidly through the surveillance photos Rigel had taken not long before his shocking demise. Her lips peeled away from her fangs, and she hissed venomously at the sight of the two murderous lycans in their street clothes. *If only I could have exterminated both of you,* she thought, gripped by an insatiable hatred that knew no relief; it would take more than the blood of just a single lycan to avenge the death of a Death Dealer.

Erika passed behind her, holding up an elegant dress. The turquoise gown, a hand-beaded silk georgette imported directly from Paris, had been fitted to Selene's exact measurements, which conveniently had remained unchanged for generations. The eager young maidservant had followed Selene back to her quarters, apparently at Kraven's instructions. Selene wished that Kraven were as concerned about the lycans' suspicious activities as he was about tonight's big reception.

The blond vampiress strolled up to a chrome-accented mirror mounted on a stark white wall. She posed before the mirror, holding the clingy embroidered gown in front of her. "Oooh, yes," Erika said girlishly. "You should definitely wear this one. It's perfect." She did a graceful twirl before the mirror, then added under her breath, "Maybe too perfect."

Even concentrating on the digitized photos, Selene couldn't miss the undercurrent of envy in the younger vampire's voice. Erika was decades away, in both power and prestige, from rating such posh attire. The servant girl's own flimsy little frock was considerably cheaper and more tawdry, making Erika look more like a London showgirl than an undead aristocrat.

The girl's jealousy was the least of Selene's concerns, however, as the zealous Death Dealer searched the digital images for some clue to the lycans' mission in the city. *Where had they intended to take the Metro to?* she wondered, having no doubt that the roaming lycans were up to no good. *There's something afoot.*

A head of sopping brown hair, attached to an attractively guileless face, caught her eye. *That's odd,* she thought, recognizing the good-looking American she had noticed back in Ferenciek Square; to her surprise, the handsome youth showed up in more than a few of the photos earlier that night. Although often out of focus or consigned to the fringes of the photo, the nameless American was nonetheless a continuing presence in the images flashing across her screen. *A coincidence,* Selene wondered, *or something more?*

Closing her eyes, she searched her own memories. In her mind, she saw once again the young man hurrying through the soaking downpour, then riding the crowded escalator down to the subway platform, followed moments later, she now realized, by Raze and Trix, stalking through the throng of commuters with malignant purpose, like hungry wolves tracking their next meal. She remembered the smaller lycan charging at the young American with outstretched claws. . . .

Her dark eyes snapped open. "They were after you," she murmured, suddenly comprehending.

But why?

Gripped by a renewed sense of urgency, she feverishly worked her laptop's keyboard and mouse. Quickly selecting the best photo of the unnamed pedestrian, she enlarged the image and adjusted the focus. The youth's chiseled features came into sharp relief, confirming that he was indeed the same individual she had noticed back in the city. Some sort of ID badge was clipped to his jacket, and she zoomed in on the small laminated rectangle, which turned out to be a hospital employee badge bearing the name "Michael Corvin."

Selene leaned back in her chair, staring speculatively into the warm brown eyes of the mysterious stranger. *Who are you, Michael Corvin?* she pondered, resting her chin on her steepled fingers. *And why were those lycans after you?*

She had lost track of Corvin once the shooting started but doubted that he had ended up in the subway tunnels with her and Raze. Selene remembered the gratifying sound of her silver throwing stars smacking into the werewolf's hairy chest. Chances were, the injured beast had been forced to abandon his prey, at least for a time. *Probably off licking his wounds somewhere,* she guessed.

But for how long?

Although she couldn't have explained why, Selene knew that it was vitally important that she locate Michael Corvin before Raze and his lycan compatriots did. He meant more than just fresh meat to those wolves.

"Mmm, he's cute," Erika commented, peeking over Selene's shoulder. Selene had briefly forgotten that the servant girl was still in the room. "For a human."

"Who's cute?" a third voice asked.

Both Selene and Erika looked up to see Kraven, resplendent in a black Armani suit, standing in the doorway. An irked, petulant expression compromised his dashing appearance. For herself, Selene suppressed a flare of irritation at the intrusion; Kraven hadn't felt it necessary to knock first.

Erika, on the other hand, immediately went into humble servant mode. Lowering her eyes, she bowed demurely and shuffled out of the room with a minimum of fuss, ducking beneath Kraven's arm as she passed through the door into the hallway outside, leaving Selene alone with Kraven.

Without waiting for an invitation, he sauntered into Selene's private quarters, his hands clasped behind his back. He strolled over to the balcony window and peered out into the stormy night. "Need I remind you," he said peevishly, "that we're expecting important guests?"

"No," Selene answered archly. "Erika's done that at least twenty times in the past hour."

Kraven turned away from the window, flashing her a wounded look. "Then why haven't you slipped into something more befitting?" He glanced at the empty silk gown, which Erika had left draped on the divan. "You know I was planning for you to be at my side this evening."

Selene could not think of a less appealing prospect, even if she didn't have more important matters to attend to. "I'm not in the mood," she declared. "Take Erika. She's just dying to be at your side."

Kraven grinned, evidently amused by the servant girl's hopeless infatuation. He walked over to where Selene was sitting, then leaned down toward her, bringing his ruddy face much too close for her liking.

"I'm sure she is," he whispered, "but everyone knows it's you I desire."

So what else is new? Selene thought, weary beyond measure of Kraven's advances. They had played this scene far too many times in the past. *You'd think that after all these years, he'd take the hint.*

His breath, hot and reeking of plasma, was unpleasantly warm upon her cheek. He moved to kiss her, but she deftly edged away from him at the last minute, a trick she had sadly had cause to perfect over the decades.

Kraven bristled at her rebuff, stiffly raising himself to his full height and throwing back his leonine black mane. Scowling, he swept a disdainful eye over her muddy boots and leathers, still besmirched by grimy souvenirs from Budapest's moldering sewer system.

"If you ask me, you take this entire warrior business far too seriously." He glanced at the framed family portrait resting on her desk. "You can't undo the past, no matter how many lycans you kill." His callous gaze left slimy, imaginary tracks across the precious portrait. "You do realize this, don't you?"

Selene shot him a warning look. He was coming dangerously close to trespassing upon sacred ground. Perhaps realizing that he had gone too far, he backed off a bit. He smiled amiably, as if to remove the sting from his sarcastic query.

"And besides," he continued, taking a less confrontational tack, "what's the use of being immortal if you deny yourself the simple pleasures of life?"

Hard to enjoy those pleasures, she reflected mordantly, *while a lycan is tearing out your throat and making a feast of your intestines.* She took a deep breath, not wanting to refight old battles. *Maybe I should make the most of Kraven's presence, while I actually have his attention.*

She pointed at the enhanced photo on the computer screen. "Do you see this human?"

Now it was Kraven's turn to sigh impatiently. He took a moment to inspect his well-manicured nails, which were apparently of more interest to him than the last moments of two Death Dealers. "What of him?"

"I can't be positive," she began, "but I'm beginning to think that the lycans—"

Kraven cut her off as the sudden glow of headlights flashed across the window. Selene realized that Soren had arrived with the visiting dignitaries from the New World Coven.

Damn, she thought. Their guests' timing could not have been worse. *Just when I was about to tell Kraven my theory!*

Kraven beamed happily, his truculent mood instantly lifted. "Now, please, put on something absolutely stunning, and be quick about it." His chest expanded beneath his elegant evening wear, like a rooster strutting in a hen yard. "I have a glorious evening planned. You'll see."

He headed for the exit, but Selene had not yet given up on the idea of sharing her concerns regarding the lycans. For better or for worse, he was the designated leader of the coven, and he needed to hear this.

"Kraven, this is serious," she called after him. "I think the enemy was following him."

He paused in the doorway and looked back at her with a puzzled look on his face, as if he'd just heard a bad joke whose punchline he didn't quite understand. "That's absurd," he said. "Other than for food, why would lycans stalk a mere human?"

Chapter Seven

$\mathcal{M}$uffled groans and whimpers escaped from the gagged mouths of the two captive humans. Strung up like sides of beef, and stripped to the waist, the men hung limply from a metal bar running the length of the abandoned subway station. Nylon webbing stretched across their mouths, while their mortal flesh was battered and bruised.

Singe paid no attention to the men's incoherent bleatings. They were just test animals, after all; he was interested in their blood chemistry, not their conversation.

The derelict Metro station had been converted into a makeshift laboratory and infirmary. Test tubes, beakers, retorts, and other chemical apparatus were arranged on crude benches fashioned of splintered plywood and salvaged metal struts. Grungy plastic sheets dangled from the ceiling, dividing the chamber into separate compartments. Jury-rigged fluorescent lights provided just enough illumination to allow Singe to get on with his work. The dark, dingy locale was somewhat less than completely sterile, the lycan scientist acknowledged, but what could you do? Hiding out underground had its disadvantages.

Photos, maps, and scribbled notes were plastered all over

the cracked tile walls. Dog-eared pages bore long lists of names, each appellation meticulously scratched out. At the center of the collage of papers was an elaborate family tree headed by a single name written in large block letters: "CORVINUS."

It may or may not have been of interest to the two trussed-up humans that their names and faces were among those displayed on the cluttered walls. Under the circumstances, Singe rather doubted that his two unlucky specimens were much concerned with the finer points of their ancestry. *Too bad,* he reflected. *It's a fascinating story.*

A weather-faced lycan wearing a stained brown lab coat, Singe had a receding hairline, a wrinkled brow, and a sly, foxlike expression. He calmly fitted an empty syringe with a twenty-three-gauge hypodermic needle, then approached the mortal he'd designated Subject B. The human's eyes widened in alarm at the sight of the massive needle, and his stifled cries took on a shriller tone. He thrashed helplessly within his restraints, unable to free himself.

Singe slunk behind the terrified specimen and waited quietly for the human to abandon his futile efforts. Within moments, the exhausted mortal gave up his struggles and slumped with his bonds, surrendering to the inevitable. Singe raised the syringe and nonchalantly jabbed it into the specimen's jugular vein.

Subject B writhed in agony. A muffled shriek came through his gag, and his tortured veins stood out like vines of clinging ivy.

"Come on, stop whining," Singe said impatiently. He was hardly known for his soothing bedside manner. An Austrian accent gave away his nationality. "It can't be that bad."

He tugged back on the plunger, and the thick syringe filled with dark venous blood. He waited until he had several cc's of the vital fluid, then abruptly withdrew the needle from the specimen's throat. Blood continued to stream from the site of the venipuncture, so Singe quickly slapped a bandage over the wound, just in case he needed to keep this specimen alive.

An identical bandage already graced the throat of the other specimen, a.k.a. Subject A.

Leaving the trembling human behind, he crossed the floor of the infirmary to a roughhewn counter, where he coolly and efficiently squirted the contents of the syringe into a pre-prepared glass beaker labeled B. Shrewd brown eyes examined the beaker, eager to see how this subject's blood reacted to the catalyst. An electronic timer ticked off the seconds.

A pity I can't report my findings to any of the established medical journals, he reflected. Singe had been a prominent biochemist in his native Austria before being recruited into the pack by Lucian himself, who had offered the dying scientist immortality in exchange for his loyalty and genius. *But I suppose wartime always imposes an element of secrecy.*

A door at the rear of the station slammed open, and Lucian swept into the laboratory, accompanied by a palpable aura of strength and authority. His glossy brown coat swept the floor.

He did not waste time with pleasantries. "Any progress?" he asked.

Singe dipped his head in deference to his pack leader. He opened his mouth to reply, only to be preempted by the sharp beep of yet another electronic timer. *Ah, perfect timing!* he thought with a smile. "Let's find out."

He turned his attention to a different beaker, this one labeled A. He gave it a gentle swish, to mix the contents thoroughly, then watched in disappointment as the crimson solution turned completely black.

"Negative," he announced sadly. *Again.*

Lucian frowned, clearly unhappy with the results of the experiment. Singe understood, however, that science was a matter of trial and error. *Sooner or later, we're bound to locate just the right specimen.* He thrilled in anticipation of that glorious day, when they finally would gain the means to dispose of their vampiric cousins once and for all.

But not today, it seemed.

A philosophical expression creased his vulpine features as Singe trudged over to one of the lengthy lists of names posted to the walls. With a sigh of weary resignation, he scratched out the name of Subject A: "JAMES T. CORVIN."

Michael Corvin read the faded printing on the door of his locker at Karolyi Hospital. A wrinkled set of puke-green scrubs hung inside the locker as Michael clanged the metal door shut. Yawning, he pulled a plain black T-shirt over his head, getting ready to head home at last.

It was five-thirty in the morning. Nearly nine hours had passed since the shoot-out in the subway station, and the blood on his street clothes had completely dried, but Michael still felt shell-shocked and on edge.

"Heading home?"

Michael turned to find his colleague, Adam Lockwood, standing behind him. A lanky man with short black hair, the other American resident was in his mid-twenties, but heavy-duty fatigue made him look older. His horn-rimmed glasses failed to conceal the dark, puffy circles shadowing his eyes. A stethoscope hung around his neck, and a pair of metal hemostats peeked from the corner of his rumpled white lab coat, as he sipped on his ninth or tenth cup of coffee.

"Yeah," Michael answered. "Nicholas gave me a few hours off."

Adam nodded sympathetically, and Michael wondered if he sounded half as wiped out as he felt. *Probably,* he thought.

"By the way," Adam added, "he said you did a terrific job tonight with that girl."

Michael managed a grim smile before grabbing his windbreaker and shuffling wearily toward the exit. He couldn't wait to get back to his apartment; with luck, he'd be in bed before the sun came up. But there was somewhere else he needed to visit first.

Moments later, he was in the Intensive Care Unit, staring through a large glass window at the injured girl from the subway. The Hungarian teenager was fresh out of surgery, unconscious and on life support. Michael felt a flare of anger on the girl's behalf. The poor kid had done nothing to deserve getting caught in that cross fire. She had just been in the wrong place at the wrong time.

Like Samantha, he thought bleakly.

He gazed at the injured girl. An electronic monitor, displaying illuminated green wave forms, kept watch over her blood pressure, temperature, and heart rate. Bags of whole blood flowed down IV tubing to replace the blood she had shed beneath Ferenciek Square.

The surgeons had stabilized her condition, at least. With luck, she'd make it.

This city is going straight to hell, he thought glumly.

Hell, in fact, was several meters beneath Budapest, in a vast subterranean bunker system built during the Second World War. The cavernous excavation once had been used as a storehouse but had been forgotten long since and allowed to fall into jumbled disrepair. Chunks of rubble were strewn across the floor of the bunker, amidst filmy pools of stagnant water. Rusted chains dangled from the vaulted ceiling high overhead, scraping against the mangled remains of dilapidated metal catwalks. Spiders, cockroaches, and other vermin infested every corner of the forgotten sanctuary, scuttling along the walls, yet the hangar-sized enclosure remained curiously free of rats or mice; even the hungriest rodent knew better than to venture into this man-made purgatory.

Now employed as rudimentary hovels and barracks, the decaying bomb shelters teemed with predatory life. Flickering lights shone through cracked and sooty windows. Humanoid lycans went about their business, while other pack members, who preferred their canine form, lounged amid the scattered debris like junkyard dogs. Bestial blue eyes glowed from the shadows.

Water dripped from the leaky ceiling, the constant tiny splashes echoing off the crumbling, mildewed walls. The fetid air was thick with the smell of unwashed bodies, both human and lupine, but despite the sizable population inhabiting the dismal bunker, not a single campfire burned. On two legs or four, lycans liked their meat raw and bloody.

Beyond the huge central chamber, a dark and twisted maze of war-torn passageways, gloomy chambers, barred windows, and shattered porcelain tiles extended through the ruins of the old bunker system, like an expressionist lunatic asylum designed and built by the inmates themselves.

Naked and bloody, Raze came staggering through one of these tenebrous corridors. He stumbled beneath the weight of Trix's bullet-filled body, wincing in pain from the shining metal stars embedded in his own lacerated chest. He cursed the bloods in general and that star-throwing vampire bitch in particular with every agonizing step.

Their time is coming, he remembered, drawing strength

from grisly imaginings of the carnage in store. *Just two more nights, then the stinking vampires will get what's coming to them! Lucian has it all planned . . .*

At long last, after what felt like an endless, arduous trek through the underworld, he made his way to the crudely constructed infirmary, where he found both Lucian and Singe. A pair of dead humans, their throats cleanly ripped out, still hung from the subway station's soot-stained ceiling. From their lifeless state, Raze guessed that these latest experimental subjects had proven just as unsatisfactory as the many others before them, which only made Raze all the more upset and embarrassed about letting that American medical student get away.

Damn bloods! he cursed again. *It was all their fault!*

He dumped Trix's bloody corpse onto an empty metal exam table, then looked over at Lucian and Singe. Pain and exhaustion were written all over his face, but he knew that Lucian would want his report before he could even think of getting rest or medical assistance.

"We were ambushed," he said tersely, leaning against the metal table for support. His deep voice rumbled like a kettle drum. "Death Dealers, three of them. We killed two, but one got away. A female."

Lucian greeted this news with a stern, inscrutable expression. "And the candidate?"

Raze lowered his head. If he'd had a tail, he would have tucked it between his legs. "We lost him," he admitted.

Lucian expelled a slow, exasperated breath. Clenching his fists at his sides, he turned to stare morosely out the grease-smeared windows. "Must I do everything myself?" he muttered under his breath.

Raze considered replying, then thought better of it. *Better to redeem myself through action, not words*, he decided, vowing not to let Michael Corvin—or any other future candidates—escape him again. *And heaven help any sun-shirking vampire who gets in my way!*

The body on the table attracted Singe's attention. "Look at this mess," he said, *tsk-tsk*ing at the gory bullet holes desecrating Trix's chest.

"AG rounds. High content," Raze supplied. "Kept him from making the change."

The Austrian scientist didn't appear too broken up by Trix's violent demise. He grabbed a pair of stainless-steel forceps and began rooting around in the dead lycan's gaping chest wounds. Raze recoiled from the squishy noises made by the doctor's ungentle explorations, but within moments, Singe had extracted the mushroom-shaped remains of a shiny silver bullet.

"No use in digging out the rest," he declared. Taking pains not to touch the toxic slug himself, the scientist dropped the squashed bullet onto a blood-stained metal tray. "Silver's penetrated his organs. Regeneration's impossible at this point."

Raze had figured as much. He knew a dead lycan when he smelled one. *I owe you, bitch,* he thought, picturing the female Death Dealer in his mind. *You and the rest of your kind.*

Having written off Trix, Singe cast an appraising eye on Raze himself. "Ah, but there's still hope for you, my friend." He approached Raze, inspecting the larger lycan's injuries. The silver points of the *shuriken* jutted from Raze's dark skin. "So let's take a closer look at these nasty little stickers, shall we?"

He traded in his now bloody forceps for a black steel hex wrench and took hold of one of the throwing stars in Raze's broad, hairless chest. The wounded lycan tensed in anticipation of the pain to come.

"Relax," Singe told him, sliding the wrench into a depression and slowly applying pressure. He turned the wrench, and Raze winced in agony. He bit down hard, clenching his jaws to keep from screaming, but a tortured grunt still escaped him. Undeterred by the other lycan's obvious discomfort, Singe used the wrench to activate the star's arming mechanism. *Click.* The points of the star retracted back into the silver disk, and Singe slowly worked the unlocked weapon out of Raze's flesh, millimeter by excruciating millimeter. "See," the doctor announced, holding up the bloody silver coin. "Not so bad."

Easy for you to say, Raze thought, glowering at the beaming lycan scientist. The extraction process had hurt like blazes, and there were still three more stars to go!

Several paces away, Lucian finally emerged from his brooding silence. He turned and locked eyes with Raze. "The vampires didn't realize you were following a human . . . did they, Raze?"

The urgency in his voice cut through the pain of Raze's ongoing ordeal. "No," the bleeding lycan replied, even as Singe slid the hex wrench into the next star. "Aaarrgh!"

Click. The second star was pulled from his chest. Raze gasped and swallowed the pain before speaking again. "I mean, I don't think so."

Lucian pounced on the uncertainty in his voice. He advanced on Raze, extracting information the same way Singe was extracting the poisonous stars. "You don't think, or you don't know?"

Singe inserted the wrench into **the third** star, and it took all of Raze's self-control not to flinch. "I'm not sure," he blurted, on the cusp of another starburst of pain. "Rrgggg!"

Click. The star released its locking blades but refused to let go of Raze's throbbing muscle and bone. Singe had to wiggle the star back and forth for a while, which hurt like hell, before the silver disk finally came free.

"Ooh, that one was really in there," Singe commented breezily, dropping it into the waste bin along with the rest of the silver detritus. Raze noticed that garbage bag was marked with the universal symbol for biohazardous waste; as far as lycans were concerned, silver was as toxic as plutonium.

Tell me about it, he thought irritably. The beginnings of a growl rumbled at the back of his throat. His hands cramped into claws, the jagged nails extending imperceptibly.

An electronic timer beeped, calling Singe away from him and granting Raze a momentary respite. The Austrian scientist hastily inspected a row of glass beakers, all of which contained an opaque black fluid. Raze had spent enough time around the laboratory to know that these were not the results Singe and Lucian were hoping for.

"Negative, the lot," Singe said, shaking his head. "We're rapidly running out of candidates." He walked over to the family tree on the wall and drew a bright red line under a single name located near the bottom of the complicated genealogical chart. "So I really must insist we have a look at this Michael Corvin."

Lucian gave Raze a scathing look, then stalked wordlessly out of the infirmary. Singe turned toward Raze, an amused expression upon his wizened face. "Congratulations. I think you just made the top of his shit list. After the vampires, of course."

It wasn't my fault! Raze thought indignantly. He wasn't sure what angered him more, Lucian's unspoken scorn or the doctor's mockery. Infuriated, he didn't wait for Singe to apply the wrench to the fourth and final throwing star.

Snarling like a rabid hound, he yanked the offending missile from his flesh with his bare hands, ignoring the scalding heat of the exposed silver. The star's razor-sharp barbs shredded his raw and mutilated flesh. Blood spurted from the wound, and steam rose from his fingertips, as Raze threw back his head and roared with all his might.

Chapter Eight

The atmosphere in the grand salon was refined, civilized. Bach's *Das wohltemperierte Klavier* played softly in the background as the elite of the coven welcomed their distinguished visitors from America. Crimson nourishment, of a particularly choice pedigree, flowed freely, sipped from sparkling crystal chalices. Vampire ladies and gentlemen, in their finest and most stylish raiment, flirted decorously with their honored guests.

Kraven should have been in his element. The gala reception was precisely the kind of chic, tony soiree he thrived on. Holding court near the entrance of the salon, accepting fulsome compliments from the visiting dignitaries while flattering them in turn, he found himself distracted and unable to enjoy himself. His eyes restlessly searched the faces of the crowd, looking for one particular vampiress, but Selene was nowhere to be seen.

Devil take the woman! he thought, concealing his growing vexation from the distinguished guests conversing with him. *Where in blazes is she now?*

He glanced over at a tall, black-haired vampire standing watch over the reception from a discreet corner of the room.

This was Soren, the imposing head of Kraven's not-so-secret police. Although reputed to be nearly as old as Viktor himself, Soren was usefully unambitious, preferring to place his considerable strength and lack of scruples at the disposal of his chosen leader. Of Black-Irish descent, he had the broad shoulders and baleful looks of his fierce ancestors. Soren once had been Viktor's personal bodyguard; now he was Kraven's.

The looming janissary looked somewhat out of place among the mingling socialites, but Kraven felt better to know that Soren and his hand-picked team of vampire enforcers were on hand should anything untoward occur. Kraven had long ago seen the need for a security force of his own, independent of the obsessed and often intractable Death Dealers, and Soren—ruthless, pragmatic, and brutal when necessary—had proven just the right vampire to carry out the more draconian elements of Kraven's agenda.

Unfortunately, it appeared that not even Soren could guarantee Selene's attendance at even so glittering an affair. He shot Soren a questioning look, but the stony-faced enforcer shook his head curtly. Kraven resisted an urge to charge up to Selene's room and personally drag her down to the party. *I've had quite enough of her willfulness and insubordination,* he fulminated silently. *My patience is wearing thin.*

A gaunt, epicene vampire wearing a red silk sash across the front of his tuxedo stepped into the center of the room and tapped a long white fingernail against the side of his chalice, calling the room to silence. Kraven recognized Dmitri, the eldest of Amelia's envoys. The ageless diplomat waited patiently for the chamber's conversations to subside, then cleared his throat. Kraven realized, with a touch of impatience, that the old fool was going to make a speech.

"Our noble houses may be separated by a great ocean,"

Dmitri intoned sonorously, "but we are equally committed to the survival of our sacred bloodlines. When the illustrious Amelia, whom I have the honor of serving, arrives to awaken the slumbering Marcus, in just two nights' time, we will once again be united as a single coven." He raised his chalice high, leading the assembled aristocrats in a toast.

"*Vitam et sanguinem,*" he recited.

Life and blood.

A chorus of clinking crystal seconded the toast, and Kraven raised his own glass, grateful that the pompous envoy had kept his remarks short. Kraven snuck a peek at the open doorway, hoping to see Selene make a tardy arrival, but he was disappointed once more. *I swear,* he thought in righteous indignation, *if she were not my intended queen, I would never let her get away with such effrontery!*

A cool hand tugged on his elbow, and he turned to see that same blond servant wench—Erika—standing at his side. She was wearing, in keeping with the occasion, a dark sequined dress, with elbow-length black gloves, which did not look too conspicuously threadbare amidst the more dazzling finery of the vampire nobles. *What the devil does* she *want?* he wondered, irked by the intrusion.

The elfin maidservant pointed demurely at her lips, then beckoned for his ear. Curious, Kraven bent over and let Erika whisper in his ear. His annoyance at the servant girl was instantly superseded by a more volcanic fury directed at another. *I don't believe it!* he thought, aghast. *How dare she?*

Without bothering to make his apologies to his esteemed guests, he stormed out of the salon. He dashed up the mansion's grand staircase, taking the steps two at a time, until he came to the heavy oak door guarding Selene's room. He threw open the door and charged inside, quickly confirming that the chamber was just as deserted as Erika had predicted.

A car engine roared to life outside, and Kraven ran to the window just in time to witness Selene's sporty Jaguar speeding past the estate's outer gates, tearing off into the night.

Damnation! He gnashed his fangs in fury as he watched the Jag's taillights disappear into the distance. He glanced at his wristwatch. It was after five A.M. The sun would be rising in a matter of hours. *So where in Hades could she be going in such a confounded hurry,* he wondered angrily, *and tonight of all nights?*

Kraven retreated from the window, perplexed and grievously offended. Scanning the room for some clue to Selene's inexcusable behavior, he noted her laptop sitting open on the desk; in her unseemly haste, she had left the machine up and running.

Frozen on the screen was the profile of some insignificant mortal, apparently lifted from a hospital employee database. A color photo of a brown-haired youth was accompanied by the human's name, Michael Corvin, and various pieces of personal information: age, nationality, address, and so on. Kraven noted with disdain that this Corvin creature was a mere twenty-eight years old. He was a callow pup even by mortal standards.

Who? Kraven vaguely remembered Selene saying something ridiculous about the lycans stalking a particular human, but he failed to see what could possibly be so important about one nondescript mortal. *For this,* he thought indignantly, *she left me without an escort at my own reception?*

Whoever this Michael Corvin was, Kraven already disliked him intensely.

The grungy apartment building was a far cry from the stately decor of the manor. The carpeted hallway was badly in need of vacuuming, while the plaster walls were scuffed and cracked in places. Harsh fluorescent lights hummed and crackled.

Good, Selene thought. These were exactly the sort of low-rent lodgings where she would expect to find a struggling medical student. *Must be the right place.*

According to his employee file, the mysterious Michael Corvin lived on the top floor of the five-story apartment building, which was located within walking distance of the Metro station at Ferenciek Square. Striding down the empty corridor, she counted down the numbers toward Corvin's apartment, 510. Tarnished brass numerals, nailed to a cheap plywood door, confirmed that she had arrived at her intended destination.

She paused outside the door, consulting her watch.

Five-fifty. Less than an hour to sunrise.

With little time to spare, she did not waste precious minutes picking the lock. Instead, she effortlessly kicked the door open with a single burst of superhuman strength.

Unlike the vampires of myth and movies, she required no invitation to enter the apartment.

The ICU at Karolyi Hospital smelled unpleasantly of antiseptic. Pierce was grateful that in his human form, his nose was not nearly as acute as when he was a wolf.

He and Taylor had arrived at the hospital, disguised in the distinctive blue uniforms of Hungarian policemen, in search of the elusive Michael Corvin. Pierce looked forward to succeeding where Raze had failed—capturing the human, pleasing Lucian, and thereby raising his and Taylor's standing in the pack.

Unfortunately, Corvin apparently had left the hospital already, and his colleague, a frazzled-looking human named Lockwood, was not proving of much assistance.

"Sorry," the lanky physician said with a shrug. "You just missed him."

Pierce had given Lockwood the impression that he and his fellow "officer" just wanted to ask Corvin a few more questions about the incident in the underground. The lycan's long black hair had been pulled back into a ponytail, the better to impersonate a cop. "You know where we can find him?"

Lockwood threw up his hands. "He's working a split shift. You'll either have to try him at home or wait until he comes back."

Scowling, Pierce exchanged an impatient glance with Taylor. The other lycan still had an ugly-looking cut on his cheek, left over from their gladiatorial battle down in their lair. Pierce remembered inflicting the wound with his own bloody claws and regretted that Lucian had aborted the contest before either of them could have claimed victory. *I know I could have beaten him!* Pierce thought savagely. *My jaws were strong, my teeth were red!*

Perhaps Lockwood noted the bloodthirsty gleam in Pierce's eyes, or maybe he just picked up on the two lycans' tense and edgy mood; in any event, a worried tone entered his voice:

"Michael isn't in any kind of trouble, is he?"

Despite the early hour, Michael Corvin was not at home. Selene did not find this too surprising; she was well aware that student doctors often kept ungodly hours. *Not unlike vampires,* she thought wryly.

That was not the only thing she had in common with Corvin. Like her own rooms back at Ordoghaz, the human's apartment had a stark, utilitarian feel. The furniture was functional, not decorative, and the barren, off-white walls offered little insight into the American's personality and tastes. The bland, featureless apartment almost could have passed as a hotel room.

Why would the lycans be interested in this human? Selene took advantage of Corvin's absence to search his apartment, hoping to discover some clue to the mystery. Moving with near-surgical precision, she conducted a thorough sweep of the premises, sifting through his sparse personal effects. There was no need to turn on the lights; vampire vision was all she required to probe the shadowy corners of the apartment.

A stack of mail piled on an end table yielded nothing incriminating, only bills and junk mail. His bookshelf was equally innocuous, holding only an assortment of medical textbooks, an English-Hungarian dictionary, and a couple of paperback novels, in English, of course. Mysteries and thrillers mostly. Nothing remarkable, not even a dog-eared copy of *Dracula* or *The Werewolf of Paris*.

The apartment was also devoid of guns, drugs, pornography, or anything remotely illicit or dangerous. No silver bullets, no wooden stakes, no garlic . . . nothing. His small refrigerator contained only TV dinners, not plasma or human flesh. Michael Corvin appeared to be exactly what he seemed: a perfectly normal human being, albeit rather far from home.

So why were Raze and that other lycan stalking him?

She was on the verge of giving up her search, when she stumbled upon a battered manila envelope, tucked away at the back of his desk drawer, where she had missed it before. Carefully opening the envelope, she discovered a sheaf of color photographs.

A cavalcade of unfamiliar faces smiled at her. Corvin's friends and family, she guessed. The brown-haired youth appeared in a number of the photos himself, his smiling semblance captured in a variety of unsuspicious contexts: birthday parties, graduations, camp-outs, beaches, ski trips, and so on.

The sunny images, radiant with warmth and fun and fellowship, provoked a peculiar melancholy in the driven vampiress. Her throat tightened as she flipped through the carefree photos, which suddenly struck her as painful reminders of the humanity she had lost over the course of time. She remembered the faded portrait residing on her own desk and wondered why Corvin chose to keep these golden memories hidden away and out of sight.

Doesn't he realize how lucky he is?

She came upon a heartbreaking photo of Corvin and an unknown woman posing arm-in-arm in front of a breathtaking sunset, of the sort that Selene had not seen since she had first learned to fear the sun. There was no mistaking the obvious affection and intimacy between the couple. They were deeply, happily, hopelessly in love.

Selene felt a yearning that was almost physical. Her brown eyes gleamed moistly. Had she ever known a love like this? Not truly, she admitted. She had been a mere slip of a girl, fresh-faced and virginal, when Viktor had first turned her, ages ago. Since then, her immortal existence had been consumed by her sacred war against the lycans, so that she had all but forgotten the simple, everyday joys of friends and family.

Let alone love.

The same woman, sun-kissed and radiant, appeared in several of the photos. Corvin's sweetheart? Girlfriend? Fiancée? Wife? Selene felt a sudden, irrational surge of jealousy.

Enough, she thought firmly. She was wasting time. It was

clear the innocent snapshots held no explanation for the lycans' unaccountable interest in Corvin.

Dropping the photos onto the floor like so much trash, she wandered back toward Corvin's overstuffed bookshelf, just in case she had missed something earlier. She ran a gloved finger along the spines of the books, once again finding nothing but a surplus of medical tomes. *Perhaps the lycans are trying to draft a medic?* she speculated. Someone had to pry the silver bullets out of their mangy hides. *But why Corvin? Why now?*

A stethoscope hung on a nail not far from the bookshelf. She fingered the rubber tubing thoughtfully, while wondering just how long she intended to wait for Corvin to return home. Dawn was near, and she was far from the mansion . . .

The phone rang, startling her.

Chapter Nine

Michael heard the phone ringing as he trudged down the hall toward his apartment. He briefly considered making a dash for the phone, but it was late, and he was too damn tired. That's what answering machines were for.

He had to wonder, though, who was calling him in the wee hours of the morning. Had one of his friends back in the States forgotten about the six-hour time difference between Long Island and Budapest? *Probably just a wrong number,* he figured. Or maybe Nicholas wanting him to work an extra shift.

No way, he thought. Between the bloodbath in the underground and the not-quite-full-moon madness in the ER, he had paid his dues for the evening. All he wanted now was a couple hours of unbroken sleep.

His groggy eyes widened in surprise, however, as he found the door to his apartment ajar. *What the hell?* he wondered, even as his answering machine finally kicked into gear. Michael heard his own voice, oddly distorted by the cheap electronic device, issue from the darkened apartment: "Hey, this is Michael. You know what to do."

The greeting was delivered first in English, then repeated

in somewhat shakier Hungarian, while the real Michael cautiously entered his defenseless apartment. *I don't frigging believe this,* he thought, torn between alarm and exasperation. *First the shoot-out, now this!* Was he interrupting a burglary in progress, or had the perpetrators already fled the scene? Michael fervently rooted for the latter scenario. After all, it wasn't as if he had anything worth stealing . . .

The answering machine beeped loudly, and Michael froze in his tracks as the machine recorded a frantic message: "Hey, Mike, it's Adam." Michael heard an uncharacteristic degree of anxiety in his friend's voice. "Look, the police were just in here looking for you, and I got the definite impression that they're convinced you were involved in the shoot-out. I told them there was no way you'd be mixed up—"

The police? Michael reacted in surprise, a second before a shadow exploded from the darkness and viciously slammed Michael against the wall, pinning him there. He glimpsed a feminine face, obscured by the darkness. Powerful fingers, amazingly strong, gripped his throat tightly. A cold, hard voice demanded answers.

"Who are you? Why are they after you?"

Michael was too shocked and bewildered to reply. He glanced down and was startled to see that his feet were a good six inches off the floor. *How is that even possible?* he wondered, dumbfounded. *Who the hell is this? Darth Vader?*

His assailant leaned forward. A shaft of light from the hallway exposed her face, and he was stunned to see that it belonged to that gorgeous, dark-haired woman from the subway station. Recognition flooded his face.

"You."

Before he could even begin to process what was happening, the entire apartment trembled. Plaster rained down from the ceiling as three heavy objects landed on the roof. *Huh?* he thought, unable to keep up with the flood of unexpected jolts. *What just smacked down on the roof?*

Hissing like a cat, the mystery woman let go of Michael, dropping him back onto the floor, and drew a lethal-looking automatic pistol from beneath the folds of a black leather trench coat. Without a moment's hesitation, she unloaded an entire clip into the ceiling. Michael's ears rang with the explosive thunder of automatic weapons fire.

Her high-caliber assault on the ceiling provoked a chorus of ferocious roars from whoever—or whatever—was on the roof. Shaking like a leaf, Michael wasn't sure what terrified him more, the blaring gunfire or the horrendous howls.

"Stay down!" the woman shouted at him.

Screw that! Michael thought, and bolted for the door.

Unlike Michael, Selene knew exactly what was on the roof. Expert ears recognized the monstrous tread of three fully transformed werewolves. *They must be desperate to get Corvin,* she realized, *if they're willing to reveal their beast forms so readily.*

Her trusty Beretta discharged an empty clip, and she hastily reloaded before turning to check on the baffled human, who so far had shown no sign of understanding what was happening. To her dismay, she found herself alone in the apartment.

Michael Corvin was gone.

Damn! she cursed in frustration. She raced out of the apartment into the hall, just in time to see a pair of elevator doors closing on Corvin.

He was getting away!

Wood and glass exploded to her right as, one after another, three snarling werewolves burst through a fire escape window at the far end of the hall. Fangs bared, cobalt eyes gleaming, they bounded down the dimly lit corridor, heading straight for her. Foam dripped from their frothing jaws.

Selene looked hurriedly for an exit. Alas, the other end of the hallway ended in a closed apartment door. Worse still, the only stairs were at the opposite end of the corridor, *beyond* the charging werewolves.

She was trapped—or was she? Thinking quickly, she opened fire on the rampaging beasts while simultaneously yanking a second Beretta from her belt. The barrage of silver bullets barely slowed the ravening werewolves; they were in a berserker fury now, and nothing short of a clean kill was going to stop them. There was no way she could take out all three wolves before one or more of them tore her apart.

Time for a quick getaway. Spinning on her heels, she fired at the floor with her second gun, tracing a circular pattern around her boots with automatic fury. Splinters flew wildly about her ankles, and a jagged hole opened up beneath her.

Gravity seized her, and she dropped through the gap to the next floor down, landing hard in a dusty avalanche of shredded wood and carpet. She glanced quickly at the elevator, only to see it bypass this floor, heading toward the lobby. *Great,* she thought sarcastically. Corvin was still getting away from her.

She whirled around toward the stairwell, her only escape route. It was at the far end of the hall, approximately thirty paces away. If she hurried, maybe she could still elude the werewolves and beat Corvin to the ground floor.

A deafening roar sounded overhead, and a fearsome claw reached through the gaping hole in the ceiling. Selene ducked just in time, barely escaping decapitation. She fired back at the werewolves, strafing the ceiling with red-hot silver as she scrambled for the stairs.

The narrow hallway turned into a hellish gauntlet as yet more lycanthropic arms came thrusting through the ceiling, seeking to snag her before she reached the safety of the stairs. Sparks flew from fractured light fixtures, and knife-like claws raked the air around her. The clamor of the howling werewolves awoke the sleeping apartment building. Selene heard clumsy stirrings and fearful exclamations coming from behind the flimsy plywood doors.

A lupine paw grabbed her long brown hair, the points of its bony claws brushing against her scalp, and Selene put on a burst of speed, tearing herself free of the creature's murderous grasp. *That was close,* she realized, wishing she had a full cadre of Death Dealers on hand to back her up. The odds against her were three to one—or worse.

Maybe coming after Corvin herself hadn't been such a bright idea.

Inside the elevator, Michael cringed at the thunderous growls and gunshots penetrating the dubious security of the descending metal compartment. His anxious brown eyes tracked his progress toward the lobby as he willed the creaky elevator to greater speed. His distraught mind worked feverishly to make sense of it all. Who was that woman, and what were those animals on the roof? *It sounds like a jungle safari gone wrong out there,* he thought, feeling as though he were trapped in a particularly incoherent nightmare. Shoot-outs in subways were one thing; that was just modern urban warfare in the early twenty-first century. Nasty but not unprecedented. But a leather-clad super-babe blasting away at roof-prowling beasts in his own apartment at six o'clock in the morning? Where the heck had that come from—and what did it have to do with him?

The elevator bumped to a stop on the ground floor, and Michael expelled a gasp of relief. "Come on, come on," he muttered, waiting endlessly for the sealed car to release him. His sneakers tapped impatiently on the floor, until the metal doors finally slid open—to reveal a stranger waiting in the lobby.

"Hello, Michael," the man said, speaking English with a crisp British accent. A slight, bearded man, maybe thirty-five years old, with cunning gray eyes and shoulder-length black hair, the stranger stood calmly in front of the elevator, his hands clasped behind him. Much like the gun-wielding amazon who had invaded Michael's apartment, the nameless individual wore a long brown coat over equally dark attire, including a pair of dark brown gloves. A gleaming metal amulet dangled around his neck. He smiled at Michael with teeth that seemed altogether too white and sharp.

As far as Michael knew, he had never seen this person before, not even in the subway earlier.

Before either of the men could say another word, shots suddenly rang out in the lobby. The stranger stiffened as the bullets struck his body. Another shot grazed his right temple, opening a bloody gash along the side of his skull.

Startled by the impact, the wounded man dived into the elevator, knocking Michael over as he did so. They hit the floor hard, the jolt knocking the wind out of Michael. He found himself lying flat on his back, tangled in a jumble with the other man. Rivulets of dark red blood streamed down the stranger's face, as he instinctively reached for his head. He grimaced in pain, looking more pissed off than afraid.

Who the heck is this dude? Michael thought. Strangely, he was more scared of the gunshot victim than for him. *And who is shooting at us?*

Looking up, past the injured man's shoulder, Michael saw the woman from his apartment suddenly appear in the doorway of the elevator. She thrust her smoking pistols into her belt as she ducked down and grabbed hold of Michael's leg. Once again, he was caught off-guard by the astounding strength of her grip.

Tugging on his ankle, she effortlessly dragged him across the floor of the elevator toward the lobby beyond. Before she pulled him completely clear, however, the other man lunged at him like a blood-soaked demon, sinking his teeth into Michael's shoulder.

Shit! He bit me!

He yelped in shock, feeling razor-sharp incisors slice deeply into his flesh. But the strength of the mystery woman was too powerful to be denied; in an instant, he was yanked away from the piercing fangs and into the lobby of his apartment building, where she rapidly jerked him to his feet.

Blood gushed from his punctured shoulder, but the leather-clad mystery woman seemed in too much of a hurry to notice. Grabbing him by the wrist, she dragged Michael with her as she raced for the door leading to the grimy alley outside. Michael didn't even try to resist; he was just as eager to get away from the psycho in the elevator as she was.

She kicked the front door open, and they hastily fled the building. The rain was coming down hard again, pelting the hood of a snazzy silver Jaguar parked right outside.

Nice wheels, he thought absurdly as she threw open the passenger door and shoved him inside.

* * *

Lucian's mouth was filled with the human's blood. Still sprawled on the floor of the elevator, the injured lycan resisted the urge to swallow the hot, tangy fluid. Instead, he groped about in his pocket until he retrieved a tiny glass vial, which had somehow miraculously survived the vampire's attack. Uncapping the vial, he spit a mouthful of fresh blood into the sterile glass receptacle.

Mission accomplished, he thought coolly.

Still, he couldn't allow Michael Corvin to fall into the hands of the vampires, not if the American was indeed the one they sought. Even if the bloodsuckers were unaware of Corvin's potential significance, Lucian had waited too long to let any candidate slip from his clutches.

First, though, he had to do something about the wretched silver.

The vampire's bullets burned hellishly within his flesh. Unless he rid himself of their presence soon, the poison would spread throughout his system, killing him just as surely as if the female vampire had sliced off his head. The caustic taint of the silver blazed like acid beneath his skin.

He climbed to his feet, ignoring the throbbing agony, and ripped open his shirt. A trail of gaping entry wounds riddled his chest, enough to kill any ordinary man or lycanthrope. Lucian counted at least a half dozen bullet holes. *This isn't going to be easy,* he realized.

He took a deep breath and stared at the ceiling. A look of intense concentration came over his bloodstained face as he closed his eyes and focused on expelling the poison from his body. Straining muscles rippled beneath his skin, while the tendons in his neck stood out tautly, like steel cords. Blood pounded at his temples. His jaws clenched as tightly as his fists.

At first, nothing happened. Then, one by one, the yawning wounds contracted, disgorging warped silver slugs in what looked like a grotesque mockery of the miracle of birth. A single blood-red bullet clattered onto the floor of the elevator, followed by a string of identical pellets hitting the ground.

Lucian's ashen face remained a mask of utter concentration. It had taken him centuries to master this trick, and even now it required all his mental energy and discipline. Agonizing hours seemed to pass, but, in fact, it took him only a matter of minutes to extrude every trace of silver from his immortal form.

He let out an exhausted gasp, and his shoulders slumped with released tension, as the last silver projectile clinked onto the floor.

Now then, he thought, licking the last of Michael's blood from his teeth. *Time to catch up with Mr. Corvin—and that trigger-happy vampire bitch.*

"What the fuck is going on?" Michael demanded, strapped into the passenger seat of the sleek silver Jag. He didn't know if he was being kidnapped or rescued or both.

The mystery woman ignored his frantic query. Putting the pedal to the metal, she sent the Jag screeching out of the alley. The sudden acceleration threw Michael back against his seat, silencing him for the moment.

He whipped his head around, peering back through the Jag's rear window at the apartment building, his home away from home in Budapest, and was shocked to see the lunatic from the elevator come striding out of the lobby, blood dripping from his forehead and bared chest. *What the fuck?* Michael thought, flabbergasted. His shoulder stung like hell where the bloodthirsty Brit had bit him. *I thought she shot him full of bullets.*

The stranger sure didn't look like a man who had just suffered multiple gunshots. Spotting the Jaguar, he raced after it with impossible speed. *This can't be happening!* Michael thought in stunned disbelief. The blood-streaked madman was actually *gaining* on the sports car, as if he were the Six-Zillion-Dollar Man or something. Michael's jaw dropped as the carnivorous stranger pounced at the car like a wild beast, leaping through the rain as though jet-propelled.

Ka-runch! Their pursuer crashed down onto the trunk of the Jag, causing both Michael and the mystery woman to start forward in their seats. Michael's eyes bulged from their sockets as he watched the indefatigable stranger scramble up the back of the car onto the roof, never mind the wind or the rain or the fact that the Jag was going at least sixty miles per hour!

This was getting more insane by the second. *Who are these people?* Michael wondered desperately. *And what do they want from me?*

The rain-slick metal was cold and slippery, but Lucian's powerful fingers found purchase anyway, digging into the bonded aluminum with clawlike nails that were several centimeters longer than they had been a second ago. It would take more than bad weather to cheat him of his prize, not after all the centuries he'd spent plotting and planning his revenge against the vampires. Michael Corvin might well be the key to Lucian's ultimate victory, and he wasn't about to let some slinky vampire minx abscond with the hapless American.

The icy wind hurled the rain against his face, washing away much of the blood from his head wound, as Lucian clambered up the back of the car onto the roof. His long black hair whipped back and forth in the gale. His left hand held on tightly to the chrome trim on the left side of the roof while he reared back in fury and raised his clenched right fist.

Sha-shank! A black carbon steel blade, double-edged and thirty centimeters long, snapped out of his sleeve with spring-loaded force. *Who needs to transform,* he thought wryly, *when you've got modern technology on your side?*

Michael stared in fear and confusion at the roof of the Jaguar. He couldn't see the bloodthirsty, seemingly indestructible stranger anymore, but Michael knew the other man was up there, only inches above their heads. He suddenly recalled the heavy whatsits landing on the roof of the apartment building, right before he ran like crazy out of his apartment. Had that been only five or ten minutes ago? It was hard to believe.

Everything was happening way too fast. Michael held his breath, fearful and uncertain about what was coming next. What could the stranger do to them, up on top of the car as he was? *Something bad,* Michael guessed, none too eager to find out. *Something really, really bad.*

A sharp black knife, thrusting through the metal roof of the accelerating Jaguar, fulfilled his dire expectations. The double-edged blade stabbed repeatedly through the rooftop over the driver's seat, trying to skewer the unknown woman behind the wheel.

"Watch out!" Michael shouted too late. The blade found its mark, sliding all the way through the woman's shoulder. She yelped in shock, then slammed on the brakes, which squealed like banshees as the Jag abruptly screeched to a halt. Michael thanked God for his seatbelts, which were all that kept him from flying headfirst through the rain-streaked windshield.

Their attacker was not so lucky. The sudden stop catapulted him off the roof of the car. Michael watched with eyes agog as the madman hit the street, rolling to a stop several yards in front of the car. He lay facedown on the rain-drenched cobblestones. Michael feared that the man was seriously injured—until he raised his head and started to get up.

What was it going to take to stop this guy?

Blood streaming from her impaled shoulder, the woman floored the gas pedal. The Jag lunged forward, heading straight for the stranger, who was already clambering back onto his feet. Tires squealed against wet pavement. "No!" Michael yelled instinctively.

The Jag slammed into the stranger with a sickening thud, launching him into orbit.

The car hit Lucian head-on, its front end striking his entire body from the shoulders down. The force of the collision shattered ribs and knocked the breath from his body. Against his will, his feet left the pavement as he tumbled toward the moonlit sky.

An ordinary human would be unconscious already, if not dead on impact, but Lucian, a pure-born lycanthrope, was not human and never had been. Although fundamentally more canine than feline, he twisted in the air like a panther, landing on his feet many meters behind the female vampire's speeding sports car. Dark eyes smoldered with stringently controlled rage as he watched the Jaguar's taillights pull away from him, disappearing into the night.

That had to be Selene, he guessed, recalling the formidable reputation of a certain infamous female Death Dealer. His mole inside the vampires' coven often had spoken of Selene and her intense hatred of all things lycan. Lucian always had suspected that their paths would cross someday, but this was not exactly the outcome he had intended. He sniffed the air, smelling the vampire's cold blood upon his blade.

The black knife retracted into his sleeve with a metallic click. Gloved fists clenched in frustration. Fractured ribs began to reknit themselves painfully. Lucian had scored first blood against Selene, yet somehow she had escaped with his prize.

Not for long, he vowed. Michael Corvin was too important to his plans. Lucian checked his pocket and was relieved to discover that the precious vial of blood had survived his close encounter with the Jaguar's front end. *A partial victory, then,* he concluded.

He had the human's blood. That would have to do.

For now.

Chapter Ten

The Jaguar came power-sliding out of an alley, taking the curve at more than fifty miles per hour. The hair-raising turn threw Michael against the passenger door. His right shoulder flared in agony where the crazed stranger had bitten it.

Despite his own injury, Michael was more worried about the mystery woman's speared shoulder. The wound was bleeding profusely, much more than his. Years of medical training kicked in as Michael frantically attempted to apply pressure to the gash carved out by the madman's knife. To his surprise, the woman's blood felt strangely cool against his palm.

"Stop the car!" he shouted. It was hard enough to try to treat a wound like this with his bare hands, let alone to perform first aid in a speeding vehicle. He'd ridden in rushing ambulances that had raced through city streets slower than the Jaguar was going now. "Stop the car!"

The woman angrily slapped his hand away with her free hand, then snatched up her pistol and aimed it at Michael. "Back off!" she ordered.

Michael took the hint and did just that. He sank back

into his seat, nervously eyeing the gleaming firearm. From what he'd seen so far, he didn't think she was bluffing.

"Okay, okay," he assured her, holding up his hands in a conciliatory gesture. He took a second to glance back through the rear window, but there was no sign of the nut with the knife, not that Michael much expected to see one. The Jaguar already had left the scene of the hit-and-run attack a couple of blocks behind. Michael found it hard to imagine that the stranger could still come after them after being turned into roadkill, but at this point he didn't know what to believe.

The Jaguar was heading west toward the Danube, zipping through the cobblestone streets and intersections as if there were a tyrannosaurus on their tail. The rain pouring down outside reflected the lights of the passing street lamps and traffic signals, giving them a fuzzy red, green, or yellow aura that only made the deranged drive seem all the more unreal and dreamlike. Sheets of water poured down the windshield, obscuring his view, but Michael glimpsed the imposing steel skeleton of Erzsebet Bridge, named after a nineteenth-century empress who was stabbed to death by an anarchist.

His worried gaze was drawn back to the Jaguar's wounded driver. The woman's face was, if possible, even whiter than usual. She kept one hand locked on the steering wheel while the other held the gun in Michael's face.

"Look," he said, trying to reason with her. "You've lost a lot of blood." Recalling the unnatural coolness of her blood, he guessed that she already had gone into shock. "If you don't pull over, you're going to get us both killed."

"Want to bet?" she said defiantly, smiling thinly through her pain. She slammed her foot down on the gas, throwing Michael back against his seat. The towering white spires of

106

Erzsebet Bridge loomed dead ahead, growing larger by the second.

Michael had dealt with uncooperative patients before, but never like this. "I'm not screwing around!" he shouted over the roar of the Jaguar's powerful engine.

"Neither am I!" she shot back. Her gaze was glued to the road in front of them. Was it just his imagination, or were her eyelids starting to droop alarmingly. "Now shut up and hold on! I'll be fine."

Michael didn't believe it for a second. He gripped the dashboard in horror as the crazed woman drove down Szabadsajto Avenue like a maniac. *Who does she think is chasing us?* he wondered. *The entire Hungarian army?*

Once again, he recalled heavy shapes landing loudly on the roof of his apartment, followed by the roaring of inhuman beasts . . .

The entrance to the bridge was right in front of them. At first, Michael thought she was heading over the river, but, at the last minute, she took a sharp turn onto the Belgrad Parkway, zooming north along the eastern shore of the Danube. Fashionable boutiques and department stores rapidly gave way to dockside piers and warehouses as the Jaguar rushed past the sleeping waterfront. Towering steel cranes, silent and inactive, perched like praying mantises over dilapidated wharves, while rusty freighters, bearing goods from all over Europe and beyond, were anchored along the shore, waiting for dawn to disgorge a horde of freshly awakened longshoremen and stevedores. Barbed-wire fences guarded wooden pallets stacked high with miscellaneous bales, crates, and bags.

Where the hell is she taking me? Michael worried, peering anxiously out the windows. *And do we stand a chance of getting there alive?*

107

Darkness blanketed the docks in shadows, but to the east, a faint trace of pink colored the sky, visible only through the vertical gaps between downtown Pest's modest high-rises. Sunrise was not far away.

Thank God, Michael thought. He couldn't wait for this ghastly night to be over, one way or another. He eyed the injured woman carefully and was horrified to see her shake her head groggily. Her eyes blinked fitfully, as if she were having trouble keeping them open. The gun in her hand shook like a Parkinson's victim.

I knew it! Michael realized in dismay, not at all happy to have been proven right. Before his panicked eyes, the bleeding woman passed out behind the wheel. Her head slumped forward, and the loaded automatic slipped from her fingers, landing on the black leather console between her and Michael.

Out of control, the Jaguar swerved wildly. Michael grabbed desperately for the steering wheel, but the car was going too fast, and the woman's limp body got in the way. Tires squealed on slippery asphalt as the Jag veered to the left, crossing two lines of traffic to careen madly toward the docks.

Frozen in fear, Michael couldn't look away from the windshield. He watched helplessly, his heart pounding like a snare drum, as the Jaguar plowed through a metal guard rail, throwing off fiery orange sparks. The Jag bounced down a rocky embankment, its state-of-the-art, computerized shock absorbers doing little to relieve the bone-jarring jolts that tossed Michael up and down and from side to side. His brutalized shoulder shrieked in agony, joining the high-pitched scream tearing its way out of Michael's lungs.

The front end of the Jag hit a jagged block of concrete, and the plummeting car tumbled end over end toward the river below. Michael felt as if he were being beaten to a pulp inside a blender. *This is it,* he grasped in a moment of staggering clarity. *I'm going to die.*

And he didn't even know why.

Then the Jaguar was airborne, and for an instant an eerie silence replaced the ear-pounding screeching and crashes. Michael heard his own heart racing and listened to the breathless pants issuing from his lips. Curiously, he heard nothing at all from the unconscious woman. He couldn't even tell if she was breathing . . .

Through the front window, he saw the moonlit surface of the Danube rush toward them like a tidal wave. The Jaguar crashed nose first into the river with a tremendous splash. Michael's overtaxed seatbelt came loose, and his head rammed into the windshield like a cannonball, cracking the glass.

Seeing stars, he struggled to remain conscious despite the ringing in his skull. If he passed out now, he would never wake up. Already, the floating Jaguar was slipping beneath the surface of the river. Michael realized he was only minutes away from drowning.

Rippling darkness swallowed them whole as the car sank toward the bottom of the Danube, its spinning tires churning up a flurry of bubbles and debris. Through the spider web of cracks across the windshield, Michael could see only opaque green shadows.

He frantically tried to open the passenger door but discovered that his mysterious abductor had locked it electronically, probably to keep him from bailing out of the Jaguar the minute it slowed below fifty. He shot an aggrieved glance at the unconscious woman, then spotted her handgun lying on the center console. A crazy idea occurred to him, and he snatched up the gun and fired it at the window.

The sharp report of the gun echoed painfully inside the cramped confines of the sinking Jaguar. Glass shattered, and a cascade of freezing water rushed in, soaking Michael to the skin and splashing against his face. He took a deep breath, filling his lungs with as much oxygen as he could manage, in preparation for a death-defying swim to the surface. Maybe there was still a chance to get out of this alive.

He looked across the flooding compartment at the helpless woman. Still dead to the world, she made no effort to save herself, even as the cold, dark water engulfed her. Michael hesitated, torn between self-preservation and a surprisingly powerful urge to rescue the endangered woman. She had done nothing but threaten and kidnap him, yet Michael found himself horrified at the possibility of her dying before he even found out her name.

What the hell. He dropped the gun, letting it sink to the floor, and grabbed the woman beneath her arms. Dimly remembered lifeguard training, forgotten and unused since that summer he had worked at Coney Island, came back to him as he propelled them both through the shattered window into the murky depths of the river itself.

He kicked strenuously toward the surface, trying to ignore the bone-numbing chill of the water. October was no time to go swimming in the Danube. The insensate woman was dead weight in his arms, as limp and lifeless as a sack of potatoes. He held her tightly beneath her armpits, his hands locked together beneath her breasts. Her loose brown hair caressed his face, the dark tresses drifting in the current like seaweed.

Moonlight, penetrating the watery darkness, called to Michael like a beacon, letting him know which way was up. Gravity dragged at his heels as he climbed toward the shimmering silver light with agonizing slowness. His lungs burned, yearning for air, and he had to bite down hard to keep from inhaling the river itself. He could swim faster, he knew, with his arms freed, yet he held on tightly to his beautiful burden.

His meager supply of oxygen was all but exhausted when his head and shoulders finally broke through the surface of the river. Choking and sputtering, he gulped down heaping lungfuls of fresh air as he bobbed upon the waves. Only a few inches away from his face, the woman's head slumped limply to one side, and he took care to keep her mouth and nose above the water. Her lovely features were as cold and white as polished bone. Blood darkened the shallow waves lapping at her wounded shoulder.

Who are you? he wondered, shifting position so that he kept one arm around the woman's slender waist, while freeing up the other arm to swim with. *And why is that so important to me?*

Fighting the current, which rapidly carried them away from the site of the Jag's final resting place, Michael sidestroked toward the shore. Night still shrouded the docks in shadow, despite the rosy promise of dawn. Feebly, he called out for help, but exhaustion sapped the carrying power of his voice, and after swallowing several mouthfuls of brackish water, he abandoned the effort, concentrating instead on making it to the eastern bank of the river.

His pathetic cries didn't even rouse the woman in his arms. Michael worried about hypothermia, uncertain if the dark-haired stranger was still alive. *I'm going to feel really stupid,* he thought, *if I drown trying to rescue a dead woman.*

It seemed to take an eternity to reach the shore. Michael's shivering body felt numb from the neck down by the time he crawled onto the muddy slope beneath a rotting wooden dock. Moss and slime coated the weathered rocks protruding from the embankment, making it hard to get a grip as he dragged himself and his uncomplaining companion into the damp, claustrophobic space. The slick green underside of the pier was only inches above his soggy scalp, providing them with precious little headroom in which to maneuver. Garbage, washed up along the shore, littered the filthy riverside burrow. Michael felt a curious kinship with the broken bottles, crumpled beer cans, discarded cigarette wrappers, greasy rags, and other assorted bits of flotsam cast up onto the uncaring embankment. Like them, he had no idea how or why he had ended up, soaked and disheveled, beneath the docks.

At least I'm still alive, he thought. *That's something.*

Breathing hard, he gave himself a moment to recover from the grueling swim. He wanted to put his head down and sleep for a year or two but knew he couldn't collapse entirely until he had seen to the woman. For all he knew, she required immediate medical attention.

Water gurgled from her mouth as he laid her down sideways atop muddy rocks. He caught a glimpse of pearl-white teeth and oddly pointed incisors. Her eyes were closed, hiding the striking brown orbs he remembered from the subway station. He gently raised her eyelids to check her pupils, which were widely dilated. He felt a thready pulse at her throat. Michael guessed that she was suffering from shock, hypothermia, blood loss, or all of the above, not to mention a close brush with drowning. In a way, it seemed a miracle that she was alive at all.

Her wound, he noted, had finally stopped bleeding. *Thank heaven for small favors,* he thought.

There was no time to lose. His teeth chattering like castanets, he rolled her onto her back, then clasped his hands together and pressed down sharply on the woman's abdomen—once, twice, three times. *C'mon!* he urged her silently. Water streamed from his hair and whiskers, raining down on his patient's leather-clad form. His eyes scoured her face for some sign that she was responding to his urgent ministrations. *Breathe for me. Breathe!*

He refused to give up on her. *You can't do this to me!* he thought. He recalled the defiant glint in her eyes as she pulled the gun on him, remembered the cold smile on her porcelain face as she fearlessly raced the Jaguar through the city streets, snatching him away from that nut in the lobby—and whatever was prowling about on the rooftop. For the first time, it dawned on him that she might very well have saved his life, although he couldn't begin to guess why. *You can't die!* he protested vehemently, staring in anguish at her lifeless, lovely features. Even unconscious and streaked with mud, she was still the most beautiful woman he had ever seen. *I don't even know who you are!*

She gagged suddenly, frigid water gushing from her mouth and nose, and his heart leaped in relief. She coughed and sputtered, lifting her head a few inches above the sludge. Her eyes flickered open, just long enough to look up and see Michael kneeling above her.

He tried to flash her a reassuring smile, employing his best bedside—or dockside—manner. His medical training came to his rescue again, and he tugged open her shirt to check on the extent of her injuries. It was possible, after all, that she might have been hurt in the crash, on top of the knife wound in her shoulder.

Her skin beneath the waterlogged black fabric was as smooth and white as ivory. He reached down to probe her ribcage gently, only to succumb suddenly to a wave of dizziness that sent his head spinning. His vision blurred, and darkness encroached on the periphery of his sight. He

113

shook his head groggily, trying and failing to overcome the sense of light-headedness washing over him. He touched his forehead and winced in pain. He tugged back bloody fingers.

Shit, he thought, remembering his head-on collision with the windshield. *I have a concussion.*

Chapter Eleven

Pierce and Taylor reported back to the infirmary empty-handed. *This is growing bothersome,* Singe thought. How was he supposed to continue his experiments without an adequate supply of suitable subjects? He glanced over at the genealogical chart on the wall. This Michael Corvin was proving more elusive than all of the previous specimens combined.

The lycan scientist paced back and forth impatiently, while the two failed hunters briefed him on their botched mission topside. Stolen police uniforms, somewhat the worse for wear, clothed their brawny physiques. Singe regarded Pierce and Taylor skeptically; like most lycans, they relied more on their animal strength, and sharpened teeth and claws, than on their brains. Singe himself was an exception in that regard.

As was Lucian.

At least the hulking pair had fared better than Raze, in that they hadn't returned to the underworld peppered with silver. No medical exertions were required of Singe, although he would have welcomed a surgical challenge to keep his hands and mind occupied while he awaited word of Lucian's own excursion to the city above. He prayed to the strictly metaphorical gods of pure science that Lucian would succeed where his brutish minions had not.

A door slammed open at the rear of the converted Metro station, and Lucian strode into the cluttered infirmary. Singe's hopes were dashed when he saw that their pack leader also had returned *sans* quarry. He tried not to let his disappointment show, for fear of provoking the other lycan's wrath.

Lucian's leather jacket was riddled with bullet holes, and the shirt beneath was torn open, exposing a hairy white chest liberally streaked with blood. Singe peered quizzically at the telltale puncture marks, but Lucian shook his head. Apparently, the solitary lycan did not require medical attention, either. Singe was not surprised; he knew full well that their immortal leader was perfectly capable of tending to his own minor (and not so minor) injuries.

But even that highly impressive talent would be nothing compared with the awesome capabilities that would be Lucian's should Singe's meticulous research bear fruit. *We are on the verge of a revolutionary breakthrough,* he thought avidly, his bright, intelligent eyes gleaming at the staggering possibilities promised by his experiments. *My theories are perfect, I know they are. All I need now is just the right human subject . . .*

"Another escape," the scientist said with a sigh, contemplating Lucian's empty hands. "Impressive. Perhaps Raze wasn't overstating matters."

Have the vampires indeed caught on to our hidden designs? Singe worried. He feared how far the enemy might go to thwart the great experiment. *No, that's impossible. The bloodsuckers are too vain and decadent to comprehend the genius of my endeavor. They're just harrying us for sport, as they always have.*

A triumphant grin stretched across Lucian's face. He casually reached into one of the inner pockets of his coat and drew forth a capped vial filled with a rich scarlet fluid. "Raze didn't bring this back," he observed.

Singe's face lit up as Lucian tossed him the vial. The middle-aged scientist eagerly held up the vial to the harsh fluorescent light. Thanks to the anticoagulant inside the vial, the blood looked as though it had been freshly bled mere minutes ago. *Hello, Michael Corvin,* Singe thought, staring exuberantly at the gently sloshing red sample. *I've been looking forward to meeting you.*

A worrisome thought disturbed him. Pierce and Taylor both had reported seeing Corvin in the company of a female Death Dealer, probably the same one who had killed Trix several hours ago. He looked over at Lucian, letting his unease show on his weather-beaten face. "If Michael is indeed the Carrier," he began, "the vampires could—"

Lucian dismissed Singe's concerns with a wave of his hand. "Relax, old friend. I've tasted his flesh. Just two more days until the full moon. Soon he will be a lycan." Lucian's wolfish grin grew wider by the moment. Singe nodded in understanding, his fears allayed by this intriguing new revelation.

"Soon he will be looking for us."

Protective metal shades began to descend over the patterned bay window in Kraven's suite, signaling the arrival of dawn. The reception in the salon had long since wound down, as both the mansion's distinguished guests and its permanent residents retired for the morning, but Kraven could not rest. He stared out the window at the estate's front gate until his view was completely cut off by the lowering shades.

Where in blazes is that infernal woman? he thought, his

handsome face disfigured by bitterness and resentment. Any other vampiress would be punished severely for such egregiously disrespectful behavior, yet Selene continued to defy him with impunity. "Frigid, castrating bitch," he muttered beneath his breath. She was taking advantage of his own deep feelings for her, the ungrateful vixen.

A sliver of sunlight crept across the carpet at his feet, and he backed away instinctively. A second later, the sun-proof metal shades reached the bottom of the window, banishing the obscene radiance from the suite entirely.

Kraven hoped that Selene, wherever she was, had found some shelter from the sun. *It would be just like her,* he thought indignantly, *to die before I have an opportunity to confront her about her waywardness!*

Once and for all.

The sound of water lapping against the shore roused Selene, who awoke not entirely certain where she was. Slowly opening her eyes, despite a throbbing ache beneath her skull, she found herself stretched out on her back beneath some kind of reinforced wooden structure. Algae-covered timbers formed a roof maybe twenty centimeters over her head. She heard the steady flow of a river down by her feet.

A dock, she grasped with no little confusion. *I'm under a dock, probably down by the Danube.*

But how?

It took her another moment to realize that she was not alone. A male figure lay next to her, resting his head upon her shoulder like a lover. For one horrific second, she feared that she finally had succumbed to Kraven's never-ending blandishments, then noted with relief the tousled brown hair on the sleeping figure, quite unlike Kraven's flowing ebony locks. *Praise the Elders!* she thought.

She blinked her eyes as the fog cleared from her mind. *Of course,* she realized, recognizing the unconscious mortal beside her.

Michael Corvin.

Much of last night's exploits came back to her, although she remained distinctly puzzled about how she and Corvin had ended up camping out beneath Budapest's thriving waterfront. The last thing she remembered was driving her Jaguar madly away from one unusually persistent lycan. And a vicious blade stabbing through the roof of the car into her shoulder . . .

Turning her head, she discovered that the shoulder in question had been crudely bandaged with what looked like a torn portion of Corvin's black T-shirt. *He dressed my wound after I assaulted him at his home, then abducted him at gunpoint?* She didn't know whether to be grateful for his efforts or appalled by his naïveté. *Well, he is a doctor,* she recalled. *Guess he takes his Hippocratic Oath seriously.*

Marshaling her strength, she tried to sit up as far as the overhanging dock would permit. A glare to one side hurt her eyes, and it suddenly registered that there were scorching sunbeams all around her, blazing down through minute cracks and knotholes in the dock above. The golden rays surrounded her like an array of deadly lasers.

"Perfect," she muttered archly.

Dismayed by her precarious situation, she automatically reached for her guns, only to find both holsters empty. Had Corvin disarmed her at the same time as he had so thoughtfully tended to her injured shoulder? Uncomfortable without a weapon in her hand, she searched the silty muck at her sides with her fingers, only to venture too near a caustic sunbeam.

Pfffttt! The beam touched the back of her hand, causing the exposed white flesh to sizzle instantaneously. She yanked the hand back, wincing in agony as thin gray tendrils of smoke arose from her scalded knuckles. She thrust the burned hand deep into the chilly muck, then exhaled loudly as the icy dampness did its best to cool her scorched skin. *Dammit,* she thought. *I knew I should have worn gloves on this mission.*

Having learned her lesson, she kept absolutely still, not moving a muscle as she cautiously eyed the luminous rays shooting down from above. The fragmented sunlight had her effectively pinned in; she could barely stir without running into one of the malevolent beams.

Not that she knew where she could escape to now that the sun had very obviously risen or how she could even leave this place in broad daylight. For the first time, it occurred to her to wonder what had become of her trusty Jaguar. *I probably don't want to know,* she thought.

How long would she be trapped here? She risked a peek at her expensive waterproof wristwatch, which had survived whatever calamity had stranded her beneath the docks, and was chagrined to see that it was not even nine A.M. Sunset was a good ten hours away.

Selene groaned. It was going to be a *long* day.

Singe used a bulbed pipette to add five drops of Michael Corvin's blood carefully to a glass beaker filled with a clear plasma solution. Lucian held his breath as he intently watched the brilliant scientist conduct his experiment.

Could it be, Lucian thought, *that we are finally nearing the end of our quest?* Was the hapless American the one they had been seeking for so long?

"It's a shame we don't have more," Singe commented, regarding the depleted supply of blood in the tiny vial. He and his leader were alone in the lycans' squalid infirmary.

Have no fear, my sagacious friend, Lucian thought, his eager gaze never leaving the beaker on the counter. He could still taste the human's blood upon his tongue. *If this sample tests true, then all the vampires in creation will not stop me from dragging Michael Corvin back to this laboratory, so that our ultimate destiny can be fulfilled at long last.*

Singe set a timer, then stirred the contents of the beaker with a glass rod. The crimson droplets reacted with the catalyst immediately, much faster than either he or Lucian had expected. Violet swirls materialized within the solution, chasing the stirring rod like miniature contrails aglow in the setting sun. Unlike before, this mixture did not display the familiar black tint of failure.

"Positive," Singe announced. His wrinkled face was positively beaming.

Lucian could scarcely believe his ears—or eyes. After so many defeats and disappointments, could this really be true? He knelt down in front of the counter, lowering himself so that he could stare directly into the swirling fluid; still there was no sign of the hated black transformation. His bearded face held a look of childish wonder as his rapt eyes tracked the swirling violet wisps. He had waited a very long time for this moment.

Victory is ours, he thought with certainty.

Once I retrieve Michael Corvin, that is.

Daylight chased Selene toward the sleeping human. As the sun slowly crossed the sky above the waterfront, the deadly sunbeams crept steadily nearer to Selene, forcing her to inch closer and closer to Corvin's unconscious form in order to avoid being burned alive.

Along with the incandescent rays, the sounds of the day penetrated the massive timber dock above her head. Footsteps pounded on the wharf as teams of Hungarian long-shoremen went about their business, loading and unloading the greedy freighters cruising up and down the Danube. Tugboat horns brayed, competing with the raucous cawing of the gulls. Selene pined for the silence and safety of her suite back at Ordoghaz, while counting on all the hustling activity to hide her presence beneath the pier.

The last thing I need is some well-meaning mortal stumbling onto me down here. She shuddered at the thought of a crew of would-be rescuers dragging her out into the lethal daylight. *I'm in enough danger as it is.*

Relentless in its approach, a merciless sunbeam glided toward her. Corvin's body blocked her escape route, and, biting down on her lip, she realized that there was no other way to go.

Time to get to know Mr. Corvin a bit better . . .

Rolling over onto her stomach, and away from the advancing sunlight, she pushed off from the muddy slope and slid her leather-encased body over onto Michael Corvin's supine form. Her svelte legs straddled his waist as she rested her weight atop him, staring down at his upraised face.

"Pardon me," she remarked wryly, faintly embarrassed by her intimate proximity to the comatose human. *And to think we haven't even been introduced!* She couldn't help noticing once again Corvin's rugged good looks. Despite everything he had been through, and a purplish bruise on his forehead, his youthful features were undeniably appealing, while his soaking windbreaker and torn black T-shirt clung to a slender, athletic torso. *If I had to spend a day on top of a strange human,* she reflected, *there are worse specimens I could have ended up with.*

Selene squirmed awkwardly astride the mysterious Michael Corvin, trying to make herself more comfortable.

She felt the heat radiating off the man's body and regretted that she had so little of her own to share. Her gaze was irresistibly drawn to the juicy vein pulsing at Corvin's throat; it had been hours since she last fed, and Selene was sorely tempted to nip the stranger's defenseless neck with her fangs. She licked her lips thirstily. Perhaps just a taste?

No, she resolved firmly, forcing herself to look away from the throbbing vein. Unlike some vampires, she did not take advantage of unwilling humans.

The questing sunbeam, heading northwest, missed her by centimeters, gliding instead across Corvin's handsome cheekbones. Selene watched in unaccountable fascination as the traveling ray illuminated the mortal's features, bathing his face in golden light. Sweat beaded on his forehead as his closed eyes squinted even more tightly against the intrusive radiance

He stirred beneath her, moaning softly, but did not awaken. Selene shifted her weight slightly, unable to look away from the enigmatic stranger.

Who are you, Michael Corvin? she wondered. *And why do the lycans want you so?*

Chapter Twelve

*F*everish images paraded backward across Michael's mind:

Shards of black glass converged before his eyes, the shattered fragments flying through the void in reverse, converging into a pattern he couldn't quite discern . . .

Severed iron chains snaked toward a dank granite floor, the broken links jangling loudly as they snapped back together, binding the chains tautly to the floor . . .

A beautiful dark-haired woman, clad in the torn remnants of a once-elegant gown, dangled in the fearsome clutches of a medieval torture device. A garbled scream pulled her jaws apart, exposing strangely pointed eyeteeth beneath her crimson lips. Steel and leather restraints obscured her body below the waist. Her eerie white eyes were tinged with streaks of red. Somehow Michael knew that the imprisoned damsel's name was Sonja and that she was a princess of sorts, as well as the love of his life . . .

"Sonja," he murmured, even as the woman's face blurred before his eyes, becoming instead the woman from the Metro station, the one who had stolen him away from the madman with the knife and the bloodthirsty teeth. *Who?* he wondered. If anything, she was even more staggeringly beautiful than the captive princess. *How?*

"Lie still," the woman—not Sonja—said. A gentle hand pushed firmly against his shoulder. "Your skull's taken a good knock."

Michael blinked his eyes in confusion as he awoke, sort of, to find himself reclining upon a chaise longue. He looked around groggily, gradually realizing that he was no longer washed up below the waterfront. Paneled oak walls and antique furnishings now surrounded him instead.

"Do you have any idea why those . . . men were after you?" the mystery woman asked, peering intently at his face. Michael was relieved to see her alive and well, even though he still had no idea who she was.

"Where are—?" Michael tried to sit up, but the motion sent his head spinning. Alternating chills and hot flashes washed over him. His vision wavered sickeningly.

"You're safe," the woman assured him. She loomed above him, her pale face only inches from his own. "I'm Selene."

Selene. Michael clung to the name like a life preserver, even as darkness lapped again at his consciousness. He felt fatigued and queasy, as if his body were fighting against some kind of infection—and losing badly. His shoulder throbbed dully where that nutcase had bitten him, and a sliver of moonlight, entering the elegant chamber through an open window, sent a tremor through his entire frame. His skin tingled oddly, the hairs on his arms standing up as though electrified. A mournful howl echoed inside his skull, like a ringing in his ears.

I'm Michael, he thought, over the cacophonous howl. He opened his lips to introduce himself, but the effort exhausted him, and he sank back against the velvet cushions of the couch. He struggled to keep his eyes open, to stay awake, but the tidal pull of the encroaching darkness was too powerful to resist. Selene's face dimmed, and her voice receded into the distance, as he succumbed to oblivion once more. "Selene," he whispered, taking her name with him into the darkness.

She sighed impatiently as Corvin lost consciousness again. The blow to his head, which had left an ugly scab surrounded by a dark purple bruise, obviously had done a number on him. He had been dead to the world for at least eleven hours, long enough for the sun finally to sink below the horizon, freeing Selene from her enforced captivity beneath the waterfront.

Corvin had remained oblivious even while she had gone to the trouble of renting a car to replace her vanished Jaguar, then he'd slept like a corpse during the entire drive back to Ordoghaz. Selene regretted not being able to take the injured human straight to an emergency room, but with the lycans hunting him so relentlessly, he was safer here in her quarters.

But why are they after you? she wondered again. *What makes you so special, besides your rugged face and good Samaritan tendencies, that is.* Clearly, interrogating the depleted human was going to have to wait until he had recovered more from his ordeal the night before. With luck, perhaps he would be able to answer a few questions by sunrise.

She mopped his forehead with a damp cloth, taking extra care around the area of the bruise. *I probably should examine him more carefully,* she thought. She had only just arrived at the mansion with her insensate charge, so there had not yet been time to check beneath Corvin's bloodstained jacket for any additional injuries. It occurred to her that she had no memory of exactly how Corvin had hurt his head. *Must have happened while I was out cold myself.*

Although her wounded shoulder was largely healed, she

still felt a phantom pain where that unidentified lycan had stabbed her. A glimpse of a metal pendant flashed across her memory, and she wondered once more who that lycan in the lobby had been. She had not recognized his face from any of the Death Dealers' copious surveillance files on their enemies.

"So," a pert voice interrupted her musings, "for once the rumors are true."

Selene turned away from the chaise to see Erika strolling blithely across the suite. She frowned, annoyed. The pert blond servant girl was invading Selene's quarters so regularly that the older vampiress was starting to feel as if she had an unwanted roommate. Besides, this was none of Erika's business.

"The whole house is absolutely buzzing about your new pet," Erika chirped enthusiastically. She approached the chaise longue, examining Corvin with open curiosity. "Oh, my God. You're going to try to turn him, aren't you?"

Selene rolled her eyes. "Of course not." She had never converted a human into a vampire, voluntarily or otherwise, in all of her long years among the undead. Killing lycans was her life's work, not seducing the innocent. And she couldn't care less what Kraven and his crowd of ageless dilettantes said about her.

Erika nodded, as if she understood where Selene was coming from. The sylphlike vampiress made a slow circle around the chaise longue, dragging her painted fingernails along the edge of the burgundy-colored velvet pillows. "Your stance on humans is a matter of record," she acknowledged.

As far as Selene was concerned, mortals were strictly innocent bystanders in the war against the lycans, but beyond that, she had always given them little thought. "I have no

127

stance," she insisted, perhaps a little defensively. "I have nothing to do with them."

"Exactly," Erika pointed out with a mischievous gleam in her eyes. Her white shoulders spilled from the top of her frilly black frock. "So why bring him here?"

Touché, Selene thought. The silly girl had a point, as much as Selene was loath to concede it. Why had she gone to such lengths for this human, aside from a natural instinct to deprive the lycans of their prey? Mystified, she searched her own soul as she stared down at Corvin's attractively tanned face. If thwarting the lycans were her only goal, why was she here nursing the comatose human like some sort of vampiric Florence Nightingale? Why did she care if he lived or died?

"He saved my life," she said softly, after a moment's thought. She did not know exactly what had happened after she had passed out behind the wheel of the Jaguar, but she felt certain that she would not have made it safely to the shore without Corvin's assistance. And who else could have bandaged her lacerated shoulder?

Erika's jaw dropped, revealing dainty white fangs. She was clearly flabbergasted at the notion of a mere human coming to the aid of a vampire—and a Death Dealer, no less! She glanced down at Corvin with greater interest, and perhaps a flicker of jealousy. Did she envy Selene her human Prince Charming?

Selene watched over Corvin protectively. It dawned on her that Erika had offered no explanation for her arrival. Selene's eyes narrowed suspiciously. "Why are you here?"

Erika wilted somewhat before Selene's forbidding gaze, backing away from the chaise and its slumbering occupant. "Kraven sent me," she said with a gulp. "He wants to see you. Now."

*　　*　　*

Thunder boomed outside, and rain slashed the windows, as Kraven and Selene argued within his palatial suite. The two high-ranking vampires were at each other's throats, figuratively if not literally.

"Completely unacceptable," Kraven railed indignantly, stalking back and forth across the handmade Persian carpet. His furious gestures sliced the air. As usual, he was dressed to the nines, in a tailored black suit. "You go against my orders and spend the daylight hours away from the shelter of the mansion—with a human? A human you have since brought back into *my house!*"

Selene did not back down. Unlike Kraven, she neither paced nor waved her arms as she spoke, remaining as still and composed as a hibernating Elder. "As far as I'm concerned, this is still Viktor's house."

Kraven shot her a poisonous look; he didn't like being reminded that he was only the master of the manor in Viktor's absence. Growling in anger, he stomped over to the window and peered out into the stormy night. Selene glimpsed a bright gibbous moon peeking out from behind the churning thunderclouds.

"Look," she said, lowering her voice. Her tight-fitting leathers were still streaked with blood and mud; there had been no time to change since returning to Ordoghaz. "I don't want to argue. I just need you to understand that Michael is somehow important to the lycans."

He spun around to confront her, his dark eyes smoldering with suspicion. "So, now it's *Michael,*" he mocked her in an accusing tone.

Selene repressed an impatient sigh. The last thing she needed right now was Kraven's adolescent jealousy. Too much was at stake. "Kraven, would you just hear me out?"

She took a deep breath before trying to enlighten him once more. "There's something—"

He cut her off abruptly. "It's beyond me why you're still obsessing over this ridiculous theory." He dismissed her concerns with an airy wave of his hand. "Lucian wouldn't be the slightest bit interested in a human!"

Lucian? Selene could not conceal her surprise. Why was Kraven invoking a long-dead lycan? The infamous Lucian had been killed centuries ago. *I don't understand,* Selene thought, her brain struggling to process Kraven's peculiar remark.

Fortunately, he mistook her baffled expression for something entirely different. "Wait," he said dramatically, like a prosecutor playing to a jury. "You're infatuated with him. Admit it."

"Now, *there's* a ridiculous theory," she retorted, although somewhat less forcefully than she had intended. Her words rang oddly false even to her own ears.

Kraven seized on the hint of indecision in her voice. Sneering, he surged toward her, her face flushed with frustration and resentment. "Is it?" he demanded.

A flash of lightning outside was followed by a booming thunderclap that rattled the glass in the window panes.

The storm was building.

Left alone in Selene's private quarters, which were ever so much finer than her own, Erika considered the unconscious human collapsed upon the chaise longue. He really was quite handsome, if not quite the Greek god that Lord Kraven was. *Not bad for a human,* she decided, *if you like that sort of thing . . .*

Bored, she cuddled beside him, enjoying the warmth of

his mortal body against her cool flesh. She playfully tickled his neck, running a teasing nail along his jugular, and twirled his tousled brown hair around her fingers. All the while, she tried not to think about the fact that Selene was alone with Kraven in his opulent suite. *Don't be silly,* she scolded herself, driving away the jealous fantasies bedeviling her mind. Kraven had been positively incensed by Selene's antics when he'd dispatched Erika to find her. Judging from the irate look on his face, he was more likely to horsewhip Selene than make love to her.

Or so Erika hoped.

Frankly, I wouldn't mind a good spanking from Lord Kraven, she thought, *as long as it was for the right reasons.* It was all horribly unfair; Selene was getting all of Kraven's attention, and she didn't even appreciate it!

Amusing herself with Selene's boy toy gave Erika some small bit of revenge. She inspected the human's exposed throat, only to notice a series of tiny rips in the shoulder of his jacket. *What's this?* she thought, violet eyes widening. Had the haughty Selene, despite her protestations, been unable to resist nibbling on the merchandise?

Intrigued, Erika peeled back the human's collar. Looking for the telltale mark of a vampire's kiss, she was shocked to discover instead an ugly, swollen red bite wound on the mortal's inflamed right shoulder. The vicious-looking teeth marks were rough and jagged, quite unlike the discreet imprint of a vampire's fangs, and tiny, bristling black hairs sprouted from the depths of the bloody indentations.

"Holy shit!" Erika exclaimed, suddenly losing all interest in sampling the sleeping human's blood. Not a Death Dealer, she had never seen a victim of the lycans before, but she knew a lycan's bite when she saw one. *He's been turned,* she realized in alarm and disgust, recoiling from the touch of his infected flesh. *He's one of them!*

A blinding flash of lightning lit up the room. Thunder boomed, and the human suddenly snapped awake, screaming at the top of his lungs. This was too much for Erika, who sprang straight up like a startled cat, sticking to the ceiling while hissing at the shrieking human below. Her claws dug into molded plaster, close to two meters above the human's head, as the stunned mortal stared up at her, eyes blinking in horrified amazement, like a man trapped in a never-ending nightmare.

Erika didn't know how long it took to turn a human into a lycanthrope, but she wasn't taking any chances.

Kraven's boots echoed down the portrait-lined hallway, in unison with the thunder roaring outside, as he marched with virulent purpose toward Selene's quarters in the eastern wing of the mansion. Selene chased after him, fearful for Michael Corvin's safety.

"What are you planning to do to him?" she called out urgently.

Kraven would not even look back at her. "Whatever I please!" he declared, letting nothing slow his murderous trek through the mansion. His outstretched claws twitched at his sides, as though they were already tightening around Michael's neck.

No! Selene thought anxiously, quickening her pace as she raced after Kraven. She realized Michael was in deadly danger; despite Kraven's foppish airs, the lordly vampire could be brutally lethal when crossed. *I can't let him kill Michael,* she despaired.

But was there any way to stop him?

*　　*　　*

I have to get out of here!

Michael looked around frantically, desperate for a way out. This whole situation was insane—guns and knives and levitating blondes. He had no idea where he was or what had happened to Selene, but he knew that he had to get away from all these gun-wielding lunatics.

A moonlit window caught his eye, and he dashed unsteadily over to it and shoved open the glass. It was raining like hell outside, and a gust of cold wind spattered his face with icy wetness. Michael ignored the rain and peered over the edge of the window. To his dismay, he discovered that it was a good twenty-foot drop to the ground.

"Shit!" he muttered. Having second thoughts about the window, he turned back toward the room—just in time to see the blonde drop from the ceiling onto the floor, blocking the doorway to the hallway outside. The golden-haired nymphet glared at Michael, hissing like a pissed-off cat. She raised her hands in front of her defensively, her sharpened fingernails extended like claws. She bared shiny white teeth, complete with pointed fangs that looked like something out of a Hollywood horror movie.

Screw this, Michael decided, preferring to take his chances with the window. He scrambled onto the sill and jumped into the beckoning night.

He plummeted two stories, tumbling head over heels, before slamming down onto the wet lawn below. The crash landing stunned him, and for a second, everything went black. His eyes drooped shut, and Michael suddenly found himself somewhere else.

Black glass exploded outward as he dived headfirst through a stained-glass window. The tinkling of the broken glass rang in his ears as he landed with a crash on the rocky ground below. The scent of the nearby forest tantalized his nostrils, offering the promise of freedom and safety.

He rolled over onto his back, and the night sky came into view, cold and unwelcoming, the distant stars looking down on him without mercy. A blood-red moon, full and gigantic, hung between billowing storm clouds like an angry portent, casting an eerie light onto high stone walls of an ancient fortress . . .

Fierce barks and growls intruded upon the scene, yanking Michael harshly back to reality. His eyes snapped open, and he realized he was lying on the lawn. The stately Gothic mansion loomed behind him, looking very different from the forbidding stone edifice in his . . . what? Dream? Vision? Memory?

Where the fuck did that come from? he asked himself, bewildered. The bizarre, hallucinatory experience had felt more vivid than a dream, closer to a memory, but he knew he had never lived through anything like that before. *I think I would remember jumping through a glass window!*

The barking grew louder, closer. He blinked repeatedly to clear his mind and lifted his aching head from the soggy grass. "Holy shit!" he exclaimed as his eyes focused on the alarming sight of three snarling Rottweilers racing toward him across the lawn, looking like the Hound of the Baskervilles' less friendly cousins. Ivory fangs glistened in the moonlight.

Panic spurred Michael into action as he hurriedly scrambled to his feet and, limping like mad, took off for the estate's perimeter fence, the yowling attack dogs in hot pursuit.

Somehow he knew that no one was going to be calling the hounds off.

Kraven stormed into the room, startling Erika, who let out a high-pitched yelp. Ignoring the servant wench, Kraven searched the chamber for this Michael Corvin whom Selene was so obsessed with. *I'll break his neck before her very eyes,* he vowed, *and drink his blood to the last drop.* He smiled cruelly at the thought. *That will teach her to place her fickle infatuations above her duty to the coven—and to me.*

But the inconvenient human was nowhere to be seen. Frustrated, Kraven shot an inquiring look at Erika, who nodded sheepishly toward the open window. A cold draft blew against Kraven, rustling his inky locks and silk jacket, as he heard the hounds baying loudly outside.

"Damnation!" he cursed. Why couldn't this miserable human stay put?

The hellhounds lunging at his heels, Michael clambered up and over the slippery iron fence. He panted in exhaustion, his ragged breaths frosting in the chilly air. Taking care not to impale himself on the fence's rusty spikes, he splashed down on the opposite side of the barrier. The furious dogs thrust their muzzles through the metal bars, snapping and barking at their elusive prey.

Bye, bye, doggies, Michael thought sarcastically as he stumbled away from the fence. A shadowy line of naked oaks and beeches promised shelter and concealment, and he limped through the storm toward the swaying trees. The wind pelted his face and hands with icy rain, and thunder punctuated every other anguished minute.

Was he heading north or south, toward the city or away from it? Michael had no idea, nor did it matter. All he cared about now was putting distance between himself and the dogs—and that entire freakhouse mansion.

His infected shoulder burned like hell.

Kraven strode impatiently to the window, even as he heard Selene rush into the room behind him. Perhaps the dogs already had claimed the human, he speculated. It would not be as satisfying, true, as slaying Corvin himself, but Kraven decided he could live with having Selene's pet torn apart by the hounds. *A fitting end,* he decreed silently, *for so insignificant a creature.*

His undead eyes easily penetrated the darkness outside. To his disappointment, however, he did not see the Rottweilers enthusiastically savaging Corvin's bleeding carcass. Instead, he saw the dogs yapping impotently at the fence and was forced to arrive at a singularly galling conclusion.

The human had escaped.

Lightning strobed the night, casting aside the darkness micro-seconds at a time. Thunder pealed overhead, all but drowning out the lupine howling inside Michael's skull. He tore through the woods like an escapee from a chain gang, cold and wet and gasping for breath. His heart pounded wildly, and he kept glancing back over his shoulder, fearful of whatever might be following him. He stumbled clumsily over the uneven terrain, tripping over dimly glimpsed branches and vines. He toppled forward, scraping his palms on the underbrush, but kept on hurrying ahead even as he painfully dragged himself back onto his feet. Muddy puddles caught him by surprise, soaking his bedraggled socks and sneakers all the way through. The baying of the hounds rang out behind him, urging him onward.

What if someone opens the gate? he worried, visualizing the baying Rottweilers following his scent into the woods. *What if they set the hounds on me?*

Utter blackness enveloped him, only to be rent instants later by another blazing shaft of lightning. The shadows lifted, leaving Michael somewhere else. Another time, another place.

He ran barefoot through the immense black forest, hearing his pursuers crash through the dense brush behind him. Looking back, he glimpsed them faintly in the foggy night: shadowy figures weaving through the evergreen tree trunks, flecks of moonlight glinting on exposed pieces of chain mail and plate armor. He felt woefully naked and defenseless compared with the warlike figures.

They burst from the swirling white mist, brandishing crossbows loaded with deadly silver. Heartless dealers in death, they bounded and dodged around the bushy pines and firs, racing to catch Michael in their lethal sights.

Multiple whooshing noises sliced through the night, and volleys of solid-silver crossbow bolts whistled past his shoulder, narrowly missing him, and sank deep into the trunk of a sturdy pine only a few paces away. The argent sheen of the deadly shafts filled his soul with fear and revulsion.

An angry snarl built at the back of his throat. A savage part of his soul yearned to turn and face his oppressors, to meet arms and armor with unleashed tooth and claw, but he knew he was too weak, too depleted by torture and captivity. Another time, he vowed. Another night.

For now, he could only run and run, ducking the barbed silver missiles that hurled past his ears . . .

Michael flinched, half expecting to see a bloody arrowhead protrude from his chest. Then the darkness fell and lifted again, bisected by another blinding flash of lightning, and he found himself back in the rainy woods.

He looked about in confusion. There were no silver crossbow bolts, no shadowy archers, only the angry barking of the guard dogs, which diminished in volume as he steadily distanced himself from the nameless mansion and its surrounding estate. The mountainous pines, with their bristling needles, once more had become the denuded, leafless oaks and beeches from before.

What's happening to me? he fretted. Nothing made sense anymore, not even the febrile imaginings of his own mind. His wounded shoulder throbbed in sync with his racing heartbeat. He shivered uncontrollably, from both the cold and a mounting sense of extreme dread. Murderous kidnappers and gangsters were bad enough, but now even his own senses were betraying him. *I don't understand any of this,* he thought, staggering through the unfamiliar woods without any idea of how far he was from Budapest and everyday life as he knew it.

Am I going insane?

Kraven turned away from the open window. Selene could tell from the sour, truculent look on Kraven's face that Michael had somehow gotten away—from Kraven and the Rottweilers alike.

She was overcome with relief, which she did her best to conceal from Kraven. The imperious vampire regent was in a bad enough temper as it was. *Damn Kraven and his infernal jealousy,* she cursed silently. *It's not as if I've ever encouraged his amorous attentions!*

Erika cowered apprehensively near the door, no doubt fearful that Kraven would blame her for the human's escape. Selene suspected that the lissome maidservant had little to fear; Kraven's dire wrath appeared directed at Selene alone.

"Leave us!" he snapped at Erika, who readily complied by darting out the door, leaving Selene alone with the de facto master of the mansion.

Selene faced him, unafraid. She was fully prepared to accept the consequences of having brought Michael to Ordoghaz, but she was not about to apologize for her actions, let alone appeal for forgiveness. Michael was vastly important somehow, and not just to her, no matter what Kraven might think.

The safety of this coven is my only concern, she asserted inwardly. *Or am I protesting a bit too much?*

Kraven crossed the floor to where she was standing. His smoldering eyes glared crossly into hers. Selene maintained a stony, resolute expression, ready for whatever threats and ultimatums the other vampire had in store.

A simmering moment passed, and Kraven opened his mouth to begin his tirade. Selene tensed in anticipation, but, at the last second, Kraven suddenly changed his mind—and viciously backhanded her instead.

Chapter Thirteen

$\mathcal{A}$ ceramic bust, bearing a notably feral expression, snapped out from beneath an ornate concrete pillar. *Blam-blam-blam!* The sculpture exploded into hundreds of white shards as a burst of rapid gunfire blasted it apart.

Scowling, Selene waited impatiently for another target to present itself. A whiff of gunpowder rose from the smoking muzzle of a brand-new Beretta automatic.

Her face still smarted where Kraven had slapped her. She had hoped to blow off steam here at the firing range, but so far she felt as irate as before. Only a fierce determination not to stir up more trouble and division had kept her from returning Kraven's blow with her own hand. *We can't afford to turn on each other right now,* she reasoned, *not with the lycans plotting something dire.*

Another ceramic target peeked out from behind a metal façade. This one bore the bestial features of a semitransformed female lycan. Selene efficiently shot it to pieces, firing continuously until the Beretta's slide snapped back. She swiftly ejected the empty ammo clip, grabbed a fresh one, and angrily slammed it into her gun.

An amused chuckle came from behind her. "Sure hope

you never get pissed off at me," Kahn said. The weapons master stood a few meters back from the firing range, observing her practice session with friendly interest.

Selene almost smiled but kept her gaze fixed on the far end of the range. Her finger tensed upon the trigger. She was fully prepared to blast apart every ersatz lycan in the dojo if that was what it took to get past the memory of Kraven's infuriating slap. *I can't believe he dared to take a hand to me! I've killed more lycans in the last few years than he has for centuries . . .*

"Hold on," Kahn said, before the next target could claim her attention. "Check this out."

Selene reluctantly holstered her gun and turned toward Kahn. The African immortal tugged a wicked-looking pistol from his belt and handed it to her. She balanced it in her grip, testing its weight. A serviceable weapon, she judged, uncertain what was so special about it.

Kahn tapped his boot down on a scuffed green button built into the floor. The remote mechanism triggered the appearance of another ceramic target at the far end of the firing range. Sculpted marble fangs accentuated a frozen snarl. "Go ahead," he said. "Squeeze off a few."

With pleasure, Selene thought, needing no urging to fire upon the lycanthropic simulacra. *Blam-blam-blam!* A tight grouping of bullet hits cratered the target. To her surprise, a shiny metallic liquid oozed from the ceramic wounds, like blood from a shattered skull.

"Eject the mag," Kahn instructed.

Intrigued, Selene did so quickly. Her eyes lit up. The bullets in the magazine were identical to the lycans' new ultraviolet rounds, except that these were filled with a lustrous metallic fluid. "You've copied the lycan rounds," she realized.

Kahn grinned proudly.

She removed one of the liquid-filled bullets and rolled it between her fingers. "Silver nitrate?"

"A lethal dose," he confirmed.

"Excellent," she declared, her mind swiftly grasping the distinct advantages of this new form of ammo. "So they won't be able to dig the silver out as they do with our normal rounds."

"Straight into the bloodstream," Kahn said with a smirk. Selene foresaw a welcome increase in lycan fatalities. "Nothing to dig out."

She handed the gun back to him. "Does Kraven know about this?"

"Of course," Kahn answered, as if puzzled by her question. "He approved it."

Selene was relieved to hear that Kraven was taking some interest in the war against the lycans. She assumed Kahn had presented the idea to Kraven while she'd been tracking down Michael Corvin in the city. *If only I could convince Kraven how important Michael is!*

She watched, lost in thought, as Kahn fiddled with his ingenious new brainchild. He racked the slide back, removed the barrel, and proceeded to examine the rifling. Selene leaned pensively against the wall, recalling Kraven's odd remark earlier that evening.

"Tell me, Kahn," she asked after a moment. "Do you believe Lucian died the way they say he did?"

Kahn's grin widened. "Kraven been telling war stories again?" As far as he and most of the other Death Dealers were concerned, Kraven had been coasting on his celebrated victory for nearly six hundred years.

"That's my point," she insisted. "It's nothing but an ancient story. His story. There's not a shred of proof that he actually killed Lucian. Only his word."

The scornful tone in her voice made it clear how little she thought Kraven's word was worth.

The implied accusation got Kahn's attention. His amiable grin faded, and he shot her a deadly serious look. "Viktor believed him," he reminded her, lowering his voice. "And that's all that matters." He carefully put aside the disassembled pieces of his gun and eyed her warily. "Now, where are you going with this?"

She had no immediate answer for him, only a vague, unsettling suspicion that Kraven was not telling her everything. Perhaps his unrelenting hostility to her investigation was based on more than mere jealousy?

"Nowhere," she muttered finally, not wanting to burden Kahn with her as yet unsupported misgivings. Shrugging casually, as though the matter was of little import, she drew her Beretta and turned back toward the firing range. Her toe tapped the button triggering the targets.

Another ceramic bust popped up. Selene envisioned Kraven's spiteful, arrogant expression as she mercilessly shot the target to pieces.

It didn't make her feel any better.

The incessant rain was not improving Kraven's disposition. A never-ending trickle of cold water ran down the back of his neck as he and Soren lurked in the shadows of a dismal alley in one of central Pest's less savory neighborhoods, only a few blocks away from the hooker-infested fleshpots of Matyas and Rakoczi Squares. Broken glass and cigarette butts littered the cracked pavement beneath his feet. Political slogans and vulgar obscenities defaced the sooty stone walls of the alley, while several meters behind him, churning rainwater cascaded over the side of a graffiti-ridden concrete overpass.

The only good thing about the miserable weather, Kraven reflected, was that it had emptied the adjoining avenues of unwanted tourists, carousers, and street trash. Even Budapest's growing population of homeless indigents appeared to have sought drier domiciles elsewhere.

Good, he thought sourly. He hunched beneath his black leather coat, keeping his face hidden behind his collar like a turtle retreating halfway into its shell. *The fewer eyes that witness tonight's rendezvous, the better.*

The bells of a nearby clock tower rang out, tolling the hour. Kraven glanced impatiently at his own wristwatch. It was nearly ten P.M. "Where the devil is he?" he muttered to the muscular, black-clad vampire standing beside him.

Soren shrugged his shoulders. He maintained a tight lookout over the alley and environs, alert to any hint of treachery. Kraven was glad to have the wary bodyguard along on this outing but was anxious to return to Ordoghaz as quickly as possible. He didn't want to give Selene cause to question his absence.

More rain worked its way beneath his collar, chilling his already lukewarm flesh. Kraven was about ready to say the hell with it, to give up and go home, when an ominous black limousine pulled to the curb of the dimly lit street beyond the alley.

About time, Kraven thought indignantly. His simmering resentment masked a deeper unease. Glancing about furtively, he slunk from the alley, shadowed by Soren.

A dark-skinned figure emerged from the driver's seat of the limo. Kraven recognized Raze, a particularly savage specimen of the wolfen breed. The beefy lycan appeared none the worse for being sliced up by Selene's silver throwing stars the night before. *A pity,* Kraven thought. He had never liked Raze.

144

Soren and Raze exchanged hostile glares. Two of a kind, after a fashion, the lethal warriors hated each other intensely; they were both eagerly waiting for an opportunity to settle which of them was more dangerous. Kraven's money was on Soren, merely by virtue of the innate superiority of vampire over lycan, but he had no intention of letting Soren off his leash tonight. Matters were far too delicate already.

Raze opened the limo's rear door and gestured for Kraven to get inside. Kraven swallowed hard, unable to conceal his apprehension entirely, and slid into the backseat of the car. As Raze closed the door, Kraven could not resist looking back to make sure Soren was still there. Then the door slammed shut, cutting him off from his imposing bodyguard.

Chin up, he reminded himself, striving to bolster his spirits. *Show no weakness. It is not I who need fear the outcome of this meeting. I have nothing to apologize for.*

His throat tightened nonetheless.

The interior of the limo was dark and musky. The flickering light of a nearby street lamp feebly penetrated the tinted black glass of the limo's privacy windows. Through the darksome glass, Kraven glimpsed Soren and Raze taking positions at opposite ends of the limo. They glowered at each other mutely, immortal soldiers nursing their bitter rivalry beneath the driving rain.

Kraven reluctantly looked away from the windows, turning his attention to the business at hand. More nervous about this encounter than he cared to admit, even to himself, he immediately went on the offensive.

"Engaging Death Dealers in public and chasing around after some worthless human was not what I had in mind!" he protested brusquely, mustering an impressive show of justifiable indignation. Cold, wet, and disheveled, he let his physical discomfort fuel the umbrage in his voice. "You were told to set up shop and lie low," he continued, "not—"

A hand exploded from the darkness of the seat beside him, clutching Kraven by the throat and cutting off his tirade. A black-clad figure leaned toward Kraven, his narrowed eyes showing little patience with the soaking vampire's histrionics.

"Calm yourself, Kraven," Lucian said. As always, his crest-shaped pendant glittered upon his chest; Kraven had never seen him without it.

The lycan's fingernails elongated, becoming razor-sharp claws digging into Kraven's flesh. The vampire winced in pain, even as he tried unsuccessfully to yank his throat free from Lucian's powerful grip. He struggled to speak but could scarcely breathe. Lucian tightened his grip, choking Kraven even harder.

"The human doesn't concern you," the lycan said calmly, as though he weren't throttling Kraven at this very moment. "And besides," he added with a wolfish grin, "I believe I've lain low for quite long enough."

He released his grip at last. Gasping, Kraven fell backward against the padded back of his seat. He glared balefully at Lucian with blood-tinged eyes. Not for the first time, he rued ever entering into an alliance with this loathsome subhuman beast. *Someday you'll pay for this effrontery*, he promised silently. Too much was at stake to jeopardize their grand endeavor now. *But someday, and soon . . .*

Recovering his breath, he did what he could to reassert his dignity. "Keep your men at bay, Lucian. At least for the time being." Lucian needed to be reminded that he was merely Kraven's partner, not his superior. "Don't force me to regret our arrangement."

146

Lucian chuckled, clearly unimpressed by Kraven's bravado. His nails retracted back to human proportions as he subjected the petulant vampire to a withering stare. "You just concentrate on your part," he instructed, his tone brooking no disagreement. "Remember, I've bled for you once already. Without me, you'd have nothing." His fearless gray eyes dared Kraven to dispute him. He spoke slowly, underlining his words for emphasis.

"You'd be . . . nothing."

Chapter Fourteen

The musty atmosphere of the archive hall felt heavy with the weight of ages. Dark oaken bookshelves sagged beneath countless volumes of forgotten lore and history. Illuminated manuscripts, painstakingly illustrated and copied by medieval monks, shared the overcrowded shelves with the abundant literary fruits of post-Gutenberg generations. Leather-bound memoirs, histories, and codexes were packed two deep in places or piled high upon the floor in tottering stacks that threatened to topple over at any minute. Dusty artifacts—souvenirs from bygone centuries—were scattered here and there among the copious written records: a ceremonial brass chalice from the thirteenth century, the curved scimitar of a long-dead Ottoman prince, an embossed silver plate commemorating the epic Battle of Vezekeny in 1654, a filigreed golden scepter bearing the royal crest of Transylvania—all precious relics from nearly nine hundred years of vampiric history.

Selene had the secluded library all to herself. No surprise there; Kraven and his hedonistic entourage were more interested in present pleasures than the accumulated debris of the past. Dust and cobwebs frosted the archaic tomes, testifying to how seldom the archive was visited by Ordoghaz's sybaritic inhabitants. Even the manor's myriad chambermaids seldom entered these cloistered chambers. As a rule, the servant girls had been selected more for their alluring faces and figures and compliant dispositions than for their diligence.

Just as well, Selene thought. She had serious research to do and no desire to be interrupted. Her eyes scanned the bulging bookshelves, looking for the specific records she required. Still clad for battle, she stalked the library in her muddy leathers. Outside, the storm was still going strong. Rain pelted the library's lancet windows, causing watery shadows to dance eerily upon the walls.

Her gaze fell on the rectangular pine door of an inconspicuous closet, tucked between two looming oak bookcases. In truth, it had been at least seventy years since she had consulted these archives herself, but she dimly recalled that the chronicles covering the early decades of the war were kept in this long-abandoned closet. In theory, the information she sought would be there.

She jiggled the antique crystal doorknob, only to find the closet door locked. *Of course,* she thought, scowling. Heaven only knew what had become of the key. Unwilling to be thwarted so quickly, she drew back her leg and—*kaboom!*—kicked the obstinate door right off its hinges. Dusty light poured into the interior of the closet, exposing its contents for the first time in uncounted generations. Selene smiled as she spotted several dozen ponderous tomes, locked away behind a thick glass case just as she remembered.

Eureka, she thought.

The cabinet inside the closet was unlocked, sparing further vandalism, and Selene sifted through the enclosed volumes, peering closely at their timeworn spines and covers.

Selecting four or five of the most promising candidates, she carried the heavy texts over to a Victorian-style maple table resting in the center of the library. She blew decades' worth of dust off both the books and the table before sitting down to inspect the ancient chronicles.

In an ideal world, she would peruse the texts at leisure, carefully reading each and every word. She sensed, however, that time was running out, so she flipped briskly but gently through the dry and crumbling pages, searching urgently for the answers she hungered for.

Columns of intricate calligraphy were accompanied by faded etchings depicting scenes from the long crusade against the werewolves. At first, Selene nodded in approval at portraits of medieval Death Dealers riding to battle, the martial tableaux filling her undead heart with pride. Yet, as she continued to peruse the elaborately detailed woodcuts, she was disturbed to see several illustrations that more closely resembled massacres than honest warfare. Ghastly images, worthy of Doré, portrayed captive beast-men and -women (recognizable by their shaggy coats and canine paws) being tortured and burned at the stake by her armored ancestors. Half-human whelps were hurled like fuel onto the rising flames or else were crushed beneath the silver-shod hooves of the Death Dealers' steeds, their childish proportions no protection against the merciless vampire warriors. Even over the gulf of centuries, the fear and anguish of the forsaken lycans came across loud and clear.

Frowning, she turned the page, only to encounter an equally unsettling illustration that showed chained lycans, both male and female, being forced to their knees and branded like cattle. Leering Death Dealers, brandishing vicious pikes and crossbows, looked on as red-hot silver was applied to the unfortunate lycans, burning the emblems of their captors into their very flesh.

"What are these?" Selene gasped out loud, recoiling from the grisly images. *Ancient myths? Medieval propaganda?*

She ran her finger down the yellowing parchment, trying to find some explanation for the book's unsettling illustrations. Her ivory brow furrowed as she struggled to decipher the adjacent text. Unfortunately, the scribbled chicken scratches appeared to be written in an archaic form of Magyar, which was somewhat beyond her abilities. She gazed in frustration at the tiny, indecipherable calligraphy, which was cleverly interlaced with rows of miniature sketches, which matched the brands being burned onto the flesh of the various howling lycans. Perhaps, she speculated, these pages constituted a catalog of the individual brands.

Peering more closely at the mysterious symbols, she couldn't help observing that although the brands varied slightly from illustration to illustration, they all had been designed around one of three ornate capital letters: *V, A,* or *M.*

Just like the insignia on the tombs of the Elders.

Viktor, Amelia, and Marcus.

Despite her snug new leathers, a shiver passed through Selene. Her mind fleeing from the distressing implications of the medieval woodcuts, she put the incriminating tome aside and reached for a different book.

To her relief, this book was written in simple Old English. Flipping through it, however, she discovered that many of the entries and illustrations had been blacked out with liberal applications of impenetrable India ink. Furthermore, dozens of pages appeared to have been torn out and discarded. She raised the book off the table and turned it over experimentally; none of the missing pages came falling out.

Interesting, Selene thought, her suspicions aroused. Why had someone gone to such efforts to cover up the past? What dark secret was being concealed?

Leafing through the plundered volume, she came across a portrait of a solitary male lycan, his lupine claws extended at his side. Intriguingly, the lycan's face had been completely burned away, leaving a circular gap near the top of the etching.

Selene examined the mutilated portrait more carefully. Visible on the faceless lycan's right arm was an elaborate cattle brand incorporating a large capital *V*.

V as in Viktor, she thought unwillingly.

A charred caption beneath the portrait read: "Lucian, scourge of immortals, master of the lycan horde."

Selene smiled grimly. *Now we're getting somewhere,* she thought. This was what she had been looking for.

Beneath Lucian's defaced portrait was another etching, depicting a heated battle between armed vampires and lycanthropes. Vampires armed with silver swords and crossbows took on a snarling pack of both humanoid and wolfen lycans, with each side inflicting grievous harm upon the other. Shrieking lycans, their bestial faces contorted in agony, were impaled three or four deep on the silver lances of vampiric cavalrymen, while elsewhere on the page, fully transformed werewolves tore unlucky vampires asunder with their dagger-sized fangs and claws. In the background, smoke and fire belched into the night sky from the mouths of several remote mountain caves. An overhanging moon, bearing the features of an outraged werewolf, looked down on the bloody scene with murder in its eyes.

Selene recognized, from Kraven's egocentric recountings if nothing else, the crucial Battle of the Alps. Her finger tracked across the gutter of the book to the adjoining page:

"Of the scores of brave souls who ventured into Lucian's infernal fortress, only a single vampire survived: Kraven of Leicester, who was richly rewarded not only for setting the great blaze but for returning with tangible proof of the lycan master's demise: the branded skin, cut from Lucian's arm."

At the bottom of the page was what appeared to be a piece of dried brown leather, folded neatly into a square. The "tangible proof" mentioned above? Wrinkling her nose in disgust, Selene carefully unfolded the paltry scrap of hide—to reveal the stylized letter *V* seared onto the fragment.

She traced the brand with her fingertip, aware of the scrap's historic significance. This was no mere scrap of leather, it was a swatch of skin cut from the flesh of a fallen lycan. Her gaze jumped back to the faceless portrait at the top of the opposite page, comparing the brand on Lucian's arm to the revolting fragment spread out before her.

The marks were identical.

How about that? she thought archly, uncertain whether to be relieved or disappointed that the archives confirmed Kraven's account of having disposed of Lucian nearly six centuries ago, a momentous feat that had elevated Kraven instantly to the upper ranks of the coven. As much as she had hoped to catch Kraven in a lie, it was good to know that the infamous Lucian was indeed well and truly dead.

Or was he?

Staring again at Lucian's burned-out portrait, Selene noticed a blackish smudge beneath the flaking hole where his face had been. Was there something beneath the ancient ashes? Wetting her fingertip, she gently rubbed away some of the loose charring, exposing a familiar-looking star-shaped pendant.

Bloody hell! She instantly recalled the identical pendant

worn by the unnamed lycan who had stabbed her in the shoulder, nearly killing her, yesterday night. *I don't believe it,* she thought, dumbfounded by her discovery. *Could that actually have been . . . Lucian?*

If so, then Kraven's slip of the tongue earlier had been even more revelatory than she had feared—and her people's greatest enemy was still alive and well.

She slammed the book shut, her every nerve vibrating with alarm. She needed to do something, tell someone, before it was too late. Lucian, lord of the werewolves, was aprowl in the night—and he was after Michael!

She lurched out of her chair and whirled toward the exit. To her surprise, she found the ubiquitous Erika standing in the doorway. *Again?* Selene thought impatiently. *I need to fasten a bell to this inquisitive little domestic.*

"I've been looking for you everywhere," the blond servant vamp explained, sounding a trifle put out. She glanced around the musty archive hall with disdain, as though no vampiress in her right mind would frequent such a tedious locale.

So what else is new? Selene thought in response to Erika's complaint. "Not now," she said brusquely. If Lucian were back and plotting against her coven, then appeasing Erika was the least of Selene's concerns.

She moved toward the exit, expecting Erika to step aside. Instead, a slim white arm shot out, blocking the doorway. "He's been bitten. Your human," the petite maidservant blurted. "He's been marked by a lycan."

Selene blinked in surprise. Was this some sort of twisted joke? Surely, Erika could not be serious. "Did Kraven put you up to this?" she asked suspiciously.

"No!" Erika shook her head. "I saw the wound with my own eyes. I swear it!"

Could she be telling the truth? Selene's mind raced back to the night before, when she had rescued Michael from that lycan (Lucian?) at the apartment building. She remembered dragging Michael out from beneath the lycan, after the wounded beast-man fell atop Michael in the elevator. Had the lycan somehow managed to bite Michael before she had extracted the panicked human from the stranger's grasp? Perhaps, she conceded reluctantly. In the speed and confusion of that hasty escape, anything was possible.

Was Michael now the enemy? Had he been lost to her irrevocably? *No,* Selene decided abruptly. *I refuse to accept that.* Michael was too important, to all of them, to give up on so readily. The thought of him becoming just another rapacious, subhuman monster tore at her heart in ways she could scarcely bring herself to comprehend. *One way or another, I'll find some way to save him.*

She locked eyes with Erika, then shot a cool glance at the servant girl's outstretched arm. Wilting before Selene's steely gaze, Erika lowered her arm and stepped aside, allowing Selene to pass over the threshold into the corridor beyond. "But what about the Covenant?" Erika asked nervously as the other woman left the library behind.

The inexperienced maid hardly needed to remind Selene of the Covenant of the Blood. This was the sacred code by which the older vampiress had lived and hunted for her entire undead existence. To fear for the safety of one whom the wolves had claimed for their own went against everything Selene had always believed and fought for.

I don't care, she thought, storming off toward the questionable privacy of her own quarters. Erika's plaintive wail followed her down the lonely corridor: "You know it's forbidden!"

*   *   *

Dr. Adam Lockwood yawned as he made his rounds at the hospital. It was a busy night on the casualty ward, made all the worse for them being short-handed. For the hundredth time this evening, he wondered what had become of Michael Corvin. The other American already had missed two shifts and failed to answer any of the supervisor's increasingly urgent phone messages. *I hope he's all right,* the overworked intern worried. *Michael's always been so responsible before.*

The antiseptic atmosphere of the hospital filled his nostrils as he walked through the ward on his way to the doctors' lounge. A fresh pot of coffee was calling his name, and Adam figured that a prompt infusion of caffeine was just what the doctor ordered. No stimulants were required to jump-start his heart, however, when the door to his right suddenly flew open and powerful hands grabbed him by the shoulders and physically yanked him into an empty examining room.

What the hell? Adam tried to call out, but a sweaty palm clamped down over his mouth. *I don't believe this!* he thought frantically. *I'm being mugged in my own hospital!*

The door slammed shut, trapping Adam inside the room with his assailant. A hoarse voice whispered in his ear: "Don't be afraid. It's me, Michael!"

Michael?

The frightened doctor nodded, acknowledging the message, and the intrusive hand came away from his face. Adam resisted the urge to shout for assistance, electing to find out a little more about the situation before pushing the panic button. He owed Michael that much, for friendship's sake.

Michael is a good guy, Adam reasoned. *He can't possibly be dangerous . . . can he?*

Another hand let go of his shoulder, and Adam slowly

turned around to face his fellow resident. Moonlight entered the exam room through a closed glass window, and Adam was shocked by what the eerie silver radiance revealed.

Michael looked like hell. He was still clad in the same bloodstained jacket and pants he'd been wearing the night before, after he got caught in that bloodbath in the Metro station. Mud and grass further stained the bedraggled garments, which looked as if they'd been dragged, along with Michael himself, through some godforsaken war zone.

Michael's face was pale and slick with perspiration. His eyes were bloodshot, and an ugly purple bruise besmirched his forehead. He shivered uncontrollably, his hands shaking like branches in a gale. Numerous small cuts and scratches went untreated on his face, neck, and hands, while livid black shadows hung beneath his manic brown eyes. He looked sick, feverish, out of control. Adam barely recognized the capable young doctor he had come to know over the last several months.

"For the love of God, Michael, what's happened to you?"

Michael's explanation, such as it was, did not reassure the other doctor, who listened with mounting alarm as his distraught colleague launched into a bizarre, irrational story of car chases, shoot-outs, levitating women, attack dogs, and growling monsters on the roof. It was totally preposterous, yet Michael seemed scarily sincere, describing each nightmarish event with paranoid intensity. He paced erratically as he spoke, tracking back and forth across the room like a caged animal.

"And ever since he bit me," he insisted, "I've been having these, I dunno what you'd call them . . . hallucinations, delusions?" He stared inwardly at hellish sights only he could perceive. "All I know is that it feels as if my skull is splitting in half."

Adam tried to keep up with the outré narrative. "A full-grown man bit you?"

Michael tugged down his collar, exposing an appalling-looking bite wound on his right shoulder. Stepping forward to take a closer look, Adam saw that the wound consisted of four deep puncture marks in Michael's well-developed trapezius. To Adam's dismay, the area around the bite was hot and discolored; the site was very obviously infected.

"Sure it wasn't a dog?" Adam asked. He peered at the marks through the smudged lenses of his glasses. From the bite radius, he guessed a largish hound was responsible. A Great Dane, perhaps, or a German Shepherd.

Michael angrily swatted his hand away. "I said it was a man!"

Adam backed away warily, startled by the other man's violent outburst. "Okay!" he said, in the same placating tone he used with grieving relatives and strung-out drug addicts. "But you're the one talking about hallucinations here, not me."

Michael sagged visibly, as though his momentary flare-up had exhausted him. Wondering once more if he should call security, Adam cautiously guided Michael over to the exam table. A nearby desk and clothes cabinet completed the room's meager furnishings. "Come on, take a seat."

Paper crinkled as Michael grudgingly complied. He sat sideways on the padded table, his legs dangling several centimeters above the floor. He looked calmer now, but Adam was still shaken by Michael's disturbing behavior a few moments ago. *He's not himself tonight, that's for certain.*

Summoning up his most soothing bedside manner, Adam timidly approached Michael again, taking a closer look at the swelling purple bruise on the injured resident's forehead. "Nice," Adam observed sarcastically. "From the looks of this, I'm betting you have a mild concussion."

He feared, however, that a concussion was the least of Michael's problems. *Is he on drugs?* Adam wondered. Michael hadn't seemed like the type, but you never knew. It dawned on Adam that he knew very little about Michael's life away from the hospital.

Why were those policemen so interested in him yesterday?

Removing a digital thermometer from the pocket of his lab coat, the lanky doctor inserted the instrument into Michael's ear. Meanwhile, Michael grabbed some medicinal supplies off the nearby table and began dabbing the infected bite marks with an alcohol swab. Judging from the lurid discoloration around the puncture wounds, Adam guessed that alcohol wasn't going to be enough. Michael probably was going to need antibiotics.

"Concussion or not," Michael rasped, "this guy was definitely after me, just like those cops . . ."

Adam swallowed guiltily. He had just been thinking the same thing—about the police officers, that is. Was Michael in trouble with the law somehow? Did he have something to do with the gunfight in the underground? *Hard to believe,* he thought. Then again, he had never seen Michael look or act like this before.

The thermometer beeped electronically, and Adam withdrew the device from his patient's ear. His vague misgivings about Michael's recent activities were displaced momentarily by his shock at the young man's temperature, which was an alarming forty degrees Celsius.

"Jesus Christ," he blurted. "You're burning up."

But Michael was too caught up in his crazed, delusional narrative to react to Adam's pronouncement. He rambled morosely as he applied a dab of ointment to his shoulder and began bandaging the wound there. "And the woman from the subway, Selene, I'm not sure, maybe . . ." His red eyes took on a manic gleam as a hysterical edge crept into his voice. "Hell, for all I know, they were all in on it together!"

He was definitely freaked out, Adam concluded, more than a little spooked by the way the other man was acting. "For heaven's sake, Michael," he exclaimed, hoping to yank the delirious resident back to reality. "In on what?"

"Haven't you been listening?" Michael snapped. Adam backed away from the exam table. "She took me hostage!"

Sure she did, Adam thought skeptically. Chances were, Michael's gun-toting mystery woman was just one of the hallucinations he'd mentioned. *This is more than I can deal with on my own,* Adam decided, glancing at the door. *He's too far gone.*

"All right, all right," he said, humoring Michael. "Calm down. I'm going to help you get this all sorted out." He edged slowly toward the exit, but his attempted departure provoked Michael, who lunged off the table and grabbed the doctor tightly by the arm. Adam's heart pounded wildly as he suddenly feared for his life. "Whoa! I'm just going to run to my office and grab a number." *Please,* he thought, scared to death of his fellow resident. *Don't hurt me, I beg you!* "A good friend of mine is a lawyer. He'll know what to do."

Would Michael buy this? Adam held his breath, waiting anxiously for the agitated man's reaction. An endless moment passed, during which time Adam's life and semi-promising career passed before his eyes, before Michael finally let go of his arm and slumped back against the exam table.

"Sorry," he apologized weakly. "I'm just . . ."

An overpowering sense of relief left Adam weak at the knees. *That was close,* he thought, exhaling at last. Michael was clearly out of control; he might be capable of anything. *I must be crazy staying alone with him in here. I need to get help—stat!*

"It's okay," he assured Michael, flashing a reassuring (and entirely fraudulent) smile. Once again, he backed slowly for the door. His fingers groped clumsily behind his back for the doorknob. "Relax. I'll be right back, I promise."

He fully expected Michael to pounce on him like a madman the moment he turned the knob, but to his blissful surprise, the crazed resident actually permitted him to slip out the door into the hallway. Adam gently pulled the door shut again, wishing he had a key with which to lock it, before allowing all his pent-up fear and anxiety to leave him shaking and pale outside the exam room.

I made it! he thought, gasping in relief. *Thank God!* Beneath his lab coat, a layer of cold sweat glued his white cotton shirt to his spine. Closing his eyes, he took a moment to recover from the psychological strain of his nerve-racking encounter with Michael before fishing around in his pockets for the card those two policemen had left with him yesterday. Where the heck had he put it, anyway?

Ah, there it was. Drawing his cell phone, he hastily dialed the number on the card.

The two officers, Pierce and Taylor, arrived with surprising speed, less than ten minutes after receiving Adam's call. *Whatever they want Michael for,* the doctor deduced, *it must be serious.* He felt certain that he had made the right decision in contacting the police.

"Thank you for coming," he murmured to the uniformed officers. He kept his voice low, just in case Michael was listening. Throughout the ward, puzzled nurses and patients watched curiously as he guided the cops toward the examination room now occupied by the agitated intern. "I don't know what's the matter with him," Adam babbled fretfully. "I've never seen him like this before."

The burly officers nodded brusquely, striding toward the closed door with their hands on the grips of their pistols. Adam hoped they wouldn't be too rough on Michael, whatever trouble he was in. *I probably should notify the American embassy,* he thought, *unless the police usually handle that.* He wasn't exactly sure about the procedure.

They were almost at the exam room when a loud crash came from the other side of the door. Glass shattered noisily, electrifying Pierce and Taylor, who sprang immediately into action. Guns drawn, they charged the door, slamming it open with their shoulders. Adam followed them, prudently keeping a safe distance behind the cops. He flinched in anticipation of violence and gunplay, but the only sound that came from the besieged exam room was the mournful keening of the wind.

I don't understand, he thought. He had been watching the door the whole time he'd been waiting for the police to arrive. Michael couldn't have got away. *And what was that crashing sound?*

He peeked sheepishly through the doorway into the examination room. Wind and rain entered through a broken window at the far end of the room. The taller of the two policemen, Pierce, ran to the window and peered through the empty pane at the street below. Scowling, he turned toward his partner and shook his head. Adam guessed that Michael was nowhere to be seen.

The frustrated cops glared at Adam.

"He was right here!" the doctor insisted. He threw his hands in the air, pantomiming helplessness. *It's not my fault,* he thought defensively, *if your prime suspect jumps out the window. I'm lucky he didn't attack me, given his deranged state of mind!*

Pierce and Taylor exchanged ill-tempered looks, then thundered out of the empty exam room, ignoring Adam completely as they shoved past the doctor on their way out. A cold wind blew against Adam from the broken window, and he pulled the door shut to cut off the draft. He watched the policemen depart, disturbed by the unconcealed fury he had glimpsed in the men's dark eyes.

"Hey!" he called after them. He hurried to catch up with the cops before they left the building. "You're not going to shoot him, are you!"

Michael waited until he heard Adam's footsteps recede into the distance, then warily opened the door of the cabinet. Taking care not to rattle the metal clothes hangers dangling around his head and shoulders, he peered through a crack-sized opening at the moonlit exam room. A flash of lightning outside exposed every shadowy corner of the room.

The coast looks clear, he decided. Grateful that both Adam and the police had fallen for his trick with the window, he slipped stealthily out of the cabinet onto the tile floor of the examination room. He looked around apprehensively, wondering how long he had before someone decided to check this room again. *I have to get out of here, but to where?*

Going to the police was out. According to Adam's message yesterday, the local cops already suspected that he had something to do with that bloody gunfight in the subway—and Michael wasn't sure he could convince them otherwise, given everything that had happened to him since. He appeared to be right in the middle of this murderous mess, whatever it was all about.

The American embassy, over at Liberty Square, was no good, either. If even Adam thought he was crazy, what would the sensible folks at the U.S. embassy think when he tried to explain what had happened to him? *Hell,* Michael thought, *even I'm starting to question my own sanity!*

Nausea struck him, and he bent over convulsively, clutching at his gut. He clenched his jaw tightly shut to keep from vomiting and fought like mad to ride out the seizure. Sweat beaded on his forehead while his insides felt as if they were turning inside-out. *Jesus Christ, what's wrong with me?* Michael wondered in anguish. None of his hard-won medical training pointed him toward a reasonable diagnosis for his condition. His vision flickered in the moonlight, briefly going color-blind before reverting to normal again. His infected shoulder throbbed in sync with dreadful pounding inside his skull. His teeth ached within his gums, as if they were being twisted out of shape.

But he was more than just physically ill. He was going crazy, too. Phantom warriors, wielding silver crossbow bolts, lurked at the fringes of his vision. Fragmentary impressions and images that had no relation to the life he remembered were shuffled in among his memories like an extra ace in some devious card trick. He closed his eyes for an instant, and he was back in that primeval forest again, being chased through the moonlit woods by shadowy figures in chain mail and armor.

That's not me! he thought violently. *That never happened!* But he could still feel the spongy forest floor beneath his bare feet, smell the sap flowing through the trees, as he ran for his life through that murky sylvan dreamscape. The cursive brand on his arm burned like a red-hot flame. He tasted his own blood upon his tongue . . .

I'm sick, Michael realized in despair. *I need help.*

But whom could he turn to? In desperation, a face

flashed across his memory. Inscrutable chestnut eyes beneath a mane of long sable hair. Skin as white as untouched snow. An exotic apparition, wild, mysterious, enticing . . .

For better or for worse, there was only one person who might be able to see him through this nightmare.

Selene.

Chapter Fifteen

*R*unning water was said to be anathema to those of the vampire breed, but that was just a myth; otherwise, Selene could not have enjoyed the much-needed shower now scouring her naked body with a steady blast of deliciously hot water.

Billowing steam filled her private bathroom as the invigorating spray pelted her flesh, at long last washing away the sweaty, muddy, bloody residue of her ill-fated excursion to the city. Dirty water collected at the bottom of the pure white marble stall, circling the drain before disappearing into the mansion's plumbing. Selene wondered how long it would take the bloody stream to reach the dank city sewers where she had battled those two lycans.

There's something down there, she knew in her heart. *Maybe an enormous pack of somethings.*

Sadly, the scorching shower could not wash away the malignant fears troubling her mind. Was Lucian alive? Kraven had accidentally referred to Lucian in the present tense before, but did that prove Kraven knew about Lucian's possible return? And what about Michael? Was Erika telling the truth, had Michael truly been conscripted by the enemy?

Please, no! she thought passionately. The soothing water rinsed the soap and shampoo from her dark hair and porcelain skin, but Selene knew that she could not hide in the shower forever. There were too many vital questions to be answered, and time was running short. *The Awakening is almost here,* she recalled. *Amelia and her entourage will be arriving after sunset tomorrow.* On what, thanks to an unlucky coincidence, just happened to be the first night of the full moon.

Selene shuddered at the thought of what that moon might bring, to Michael as well as to the entire vampire nation. A desperate ploy came to mind, one that she ordinarily would have rejected as too extreme but which now struck her as the only option remaining to her. *I have to risk it,* she decided. *There's no other choice.*

Reluctantly, she turned off the shower and let the last of the hot water trickle down her body. Stepping out of the stall into the luxury-sized bathchamber, she toweled herself quickly, then pulled on a dark blue cotton bathrobe.

Steam clouded the queen-sized vanity mirror above the sink. Her mind made up, she strode decisively up to the sink and reached out to touch the foggy mirror. Her fingertip gently traced a string of letters across the glass:

VIKTOR.

She paused for a moment or two, humbled by the exalted name she had invoked. Then she wiped her hand across the mirror, erasing the message.

"Please forgive me," she whispered, bowing her head in reverence. Although the mirror held only her own reflection, that was not at all whom she was addressing. She lifted her head, entreating the mirror with anguished eyes.

"But I desperately need your guidance . . ."

* * *

The taxi rushed down the lonely forest road, carrying Michael back toward the manor. Night shrouded the skeletal oaks and beeches lining the road as he peered out the window of the cab, praying that he was remembering the directions right.

Ashen and trembling, he slumped in the backseat, clutching a handful of fresh bills that he had extracted from an ATM back in the city. A map of the towns and villages north of Budapest was spread out on his lap. As far as he could tell, he was successfully retracing the route he had taken from the mansion back to the city earlier that night. *Szentendre,* he reminded himself repeatedly, as though the name might slip out of his bruised and battered brain. *Selene's mansion was just outside Szentendre . . .*

The taxi hit a pothole, and the bump caused Michael's throbbing head and bones to protest forcefully. He hugged himself tightly, hoping he wouldn't be sick in the cab. The howling in his ears roared like an upset menagerie, and every glimpse of moonlight caused his teeth and gums to ache something fierce. The moon was almost full, he noticed, waxing brightly above the shadowy forest outside.

Am I doing the right thing? he worried. He remembered the savage Rottweilers baying at his heels and wondered if he was crazy to come within fifty miles of that creepy mansion again. Then he recalled Selene's lovely face looking down at him, wiping his febrile brow with a damp rag, and realized he had nowhere else to go. *I just hope Selene, whoever she is, is really on my side.*

The cab's interior smelled of tobacco, beer, and goulash, which didn't do Michael's queasy stomach any favors. He couldn't recall the last time he'd eaten, back before his life went insane, yet he still felt more nauseated than hungry. He struggled to keep his eyes open, afraid of the visions waiting in the darkness, but it was no good. A violent tremor shook his body, and his eyes rolled up inside his head, so that only the blood-streaked whites were visible.

CRACK! A spinelike whip, seemingly forged of solid silver vertebrae, snapped out of the void. The gleaming whip lashed his head and shoulders, burning and stinging at the same time. The lash opened his flesh, causing hot blood to stream down his back, over countless overlapping layers of old scar tissue, before the scalding silver cauterized the freshly opened wound. Then the whip cracked again, and he felt its agonizing bite once more . . .

"No!" Michael exclaimed. His eyes rolled back to normal as he escaped the vivid hallucination. He reached instinctively for his back, to make sure the scars were strictly imaginary. *That felt so real,* he thought, gasping, *as if the flesh were being flayed from my body!*

"Are you all right, sir?" The cab driver, a chunky Armenian immigrant, glanced back over the seat. He looked as if he were having profound second thoughts about accepting the ailing young American as a fare. "You were having some kind of—how you say?—seizure?"

"I'm fine," Michael lied. He nodded to assure the worried driver that he was okay, even though he felt anything but. *What the hell is wrong with me?* he fretted anxiously. *I can't take this much longer!*

Perhaps Selene could explain what was happening to him. If not, he wasn't sure what else he could do. He forcibly yanked his mind back into the present, away from silver whips and bloody torture, and tried to concentrate on the road ahead of him. An intersection approached, and Michael groggily consulted the map on his lap. "Turn here," he instructed, gesturing toward the right.

Selene has to be able to help me.

She has to!

Chapter Sixteen

*T*he guard looked up as Selene entered the security booth, clad in a fresh set of slick black leathers. Watching over the crypt and its hibernating inhabitants was a tedious job, so no doubt he welcomed the unexpected company. *Careful,* Selene warned herself. *Don't give away your intentions.*

"Kahn wants to see you," she said tersely.

That got a reaction. Selene knew that the guard, Duncan, had aspirations of rising in the ranks of the Death Dealers. He jumped up from his seat behind the security monitors, eager to report to the dojo upstairs. He halted at the exit, though, and glanced back uneasily at his post.

"Don't worry," she told him. "I'll hold down the fort."

He nodded gratefully and rushed out of the booth. Selene waited until his retreating footsteps completely disappeared before pressing an electronic button to open the entrance to the crypt itself. *I have to hurry,* she thought. Duncan would soon discover that he had been tricked.

She descended the timeworn granite steps to the sunken stone floor below. The temperature seemed to drop a couple of degrees with each step, so that her blood felt even colder than usual by the time she reached the bottom of the crypt.

Am I actually going through with this? she thought uncertainly, daunted by the sheer enormity of what she was contemplating. *Until tonight, I never would have dreamed of disturbing an Elder's sleep.*

The crypt was hushed and dimly lit. Selene's eyes penetrated the umbrageous twilight to focus on the three bronze hatches resting at the center of the bottom floor's interlaced Celtic circles. Only two of the tombs were occupied, she knew. Amelia's sarcophagus was empty, awaiting the female Elder's arrival tomorrow night, when Marcus would emerge from his sepulchral resting place to take his turn as sovereign of all the covens of the world. At least, that was the plan.

Selene had other ideas. Ignoring the other two hatches, she went straight to the polished bronze circle marked by a stylized letter *V.* She knelt beside the tomb, hesitating only an instant before inserting her fingers into the cold metal groove surrounding the *V.* Untouched for almost a century, the ancient hatch resisted her at first. Exerting her strength, however, she succeeded in rotating the circular bronze disk, which activated the dormant locking mechanism. The intricate designs adorning the hatch began to turn mechanically as Selene heard the muted rumble of hidden machinery awakening from slumber. The bronze hatch split apart into four triangular segments, exposing the sarcophagus beneath.

The ponderous sound of stone sliding across stone violated the funereal stillness of the crypt. Selene rose to her feet and, holding her breath, stepped back from the tomb. She was committed now. There was no turning back.

Accompanied by the automated reverberation of a concealed motor, a large vertical slab rose from the floor like a coffin-sized elevator. The slab thrust upward until it was several centimeters taller than Selene, then pivoted on its axis. Moving steadily, it snapped into place horizontal to the floor.

A supine figure was laid out upon the slab. Selene stepped toward the bier, suppressing a gasp at the shocking sight before her.

After nearly one hundred years of unbroken slumber, Viktor bore little resemblance to the regal monarch she remembered. The skeletal figure on the slab looked more like a mummy than a vampire: dry, withered, and seemingly lifeless, like a collection of fragile bones shrink-wrapped in papery brown skin. His closed eyes lurked at the bottom of sunken black sockets, while his desiccated lips had peeled away from his gums, exposing yellowed fangs locked in a death's-head grin. Once-powerful limbs were now spindly sticks wrapped in jerkylike strips of meat, and his plunging abdomen had collapsed below the exposed ribcage. Black satin trousers spared her the sight of his shriveled manhood.

Oh, my sire, she lamented, *what has your long repose done to you?* Even though she had expected to find Viktor in just this condition, the ghastly reality still came as a jolt. She had to remind herself that Viktor had submitted to his interment willingly, as part of a hallowed tradition that stretched back through the ages. The everlasting cycle of the Chain served two vital functions: first, as an ingenious power-sharing arrangement among the three Elders, avoiding conflict among them by ensuring that only one of them was in command in any given century; and second, to provide each Elder with a much-needed respite from the demands of eternity.

"Immortality can be wearing," Viktor had once explained to her, shortly before entering his tomb a century ago, "watching the never-ending tides of history ebb and flow, striving to keep up with the dizzying changes in science and civilization. Even the most resilient Elder feels the need to retire from the fray from time to time, to spend a century or

173

two in silent repose, before rising to confront the future with renewed wisdom and clarity."

That had been nearly one hundred years ago. Selene shook her head, trying to reconcile the majestic immortal in her memory with the cadaverous figure upon the slab, which was disturbingly silent and immobile, its bony chest neither rising nor falling as the fleeting moments passed. If she hadn't known better, Selene would have sworn that the apparent corpse on the slab was well and truly dead, beyond all hope of resurrection. Indeed, by the blinkered standards of modern medicine, Viktor *was* dead.

But appearances could be deceiving. Gleaming copper implants mottled Viktor's emaciated throat, the female components on an elaborate intravenous feeding system. More connections, she knew, were hidden beneath the comatose vampire's back, designed to sustain Viktor during his centuries-long period of hibernation.

The apparatus had kept him alive for ninety-nine years and exactly 364 days. Left undisturbed, it would preserve him for another century as well.

Selene couldn't wait that long.

Quickly, she thought, knowing that Duncan could return at any minute. She tore her gaze away from Viktor's seemingly lifeless carcass to inspect the meticulously crafted framework surrounding him. A series of shallow silver bowls were built into the raised edge of the sarcophagus, leading to a delicate metal spigot. Both the bowls and the spigot were carefully etched with precise calibrations, and a telescoping metal arm connected the apparatus, which was collectively known as the catalyst drip, to the bier itself.

Trepidation warring with resolve, Selene watched apprehensively as the metal spigot motored along the inside of the casket, positioning itself above Viktor's mummified face.

174

Here comes the tricky part, she thought. To her knowledge, an awakening had never been attempted by one such as she. The Elders alone held the power to organize their thoughts and memories into a single, cohesive vision, forming a detailed record of their reign. Selene could only hope that Viktor would hear—and comprehend—her desperate plea.

She unzipped her sleeve and raised her arm to her face. Her lips parted, exposing her fangs, and she took a deep breath. *Please let this work!* she entreated. *The outcome of the war may depend on it.*

Without further delay, she bit into her wrist, feeling her own deadly fangs slice through her ageless white skin. The sharp sting of the incision made her wince, and the briny taste of her own blood exploded upon her tongue, yet she resisted the urge to drink deeply of her crimson essence, just as she took care to cut only deeply enough to sever the veins, sparing the vital arteries buried further beneath her flesh. She needed only a tiny stream of blood for this solemn rite, not a spurting red geyser.

Allowing herself only a sip of her cool vampiric plasma, Selene reluctantly pulled her wrist away from her blood-smeared mouth. *There's nothing like the real thing,* she admitted with a stab of regret, *even when stolen from my own veins.* She had subsisted on sorry substitutes for far too long.

But her frustrated craving was not what mattered now. She held her wrist out over the leading bowl of the catalyst drip and squeezed the wound to hasten the flow. Dark venous blood spilled from her opened wrist into the shining bowl, beginning its slow and winding progression from bowl to bowl. An arcane chemical catalyst, absorbed via an osmotic filter at the base of each bowl, mixed with Selene's shed blood to undergo a sublime alchemical transformation even as the thin red serum descended toward Viktor's desiccated maw.

Selene peered ruefully at the crimson stream. She was all too aware that she lacked the mental strength and discipline to precisely regulate the flow of memories being carried by her blood. All she could do was watch the dark red fluid make its way toward the open spigot and pray that her entreaty had not been garbled too badly.

Leaving Viktor and the equipment alone for a moment, she hurried across the bottommost floor to the rear of the crypt, where a sealed plexiglass chamber lurked just beyond the subdued halogen lighting over the Elders' tombs. A pair of rectangular marble pillars framed the entrance to the sealed compartment, whose sterile, futuristic design contrasted sharply with the somber medieval majesty of the ancient crypt.

This was the recovery chamber, employed only once every hundred years. The transparent plexiglass walls were a new addition to the facility, part of a never-ending program to update and improve the chamber in accordance with the steady progress of technological innovation. The Elders demanded and deserved the best that modern science could provide, even if their memories extended profoundly back through history.

Selene rushed into the recovery unit and flicked on the lights. A wheeled metal gurney occupied the center of the room, surrounded by antiseptic chrome counters and sophisticated diagnostic monitors. A complicated array of plastic tubing dangled from the ceiling like a bizarre biomedical chandelier.

Ducking her head beneath the overhead tubing, Selene went straight for a refrigerated metal cabinet, whose locked door proved no match for her preternatural strength and determination. Dozens of plastic IV bags filled with preserved human plasma and hemoglobin rested inside the cabinet, and Selene helped herself freely to the supplies, piling them high atop a burnished steel counter next to the gurney. *Is this enough?* she fretted, wishing she didn't have to figure all this out on her own. *Too bad Michael isn't here,* she thought wryly. He was a doctor, after all, although Selene seriously doubted that he had ever taken part in a procedure like the one she was now attempting.

While Selene hastily prepared the recovery chamber, the first few drops of her catalyzed blood completed their circuitous journey through the sequence of bowls. A swollen scarlet bead dangled beneath the lip of the burnished copper spigot, the globule bulging in size until gravity finally wrested it from its precarious perch.

The bright red droplet plummeted through space to land with a *splat* upon Viktor's cracked and arid lips. From there, it trickled over the brink into the yawning chasm between the mummy's lips, falling like rain upon the sere and barren landscape at the back of his throat.

More bloody raindrops plunged from above, watering the inanimate tissues with miraculous results. Parched membranes greedily soaked up the magic elixir. Inert cells and corpuscles rose from the dead, pulsing back to life at a geometric rate. Dried veins and capillaries resumed their ancient duties, carrying Selene's heartfelt libation deep into the petrified recesses of Viktor's undead heart and mind, along with a flood of jumbled memories and images.

Selene, bathed in candlelight, her lovely face wan and bloodless, stands before a window, staring at her reflection. A pristine white nightgown is draped upon her shapely form. Her eyes wide, she tugs down the collar of her gown, inspecting the fresh bite wound on her slender throat: two livid red spots directly above her jugular. Her lower lip quivers tremulously as her slen-

der fingers gingerly explore the wound. Her fear-stricken eyes are those of a traumatized innocent, quite unlike the hardened Death Dealer she would someday become.

A shadowy figure, only dimly reflected in the glass, strolls up behind her, placing a reassuring hand upon her shoulder. Viktor's hand, as yet untouched by time . . .

The images came faster, burning past his mind's eye with blazing intensity. The memories were disordered, chaotic, and out of sequence, as though being fed to him by a clumsy amateur.

Selene stands before a foggy bathroom mirror, unintentionally echoing her pose from that night long past. Her dark brown hair is freshly wet from a shower. A dark indigo bathrobe partially conceals her moist, alabaster flesh . . .

Three frenzied werewolves, their misshapen bodies bristling with pitch-black fur, charge down a dingy corridor faintly illuminated by sputtering electrical lights. Their yellowed fangs glint sharply beneath the fluorescent glow. Spume drips from the corners of their gaping jaws . . .

Selene and Kraven argue heatedly in a palatial suite. Their eternally youthful faces radiate extreme emotion and mutual contempt. Kraven raises his hand, which smacks against her ivory cheek like the lash of an angry whip . . .

Back before her mirror, Selene writes Viktor's name across the befogged looking glass . . .

The disjointed memories flickered and warped as they paraded frenetically across his consciousness. Waking slowly, he attempted to make sense of the confused images, but the kaleidoscopic barrage of visions defied his control.

As Selene looks on with disdain, Kraven presides over a sanguinary orgy in the grand salon. Supple vampiresses, in various states of dishabille, offer their exposed throats and breasts to Kraven, who greedily partakes of the proffered white flesh and crimson refreshment. A surfeit of blood trickles down his chin, staining his ruffled white tunic, as his sybaritic acolytes couple, triple, and even quadruple with abandon, turning the elegant salon into a scene of wanton debauchery.

Discarded items of clothing, fashionably expensive and otherwise, litter the floor. Thirsty mouths seek out willing veins, so that every square centimeter of naked flesh receives the razor-sharp kiss of striking fangs. The collective essence of the cavorting vampires circulates through their intertwined bodies like the bloodstream of a single vast organism. Human slaves and initiates, imported at great expense from Budapest and beyond, season the licentious repast, adding an infusion of mortal heat to the cold-blooded sensuality of the undead. Slurping and sucking noises pervade the scene, punctuated by ecstatic grunts and moans . . .

The voluptuous images stirred his own sluggish blood, but the choppy cascade of memories swiftly moved on, its relentless current carrying him elsewhere.

A human youth, his hair and clothing drenched as from a heavy rain, rides an escalator down to a crowded subway platform . . .

Viktor's own body lies upon a padded bier, his undying flesh mummified by his long interment beneath the mansion . . .

A woman's wrist—Selene's—bleeds above the open bowl of the catalyst drip, beginning the time-honored process by which she shares her turbulent memories with the body upon the slab . . .

Enough. He froze the bleeding wrist within his mind. Exerting his returning powers of concentration, he halted the flood of fractured memories, then turned back the stream so that the preceding images zoomed by fleetly in reverse. He scanned Selene's jumbled recollections, maintaining tight control over the visions, until he found the moment he sought, the one she had clearly wished him to experience.

She stands once more before her bathroom mirror, entreating her reflection with anxious eyes. "Please forgive me," she says solemnly, "but I desperately need your guidance. I apologize for breaking the chain and awakening you ahead of schedule, but I fear we may all be in grave danger. Especially you, my lord, if left in your weakened state, for I believe the fearsome Lucian is alive and well. Here. Now. In this very city, preparing to strike out at us during the Awakening." She swallowed hard, visibly troubled by this unnerving prospect, before speaking again. "Even more disturbing is the realization that, if I am correct in my suspicions, Kraven himself is in league with our greatest enemy."

Chapter Seventeen

*H*is face locked in a frozen scowl, Soren approached the security booth outside the crypt. Kraven had instructed him to make sure the Elders remained undisturbed, and Soren intended to take no chances.

His already sullen expression darkened as he saw that the enclosed booth was conspicuously empty. *Where is the guard?* he wondered right away, instinctively reaching for the 9mm P7 pistol holstered at his hip. *I don't like the look of this.*

Eyes wary, he entered the booth. His meaty finger stabbed a button on the control panel, and he watched impatiently as the adjacent wall split in half, exposing the crypt itself to view. Peering through the thick transparent glass, he was both relieved and surprised to see that the crypt appeared undisturbed. The three bronze hatches marking the Elders' tombs rested securely in place, just as they had for very nearly a century.

Puzzled, he looked around the booth, detecting no evidence of a struggle. Perhaps the missing guard was simply shirking his duties, slipping away to enjoy a furtive tryst with one of the servant girls?

Soren sneered scornfully. Kraven would have the guard's hide for this breach of security, if Kahn didn't get to him first. Not that it much mattered, Soren realized; after tomorrow night, everything would be different. And protecting the Elders no longer would be a cause for concern.

Her back pressed tightly against the cold stone walls of the crypt, Selene hid in the shadows just outside the circle of illumination cast by the soft halogen lights. She could see Soren prowling about the security booth, but, with luck, he wouldn't spot her, especially since the crypt appeared undisturbed. Thank heaven that she had returned the elevated slab and the bronze hatch to their usual locations before Soren arrived! Being surprised by Duncan would have been bad enough; the very last thing she needed was to be caught red-handed by Kraven's personal pit bull.

There would be time enough to face the consequences of her drastic actions. For now, she had no desire to justify her decision to Kraven and his thugs. *I will answer to Viktor himself when the moment of reckoning comes.*

She held her breath while Soren stared suspiciously at the silent crypt. Would he discover her after all? Grueling seconds dragged on interminably until the ageless janissary finally turned away from the glass. He pressed a button on the control panel and a set of opaque faux-stone doors slid shut, hiding the interior of the crypt from view.

Selene expelled a sigh of relief. *That was a close one,* she realized. She wondered how long she would have to hide in the shadows before it was safe to slip out of the crypt.

It was, she conceded, a rather too apt situation for a vampire to be in.

*   *   *

Something stinks, Soren thought metaphorically. Even though there was no sign of any intruder, aside from the unexplained absence of the guard, the seasoned bodyguard remained on edge. Instincts honed over generations of service to the coven and its masters told him that there was trouble afoot. Vague misgivings nagged at his mind like the gnawing of phantom wolves. *Perhaps I should search the crypt by foot?*

He reached for the control panel, intending to unlock the entrance to the crypt, only to be distracted by what he witnessed on one of the booth's numerous surveillance monitors.

A taxi, of the sort routinely seen on the streets of Budapest, had pulled into the driveway outside the mansion's front gate. "What the devil?" he snarled. Amelia and her entourage were not expected until tomorrow night at the earliest, so who the hell was this unexpected visitor?

The crypt forgotten, Soren hastily tugged out his cell phone. Kraven needed to know about this—ASAP.

"This is it," Michael croaked hoarsely to the cab driver, confirming that they had reached the correct destination. The stolid Armenian cabbie eyed Michael doubtfully in his rear-view mirror. He looked all too eager to unload his pale and disheveled American passenger.

Michael couldn't blame him. *I must look like a mess,* he realized, collapsed against the backseat of the cab. The rain earlier had washed most of the sludge and blood from his jacket and pants, but Michael still felt badly in need of a shower, among other things. His skin was clammy and slick with perspiration beneath his torn and rumpled attire. His head felt as if a scalpel were jabbing into his brain, and painful spasms periodically wrenched his insides, causing him to clutch his stomach while groaning out loud. Feverish and light-headed, he forced himself to sit up and thrust a wad of pinkish-blue bills at the driver. He was probably overtipping the man egregiously, but Michael didn't have the strength or the mental acuity to calculate the proper amount.

"Thanks for the ride," he said weakly. His breath came in halting pants as he laboriously climbed out of the taxi. The cabbie nodded brusquely, then wasted no time turning the yellow sedan around and accelerating back toward the main road, as if he couldn't wait to leave both Michael and the mansion behind.

Wonder if he knows something I don't, Michael thought, watching the taxi's taillights disappear into the night, the fleeing cab trailing streamers of reflected yellow light over the rain-soaked asphalt. Tonight's nonstop deluge mercifully had faded to a slight drizzle, but Michael's damp sneakers squished noisily as he reluctantly turned away from the outer limits of the driveway toward the forbidding cast-iron gates directly in front of him.

Beyond the high spiked fence, the mysterious mansion loomed ominously, its Gothic turrets and battlements stabbing upward at the lightening night sky. Sharply pointed arches and gables added to the manor's daunting façade. It looked like something out of *Dark Shadows,* he thought, or maybe *The Rocky Horror Picture Show.*

A layer of heavy fog blanketed the lawn outside the mansion. Michael remembered running for his life across that very same lawn earlier tonight—had that really been only hours ago?—and wondered for the umpteenth time if he was making a terrible mistake coming back to the mansion of his own free will. Baying Rottweilers, their jaws snapping at his heels, surged out of his memory, along with a hissing blonde glued inexplicably to the ceiling.

Michael shuddered, unable to tell if it was fear or sickness that left his body trembling. *There's no turning back now,* he reminded himself bleakly as he staggered toward the gate. The waxing moon peeked through the cloudy night sky, so blinding in its intensity that Michael could not look at it directly. Its incandescent silver glow felt hot upon his face and hands. Every hair on his body rose as though electrified by the vibrant moonlight.

Please, Selene! he thought desperately, unable to fathom the volcanic convulsions racking his mind and body. *Please be there for me!* The enigmatic, dark-haired beauty was the only person he knew who might be able to explain this waking nightmare—and help him find a way out of it.

If there was a way.

A gaggle of excited servant girls following in his wake, Kraven stormed into the viewing chamber. He ignored the mindless whisperings of Erika and her ilk, concerned instead with finding out why Soren had summoned him from upstairs. *It's nearly four A.M.,* he fumed silently. *I had hoped to retire for the morning soon.*

After all, he had an important night tomorrow.

Soren spied him through the two-way mirror and quickly activated the automatic doorway, admitting Kraven to the security booth. The lord of the manor casually noted the absence of the usual guard but failed to see what might warrant his own presence in this morbid locale. "Well?" he demanded crossly. "What is so pressing?"

Soren simply pointed at one of the black-and-white monitors mounted above the control panel. Kraven blinked in surprise at the sight of an unusually bedraggled-looking human male, perhaps twenty-five years old, peering stupidly into the security camera at the front gate. *Who?* Kraven wondered in confusion. The face looked vaguely familiar, but the vampire regent felt certain that he had never met this mortal before.

What brings him to our door? Kraven frowned unhappily. The timing of the stranger's arrival, less than twenty-four hours before the Awakening, was singularly inauspicious. *Why here?* he worried. *Why now?*

The vaulted sanctity of the viewing chamber was packed with chattering maidservants, competing to get a better glimpse of what was happening in the security booth. Selene took advantage of the commotion to slip unnoticed out of the crypt into the crowded chamber outside.

Her midnight-black fighting gear contrasted sharply with the flimsy, frilly uniforms of the tittering servant girls, yet all eyes remained fixed on Kraven and his surly janissary, allowing Selene to join the scene unnoticed, at least for the moment. *What's this all about?* she thought, puzzled and concerned by Kraven's abrupt visitation. As far as she knew, her tampering with Viktor's tomb remained undetected, but why else would Soren have alerted his heinous master?

Part of her was tempted not to look a gift distraction in the mouth. *Just get out of here,* she urged herself sensibly, *before Kraven finds out what you've done.* Another part of her, however, driven by an intuitive conviction that whatever was happening was vitally important, compelled her to edge slowly toward the open doorway to the security station. She shouldered her way through the clustered female domestics until only the ubiquitous Erika stood between her and the entrance to the booth. Selene crept up behind the young blond vampiress, straining to see what exactly had Soren and Kraven up in arms.

Kraven almost never visits the crypt, she recalled. Doubtless, he disliked any reminder that he ruled the mansion only as Viktor's surrogate. *So what has lured him down here?*

But before she could catch a glimpse of the relevant security monitor, a distraught voice crackled over the loudspeaker in the booth:

"Let me speak with Selene!"

Her eyes widened in alarm. Hoarse and ragged though it was, she instantly recognized Michael's voice. *Bloody hell! Whatever possessed him to come back here?*

Shoving Erika aside, she rushed into the security booth, where her horrified eyes rapidly confirmed what her ears already had told her. There was Michael, staring forlornly at her from the monitor. To her dismay, she saw that he looked even more sick and panic-stricken than he had been many hours ago.

"He's been bitten, your human." Erika's shocking warning, delivered hours ago in the archive hall, flashed unwanted across Selene's mind. *"He's been marked by a lycan."*

Could it be true? Had Michael been infected with Lucian's foul contagion?

Kraven gave her no time to react. Quickly putting two and two together, he whirled around to confront her. His face was livid with rage, and he shook an accusing finger at the monitor. Descending raindrops streaked the image on the screen, like tears running down the human's face. "Is that Michael?"

The only good thing about Kraven's jealous pique was that it never occurred to him to question what Selene was doing outside the crypt. Ignoring his outburst, she reached out and adjusted a digital WebCam mounted atop the control panel, turning the unblinking eye of the camera toward her.

"Is it Michael!" Kraven demanded, his voice rising to an intemperate pitch.

Of course it is, she thought acerbically. The real question was what she would do now.

Shivering in the cold, Michael stood in front of the remote-operated security camera, marching in place in a vain attempt to keep warm. The swirling gray fog seemed to soak into the very marrow of his bones, chilling him utterly, while he waited for somebody inside the mansion to notice he was there. Preferably, a certain gun-toting femme fatale of uncertain origin and intentions.

Selene.

She was named after the moon, he suddenly realized, and appropriately so. Like that shimmering lunar orb, she seemed to exert an almost tidal pull upon his mind and body, drawing him here despite his better judgment, holding him in place outside the last place on earth he ever wanted to come back to.

How long am I going to stand out here, freezing my butt off? He hugged himself tightly, trying to keep his last vestiges of body heat from seeping out into the mist. Despite his impatience, he knew that he wasn't going anywhere until he found out whether Selene was somewhere inside the spooky stone edifice on the other side of the locked iron gates. *Great,* he thought sarcastically. *Now I'm a fugitive and a stalker.*

A blank electronic monitor above the camera flared to life abruptly, setting his heart racing. His bleary eyes snapped open as Selene's luminous features appeared on the monitor. *Thank God!* he thought, lunging toward the elevated camera. His shaking finger poked the talk button on the intercom.

"I need to talk to you!" he shouted frantically into the speaker. A faint spark of hope flickered within him. "What the hell is going on? What's happening to me!"

Selene leaned across the control panel toward the intercom. She pressed down on a button. "I'll be right out," she promised tersely.

There was no time even to try to answer any of Michael's anguished questions. She knew his life depended on getting him away from Ordoghaz as quickly as possible. Even if Erika were wrong, and Michael wasn't becoming a lycanthrope, Kraven's insane jealousy placed the unsuspecting human in mortal danger.

"If you go to him," Kraven warned, drawing himself up like a rooster puffing out its chest, "by God, you'll never be welcomed in this house again!"

Turning away from the control panel, Selene could not resist giving him a nasty surprise. "Now that Viktor's awake," she stated, looking Kraven dead in the eye, "he'll have something to say about that."

The horror-stricken look on his face was priceless. For the first time in perhaps six hundred years, Kraven had been rendered speechless. Stunned mystification caused his eyes to bulge.

Selene didn't wait for the dumbfounded regent to recover from his shock. She swept out the door of the security booth, passing Erika, who was fluttering right outside the exit, observing the unfolding drama with eyes agog. The servant girl's jaw dropped as Selene plowed like an ice-breaker through the flock of vampire maids. "Wait!" Erika called after the other woman. "What are you doing?"

The only answer she received was the echoing ring of Selene's bootsteps as the female Death Dealer disappeared down the marble corridor. *Has Kraven checked the crypt yet?* Selene wondered maliciously. *Or is he still working up his nerve?*

Too bad she couldn't stay to find out.

The iron gates slid open automatically, and a dark gray sedan came screeching out into the driveway. Selene wasn't kidding, Michael realized, when she said she would be right out; less than five minutes had passed since she'd vanished from the monitor screen.

She flung the passenger door open. "Get in!" she snapped with an urgency that scared the hell out of him.

Michael couldn't help remembering that the last time he had gotten into a car with this woman, he had almost ended up at the bottom of the Danube. *This is what I came here for,* he reminded himself. He glanced uncertainly at the fore-boding mansion. *Isn't it?*

Gulping, he climbed into the car.

Viktor . . . awake?

Kraven couldn't believe his ears. *She can't be serious,* he thought desperately. *She must have been joking.*

Not that Selene had ever been known for a puckish sense of humor.

The agitated regent dispatched Soren to find the security booth's missing guardian, then charged out of the control room toward the crypt itself. He was terrified of what he might find but unable to live with the uncertainty for a heartbeat longer. The chill, ultra-air-conditioned climate of the sunken chamber matched the icy dread clutching his heart as his fearful eyes searched for the bronze plate marking Viktor's buried tomb.

There! Thank the Fates! Relief washed over him like a soothing bloodbath as he saw that the inscribed hatch remained in place above his master's sarcophagus. Looking closer, he noted that Marcus's tomb appeared undisturbed as well, as did the now-vacant repository awaiting Amelia. *All is well,* he concluded, taking a moment to compose himself. He took a deep breath, then released it slowly. Selene had merely been playing with his head, the deceitful bitch!

He turned to exit the crypt, his mind already devising the diabolical punishments he would inflict on Selene if she ever dared to show her duplicitous face at the manor again, and he was startled to find a jittery blond servant girl standing behind him. Her elfin face was wan, even by vampire standards, and she trembled nervously, as though an entire pack of werewolves were salivating over her dainty flesh. Panicked violet orbs looked up at him.

Now what? he wondered irritably.

"I warned her," she blurted breathlessly, the words spilling over her lips in a torrent. "I warned her, but she wouldn't listen. She never listens—to anybody." Kraven assumed she was referring to Selene. "I'm sorry, I should've told you sooner. I should've—"

Kraven's ears perked up suspiciously. "Told me what?"

"Her human. Michael." She cringed as she spoke, dipping her head toward her shoulders. "He's not a human at all. He's a lycan."

His newly regained composure evaporated in an instant, as the little handmaiden's appalling revelation set his temper ablaze. Blood reddened his eyes and face, while swollen veins pulsed violently at his temples. The servant girl backed away tremulously, anticipating the storm to come.

"WHAT?" he roared like an aggrieved lion, unaware that only a few meters away in the darkened recovery chamber, ancient ears heard his bellowing cry—and listened attentively.

Chapter Eighteen

The dark Hungarian woods zipped past the sedan's windows in a blur as Selene kept her foot on the gas pedal. Spinning tires sent a whirlwind of fallen leaves swirling behind them, recklessly swooping and rising above the rainslick asphalt. Her fingers tightly gripped the steering wheel as the female vampire drove through the night like a bat out of hell, although the irony was largely lost on her.

"Look," she said forcefully, her intense brown eyes never leaving the road, "you can never go there again. *Never.* They'll kill you. Do you understand?"

"Kill me?" The strident confusion in Michael's voice testified that he very clearly did not have a clue. "Who the hell are you people?"

Where to begin? she wondered, unsure how much or how little she should share with the agitated mortal—if he even was a mortal. Risking a glance to her left, she spotted the gashes in Michael's jacket above his right shoulder. *Oh, hell,* she thought, her heart sinking. *Please don't let that mean what I think it does.*

Letting go of the wheel with one hand, she reached out and roughly yanked his jacket and T-shirt off his shoulder, exposing a red-stained bandage underneath. Her fingers dug beneath the bloody gauze and impatiently ripped the bandage from Michael's naked shoulder.

"Hey!" he yelped in surprise, but Selene wasn't listening. All her attention was focused on the ugly wound, which now consisted of a crusty scab sprouting several dark black hairs. *No!* she thought in despair, the sight of the scar hitting her like a blast of sunlight. Although the mark was already healing, there was no mistaking the savage bite of a lycanthrope.

Erika had been telling the truth. Michael was becoming one of *them.*

Selene slammed her fist into the dashboard, cracking the hard molded plastic. *It's not fair!* she thought angrily. *Not him! Not Michael!*

He stared at her, uncomprehending. The baffled innocence in his naive American face nearly broke her heart.

What the hell have I gotten myself into? The sedan accelerated through the nocturnal countryside, zooming at breakneck speed toward Budapest—and a future she couldn't even bear to imagine.

Now what do I do?

Deep within the crypt, Kraven was beside himself. "How could she choose a mangy lycan dog over me?" he ranted. The very thought of them together made his cold blood boil. "It's . . . inconceivable!"

He angrily turned on the shapely blond bearer of this highly upsetting news. "Wait," he said, a hopeful thought striking him. He peered suspiciously at the cowering servant girl, who, if memory served, was named Erika. "You're the jealous one, aren't you?"

Perhaps this was merely a clumsy, not to mention taste-less, attempt to divert his affections from Selene?

Alas, the silly little vamp reacted with horror to his implied accusation. "No! I swear, my lord, I would never lie to you!"

Sadly, Kraven believed her, which left him no choice but to accept the obscene reality of Selene's treacherous liaison with a lycan, of all creatures. *This time she's gone too far,* he thought vindictively. Death Dealer or not, no vampire could be allowed to fraternize shamelessly with the enemy.

Except for his secret alliance with Lucian, of course.

He moved to leave the crypt, only to be halted in his tracks by a dry, whispery voice that emerged unexpectedly from the shadows at the rear of the subterranean chamber.

"What is this tumult?" the voice demanded.

Kraven's blood froze. *No, it cannot be!* In his justifiable fury over Selene's criminal behavior, he had completely forgotten about her parting remark concerning Viktor. *I had thought her words nothing more than an empty taunt.*

Both he and Erika looked toward the voice, which seemed to emanate from the darkened recovery chamber. Kraven swallowed hard as a skeletal figure shuffled from the back of the chamber toward the clear plexiglass wall dividing the recovery unit from the crypt itself. An involuntary gasp escaped the servant girl at the grotesque sight before them.

Viktor, an elegant silk robe draped over his emaciated frame, looked back at them from behind the transparent barrier. Cold white eyes, like polished quartz, peered intensely from the murky hollows of his sockets. His mummified face held a cool, imperious expression. An intricate network of IV tubing rose from Viktor's neck and shoulders, connecting him to a lighted overhead feeding mechanism, so that he resembled a demonic marionette. Bright arterial blood flowed down the intravenous tubes, nourishing and restoring the newly risen Elder.

This is all wrong! Kraven protested inwardly, seeing his carefully crafted designs unravel before his eyes. Viktor was supposed to be safely interred in the earth right now, not up and about on the very eve of Kraven's greatest victory! *Can the plan still be saved,* he wondered anxiously, *or has all my bold and meticulous scheming come to naught?*

Erika dropped to her knees beside Kraven, reminding him to do the same. His mind in a whirl, his glorious future suddenly cast into uncertainty, the terrified vampire lord knelt before his dark master.

Michael held on tightly to the door of the sedan as Selene drove at top speed along the rain-soaked highway. A dented metal sign announced that they were only thirty kilometers from Budapest, but Michael was too busy listening to Selene to pay much attention to their progress.

"Whether you like it or not," she said grimly, "you're in the middle of a covert war that has been raging for the better part of a thousand years . . . a blood feud between vampires and lycans."

Michael wasn't sure he had heard her correctly. "Vampires and . . . what?"

"Werewolves," she added, noting his disoriented expression. "Lycanthropes."

Michael's jaw dropped. *Are you kidding me?* he thought in shocked disbelief. Vampires and werewolves? What did she think this was, some dopey horror movie? *This is the twenty-first century, for crissakes, not the Dark Ages!*

Despite his skepticism, bizarre memories from the last forty-eight hours flashed through his brain.

That blond girl at the mansion, sticking to the ceiling while she hissed at him through sharp white fangs . . .

The stranger in the elevator, sinking his teeth into Michael's shoulder . . .

The ceiling of his apartment building, shedding chunks of plaster as three unseen creatures landed heavily on the roof above . . .

The bloodcurdling roar of an unearthly beast . . .

"No!" Michael blurted, shaking his head. This was impossible. There were no such things as vampires or werewolves, except among deluded psychopaths and blood fetishists. *Maybe that's what's going on,* he thought feverishly, struggling to find a rational context for what Selene was saying. *This could be some sort of cult thing, maybe even a gang war between two rival sects.*

"Believe what you want," Selene said, discerning the doubt in his eyes. She raked her gaze across his pale, perspiring features. "Consider yourself lucky. Most humans die within an hour of being bitten by an immortal. The virus we transmit is extremely lethal."

Don't talk to me about viruses! he thought. *I'm a doctor. I know this is bullshit!* Selene didn't look like any sort of werewolf he'd ever heard of, so he guessed she considered herself a vampire. "And if you bit me, I suppose, what? I'd become a vampire myself?"

"No!" she said sharply, his sarcastic tone eliciting an impatient scowl. "You'd be dead. No one has ever survived a bite from both species—and, unfortunately, the lycans got to you first." She shook her head at her own reckless folly. "By rights, I should stop the car and kill you right here and now!"

Michael gulped. Vampire or not, he knew from experience just how dangerous this woman could be. "Then why are you helping me?" he asked hesitantly.

"I'm not!" she insisted, perhaps a tad too vigorously. "I track you down and kill your kind! I'm a Death Dealer! It's my duty." She stared fixedly at the winding road ahead, making a point of not looking at him. "My only interest is finding out why Lucian wants you so badly."

Death Dealer? Lucian? This was getting more confusing—and insane—by the minute. Michael slumped back against his seat, overwhelmed by an "explanation" that made no sense whatsoever. Raising his free hand, he fingered the swollen bump on his forehead, a painful souvenir of the last time he went driving with Selene. *Maybe I was wrong to come looking for her,* he second-guessed himself. *Maybe she's psychologically disturbed.*

But what if she were telling the truth?

Head bowed, Erika rose and quietly tiptoed out of the crypt, leaving Kraven alone with Viktor. He barely noticed her leave, too perturbed by his dread master's untimely resurrection to pay heed to anything else. Was Soren still waiting in the security booth? It mattered little; no bodyguard on earth could spare Kraven from Viktor's wrath should the Elder find fault with his trembling regent.

Damn you, Selene, Kraven thought. *What have you done?*

"Do you know why I have been awakened, my servant?" Viktor asked. His voice was a dry rustle, creaking from petrified vocal cords that had lain silent for nearly a century.

"No, my lord," Kraven answered. Kneeling, he stared meekly at the floor, unable to meet his master's smoldering, all-white eyes. "But I will soon find out."

Viktor gestured for Kraven to rise. "You mean when you find *her.*"

Then Viktor knew that Selene was responsible for his awakening? "Yes, my lord," Kraven said quickly, praying that the faithless Selene, and not himself, would incur the Elder's displeasure. "I give you my word that she shall be found!"

Viktor nodded thoughtfully. Calcified joints cracked and popped. "You will let her come to me," he decreed. "We have much to discuss, Selene and I. She has shown me a great many disturbing things." An ominous tone entered his bone-dry voice. "Things that will be dealt with soon enough."

Kraven quailed before the gaze of the reanimated Elder. What did Viktor mean? What had Selene shown him? For an instant, Kraven felt certain that Viktor knew everything: the alliance with Lucian, the plans for tomorrow night, everything. He shuddered at the thought. Death would be mercy if Viktor had even a glimmer of Kraven's true ambitions. More likely, Kraven would be doomed to an eternity of unceasing torture for merely daring to contemplate such an unprecedented offense.

It took all his courage not to run fleeing from the crypt this very moment. Kraven felt his resolve waning perceptibly as he forced himself to remain in Viktor's presence, while the skeletal Elder subjected him to a withering stare. Viktor stepped closer to the plexiglass divider, and Kraven clenched every bone and muscle in his body in order to remain stiffly at attention. His face became a rigid mask, betraying nothing.

"This coven has grown weak . . . decadent," Viktor pronounced, as though Kraven's harmless (albeit numerous) indulgences were written in scarlet upon the younger vampire's face and figure. Kraven felt like Dorian Gray, confronted by the incriminating lineaments of his notorious portrait. "Perhaps," Viktor continued, "I should have left someone else in charge of my affairs."

Once again, Kraven wondered what exactly Selene had managed to communicate to the newly roused Elder. A flicker of resentment helped to melt a bit of the icy dread oppressing his spirit. *Just one more night,* he thought maliciously, *and Viktor's opinion of my abilities would have been academic!* Kraven kept his secret agenda hidden deep within the most clandestine chambers of his immortal heart. Perhaps there was still a chance for success, despite the Elder's premature awakening?

Taking a closer look at the unsightly creature before him, Kraven saw that the mighty Viktor was, in fact, still recovering from his prolonged period of hibernation. He tottered momentarily upon his withered legs and raised a bony hand to his brow as he closed his eyes and squinted in discomfort, as if pained by the turbulent impressions within his ageless skull. "Still," Viktor conceded solemnly, "Selene's memories are . . . chaotic, with no sense of time or sequence."

"Then, please, my lord," Kraven asserted, encouraged by Viktor's fleeting signs of weakness, "allow me to summon assistance."

It would not be long, he knew, before Viktor was entirely himself again, but Kraven intended to make the most of the Elder's brief period of recovery. *Just one more night,* he thought again. *That's all I—and Lucian—need.* Then Viktor and his fellow Elders would regret underestimating Kraven of Leicester! "Heed me, my lord. You are greatly in need of rest."

Dry, papery eyelids peeled open. "I've rested enough," Viktor declared. "What you can do is summon Marcus. It is time I was made aware of matters as they stand."

Kraven gazed at the Elder, aghast. *By God, he does not comprehend what has truly occurred.* The dark-haired vampire's freshly restored confidence wilted at the daunting prospect of explaining to Viktor the full enormity of Selene's unspeakable transgression. *Please remember, my master,* he thought timorously, *Selene is to blame, not I!*

His mouth nearly as dry as his mummified sire's, Kraven pointed toward Marcus's tomb. "But . . . he still slumbers, my lord."

Viktor's pallid cranium drew back like a cobra's. His sunken eyes widened alarmingly, then began to burn with malignant fire. His lipless mouth turned downward in a macabre grimace. Exposed fangs gnashed angrily.

Frightened by Viktor's growing fury, Kraven stepped back across the floor of the crypt. He hastened to finish his explanation, before the Elder's simmering temper exploded at the nearest living target, namely Kraven himself.

"Amelia and the council members are scheduled to arrive here tomorrow night . . . to awaken Marcus, not you."

Wordless rage contorted Viktor's hideous countenance, turning his death's-head visage into that of a vengeful demon. Kraven stumbled backward, averting his eyes from the wrathful Elder as he nervously spelled out the entire wretched situation: "You've been awakened a full century ahead of schedule."

Chapter Nineteen

*K*raven felt as if he'd been drained by an entire coven of voracious she-vampires when he finally staggered out of the unquiet crypt. *Thank Providence!* he thought shakily, both relieved and surprised that he actually had survived his nerve-jangling encounter with Viktor. He had forgotten just how menacing his sire could be.

Ultimately, the autocratic Elder had merely dismissed Kraven from his presence, the better to ponder matters in private. Kraven was delighted to accommodate Viktor in this regard and drew some small comfort from the fact that, for the time being, the newly awakened Elder was confined to the circumscribed borders of the recovery chamber. He knew better, however, than to think that Viktor would languish in the gloomy bowels of the mansion for long. Viktor would rise from the crypt, in full possession of his former strength and majesty, soon enough.

I must be prepared, Kraven thought hastily, *before it is too late.*

To his surprise, he found the servant girl—Erika—waiting for him in the stately viewing chamber outside the crypt. The rest of the nattering handmaidens had fled the vicinity, no doubt spooked by Viktor's unsettling resurrection, yet Erika had stayed behind, perched tensely on the edge of a carved marble bench. She sprang dutifully to her feet as Kraven exited the crypt.

"My lord!"

After keeping all his fears and resentments bottled up during his grueling audience with Viktor, Kraven welcomed the opportunity to vent his emotions to someone considerably less intimidating than Viktor. This doting scullion was so insignificant in the scheme of things that he could speak freely in front of her. It was like talking to an empty room, really.

"That bitch has betrayed me!" he ranted, spewing the worst of his bile at Selene and her lycan paramour. He stomped away from the crypt's soundproofed walls, putting a healthy distance between himself and the ghastly revenant now residing in the recovery area. "Now Viktor knows everything she has been obsessing about!"

But how much did Selene truly know or suspect?

Drawing near him, Erika winced at his heated denunciation of Selene. She clearly disliked seeing his passion directed at another vampiress, no matter how bitter his disposition. Meekly, tentatively, she reached out to comfort him. Her tiny hands lit softly on his arm.

Irritated, he shoved her away roughly. *Stupid tart!* he fumed. The last thing he needed now was some lovesick menial fawning over him. His eternal life was at risk!

Choking back a sob, Erika stumbled away from him, her pale vampiric face flushing red with shame and embarrassment. The obvious depth of her heartache penetrated Kraven's brooding preoccupation, spurring him to reconsider the servant girl's advances. Perhaps he should not be so fast to toss away such a fervent devotee?

"Wait!" he called after her.

Erika froze as though thunderstruck. Her violet eyes were wet as she turned to look back at him. Crimson tears streaked her cheeks.

For the first time in nearly thirty years, Kraven really looked at Erika, inspecting her flaxen hair, silky skin, and lissome figure. Bare white shoulders and an enticing throat offered a preview of the creamy delights beneath her tarty black frock. She was a tasty morsel, he had to admit, if not quite the irresistible goddess that Selene was.

He strode across the floor to where the transfixed maid stood quaking, her slender hands cupped over her lips, as if she were afraid to give voice to the riotous emotions roiling her soul. She all but melted as Kraven dropped his hands onto her bare shoulders and gazed down into her eyes.

"Are you to be trusted?" he asked.

She nodded, beaming back at him. Her adoring eyes and radiant expression told him everything he needed to know.

His wish was her command.

The broken-down old brownstone, located in one of central Pest's less picturesque corners, was an ugly, unprepossessing pile of bricks, clearly erected sometime after the war, when the city was still under Soviet control. Decades of smog and soot had blackened every inch of the building's dingy exterior, while the steel-shuttered windows and spray-painted graffiti made it clear that the brownstone had been abandoned for some time.

Or so it appeared.

"This is one of the places we use for interrogations," Selene explained as she pulled up to the curb. The rain finally had let up for a time, but the streets and sidewalks were still wet. Greasy puddles reflected the gibbous moon shining down through the low-rise neighborhood buildings.

After parking the sedan in an adjacent alley, away from sight, she got out and led Michael up the slippery steps of the building, where she unlocked the padlock holding the front door shut. They stepped inside the murky foyer, and Michael heard rats scuttle away in a hurry, surprised by the brownstone's late-night visitors. Selene switched on a flashlight, perhaps as a concession to Michael's merely human vision, and swept the trash-strewn lobby with its cool white beam. A dilapidated staircase led upstairs, and Selene confidently ascended the creaking steps, pointing the way with the flashlight.

Michael followed her numbly, his exploding brain still trying to cope with the mind-boggling revelations Selene had imparted to him earlier. He had spent much of the subsequent drive in silence, in fact, struggling to decide how much, if anything, to believe of the whole wild story. *Werewolves and vampires . . . oh my God,* he thought.

The really scary part was that, against every fiber of his modern, rational, twenty-first-century being, he actually was coming around to the preposterous idea that, just maybe, Selene was telling the truth. In which case, he was in the deepest shit imaginable.

"So, what do you do?" he asked her warily as they climbed the stairs, floor by wearying floor. His much abused and depleted body strained against gravity with every step. "Kill people, drink their blood?"

Selene shook her head. "We haven't needed to feed on humans for hundreds of years." Unlike Michael, she sounded unaffected by the exhausting climb. "It draws needless attention."

They reached the top of the stairs, and she unlocked a

heavy wooden door on the sixth floor. She stepped inside and switched on a light, then gestured for Michael to follow her. He did so, for lack of any better idea.

Enter freely and of your own will, he thought, recalling a line from *Dracula.* He had read the book years ago, in high school, but had never expected to find himself living it. *Step into my lair . . .*

Fluorescent lights, coming on one by one, exposed a small, Spartan room equipped with minimal furnishings. There were no beds or sofas, just several sturdy metal chairs, weapons racks on the walls, and neatly stacked boxes of ammunition. The walls and floor were bare and unadorned, except for an out-of-date calendar pinned to one of the walls. *Some sort of safe house,* Michael realized, even though, up until now, his only knowledge of such things had come strictly from spy novels and movies.

Selene flicked a switch on the wall, producing a short electronic buzz. A set of rusty metal shutters slid downward to reveal an open window looking down on the street below. She approached the window cautiously, then risked a searching glance outside before nodding grimly to herself.

All's clear, Michael guessed. He tried not to think about the idea that, if her story were to be believed, Selene was looking out for werewolves.

A small portable refrigerator hummed in one corner of the room, next to a wooden ammunition crate. Selene stepped away from the window and opened the tiny fridge. Michael spotted what looked like several dozen frozen packets of whole blood. *Emergency medical supplies,* he wondered queasily, *or dinner?*

Selene snatched a packet from the fridge and casually tossed it toward Michael. To his amazement, he actually caught it, despite feeling like death warmed over.

The frozen blood was cold to the touch, like an icepack. Michael resisted an urge to press it against his aching forehead, instead inspecting the logo printed on the plastic packet. "Ziodex Industries," he read out loud.

He recognized the name. Ziodex was a big deal in the global biopharmaceuticals industry. Karolyi Hospital stocked plenty of Ziodex's products.

"We own it," Selene stated, explaining, among other things, what paid for the upkeep on that expensive mansion of hers. "First, synthetic plasma. Now that. Once it's approved, it will be our newest cash crop."

Michael flipped over the packet and read the label on the back. His bloodshot eyes bulged in shock as he realized what he was holding.

"Cloned blood," he whispered, unsure whether to be impressed or appalled. As a medical student, he had known that there had been some research and development along these lines, but he'd had no idea that Ziodex was so far ahead of the field. "Wait a second," he protested, as a point of confusion occurred to him. "You said before that . . . vampires"—he stumbled awkwardly over the word—"haven't needed to feed on humans for centuries. Surely, you weren't cloning blood a hundred years ago?"

"Of course not," Selene said. To his relief, she didn't help herself to a refreshing pint of plasma; that would probably be more than he could take right now. "We subsisted on cattle blood for ages, by the Elders' decree. Preying on human stock was immoral, as well as dangerous. We had no desire to attract the pitchforks—and wooden stakes—of an outraged populace." She reclaimed the thawing packet from Michael and popped it back into the freezer. "Synthetic plasma and cloned human blood are relatively new innovations."

Michael didn't have the nerve to ask her whether cloned blood tasted the same as the regular kind. "So vampires don't really drink blood anymore?"

In a weird sort of way, that was almost disillusioning, like finding out that Lizzie Borden didn't really hack her parents to pieces.

Selene hesitated before answering, then assumed a somewhat defensive tone. "Well, we don't *need* to drain humans for sustenance, but some vampires still like to drink real blood occasionally, for pleasure." She avoided his eyes, clearly uncomfortable with the topic. "From each other, that is, and certain human . . . donors."

"Willing donors?" Michael pressed.

"In theory," she said darkly. Michael got the distinct impression that some vampires were more scrupulous about their recreational dining than others. He thought he knew what kind of vampire Selene was, but his hand rose protectively toward his throat nonetheless. At the same time, part of him still couldn't believe that he was genuinely taking part in a serious discussion about the eating habits of vampires.

I mean, c'mon . . . vampires?

An awkward silence fell over the room. Michael's rubbery legs reminded him just how sick and tired he was, and he dropped mercifully into the nearest heavy-duty titanium chair, which felt hard and durable enough to seat a full-grown gorilla—or perhaps a monster-sized werewolf. His shell-shocked gaze drifted absently about the room, eventually falling on a massive steel table resting nearby. A tray of silver surgical instruments sat atop the table, covered by a grayish-white layer of dust and cobwebs.

"What are those for?" he asked. The doctor in him was scandalized by the distinctly less than sterile condition of the scalpels and pliers and such, many of which showed signs of rust, dried blood, or some grisly combination thereof. *Do vampires not have to worry about infection?* he wondered, reluctantly employing the *V*-word again.

"Lycans are allergic to silver," Selene informed him. She drew out one of her pistols and placed it on the table beside the tray of instruments. "We have to get our bullets out quickly, or they end up dying on us during questioning."

There was nothing apologetic about her tone; if anything, she seemed much more comfortable discussing interrogation techniques than she had been when divulging the seamier underside of the vampiric lifestyle.

Michael stared at her, aghast. He tried and failed to imagine this exquisite beauty brutally interrogating a captive werewolf. "What happens to them afterward?"

"We put the bullets back in," she said with a shrug.

Lucian and Singe made their way down a crumbling passageway far beneath the sleeping city. The lycan scientist disliked leaving his underground laboratory, but Lucian had insisted that Singe accompany him as Lucian checked on the preparations for tomorrow night's historic operation. In any event, Singe conceded to himself, there was little else he could do until the human, Michael Corvin, was successfully retrieved. The grand experiment was essentially on hold.

"It may be wise," Lucian commented, "to keep a closer eye on our bloodthirsty cousins."

Singe realized that Lucian was referring to the vampires. Unlike the less enlightened members of their pack, Singe was aware of the profound genetic link between the lycanthropes and their undead foes. Both breeds shared a common origin, now shrouded by centuries of conflict and superstition.

209

"I'll have Raze see to it immediately," he assured Lucian. A little extra surveillance couldn't hurt, especially with all that was at stake, and Raze had recovered sufficiently from his injuries to undertake such a mission.

Lucian slowed to a stop and placed a hand on Singe's scrawny shoulder. The metallic pendant on Lucian's chest caught the light from the sputtering fluorescents overhead. Singe had never seen his leader without his gilded talisman. *A curious affectation,* the old scientist thought, but one he had never chosen to question. *Odd that so knowledgeable and visionary a being would flaunt such an archaic trinket.*

"I'm afraid that I'm going to have to place my faith in you, my friend," Lucian said. "Time is running short, and I need to rely on the sharpest wits at my disposal."

Singe repressed an impatient sigh. *I'm a scientist,* he protested silently. *I belong in my lab!* But who was he to challenge his master's instructions? If not for Lucian, he would have died of leukemia generations ago.

"As you wish," he agreed.

Chapter Twenty

Michael sat uncomfortably in the steel chair, exhausted but unable to sleep. His head throbbed with every heartbeat, and his guts felt tangled into a knot. Invisible bugs crawled over every inch of his body, causing him to scratch uselessly at his arms and legs. The moonlight coming through the window hurt his eyes, but he found himself unable to look away from it for long. *Is it true?* he wondered, despite years of rigorous scientific training. *Is Selene right? Am I turning into a werewolf?*

It was insane, ridiculous even to consider for an instant, and yet . . . why did he still hear that unearthly howl echoing inside his skull?

He looked over at Selene, afraid to ask her what his debilitating symptoms might mean. The leather-clad Englishwoman stood vigilantly by the open window, keeping watch over the silent street outside. Her fingers rested on the grip of her automatic pistol, as if she couldn't wait to find a target for her silver bullets.

"Why do you hate them so much?" he asked her.

Selene frowned and shifted position so that her back was to him. From her body language and from what he glimpsed of her expression, there was no way in hell she wanted to have this conversation with him right now.

"Can't you just answer the question?" he persisted. If she were going to condemn him for becoming a werewolf, he at least wanted to know why. *Am I going to become your next target,* he agonized, *once whatever happens . . . happens?*

He waited tensely, but no response was forthcoming. He stared helplessly at the glossy leather contours of her back, until he was certain she was giving him the brush-off. "Fine," he muttered sourly, turning his gaze to the bare wooden timbers of the floor. A dark brown smudge discolored the floor beneath where he was sitting. Dried blood from the victim of some past interrogation?

"They tore my family to pieces," she whispered slowly, breaking the silence. She spoke so faintly that at first Michael wasn't sure that he heard her. "Fed on them . . ."

She turned away from the window, locking eyes with Michael. In those enigmatic chestnut orbs, he thought he discerned years of unhealed grief and sorrow. Old pain colored her voice.

"They took everything from me," she said.

Kraven reclined on a red velvet divan, lost in thought. Where was Selene now, and what was she doing with that lycan trash? According to Soren, she had fled the mansion with this Corvin character while Kraven had been occupied with Viktor down in the crypt. *She could be anywhere by now,* he groused unhappily. Somehow he doubted that she would return to the mansion before sunrise.

He disliked having such a loose cannon in play less than twenty-four hours before his ultimate bid for power. Viktor risen, Selene missing, Lucian discontented . . . nothing was going according to plan!

It still can work, he thought desperately, striving to reassure himself. *I just need to be strong and not give in, not with victory so near . . .*

The door swung open, and Erika entered the suite. *About time,* he thought. He had dispatched her to notify the household staff of Viktor's resurrection, the better to prevent pernicious rumors and gossip from spreading unchecked throughout the manor. By way of damage control, he had claimed credit for the Elder's awakening, instructing Erika to spread the story that he had been acting under top-secret directives from Amelia herself, for reasons privy only to the two of them. With luck, this improvised fabrication would leave the impression that he was still fully in command of events, at least until it no longer mattered.

Soon, he promised himself, *my authority will be beyond question.*

He sat up straight on the divan. "Good, you're here," he addressed the tardy maidservant. Erika had been gone for at least fifteen minutes or so; from the looks of it, she had taken the time to touch up her makeup and let down her hair. "Now, I need you to keep what I'm about to tell you under the strictest confi—"

Erika surprised him by reaching out and pressing a finger against his lips. Her violet eyes looked into his.

"It can wait," she whispered huskily.

With a sexy smirk, she reached back and undid the clasps of her lacy black frock. The garment slid to the floor, exposing a sylphlike female form that had not aged a day since that fateful night in Piccadilly twenty-seven years ago. Her bare feet stepped free of the discarded dress, bringing her undraped flesh within a finger's reach of her seated sire.

Kraven was taken aback, to say the least. This was not exactly what he'd had in mind when he had told the eager maidservant to report back to him. He'd intended only to instruct her to monitor Viktor's activities in the recovery room, under the guise of tending to the Elder's comfort, and keep him informed of Viktor's every action and utterance.

Then again, he reflected, weighing his options, *what the hell?* His dark eyes greedily devoured the blond vampiress's enticing nakedness. Despite the weighty concerns troubling his mind, he felt his undead body responding to her generously displayed feminine charms. *Why not?* he reasoned. He needed every minion he could muster right now, and if this was what it took to secure the girl's absolute allegiance . . . well, there were worse ways to pass the hours before sunrise.

Accepting her provocative invitation, he took hold of her slim white hips and pulled her to him, wrapping his arms around her slender waist. His lips found her belly, and her taut flesh quivered uncontrollably as he kissed and licked his way up toward her breasts. Her supple skin was smooth as porcelain and cool as a refreshing mountain stream, and his hungry tongue left a moist trail across the sensuous contours of her nubile body.

Erika gasped once, then bit down hard upon her lower lip. Kraven smiled at his own amatory prowess; no doubt, the silly minx had been waiting for this moment ever since she became a vampire.

"Something was in the stable, tearing the horses to pieces," Selene said softly. She remained standing beside the open window. It felt strange to be speaking to him like this, and of such a deeply personal matter, but she couldn't help herself. It felt oddly right as well, although she couldn't have begun to explain why.

"I couldn't have saved my mother. Or my sister. Their screams woke me. My father died outside, trying to fend them off. I stood at my door, about to run to my nieces, when . . . Twin girls, barely six years old. Butchered like animals. They cried for me . . . and then there was silence."

"Jesus Christ," Michael exclaimed. Despite his own troubles and the bestial contagion wracking his body, his earnest young face was filled with unmistakable compassion and sympathy. Her throat tightened, making it even harder to speak. She couldn't remember the last time anyone had even tried to share her pain.

"The war had spilled into my house, my home." Her voice was little more than a whisper, but she could see Michael hanging on her every word. Crimson tears welled up in her eyes, for the first time in centuries. After all these years, the memory was still like an open wound. "And the next thing I knew, I was in Viktor's arms. He had been tracking the lycans for days. He drove them off, saved me."

Viktor's name provoked a puzzled expression from Michael. "Who?"

"The oldest and most powerful of us all," she explained. "That night Viktor made me a vampire. His blood gave me the strength to avenge my family. And I've never looked back."

Until now, she added silently. What was it about this human that made her want to open up like this, break free of the emotional armor that had encased her heart for ages? He was just a mortal, and one infected by the lycans.

"I saw your pictures," she blurted. She told herself she was only changing the subject, turning the focus back on

Michael, where it belonged. "Who was the woman? Your wife?"

Michael's head jerked back in surprise.

The lycans' armory was housed in an abandoned bunker many meters beneath the thriving metropolis above. Water dripped on the concrete floor outside the bunker as Lucian inspected his troops.

Fully armed with UV-compatible semiautomatic weapons, several dozen lycans were lined up in the tunnel, their backs turned to the crumbling brick walls. Humanoid figures, clad in grubby brown apparel, gripped their guns and rifles, preparing to deal out ultraviolet death to their ancestral enemies. The lycan soldiers snapped to attention as Lucian strode past them into the makeshift armory.

Excellent, he thought. The pack looked fit and ready for combat.

Although dimly lit and grimy, the armory was perfectly functional. Lycan commandos were busily going about their duties, inspecting and oiling high-caliber weapons, loading UV cartridges, and so on. A rickety aluminum table had been set up in the center of the converted bomb shelter to assist in the planning of tonight's operation. Pierce and Taylor, having traded their bogus police uniforms for scuffed brown leather, stood around the table, poring over a detailed map of the city. They looked up from the chart at Lucian's approach.

"How are things progressing?" he asked them curtly.

The two lycans smiled in answer, baring sharp white teeth.

Now it was Michael's turn to relive the worst night of his life. He stared bleakly into the past as Selene watched him from across the barren hideout.

"I tried to swerve, but he hit us anyway. Sent us right into the oncoming lane. When I came to, I realized part of the engine was now in the front seat . . . and she was pinned there, not six inches from me, in this . . . horrible position. She must've been in shock, because she just kept asking me over and over if I was all right. She was more worried about me than . . ."

He had to pause, his throat choked with emotion. Selene's heart went out to him. Considering his history, she was amazed that he had ever gotten into a car again, let alone endured her speeding Jaguar the night before. Michael had told her all about their headlong plunge into the Danube; she felt a stab of remorse for subjecting him to yet another automotive catastrophe.

Blinking back tears, he started again. "If I knew then what I know now, I could've saved her. Stopped her bleeding, treated her for shock and trauma." Selene heard guilt as well as sorrow in his voice. "No doubt in my mind, I could have saved her . . . but, instead, she died right there, not two minutes before the ambulance arrived."

To her shame, Selene felt a flicker of relief that Michael's fiancée, an American named Samantha, was irrevocably dead and buried, but she dismissed that reaction as unworthy of her. What did that matter, anyway? Michael was only a pawn in the war against the lycans . . . wasn't he?

"After that," he continued, "I really didn't see any reason to stick around in the States. My grandparents—my dad's folks—emigrated from Hungary back in the forties, after the war, and they used to talk fondly about the Old Country, so once I got my degree, I figured what the hell? I just took off, came over here to, I dunno, move on . . . forget." He shrugged nonchalantly, feigning a blasé attitude that seemed at odds with his true feelings. "Seemed like a good idea at the time."

You probably would have been better off staying in America, Selene thought mordantly. Without being obvious about it, her gaze drifted to the bloodstained bite marks on his shoulder. "And have you?" she asked him. "Moved on?"

He looked her squarely in the eyes. "Have you?"

Selene didn't have an answer for him.

Yes! Erika thought rapturously. *At last!*

Kraven's icy lips explored her breasts, his keen teeth teasing first one nipple, then the other. Kraven's strong hands gripped her rump, his demanding grasp leaving its imprint upon her pliant flesh. She ran her fingers through his luxurious black mane, clinging to his unbound hair as though her immortal life depended on it.

Erika could not believe her good fortune. Finally, her most fervent fantasies were coming true. Lord Kraven was making love to *her,* not Selene, not Dominique, not any of the other girls. The regent of the manor, the ruler of the coven, had chosen *her.* She had *arrived!*

He drew back his head, just for an instant, and used his sharpened fingernail to slice a small half moon beneath her left nipple. Erika gasped out loud as her blood began to leak from the stinging, crescent-shaped gash.

Kraven's mouth returned to her breast, lapping at the crimson stream. Erika moaned ecstatically and threw back her head, surrendering to the moment as the vampire lord suckled on her bleeding teat.

She never wanted this moment to end . . .

Outside the mansion, beyond the perimeter fence, a matte-black van slowly drove past the entrance to the estate. The unassuming vehicle crept along the road with both its headlights and taillights off, so that it was all but invisible in the deep, tenebrous night. Swirling tendrils of dense gray fog helped shroud the creeping van from watchful eyes.

Singe sat behind the wheel of the van, his lycan eyes easily penetrating the darkness outside. He slowed to a stop a few meters away from the mansion's driveway and peered through the high cast-iron gates at the secluded Gothic edifice at the opposite end of the driveway. The palatial residence, with its marble columns and towering spires, was certainly grander and more impressive than the lycans' crude underground lair.

So that is Ordoghaz, the scientist thought. He felt both excitement and trepidation at coming so near to the very stronghold of his foes. An entire coven of vampires, including scores of lethal Death Dealers, was less than half a kilometer away—and completely unaware of his presence.

Or so he hoped.

I really should be back in my lab, he groused silently. This sort of intelligence operation was the sort of thing that Raze or Pierce or Taylor should be handling. Singe took a moment to pine for his abandoned scientific equipment and experiments; he resented being pulled away from his work at such a critical juncture, just as he was nearing the very culmination of his groundbreaking endeavor. *At the very least, I should be out tracking down the elusive Michael Corvin, so that we can proceed with the experiment, not spying on a nest of unwary bloodsuckers!*

Still, his was not to reason why. With a sigh of resignation, he looked away from the nearby mansion and peered back over his shoulder at the rear of the van, where a five-man team of lycan commandos readied their weapons.

Their humanoid faces held expressions of feral anticipation. Unlike the out-of-place biochemist, the soldiers looked ready, eager, and loaded for bear.

Or, in this case, bats.

"Who actually started this war?" Michael asked.

Selene stood watch by the open window. A shaft of silver moonlight threw her statuesque silhouette onto the uncarpeted wooden timbers of the floor. Despite everything, he couldn't help noticing how beautiful she was.

"They did," she answered, "or at least that's what we've been led to believe." Her mournful eyes were turned toward the deserted streets outside. "Digging into the past is discouraged. Many things are." A trace of resentment entered her voice. "But I'm beginning to suspect that there's more to this war than meets the eye."

Like what? Michael wondered, then realized that he was giving serious consideration to the political underpinnings of a secret war between vampires and werewolves. *Am I actually buying all this?* he asked himself incredulously. He gazed closely at the exotically gorgeous woman standing by the window. In her tight black leathers, Selene looked more like Emma Peel than Anne Rice. Did he really think this woman was an honest-to-God vampire?

I don't know, he admitted reluctantly. He didn't know what he believed anymore.

Selene glanced at her wristwatch. "Almost five A.M.," she announced. "I should be heading back."

Right, before the sun comes up, Michael realized, appalled that this actually made some sort of sense to him. Was there a comfy coffin waiting for Selene back at the mansion?

"What about me?" he asked.

She paused before answering. "Viktor will know what to

do," she said finally. Michael recalled that, according to Selene, Viktor was the head honcho of all the vampires. Having his future dependent on the decisions of a real-life Count Dracula did not reassure Michael. "I'll come back tomorrow night," she promised.

No way, Michael thought, rejecting the idea of spending the next twelve hours hiding out by himself in this dismal safe house. He clambered unsteadily to his feet and pulled on his jacket. "Well, I'm sure as hell not staying here alone," he declared, trying to ignore the way his head was spinning. He steadied himself by grabbing onto an arm of the solidly built titanium chair.

"You will if you want to live," Selene said sternly. Stepping away from the window, she crossed the floor to where Michael was standing.

He closed his eyes, waiting for the dizziness to pass. The way he was feeling now, he wasn't sure he was going to last until tomorrow night. His temples throbbed with every heartbeat, and his shoulder burned where that bearded madman had bitten him. For all I know, I'm coming down with rabies.

"Look," he appealed to her, "you can help me sneak back into the hospital, or I can do it myself." A shudder passed through him as he recalled his close call at the hospital several hours ago. What if the police were still looking for him there? "Either way, I need to run a few tests on myself, see if I've been, you know, infected with . . . something."

He couldn't bring himself to say lycanthropy. That was the precise medical diagnosis, wasn't it?

Selene maintained a stony expression, apparently unconvinced by his plea. Fine, Michael thought irritably. He nodded at the recalcitrant woman and turned toward the door. Guess I'm on my own then.

221

Her hand grabbed his arm, and, once again, Michael was surprised at just how strong she was. Her closed fist felt like an unbreakable vise.

Sick as he was, he knew he had no chance of breaking away from her iron grip. Heck, he'd probably be just as stuck if he were in the pink of health. She was that strong.

Strong as a vampire?

Now what do I do? he thought helplessly. He turned back toward her, unsure whether to bawl her out angrily or plead for mercy. How did you reason with a stubborn vampire, anyway?

They stood face to face, only inches apart. Selene's dark eyes—enigmatic, inscrutable—stared intently into his. Her exquisitely crafted face offered no clue to what was going on behind those unforgettable chestnut eyes. Michael started to open his mouth, still uncertain what he was going to say, but Selene leaned forward unexpectedly and silenced him with a kiss.

Her lips were cold but lush and tender. Michael's mind was caught off guard, but his body responded instantly, as though it had been waiting for this moment all night. Perhaps it had; Michael hadn't realized until now just how much he had been wanting to kiss her. He closed his eyes, savoring the sensation, and passionately kissed her back.

CLICK-CLICK. A pair of metallic snaps intruded on his bliss, and Michael's eyes snapped open in confusion. *What in the world?* His eyes widened further as, looking down, he saw that Selene had handcuffed him to the heavy titanium chair.

"Hey, what the heck are you doing?" he gasped, feeling betrayed, frustrated, and disappointed all at the same time. Pulling away from Selene, he tugged vigorously on the cuffs, but the sturdy chair, built to withstand the frenzied efforts of a captured werewolf, was bolted securely to the floor and refused to budge.

He was trapped.

Selene stared at him implacably, showing none of the ardor and affection her moist lips had bestowed on him only seconds before. She reached beneath her coat and drew out her pistol.

Michael gulped, wondering if this was the end. Had the kiss been some sort of twisted gangland tradition, bestowing a final benediction upon the condemned, or had she simply meant to distract him long enough to put the cuffs on him? Either way, he was suddenly reminded just how little he truly knew of this woman or what she was capable of.

And I thought she was my last, best hope!

What remained of his strength evaporated, and he stumbled backward into the waiting chair. He dropped weakly into the seat, unable to stay on his feet a second longer. *Go ahead and kill me,* he thought bitterly. *Just let me sit down for a minute first.*

Gun in hand, Selene stepped toward him. She leaned down to look him straight in the eye. The voice that issued from her lips was flat and devoid of emotion: "When the full moon rises tomorrow night, you will change, you will kill, and you will feed." She shook her head ruefully, forestalling any objections. "It's unavoidable." Her steely gaze drifted to the metal cuffs holding him fast to the chair. "I can't leave you free to roam around. I'm sorry."

This is insane! Michael thought furiously, wishing he had the strength at least to rattle his bonds in defiance. *One minute you're kissing me, the next minute you're telling that I'm going to turn into a monster?*

Selene racked a round into her trusty automatic. Michael wondered how many of the bullets had his name on them.

Instead of shooting him, however, she ejected the magazine and held it up to him so that he could see the gleaming silver bullets inside.

Just like the Lone Ranger, he thought irrationally. *Thanks a bundle, kemo sabe.*

"A single round most likely won't kill you," she explained in a monotone, "but the silver should prevent the transformation . . . at least for a few hours." She reinserted the cartridge into the gun and dropped the loaded weapon into his lap. "If I don't return in time, do yourself a favor. Use it."

Later, Michael would realize that he could have conceivably pulled the gun on Selene and demanded that she free him. (Not that silver would have much effect on a vampire, probably.) Right now, though, he could only gape at her, dumbfounded and amazed just to be breathing, as she fleetly exited the room, slamming the door shut behind her. He heard the click of a lock sliding into place, followed, a few heartbeats later, by the sound of her bootsteps disappearing down the stairs.

Numbly, he lifted the gun from his lap. He stared at it as if it were an alien artifact.

"Use it," Selene had said.

She wasn't serious, was she?

Chapter Twenty-one

The sporty gray sedan came screaming toward Ordoghaz at breakneck speed, racing the rising sun. *Cutting it a bit close, are we?* Singe thought wryly, watching from inside the parked van. The vampiric inability to tolerate sunlight was a weakness that he and his lycan kinsmen did not share with their enemies. He wondered what had kept this tardy bloodsucker out so late.

The driver of the sedan was in such an obvious rush that Singe judged it highly unlikely that he or she would spot the unlit van lurking in the shadows across from the entrance to the vampires' mansion. Raising a pair of binoculars to his eyes, he saw that the driver was a dark-haired female sporting the distinctive leather garb of a Death Dealer. He guessed at once that this was the infamous Selene, who had already foiled at least two attempts to take Michael Corvin into custody.

Singe felt that this was reason enough to want her dead.

To his acute disappointment, she appeared to be alone, which prompted him to wonder where exactly Michael Corvin was now. Was the elusive mortal already sequestered somewhere within the forbidding walls of Ordoghaz, or had this undead vixen stowed him elsewhere?

If she's wasted a drop of his precious blood, he thought poisonously, *I'll see to it that Lucian has her tortured for all eternity!*

As expected, the sedan paid no heed to the skulking van, instead zipping straight toward the manor's cast-iron gates, which opened automatically to admit her. Singe watched with curiosity as Selene sped her car down the driveway toward the shelter of the mansion's sunproof walls. This vampiress, he recalled, always seemed to be on hand when Michael Corvin was in jeopardy, which made her suddenly very interesting to the sly lycan scientist.

Perhaps, he reflected, *this scouting mission is not such a waste of my time after all . . .*

Kraven was insatiable, sucking on Erika's bleeding breast until she lost all sense of time and space. Still fully clothed himself, the vampire lord held her nude body erect above the carpeted floor of the suite as his thirsty mouth drained her of volition. Blood trickled from the corners of his mouth, flowing down his chin to stain his black brocade shirt.

Erika knew she should protest, before her master emptied her beyond recovery, but she couldn't bring herself to let go of Kraven's flowing black locks, let alone tear herself away from his strong, voracious lips. This was what she had always longed for, after all, and an orgasmic thrill rippled endlessly through her palpitating body as, eyes tightly shut, she tilted her head back, offering Kraven her throat as well as her breast, should he choose to partake of her pulsing jugular. *Bite me! Drink me!* she entreated him lustily. *Make me yours!*

BEEP-BEEP! The insistent ring of a cell phone interrupted nirvana. Erika's eyes snapped open, and her lips let out a whimper of dismay as abruptly, inconceivably,

226

Kraven's mouth came away from her breast and his powerful arms let go of her body. *Wait!* she wanted to cry out, feeling his strong, masculine form slip away from her. *Don't stop!*

Tottering on unsteady legs, she watched in disbelief as the lord of the manor, who only seconds ago had been melded to her in an intimate bond of blood and desire, stepped across the room to retrieve his cell phone from a jacket hanging over the back of an eighteenth-century ebony chair. Ignoring Erika completely, he raised the phone to his ear. "What is it?" he demanded, casually wiping her immortal blood from his lips with the back of his hand.

Erika heard the voice of Soren, Kraven's dour lieutenant, emerge from the electronic mouthpiece. "She's here," he reported gruffly.

Selene, she realized instantly, her humiliation complete. *Who else could it be?*

His face still flushed and ruddy with Erika's crimson essence, his shirtfront still stained with the scarlet excess of his salacious feast, Kraven rushed out of the suite without a word, leaving Erika standing naked and alone on the Persian carpet, abandoned, discarded, and almost completely drained of blood.

Soren already had arrived at the front door when Kraven stormed into the spacious foyer. The stone-faced janissary was blocking the open doorway with his body. He clearly had no intention of letting Selene into the mansion before the sun rose.

Kraven appreciated the sentiment but was not quite ready to see Selene's flawless body reduced to ashes. "Let her pass," he instructed sourly.

Displaying not even a smidgen of gratitude for Kraven's

227

leniency, Selene shoved Soren aside and stalked into the mansion. Her eyes made contact with Kraven's, then looked away in contempt. She strode past him without so much as a word of greeting, let alone an apology for her numerous transgressions.

Astounded by her insolence, Kraven chased her down the corridor. With dawn only minutes away, most of the coven already had retired for the day, but a few stragglers still hurried to and fro about the mansion, taking care of various last-minute chores before seeking their respective quarters. These miscellaneous vampires watched the unfolding scene with curiosity and concern, all the while trying not to be too conspicuous in their eavesdropping.

Kraven's ruddy face, already encrimsoned by Erika's blood, flushed even darker. Bad enough that Selene was brazenly flouting his authority, but did she have to do so in front of an audience? The embattled vampire regent could hear the scurrilous gossip burning his ears already.

He hurled accusations at her back. "Not only have you broken the Chain, you've been harboring a lycan. A capital offense!"

Not even the threat of execution slowed Selene's determined trek through the mansion. He guessed that she was heading toward the crypt to see Viktor, blatantly going over his head. *Not if I have anything to say about it!* he vowed furiously, catching up with her before she reached the stairs at the rear of the mansion. Grabbing her arm, he forcefully steered her into the relative privacy of a secluded alcove. *Under no circumstances are you speaking with Viktor before I have words with you.*

Metal shutters descended over the tinted windows lining the alcove, throwing the unlit niche deep into shadow. Kraven spun Selene around, forcing her to look him in the face. He saw neither fear nor guilt in her scornful gaze, which only infuriated him more.

"How could you do this to me?" he raged, his fingers digging into her arm. "Embarrass me like this? The entire coven knows that I have plans for us!"

"There is no us!" she spat back defiantly. Her eyes regarded him with disgust.

Kraven lost his temper entirely. He slammed her against the sealed windows, causing the metal shutters to ring out. "You will go before Viktor and tell him exactly what I tell you. From here on out, you will do as I say." Bleached white eyes and bared fangs demonstrated the dire extremity of his displeasure. "Is that in any way unclear?"

Selene answered with a lightning-fast blow to his face. *Wham!* Her palm snapped up, smashing against his nose with expertly measured force—not enough to break anything but sufficient to send a jolt of misery straight to his brain.

He dropped to one knee, blood trickling down his face. Selene took advantage of the moment to pull away from his grasp. She exited the alcove in a flash, the tail of her trench coat snapping in her wake.

Kraven tasted his own blood upon his lips. Fortunately, after feasting on Erika, he had plenty to spare. He smirked as he licked the blood from around his mouth. At least he had provoked some sort of response from Selene, cracking her veneer of frosty detachment. *Not exactly the type of foreplay I would have preferred,* he thought lewdly, *but it will do for now.*

Climbing to his feet, he charged after her, elbowing his way through a throng of gaping *nosferatu.* He pursued her down the marble stairway leading to the crypt, arriving at its underground entrance just in time to see an impenetrable steel door slam shut. He heard the tamperproof locking mechanism clank into place as Selene sealed the crypt from inside, stranding him in the hushed viewing chamber, unable to take part in Selene's pending reunion with Viktor.

"Blast it!" he cursed, consumed with frustration. Who knew what the treacherous Death Dealer was telling Viktor at this very moment?

Selene approached the recovery chamber with apprehension, the genuine satisfaction she had taken in smashing Kraven's face fading quickly as she faced the prospect of justifying her recent actions to Viktor. Kraven was not wrong when he accused her of violating the coven's most sacred laws and traditions. She could only pray that Viktor would understand why she had been forced to do so.

I awoke him with my own blood, she recalled hopefully. *He already knows what is in my heart.*

The skeletal figure of the Elder waited for her to draw nearer, standing imperiously amid the high-tech trappings of the recovery chamber as though it were a gilded throne room. Selene saw with some relief that Viktor already had regained a portion of his former substance. Although still unnaturally gaunt and wizened, he no longer appeared quite so mummyish. There was a bit more flesh on his bony frame, and his chalky gray skin was not quite as stiff as parchment.

Sunken eyes fell upon her, holding a strange mixture of joy and sorrow. Intravenous tubing pumped oxygenated red blood into his immortal veins. He beckoned for her to approach the plexiglass barrier between them.

"Come closer, my child," he rasped drily.

The guard looked up in surprise as Kraven barged into the security booth. He was one of Soren's men, replacing the previous watchman, who had been stripped of his rank and duties for his carelessness in letting Selene trick him away from his post. If and when Kraven survived the next twenty-four hours, he fully intended to have the earlier guard flayed within an inch of his eternal life.

For now, however, Kraven had more important mishaps to contend with. Without bothering to offer the new guard a word of explanation, he grabbed the startled vampire by the shoulders and forcibly ejected him from the booth. Then he yanked the door to the service corridor shut, ensuring that no one besides himself could witness whatever was transpiring in the crypt between Viktor and Selene.

I must know what they are saying! Kraven thought frantically as he hastily fired up a security monitor. An anxious look washed over his face as he beheld a televised image of Selene approaching the risen Elder. He gulped in anticipation of what she might divulge, even as he assured himself that there was absolutely no excuse for her egregious crimes against the coven.

No excuse at all.

Selene bowed reverently before Viktor, then humbly began her explanation. "I have been lost without you, my lord. Constantly hounded by Kraven and his never-ending infatuation."

A death's-head grin appeared on Viktor's horrific countenance. "It is the oldest story in the annals of mankind," the Elder said knowingly. "He most desires the one thing he cannot have."

Selene smiled, grateful for Viktor's apparent understanding. An overwhelming rush of relief came over her. Perhaps this encounter would not be as terrible as she had feared. *Everything I've done has been to ensure the safety of the coven. Viktor surely will recognize that!*

The grin disappeared from Viktor's face, and his sonorous voice took on a sterner tone. Selene realized with a shudder that she may have counted her blessings too soon.

"Now, tell me, why have you come to believe that Lucian still lives?"

Spying from the security booth, Kraven felt a chill more than equal to the one Selene was now experiencing. This was the very topic he had been dreading. No good could come from Selene and Viktor invoking Lucian's name.

He bent closer to the booth's loudspeaker, dismayed by what he was hearing yet hanging on every word. *Keep your mouth shut, you back-stabbing slut!* he thought heatedly, wishing he could reach through the monitor to choke Selene into silence. *You can't prove a thing!*

His cell phone rang unexpectedly, startling him. "What in blazes?" he muttered, reaching for the beeping device. His anxious gaze stayed fixed on the monitor screen as he lifted the phone to his ear.

"Hello?"

I have nothing to be ashamed of, Selene reminded herself. She met Viktor's forbidding gaze with fearless brown eyes, her chin held high. "But I've given you all the proof you need," she protested. Her wrist itched where she earlier had gnawed open her veins to share her blood—and her memories—with the Elder.

"Incoherent thoughts and images," Viktor said dismissively. "Nothing more. Which is why an awakening always must be performed by an Elder. You do not possess the necessary skills."

I know that, Selene thought urgently. She had never expected that the catalyst drip would bring Viktor completely up to speed, the way it would have if Marcus or Amelia had performed the ritual. Ordinarily, under far less exceptional circumstances, the drip was the means by which the Elders maintained an unbroken progression of memories throughout the ages, with each Elder passing on two centuries' worth of accumulated knowledge and experience to the Elder who succeeded him or her. Selene could not hope to have managed such a seamless transference, yet surely, she prayed with all her heart, something of her recent discoveries and suspicions must have penetrated Viktor's newly awakened consciousness. The evidence of conspiracy was simply too alarming to ignore.

"But I did see Lucian," she insisted. "I shot him! You must believe me!"

Viktor's shriveled lips turned downward. Unmistakable anger infused his parched voice with a threatening edge. "The Chain has never been broken," he declared ominously. "Not once, not in more than fourteen centuries. Not since we Elders first began to leapfrog through time. One awake, two asleep—that is the way of it." His accusing eyes raked her over. "It is Marcus's turn to reign, not mine!"

Kraven paced back and forth within the security booth. His fretful eyes intently watched the security monitor, even as he listened to the intimidating voice on the other end of the line.

Speak of the devil, the scheming regent thought unhappily. Lucian was demanding an update on the status of tonight's operations. Kraven felt as though he were being torn in half by two equally formidable entities. *Whom do I fear more?* he asked himself. *Viktor or Lucian? The Elder or the most fierce of the werewolves?*

"There's been a complication," he stammered into the

phone, uncertain how to break the news of Viktor's revival to the unforgiving lycan leader. Would Lucian blame him for Viktor's untimely return to the waking world?

It's all Selene's fault, he fumed silently. *She and her wolfen Romeo!*

Selene tried to maintain her composure beneath Viktor's scalding gaze. "But I had no choice," she argued, knowing that her words might spell the difference between immortality and oblivion for her entire species. "The coven is in danger, and Michael is the key. I know it!"

"Ah, yes," Viktor said venomously. "The lycan."

There was a harshness in his voice that Selene never had heard before. The venerated Elder had always been like a father to her, ever since the night her mortal family perished. She would have trusted him with her life.

But did he still trust her?

"Please," she pleaded. "Just give me the chance to get the proof you require."

In the security booth, Kraven switched off his phone, his ears still ringing with the sound of Lucian's biting disapproval. The lycan had not been amused by the latest developments at the mansion. Kraven feared his prickly alliance with Lucian was now strained to the breaking point. Wiping his sweaty brow, he directed his full attention back to the security monitor, just in time to hear his own name being invoked over the intercom.

"I will leave it to Kraven to collect the proof, if there is any," Viktor declared.

Selene reacted with shock to the Elder's pronouncement, unable to conceal the hurt in her voice. "How can you trust him over me?"

"Because," Viktor thundered, "he's not the one who has been tainted by an animal!"

Kraven's face lit up. He had never seen the Elder so incensed before, yet Viktor's awesome fury seemed directed at Selene alone.

Perhaps, the regent thought, *my luck has changed.*

Heartbroken and disillusioned, Selene listened numbly as Viktor weighed forth upon her crimes. That she heard a degree of sorrow in his stentorian voice was meager consolation.

"I love you like a daughter," Viktor intoned solemnly, "but you've left me with no choice. Our rules are in place for good reason—and they are the only reason our kind has survived this long. You will not be shown an ounce of leniency. When Amelia arrives after sunset, the Council will convene to decide your fate." His austere visage and dolorous tone offered no promise of mercy. "You have broken the Chain and the Covenant. You must be judged."

She had little doubt what that judgment would be.

Erika watched as Selene was escorted through the salon and up the grand staircase by four armed guards. Grimfaced, Kraven and Soren accompanied the party as they led the accused Death Dealer toward her quarters in the east wing of the mansion. Unsurprisingly, Kraven did not even spare Erika a glance as he passed her by, despite their intimate encounter less than an hour ago.

A cluster of curious vampires gathered at the foot of the stairs, exchanging rumor and gossip in excited whispers. Was it true what they were saying? Had Selene really awakened Viktor all on her own, without Kraven's permission? Was she secretly in bed with a lycan?

Erika snaked through the nattering crowd, keeping a

close eye on Selene and her imposing entourage. The servant vamp had put her lacy uniform back on, yet her abused feelings still felt raw and exposed. She couldn't forget the way Kraven had left her naked and abandoned the instant he'd received word of Selene's return. She felt exploited, used, like an empty bottle of blood left discarded after a drunken binge.

He never really cared about me, she realized, her lacerated breast still sore from Kraven's ravenous attentions. *Not for a single moment.*

All he cares about is Selene.

Disengaging from the crush of undead bystanders, she stealthily crept up the stairs after Kraven and the others. No one noticed her depart. She was just a chambermaid, after all, meaningless, invisible. Erika followed Selene and her captors, taking care to keep a safe distance back, until the party reached the entrance to Selene's quarters. Erika ducked into a small, unfrequented alcove.

Peering around the corner, she felt a jealous pang as she observed Kraven disappear into the suite after Selene, pulling the door shut behind him. Soren and his goon squad remained in the hallway outside the suite, sullenly standing watch like bouncers at an exclusive nightclub.

Only the presence of the guards kept Erika from running down the hall and placing her ear against the door. Despite everything that had happened since the sun went down last night, or perhaps because of it, she desperately yearned to know what was going on behind the solid pine door.

What could possibly be transpiring between Kraven and Selene?

Selene wished that Kraven would simply leave her alone. Her ghastly confrontation with Viktor had left her depleted and drained of spirit; the last thing she needed right now was Kraven's egocentric gloating.

"You should have listened to me and stayed out of this," he scolded her petulantly. "Now you'll be lucky if I can convince the Council to spare your life."

When Selene declined to reply, let alone plead for clemency, he whirled around and stomped toward the door. To her surprise, Selene discovered she still had loathing enough to fire off a parting shot.

"Tell me," she asked him coldly, "did you have the nerve to cut the skin from his arm, or did Lucian do it for you?"

Kraven stumbled, missing his stride. He spun around in stunned chagrin, glaring at her as though he had just been sucker-punched. His stricken expression instantly confirmed what Selene already had concluded: Kraven was in league with Lucian and had been for a long time.

Traitor! Her pitiless eyes accused him.

Kraven gulped, then, with great effort, regained his composure. He somehow managed a sneering grin. "Mark my words. Soon you'll be seeing things my way."

He fled the room, unwilling to give Selene a chance to have the last word. The door slammed shut hard enough to rattle the light fixtures on the wall. Selene heard a key lock the door from the outside, making her a prisoner in her own chambers. Metal shutters covered the window Michael had shattered when he first fled the mansion. The shuttered aperture held no escape for her, not while the sun was shining brightly outdoors.

Knowing better, she approached the door to the hall, unable to resist the temptation to try the lock. She laid her hand on the crystal doorknob.

"Don't even think about it," Soren said gruffly from the other side.

* * *

The door banged shut, making Erika jump. Still hidden in the gloomy alcove, she listened carefully as Kraven issued instructions to Soren and his men.

"No one opens this door, understood? I can't afford to have my future queen running off with that lycan again."

Kraven's words stabbed Erika like a wooden stake through her heart.

Future queen.

Nothing had changed, she realized. Even after all of Selene's rejections and betrayals, after Erika had given freely of her own precious blood and body, Kraven was still obsessed with Selene.

Always Selene.

Erika retreated into the sheltering alcove, blending with the shadows as Kraven stormed past her down the hall. The betrayed and brokenhearted servant girl felt the last ember of her devotion die, replaced by a longing for something very new and different from what she always craved before.

Revenge.

Chapter Twenty-two

*S*unlight poured through the window of the safe house, warming Michael's bones but doing little to exorcise the fears and frustrations tormenting his febrile mind, which finally had drifted into unconsciousness after long, agonizing hours spent handcuffed to the massive chair. Drenched in sweat, he shifted uneasily in his seat, as another round of disturbing images invaded his dreams.

A spinelike whip forged of gleaming silver vertebrae lashes out at him, stripping the flesh from his bones . . .

Tears course down the face of his beloved Sonja as she struggles futilely against the iron torture device confining her. Her unearthly white eyes lock onto his, filled with a poignant mixture of fear and sorrow . . .

Like a flock of malignant gargoyles, the vampire Council perch atop regal stone pillars, glaring down at the prisoners with utter contempt. Their bone-white faces hold no mercy for either him or Sonja as they contemplate their captives' respective tortures with icy disdain . . .

Not far away, trapped behind bars of silver-iron alloy, Michael's pack brothers snarl and growl in protest. They hurl their weak human bodies against the bars of the dungeon, des-

perate to come to his aid, but their frenzied efforts come to naught . . .

The silver whip cracks forth again . . .

Michael jerked awake, his back still feeling the savage bite of the lash. He blinked in confusion, uncertain of his location. It took him several heartbeats to realize that the murky, torchlit dungeon was gone, replaced by the more mundane environment of Selene's safe house in Budapest. Without thinking, he tried to rub his eyes with his knuckles, only to have the motion halted abruptly by the metal chain cuffing him to the chair.

That's right, he remembered. *I'm trapped.*

The realization provoked an irate response. Grunting in exertion, he tugged furiously on the chain cuffing him to the chair. He rocked back and forth in the seat, throwing his entire body into the effort.

The cuffs didn't yield by even a fraction of an inch.

"Son of a bitch!" Michael gasped, out of breath from his exertions. It was no use; he and the heavy titanium chair were stuck together.

Thanks to Selene.

What was she thinking, leaving him trapped like this? *Oh, yeah,* he recalled. *She was afraid I was going to get all fanged and furry out when the full moon rose tonight.*

"Werewolf, my ass," he muttered. He refused to accept Selene's insane prognosis. True, he was definitely coming down with *something*—he still felt queasy and feverish—but lycanthropy? *Give me a break!*

As he looked around for some way out, his gaze fell on the automatic pistol resting in his lap. Loaded with silver bullets, no less, more evidence of how completely preposterous his life had become. Michael remembered using a similar gun to free himself from Selene's sinking Jaguar two nights ago.

Wait a second, he thought, as a wild idea struck him. It was a desperate, possibly dangerous measure, but what other options did he have?

Trembling, he lifted the gun from his lap. His sweaty palm wrapped around the cold steel grip of the weapon. Acting quickly, before he had a chance to talk himself out of what he had in mind, he pressed the muzzle of the gun against the implacable metal chain. He closed his eyes, turned his head, and pulled the trigger.

BANG!

The recoil and loud report were too much for Michael, who flinched spasmodically, dropping the gun. The falling weapon skittered across the naked wooden floor, eventually coming to rest a foot beyond Michael's reach. *Just as well,* he figured, opening his eyes; he doubted he had the nerve to try this harebrained stunt again. He had half expected to be killed instantly by a ricochet.

But had it worked? Breathing hard, he turned to inspect the maddeningly stubborn cuffs. His heart sank immediately.

The chain wasn't even scratched.

Kahn paced the floor of the dojo as his troops prepared for duty. A full score of Death Dealers, male and female alike, loaded their weapons with solid silver cartridges. Amelia was due to arrive at the train station within hours, shortly after sundown, and Kahn intended to make sure that the Elder was greeted by a full security detail. With all the lycan activity over the last few nights, nothing could be left to chance.

A pity, he thought, *that there hasn't been time to mass-produce the new silver nitrate rounds.* So far, the gun on his workbench was the only working prototype.

One face was conspicuously absent from the assembled brigade: Selene's. Kahn couldn't help wondering what had become of the resourceful Englishwoman, whom he had always considered one of his most steadfast and determined comrades. *Is it true what they're saying about her?* he thought, hiding his doubts behind a mask of cool professionalism. He found it hard to believe that Selene, of all immortals, would betray them out of love for a lycan.

Yet that was what Kraven had declared, presumably with the full backing of Viktor himself. Kahn had yet to confer with Viktor directly, since Kahn had restricted access to the crypt during the Elder's period of recuperation, but he couldn't imagine that even Kraven would be so arrogant as to accuse Selene of treason without Viktor's tacit approval.

And who am I to question the judgment of an Elder? Kahn shook his head, allowing a slight scowl to convey his unhappiness. Something was not right here; it had been Selene, after all, who had stood in this very loft only two nights ago, arguing vehemently that the lycans were up to something big. How could she have completely switched her loyalties over the last forty hours or so—unless her heated show of concern had been meant to divert suspicion from herself?

Kahn angrily inserted a cartridge into his own modified AK-47 assault rifle. He hated all this double-agent espionage bullshit; he was a soldier, not a spymaster. *Just give me something howling and hairy to shoot,* he thought sourly. *Preferably at close range.*

Footsteps on the stairs alerted Kahn to the arrival of Kraven to the dojo. The regent was dressed to the nines, no doubt in anticipation of Amelia's approaching advent. His silky black suit stood in marked contrast to the reinforced leather gear of Kahn and his fellow Death Dealers.

Kahn hefted his rifle, cradling it against his chest. "We're ready," he informed Kraven.

"Change of plans," the regent announced offhandedly. A self-satisfied smirk was Kahn's first warning that something was amiss. "The Lady Amelia will be picked up by Soren and his team."

Kahn's jaw dropped. "That's our job," he insisted, and with good reason; he had personally overseen the security at the last five Awakenings.

"Not anymore," Kraven said smugly, not even bothering to conceal his perverse enjoyment of the other vampire's consternation. It seemed unthinkable that Kraven had ever been a Death Dealer, let alone the esteemed slayer of Lucian.

How can he do this, Kahn thought in disbelief, *and why?* The safety of Amelia was too important to play political power games with. Wheels of suspicion began to churn behind Kahn's shrewd brown eyes as Kraven turned his back on the mansion's military commander and blithely strolled away.

Perhaps Selene was not the traitor in their ranks?

The sun set on the Nyugati train station in the northwestern corner of Pest. A row of black limousines was parked beside a glassed-in platform that had been expressly cleared of humankind. Seated within the lead limousine, Soren watched the sinking sun through the dark, polarized windows of the car, waiting until the last traces of daylight had vanished from the sky before emerging from the limo, an unreadable expression on his face.

Flanked on both sides by armed security forces, he stared expectantly at the empty platform. Off in the distance, from somewhere to the west, he heard the unmistakable rumbling of an approaching steam engine.

Right on time, he thought coldly.

Within seconds, a jet-black passenger train chugged into view, pulled by a vintage 1930s locomotive, impeccably maintained. An old-fashioned steam engine powered the locomotive's chugging pistons and connecting rods as the privately owned train came roaring into the station amidst squealing brakes and scalding blasts of steam.

Soren retrieved a laser pointer from his pocket and, as agreed, fired off three quick ruby pulses as the train slowed to a stop. The pulses were to assure Amelia's bodyguards that the station had been secured and vetted by Kraven's security forces.

His signal was promptly acknowledged by an answering pulse, visible through the tinted window of the forward passenger car. Soren visualized his counterpart aboard the train, signaling Amelia's entourage that the platform was safe. So far, all was going according to plan.

Soren's stolid features gave no indication that anything exceptional was occurring, not even as a hairy claw broke through the steam fogging the platform. He watched cold-bloodedly as four enormous werewolves, black fur bristling from their grotesque, subhuman bodies, stealthily crept up the side of the train and onto its roof.

Although nearly fifteen centuries old, the Lady Amelia had the youthful beauty and haughty carriage of an international supermodel. Her lustrous black hair bound tightly on her gracefully sculpted head, she looked out at the world through imperious green eyes. A strapless satin gown exposed slender white shoulders, while a jeweled silver pendant, large enough to shame the crown jewels of many a mortal kingdom, rested on the flawless ivory expanse of her bosom.

Accompanied by her entourage and bodyguards, she strode down the center of a plushly fitted dining car toward the exit ahead. The trip from New York, by way of Vienna, had been a long one, and she looked forward to arriving at Ordoghaz before too much time passed. There, in accordance with their ancient traditions, she would go down into the earth for another two hundred years of tranquil repose.

In truth, she yearned for the unbroken quiet of the crypt. The twentieth century had been a wearying one, rife with war and turmoil among the mortal world, and the present era looked to be no less trying. She was happy to let Marcus cope with the challenges to come. Perhaps the world would be a more orderly place when next she rose from the tomb, two centuries hence.

I rather doubt it, she lamented inwardly. Immortality had taught her realism, among other things.

The regal procession swept down the passageway, past rich cherrywood panels with polished gold fittings. Tinted orange light bulbs mimicked dancing flames atop gilded electric lamps fashioned in the shape of antique candelabra, the ersatz candlelight casting a gentle glow over the train's interior. A leather-clad Death Dealer led the way, cradling a loaded submachine gun against his chest, while Amelia's neatly groomed attendants and ladies-in-waiting trailed dutifully behind her. Distinguished members of the Council, their elegant attire adorned by badges and emblems that signified their illustrious status, kept pace with the Elder and her retinue. The oldest among them already had attended many previous Awakenings. No doubt, they expected the transition to proceed as smoothly as ever.

A peculiar noise, like something scratching at the roof of the car, caught the attention of Amelia and her attendants. She glanced up briefly at the ceiling, as did several of her ladies-in-waiting. For a second, a flicker of apprehension passed through the aristocratic immortal. Was something amiss?

She swiftly dismissed the notion. Kraven and his people had already secured the platform outside. Between her own complement of bodyguards and the additional Death Dealers from the mansion, it was foolish to imagine that any danger could await her here.

It has been an interminable journey, she reflected. *I must not let my chafed nerves get the better of me at the very end of my travels.*

At the far end of the lushly appointed dining car, a narrow vestibule preceded the car's closed steel door. Amelia waited with superhuman patience as the leader of her Death Dealers unlocked the compartment and slid open the door.

She expected to see a moonlit platform, peopled only by those vampires who had been honored with the task of transporting her to Ordoghaz She wondered briefly if Kraven would be present to greet her personally, or if he awaited her back at the mansion. It mattered little to her; Kraven was Viktor's protege, not hers.

Instead of a welcoming party, however, the sliding door opened to reveal the gigantic form of a ravening werewolf clinging to the side of the train. Saliva dripped from the monster's gaping jaws, even as two more man-beasts dropped loudly onto the platform behind him. A foul, musky scent invaded the vestibule, while bestial growls broke the silence.

By the Blood of the Ancestor! A flicker of surprise registered on Amelia's immaculate features, less than a heartbeat before the creature lunged at her with terrifying speed, throwing the startled Death Dealer effortlessly aside. Knifelike claws and teeth tore into immortal flesh . . .

*   *   *

On the platform, Soren and his so-called security team watched impassively as the grisly sounds of a massacre escaped the train. Anguished screams mixed with the roar of both gunfire and rampaging beasts. Immortal blood sprayed the polarized windows from inside, painting abstract designs of crimson on the tinted glass.

Soren made no attempt to intervene in the lycanthropic feeding frenzy, even as the pitiful cries of Amelia and her entourage gave way to a wet, sticky symphony of crunching bones and tearing flesh.

Yes, he thought once more. All was going exactly according to plan.

Chapter Twenty-three

With the fall of night, the metal shutters rose from Selene's windows, permitting her a view of the grounds outside the mansion. Armed sentries—Soren's people, not Kahn's—prowled the spacious front yard, each of the soldiers armed to the teeth, while two more guards were stationed directly beneath her window. Kraven clearly had no intention of letting her slip away again.

When did Ordoghaz become a police state? she thought bitterly. *And why has Viktor sided with Kraven against me?*

Her gaze shifted from the lawn below to the starry night sky. The storm clouds of the previous nights finally had blown away, so that nothing obscured the eerie silver radiance of the moon, which hung large and full above the horizon.

The sight of the moon instantly turned her thoughts to Michael—and to the vile infection transforming him from within. *I left him the gun,* she remembered grimly, *and the silver bullets.*

But would Michael have the wisdom to use the Beretta in time?

* * *

Still cuffed to the titanium chair, Michael dozed uncomfortably on the bare wooden floor, his back propped up against the immovable seat. He twitched and moaned fitfully as he slept, besieged by alien thoughts and memories.

Running madly through the dense Carpathian forest, the silver arrows of his enemies flying past his head like angry wasps . . .

Feeling the Change upon him, gaining strength and vigor as he gladly sheds his clumsy human form. Growing claws and fangs to match the bloodthirsty fury in his soul . . .

Moonlight fell upon Michael's unconscious form, and every hair on his body leaped up as though electrified.

The dusty utility closet was tucked away in an unfrequented corner of Ordoghaz, known only to the mansion's staff of menials. Erika doubted that Kraven could have found the closet—and the fuse box within—even if his eternal life depended on it.

Sometimes there are advantages to being at the bottom of the pecking order, the red-eyed servant girl thought. Dried tears stained her alabaster cheeks, while the sting of her shoddy treatment at Kraven's hands festered deep inside her broken heart. *If he thinks he can just throw me over in favor of Selene, well, he's got another think coming.*

The closet was dark and unlit, but Erika could see easily in the gloom. Opening a metal panel, she reached inside and laid a small white hand upon a switch. At the last minute, she hesitated, holding her breath as she reconsidered her reckless scheme. Was she really going to do this?

Hell, yes! she thought indignantly, and threw the switch.

In the recovery chamber, deep within the bowels of the mansion, Viktor reclined upon a large white chair, whose grandiose dimensions gave it the appearance of a throne. He rested motionlessly as his famished body soaked up a revitalizing infusion of fresh human blood. The intricate life-support apparatus hummed and gurgled in the background, while the soft halogen lights exposed a chalky white figure noticeably less cadaverous than before.

As the blood nourished him, Viktor considered the unusual—indeed, unprecedented—circumstances surrounding his premature resurrection. Selene's obscene betrayal was disappointing enough, yet he had grave doubts regarding Kraven as well. Clearly, he and Amelia would have much to discuss when his fellow Elder arrived at the mansion later this evening.

And then, he silently resolved, *there will be changes made.*

Without warning, the lights went out, interrupting his chain of thought. Even with his eyes closed, the sudden blackness was too jarring to overlook. An emergency siren went off, signaling a breach in the mansion's security.

Viktor's eyes snapped open, exposing their colorless, inhuman whites. *By the Ancestor,* he raged, *is there no end to this chaos?*

The lights blinked off all over the mansion, from the crypt to the dojo, where, several floors above the recovery chamber, Kahn looked up in surprise at the unexpected blackout. Red-tinted security lights switched on as emergency backups kicked in, throwing a lurid scarlet glow over the training area. Kahn saw his assembled Death Dealers looking about in confusion; the mansion had never come under attack within the memory of even the oldest immortal.

What the devil?

* * *

The ear-piercing alarm continued to shriek as Selene ran back to her window. Peering downward, she saw Soren's guards go scrambling toward the other side of the estate, guns drawn.

Her undead heart beat faster. She had no idea what the source of the disturbance was, but she knew that this was her chance. Perhaps she still could get to Michael before he started changing?

Before she could react, however, the door banged open, and Erika came rushing into the suite. Glancing past the uninvited servant girl, Selene saw that the guards posted outside the door had disappeared as well, no doubt joining their comrades to investigate whatever had triggered the alarm. *Better and better,* the captive Death Dealer thought, not inclined to look a gift horse in the mouth.

But first there was Erika to deal with. Without a word of explanation, the blond vampiress tossed Selene a bulging nylon pouch. She swiftly unzipped the bag and was surprised to discover a pair of Berettas inside.

Confused but grateful, she directed a quizzical look at Erika. Up until now, Selene had judged the pert young maidservant to be thoroughly in Kraven's thrall. "Why are you helping me?"

Erika rolled her eyes, as if amazed that Selene didn't get it. "I'm not," she stated emphatically. "I'm helping me."

Whatever, Selene decided. The servant girl's personal agenda was the least of her concerns. She smiled appreciatively as Erika threw her a set of car keys, a strange mixture of fear and exhilaration washing over the younger vampiress's face.

There was still an empty gap in the window where Michael had dived through it only the night before. Following his lead, Selene dashed to the open window and leaped over the edge.

Hang on, Michael! she thought anxiously, even as the soles of her boots touched down on the damp lawn. *I'm on my way!*

Singe had almost nodded off behind the wheel of the van when his keen ears picked up the sound of the mansion's gates sliding open. He looked up in time to see that same gray sedan come rocketing out of the manor's driveway, throwing up a spray of gravel as it took a sharp turn onto the road leading back to the city. A familiar dark-haired vampiress occupied the driver's seat.

Selene.

The lycan scientist immediately went into action, firing up the engine of the slumbering van. After having spent the entire day staked out across from the vampires' lair, he was not about to lose track of his quarry now. There had been nobody else in the car with Selene, at least not that he could see, but perhaps she was even now racing back to Michael Corvin's side.

Not without me, you're not, he resolved. The lycan gunmen in the back of the van grunted in protest as the van executed an abrupt U-turn and took off speeding down the road after the gray sedan.

The wailing alarm screamed in Kraven's ears and gnawed on his nerves as he burst from the privacy of his suite into the hall outside. Kahn and several tense-looking Death Dealers came racing down the darkened corridor, the incandescent beams of their flashlights raking the walls. The leather-clad warriors seemed to be in full-blown panic mode. Not a good sign.

"What's going on?" Kraven demanded. As far as he knew, the present upset had nothing to do with his and Lucian's plans for tonight, unless perhaps the nefarious lycan commander had double-crossed him?

An icy chill ran down his spine at the very idea.

Kahn hastily answered Kraven. "The perimeter sensor's been tripped!" he explained, clutching a loaded automatic rifle. "We're locking down the mansion!"

But it's too early, Kraven thought in alarm. *I haven't lowered our defenses yet!*

The plan was to allow Lucian and his forces to stage a successful "sneak attack" upon the mansion. Kraven would place his own people at key locations, while diverting Kahn and his Death Dealers to where they could do the least harm. Later, after Lucian personally disposed of Viktor and Marcus, Kraven would step forward to take undisputed control of both the Old and New World covens, eventually striking a historic peace agreement with Lucian that would leave Kraven covered in glory—and free to disband the Death Dealers once and for all, replacing them completely with Soren's handpicked security force, whose loyalty was to Kraven alone.

Then Selene had to complicate mattters by reviving Viktor ahead of schedule! Now the crisis was upon them, forcing him toward a perilous confrontation he had hoped to avoid. *Can even Lucian overcome Viktor,* the scheming regent pondered, *now that the Elder had regained much of his legendary strength?*

Adding to the confusion, Erika came running up behind Kahn and his security team. Kraven felt a stab of irritation—*now what does the stupid wench want?*—until her panicked face and obvious distress caught his attention.

"It's Selene!" she gasped breathlessly. "She's escaped, to go to him . . . Michael!"

A jealous fury drove Kraven's fears from his mind. The thought of Selene rushing to her mangy lover's arms infuriated him beyond reason. He shouted angrily to anyone within earshot: "I want that lycan's head on a plate!"

The gray sedan careened through the city streets, racing against fate and the insidious influence of the rising moon. Behind the wheel of the speeding vehicle, Selene glimpsed the moon shining between the thickly clustered high-rises and wondered if she was already too late.

Had Michael delayed his transformation by shooting himself with the silver bullet, or had he already metamorphosed into an unreasoning beast? The very thought of Michael physically changing into a werewolf distressed her more than she wanted to admit. She prayed that he would find the strength to resist the infection until she could make it back to him—even if it ultimately meant that she would have to kill him herself.

She breathed a sigh of relief as the safe house loomed into view. She had broken multiple speed limits, and very nearly the sound barrier, getting to Budapest from the mansion in less than an hour. Now that she had almost reached her destination, however, she found that she had no plan beyond discovering whether Michael was still human.

And if he is, she asked herself pointedly, *what then?*

She had no idea.

The sedan squealed to a halt in the deserted alley beside the safe house. No lights shone through the building's windows; the coven kept the five-story edifice conveniently unoccupied. Seconds later, Selene was dashing up the front steps of the building and unlocking the door. She slipped inside the desolate structure as swiftly and silently as a wraith.

In her haste, she failed to notice the ominous black van slowing to a stop across the street.

"After her! Don't let her get away!" Singe barked at his lycan foot soldiers. His avid eyes gleamed with the thrill of the hunt, an invigorating frisson not unlike the heady excitement of scientific discovery. For all he knew, the elusive Michael Corvin was only meters away, somewhere in the dilapidated-looking edifice the vampiress had just entered.

His heart pounded in anticipation. Once he had the specimen in his grasp, the final phase of Singe's great experiment could begin. Just to play it safe, he hastily contacted Pierce and Taylor by cell phone, alerting them to his location.

"Remember!" he called out to his men moments later, as the lycan soldiers piled out of the back of the van. Semi-automatic weapons armed with UV ammo glistened beneath the streetlights. "Take the male alive—at all costs!" He hurried after the commandos, unwilling to forgo the conclusion of their long chase. His boots raced up the steps of the building. "The vampire bitch is expendable!"

Selene took the steps two at a time, dreading what she might find on the top floor of the empty building. She was not so intent on climbing the stairs, though, that her keen ears failed to detect the alarming sound of racing bootsteps three stories below. Someone was chasing after her; from the sound of it, several someones.

Who? she wondered anxiously. She peered over the wrought-iron rail at the winding staircase behind her, half expecting to find a squad of determined Death Dealers on her tail. She had no illusions that her former comrades would show her any mercy, not after all she'd done over the last few nights. *I wouldn't trust me, either,* she acknowledged.

But instead of a crack team of undead warriors, she saw six thuggish figures in shabby brown attire. Not vampires at all, then. Lycans.

They must have followed me, she realized.

And she had led them straight to Michael!

The lycans charged up the stairs below her. Badly outnumbered, Selene realized she had only moments before the man-beasts caught up with her. Drawing her Beretta, she fired down at the oncoming lycans, who ducked away from her blistering fusillade yet kept on climbing toward her. Turning her back on the intruders, she sprinted up the last flight of stairs to the fifth floor, then ran like mad down the hall to the barren room where she had last seen Michael.

Would he still be there? Was he still remotely human? Selene held her breath as she ran, hoping against hope that there was still some trace of the unlucky American left to rescue.

Dead to the world, Michael slumped against the cold steel legs of the interrogation chair. His free hand clumsily groped at the empty air, as alien memories carried his mind back to a very different time and place.

His hand delicately sweeps along the edge of a gilded vanity table, tenderly exploring a collection of ornate combs, hairpins, and perfume bottles. The beautiful objects are all the more precious because he knows they belong to her.

He longs to touch Sonja gently again, just as he now reverently fingers her things . . .

An eruption of automatic gunfire rocked the apartment, jolting Michael from his feverish delirium. His bloodshot eyes jerked open, and he abruptly found himself back in the so-called safe house, which suddenly didn't seem all that safe. The thunderous weapons fire sounded as if it were coming from right outside the room.

Michael was still groggy and disoriented when the apartment door banged open and Selene ran into the room. As ever, she was clad entirely in black and sporting a smoking handgun. Her feline grace and beauty struck Michael even through his punch-drunk state, taking his breath away. Holstering the gun, she retrieved a key from the pocket of her trench coat and hastily unlocked his cuffs.

"We need to go," she said.

Free at last, Michael scrambled away from the chair with all due speed. "What is it?" he asked her urgently, alarmed and confused. He heard multiple footsteps pounding on the stairs outside. "What's going on?"

Selene shook her head. Clearly, there was no time to explain. Raising her pistol, she aimed at the wall separating the apartment from the hall and unleashed a blistering salvo right through the flimsy barrier. Plaster exploded beneath a hail of bullets, and bestial screams came from the hallway beyond. Michael heard heavy bodies thump to the floor even as yet more guttural voices shouted in anger.

Were those the voices of irate werewolves, he wondered, or were Selene's fellow vampires after them now? And how crazy was it that those were actually the options?

Selene's long black coat swirled about her as she spun around and opened fire at the nearest window. Shattered glass burst outward, raining down on the street below, and Selene turned to shout at Michael.

"Go, go, go!" she ordered him. "Jump!"

Michael staggered over to the shattered window and stepped out onto the sill. He peered down at the glass-strewn pavement, some fifty feet below, then looked at Selene in bug-eyed disbelief. "Are you fucking kidding me?"

Before she could answer him, four darkly garbed gunmen burst through the door. Their weapons blasted repeatedly, like a string of firecrackers, and luminous bullets popped and ricocheted off the metal window frame surrounding Michael. He recoiled instinctively from the deafening assault, stumbling backward out the window.

The sill disappeared beneath his feet, replaced by nothing but empty air and gravity. A panicked shriek tore out of Michael's lungs as he plummeted toward certain doom, his arms and legs flailing wildly. Months of gory experience in the ER painted a vivid picture of his broken body splattered all over the sidewalk. *This is it,* he thought. *I'm going to die.*

Perhaps it was just as well . . .

The cold night air whipped past his falling body. Michael squeezed his eyes shut, bracing for the inevitable (and almost certainly fatal) impact. At the last minute, however, his body instinctively twisted in midair, so that he landed feet first on the pavement, completely unharmed.

Eyes wide, Michael looked about himself in amazement, then tilted his head back to gaze up at the broken window, a full five stories overhead.

Wow, he thought.

Maybe there was something to this whole werewolf business, after all.

A spent shell casing clattered to the floor. It rolled across the rough wooden timbers until it came to rest beside four bullet-stitched bodies. Pools of blood expanded outward from the scattered corpses, adding a crimson sheen to the floor.

The last immortal standing, Selene paused amidst the carnage, her gun smoking in her grip. She nodded with satisfaction at the fallen lycans; the old-fashioned silver ammo was still as effective as ever. The scent of so much spilled blood made her mouth water.

That was a close one, she acknowledged, wishing she knew why the lycans wanted Michael so badly. *There's something I'm still not getting here.*

The screech of peeling tires drew her attention to the street outside. Rushing to the window, she stared down in dismay as a blue-and-white police car pulled up to the curb less than a meter away from where Michael was standing. A pair of uniformed officers piled out of the car and none too gently took hold of Michael, forcing him into the backseat of the squad car. Michael fought back, slugging one of the cops in the jaw, but, in his debilitated state, he was outnumbered and overpowered by the two other men.

Bloody hell, she thought. Not for a second did she think that Michael's attackers were genuine police officers. She recognized the telltale ferocity of lycans in disguise. Reinforcements, she guessed, probably summoned by the beastmen she had just killed.

She took aim with her Beretta, determined not to let these new lycans steal Michael away from her, and pulled the trigger. But instead of unleashing a fresh salvo of deadly silver bullets, the weapon merely clicked impotently.

Out of ammo, she realized. *Damn!*

Hurriedly, she ejected the empty clip, but she was already too late. Before she even had a chance to reload, the squad car took off into the night, its siren howling as though the speeding vehicle were as wolfen as its passengers. Within seconds, it had disappeared into Budapest's busy nocturnal streets.

Michael was gone.

Her shoulders slumped, and her trigger arm dropped limply to her side as she stood silently in the bullet-riddled apartment, the lifeless bodies of her enemies strewn around her. Crimson puddles lapped at the heels of her black leather boots.

Now what do I do? she thought hopelessly.

A feeble moan intruded upon her despair. Selene spun away from the window, stunned to discover that one of the lycan casualties was still alive: a scrawny sort, middle-aged in appearance, who struck her as somewhat less thuggish than his associates. He looked more like a professor than a foot soldier, with close-cropped brown hair and a deeply furrowed brow. Older than the typical lycan berserker, the surviving intruder seemed an unlikely candidate for an assault team. He writhed helplessly on the floor, unable to lift himself out of a brackish pool of his own blood.

Interesting, Selene thought.

Chapter Twenty-four

Kahn apprehensively eyed the huge amber orb hovering in the sky above him. The werewolves would be at their most feral tonight, he realized, a worried frown on his ebony features. Whose bright idea was it to schedule the Awakening on the first night of the full moon?

Flanked by a trio of heavily armed Death Dealers, Kahn patrolled the grounds of the estate, whose high iron gates no longer seemed quite impervious enough. He strode across the lawn toward a perimeter guard marching beside the front gate.

There was a rustling in the shadows, and three large Rottweilers came bounding across the grass. The fearsome attack dogs enthusiastically greeted Kahn, who doled out a round of affectionate pats to each of the eager canines. Saliva dripped from their powerful jaws.

"Hey, guys." Kahn could not help noting the similarities between the drooling guard dogs and the coven's lycanthropic enemies. The Rottweilers were arguably closer kin to werewolves than vampires, yet he had no doubts about the loyalty of these canine sentinels. *Besides,* he thought, *trained vampire bats are simply not practical.*

"Any luck?" he asked the guard, a vampire named Mason.

The other man shook his head. "We've made the rounds twice. And believe me, the dogs would have been all over it if anything had even got near that fence."

Kahn nodded, trusting Mason's judgment. He was a Death Dealer, one of Kahn's own, not a member of Soren's heavy-handed security force. If Mason said there were no lycans lurking about, Kahn believed him.

Nonetheless, he still felt uneasy. He checked his watch, scowling at what it revealed. "Amelia should have arrived by now," he observed, his deep voice filled with concern. He turned to the troika of Death Dealers accompanying him. "I want you three to slip off the property and find out what's keeping her."

He stroked his chin unhappily. In theory, Soren was personally seeing to Amelia's safety, yet Kahn found himself increasingly uncomfortable with that notion. *Something's not right here,* he thought once again. *I haven't felt this worried since Lucian was alive.*

The Lady Amelia no longer looked quite so immaculate. Beaten and bloody, she sprawled prostrate on the floor of the dining car, her bruised cheek pressed against the blood-slick floor. Loose strands of raven-black hair fell across her face, while her once-stylish gown lay in shreds and tatters on her scratched and brutalized form. The noxious stench of the werewolves' matted fur befouled the air, mixing with the deplorable tang of spilled immortal blood.

Her immortal mind struggled to cope with the enormity of the disaster. How had this atrocity come to pass? Where were the Death Dealers from Ordoghaz? Her own defenders lay in pieces around her, their sundered bodies torn apart by the werewolves' maddened claws and teeth. Even now she heard the loathsome beasts feasting on the lifeless flesh and bones of her council. Only the strength and resilience of an Elder had kept her alive so far, yet now she faced the very real possibility that her eternal existence was finally coming to an end.

No! She rebelled, unwilling to accept extinction after so many centuries of life and power. She laboriously lifted her head from the floor, ignoring the pain that racked her ravaged body. She mustered all her strength for one last desperate attempt at escape. *I must get away! I must survive!*

A massive paw slammed into her skull, pinning her to the ground. Jagged claws dug into her scalp as a snarling werewolf bent low to growl menacingly in her ear. The beast's hot, putrid breath panted against her like a blast furnace, causing her stomach to turn. Placing her palms against the sticky red floor, Amelia tried to overcome the pressure of the werewolf's heavy paw, but it was no use; she was too weak to resist.

This cannot be! her thoughts protested in vain. *I am an immortal, an Elder . . . I cannot die at the hands of an unclean animal!*

Bootsteps rang on the floor of the train, drawing near her. Twisting her head, she raised her eyes enough to see a tall black man in a brown leather jacket walking calmly toward her. Unlike his lupine compatriots, this particular lycan had retained his human guise; his shaved skull was as hairless as the werewolves' were hirsute. Amelia surmised that the newcomer was the alpha-male in charge of this blasphemous ambush.

A gleaming metal case was clutched in the lycan's hands. Without comment, he placed the case down on the floor and flipped open the lid. He reached inside and removed a set of empty hypodermic syringes. The hollow needles at the tip of the syringes were at least three centimeters long.

Amelia's white, inhuman eyes widened in fear at the sight of the vicious apparatus. *Not my blood!* she thought hysterically. *In the name of the Ancestor, don't take my blood!*

Raze smirked.

The squad car rocketed through a squalid, graffiti-ridden district of Budapest. The amber glow of the moonlight competed with the harsh white illumination of the street lamps. The police car's siren wailed relentlessly, clearing a path through the late-night traffic. Wherever they were going, they were heading there fast.

In the backseat, separated from the two uniformed police officers by a steel-mesh partition, Michael was getting sicker by the moment. His forehead felt as if it were on fire, and his whole body throbbed unbearably. A cold, sweaty film glued his dirty T-shirt to his skin. His mouth felt as dry as the Kalahari. *Jesus Christ, this just keeps getting worse. What the hell is wrong with me?*

He wanted to think that the two cops were driving him straight to a hospital, but that didn't seem too likely; he hadn't gotten the impression that the men were overly concerned with his welfare. He wondered if they were really police officers at all. It was a crazy thought, but he figured that at this point, he was entitled to be a little paranoid.

A drop of blood splattered on the knee of his muddy pants, and he raised a hand to his upper lip. His fingers came away red and sticky.

Shit. Now his nose was bleeding.

Michael stared out the rolled-up windows of the squad

car, watching morosely as the brightly lighted sidewalks and buildings zipped by. They were heading northeast, it appeared, following the route of the city's oldest subway line, built more than a hundred years ago. Right now the car was passing through the busy red-light district around Matyas Square. Michael saw throngs of local hookers brazenly plying their trade beneath the street lamps, heedless of the police car zooming past their ranks. Although illegal, prostitution was more or less tolerated in some of the city's less respectable neighborhoods.

Michael's defeated gaze drifted upward to the cloudy night sky. Suddenly, before he knew what was happening, the full moon slid from behind a bank of angry storm clouds.

The glowing white disk provoked an immediate response. Michael's brown eyes dilated, shrinking down to tiny black pinpricks. His heart pounded so loudly that his ears were filled with what sounded like the unchecked turbulence of a never-ending hurricane. His guts twisted inside him, extracting a tortured moan from his cracked and bleeding lips. His stomach felt as if it were being turned inside out.

Up front, the two cops traded a look before glancing back at their anguished prisoner. Concern flickered over their surly faces, as if they were afraid Michael was going to throw up all over the backseat.

"Hey, Taylor," one of the cops said. He was the long-haired one who was riding shotgun. "Maybe we should pull over and dose him?"

The driver peered at Michael via the rear-view mirror. "Nah," he muttered to his partner, whose name Michael had gathered was Pierce. "He'll be all right."

Taylor spoke directly to Michael. "Come on, man, hang

tough." He turned his eyes back toward the road. "We're almost there."

Almost where? Michael wondered, but all that escaped his lips was another queasy moan. Every muscle in his body spasmed beyond his control. The pounding in his ears increased exponentially. His vision wavered, the color fading from his sight as the world turned into a gray, monochromatic blur. At the same time, his sense of smell heightened intensely, so that the rancid filth of the streets outside overwhelmed him. He choked on the sickening stench and clutched at his stomach. *Omigod,* he thought, grimacing. *How can anyone feel this bad and not be dying?*

"Yeah, I know," Taylor said, responding to Michael's groans. He looked back at Michael through the sturdy metal grate. Michael thought he heard a hint of sympathy in the driver's gruff voice. "First time's a bitch, hurts like hell. But after a while, you'll be able to control it, change whenever you want. Moon won't make a shit bit of difference."

Change? The word somehow penetrated his throbbing brain. Was that what this was, the first stage of his transformation into a bona fide werewolf? *No!* Michael thought in horror, never mind the convulsions racking his aching body. *It can't be true. It's not possible!*

Unable to speak, he groaned even louder. Taylor shook his head in disgust, then turned up the radio. Blaring gypsy rock filled the squad car.

A violent spasm rocked Michael from head to toe. His back arched in agony, as though he were undergoing a jolt of electroshock therapy. He bit down hard on his lower lip, missing his tongue by only a fraction of an inch. His heart pounded like a war drum beneath his breast, even as the cartilage around it began to crackle and crunch. Abused

266

tendons twisted and snaked, causing blood-wet bones to shift position painfully.

His entire skeletal structure started to reshape itself. Horrified, Michael pulled up his T-shirt and watched, mesmerized despite his torment, as his ribs snapped and cracked before his eyes, cascading like piano keys beneath his palpitating skin. *Holy fuck!* he thought. In eight-plus years of medical training, including several grisly stints in the casualty ward, he had never witnessed anything so astounding or grotesque. Human tissue was not supposed to act like this, dammit!

A wave of dizziness came over him. Michael clutched at the edge of the seat like a drunk teenager with a humongous case of the bed-spins. He held on for dear life as the hideous metamorphosis accelerated its pace.

Pulsing blue-black veins traversed the whites of his eyes, spreading like tropical vines until Michael's sensitive brown orbs took on an unnatural cobalt hue. Wild patterns of mottled splotches bloomed across his face and neck like broken capillaries, darkening his skin. Pale, bloodless flesh acquired a coarse gray tone.

Michael's gums smarted as, starting with his canines, his teeth grew sharper and more pronounced. Soon he could not even close his mouth because of the bear trap of serrated fangs jutting from his jaws. He needed a bigger mouth . . .

Ordinary human fingernails grew at a preternatural rate, becoming hooked yellow claws that tore right into the fabric of the seat. Scuffed vinyl ripped apart loudly.

The tearing noises caught Pierce's attention. The long-haired cop twisted in his seat, turning to inspect Michael through the steel-mesh divider. "Holy shit!" he blurted.

"He's changing right here in the fucking car! Pull over! Pull over!"

Caught in the throes of the transformation, Michael kicked out wildly at the metal screen between him and the two supposed police officers. *Boom!* The ringing metallic impact briefly overpowered the rock music blaring from the car radio.

At the wheel, Taylor whirled around quickly, shocked to find himself face-to-face with Michael, who was now well on his way to becoming a full-fledged werewolf. Glowing blue eyes peered out from beneath a sloping brow, while his nose had devolved into a bestial snout with flaring black nostrils. Jagged canines and incisors protruded from a snout-like, prognathous jaw. Foam dripped from his chin as he bared his newborn fangs and let loose with a ferocious roar.

Caught by surprise, the driver lost control of the car, which swerved sharply to the right, making an unplanned turn into a grimy, cobblestoned alley, whose brick walls appeared to rush precipitously at the oncoming car. Taylor slammed on the brakes, and the cop car screeched to a halt, throwing its passengers forward abruptly. Michael's thrashing body thudded against the metal divider, denting the thick steel grating.

Unfazed by the vehicle's sudden stop, the berserk American tried to smash his way out of the squad car. He kicked savagely at one of the side windows, and a spider web of cracks fractured the glass. One more good kick, and the window was history.

Panicked, Pierce and Taylor leaped out of the car. "Get the kit!" Taylor yelled at his partner, while he hurried to subdue their unruly prisoner. "Pronto!"

Standing outside the car, Pierce bent over the passenger seat and hurriedly rummaged through the glove compartment. He tugged out an unmarked nylon case and unzipped its seal. Inside were several fully loaded syringes. Pierce grabbed one and slid the tip between his teeth before biting down on the protective cap. With a twist of his head, he wrenched the cap from the needle, then spit it out onto the dirty floor of the alley.

Meanwhile, Taylor yanked open the back door of the squad car and grabbed Michael's arms and legs. Using his full weight, he struggled to hold the half-transformed human down. Michael had not yet achieved the mass and dimensions of a full werewolf; otherwise the grunting cop would not have stood a chance, not without shedding his own mortal semblance. "Do it!" he bellowed impatiently at Pierce. "Stick him! Stick him!"

The shouted commands meant nothing to Michael, whose intellect had all but vanished beneath a tidal wave of primal rage and abandon. All he cared about now was breaking free from the suffocating confines of the squad car. He could smell the anxiety of the two frantic policemen, and the provocative scent only served to madden him further.

Fighting back, he seized Taylor by the jaw, then viciously slammed the cop's head against the metal door frame. *Thwack!* Taylor staggered backward, clutching his battered skull. Momentarily stunned, the red-haired policeman dropped to his knees outside the car. Purple rage darkened his grimacing countenance as he gnashed his teeth and glared murderously at the uncooperative prisoner inside the car.

But before Michael could take advantage of Taylor's momentary incapacitation, the second cop surged forward, syringe in hand. Michael felt a sharp pain below his chin as Pierce stabbed the tip of the hypo into his neck. Pierce pushed the plunger home, and a sudden burning sensation spread through Michael's jugular vein out to the rest of his body.

He threw back his head and howled in agony.

Chapter Twenty-five

Kraven nervously approached the plexiglass barrier surrounding the recovery chamber. Through the transparent wall, he spied Viktor standing expectantly, his silken robe drawn about his towering figure. The continuing infusions of fresh blood had obviously agreed with the Elder; Kraven was chagrined to see how much Viktor's previously emaciated frame had fleshed out. The Elder was looking more and more like his old self, which did not sit well with his designated regent.

How in blazes can I wrest control of the coven from such a being, even with Lucian's help? Kraven railed inwardly at the sheer inequity of his situation. *Damn you, Selene! Why couldn't you have left Viktor in the earth where he belonged?*

"I sent for Selene, not you," Viktor stated, in a voice not nearly so dry and raspy as before.

Kraven bowed his head in genuflection. "She has defied your orders and fled the mansion, my lord."

Fury flashed across Viktor's gaunt, angular countenance. "Your incompetence is becoming most taxing."

"It's not my fault!" Kraven protested. "She's become crazed, obsessed!" He threw up his hands in exasperation. "She thinks I'm at the core of some ridiculous conspiracy."

"And here's my proof!" a defiant voice rang out.

By the gods, no! The blood drained from Kraven's face as Selene strode past him, gripping a middle-aged lycan by the throat. Kraven thought he recognized the man as one of Lucian's underlings.

Selene threw the lycan in front of Lucian and roughly forced him to his knees. The prisoner was bruised and bloody, his shabby garments riddled with gory bullet wounds. Kraven had no doubt that Selene herself had inflicted the damage on this miserable specimen of the lycan breed.

But why had she brought the creature here? What sort of proof was she talking about?

D-shaped steel anchors snapped out of the floor. Heavy iron chains rasped across the polished stone tiles. Adamantine shackles clanged shut, and Singe found himself on his hands and knees, cuffed and shackled, like a terrified peasant groveling for mercy before his king.

His red-streaked eyes still held a glint of rebellion. *You can subdue my body but not my mind,* he thought fiercely. *Lucian is my true liege and patron, not any bloodsucking parasite!*

The refrigerated crypt was uncomfortably cold. Singe shivered within his shackles, while his misused body ached from dozens of untreated wounds and injuries. Even though Selene had removed several bullets from Singe back at the safehouse, the better to keep her prisoner alive, he could still feel the remaining silver slowly infiltrating his veins and arteries, poisoning him by degrees.

Peering upward furtively, he took stock of his dire circumstances. He was trapped in the crypt with no fewer than three powerful vampires, each of them regarding him without mercy. The Elder behind the clear plastic barrier

272

was obviously Viktor; Lucian had informed Singe via cell phone of the Elder's unexpected resurrection, which had complicated their plans to no small degree. Despite his defiant attitude, the Austrian lycanthrope could not help feeling uneasy in the presence of such a primordial and puissant entity. From his research, he knew only too well of the preternatural capabilities of this immortal; Viktor was, at most, only one or two steps removed from the very source of the vampiric bloodline, which made him dangerous indeed.

The other male vampire disturbed him less. Singe recognized Kraven from the scheming regent's covert meetings with Lucian. At the moment, Kraven looked distinctly uneasy. Singe could see in the vampire's eyes that Kraven desperately wanted to flee the crypt yet felt compelled to stay and try to bluff it out.

I can't blame him for being nervous, Singe thought, enjoying the arrogant vampire's discomfort. *Not with the secrets he has to hide.*

And then, of course, there was Selene . . .

"Tell them!" she commanded him harshly. "I want you to tell them *exactly* what you told me."

Singe hesitated, reluctant to sacrifice his usefulness by immediately divulging all he knew. Perhaps there was some way to play these vampires against each other?

But Selene gave him no time to consider his options. Grabbing his arm, she jabbed her fingers into an open bullet wound in his shoulder.

"Ahhhh!" he yelped shrilly. The excruciating pain almost made him pass out. "All right! All right!" There was no way he could resist this torture for long; it seemed he had no choice but to tell the bloodsuckers everything.

Selene loosened her grip but did not let go of his arm.

She kept her fingers in the wound, as a tactile reminder of what Singe had in store should the injured lycan defy her again. Gasping from the traumatic shock to his system, Singe had to take a deep breath before speaking.

"For years," he began, "we've been trying to combine the bloodlines . . ."

Doped up and groggy, Michael was only half aware of being dragged down a dank, murky tunnel somewhere beneath the city. A subway train thundered by several feet overhead, rattling the crumbling brick catacombs. If he'd been more alert and clear-headed, Michael might have worried about getting buried alive.

His wrists were handcuffed tightly behind his back, while a thick piece of nylon webbing was wrapped around the lower half of his face, gagging him. On the brighter side, whatever he'd been dosed with had apparently reversed, at least for now, the grotesque metamorphosis brought on by the moonlight. He was fully human once more. *Do I need a prescription for that stuff,* he wondered fuzzily, *or can I get it over the counter?*

The alleged cops—Pierce and Taylor—said nothing as they hauled Michael through a maze of subterranean corridors, merely grunting in exertion as they each held onto their prisoner by one arm. Michael dimly glimpsed, out of the corners of his eyes, other brutish figures going about their business in this stygian underworld. Shadowy men and women, their eyes and teeth gleaming vibrantly in the dark, prowled through the tunnels, sometimes gnawing on disturbingly human-looking bones. A few of the women clasped nursing infants to their exposed breasts, but the misshapen babies struck Michael as more canine than hominid. Feral children chased one another past their elders, yipping and squealing like overexcited pups, while here and there throughout the twisting labyrinth, Michael occasionally glimpsed wild-eyed men and women copulating openly. Their bestial pants and moans added to the barbaric ambience of the catacombs as the frenzied lovers mounted each other with abandon, clawing and nipping at their mates' quivering flesh. The musky atmosphere was redolent of sweat and fur and filth.

Michael's eyes blinked blurrily in their sockets as he gradually shook off the narcosis clouding his mind, becoming more and more aware of his bizarre surroundings. The stench of the tunnels reached even through the nylon gag over his mouth.

Where am I, he wondered, frightened and disoriented, *and what the hell am I doing here?*

". . . trying to combine the bloodlines," Singe continued, his memory taking him back to his cramped, cluttered laboratory under the city. He remembered placing a drop of lycan blood on a slide, then peering at the sample through the lenses of a powerful microscope.

Then he'd added another drop of blood, this time from a plastic dropper labeled "Vampyre." Through the microscope, he could discern the physical characteristics that distinguished vampiric blood cells from lycan. Both species briefly coexisted within a minute sea of plasma.

Then, just as it always did, an instant reaction occurred: the opposing blood cells turned on each other, consuming the enemy hemoglobin in a pyrrhic orgy of mutual destruction until not a single viable cell remained.

". . . and for years we failed," Singe confessed. "It was useless. Even at a cellular level, our two species seemed destined to annihilate each other." He paused in somber contemplation of innumerable failed experiments, until a painful twist of Selene's fingers prompted him to continue. "That is, until we found Michael."

A complicated genealogical chart, spanning several generations, was posted to the wall of the subway station, which appeared to have been converted into some sort of improvised laboratory or infirmary. A banner printed along the top of the chart read "Corvinus Family Tree."

Michael stared in confusion at the yellowed chart even as Pierce and Taylor strapped him to a swiveling examination table. Taking no chances on Michael escaping, the men crisscrossed Michael's body with heavy-duty strips of nylon webbing, similar to the sturdy tape stretched tightly over his mouth. Michael's wrists were cuffed behind the cold metal table, so that his arms were bent at very uncomfortable angles.

This looks bad, Michael thought. So which side were his captors on, the vampires or the werewolves? Judging from the animalistic behavior he had glimpsed on his way here, Michael guessed the latter. *Werewolves,* he marveled bleakly, having passed beyond disbelief. His near transformation back in the squad car had wrung the last drops of skepticism from his mind. *I've been captured by werewolves.*

And he was one of them, sort of.

Shit, he thought wryly, finding a trace of dark humor in his outré situation. *Eight years of schooling, a mountain of debt, and now I'm doomed to become a werewolf.* He shook his aching head in disbelief. *Un-fucking-believable.*

The two lycans, as Selene called them, swung the table upward, elevating Michael's head, so that he found himself directly facing the elaborate family tree. Many of the names on the chart had an inky black line running through them, as though they had been stricken from the list for some reason. His baffled gaze dropped quickly to the very bottom of the chart—where an extremely familiar name was circled in red.

"A very special specimen," Singe continued, his shoulder still throbbing where Selene had cruelly dug her fingers into the wound. "A direct descendant of Alexander Corvinus, a Hungarian warlord who came to power during the early seasons of the fifth century . . . just in time to watch a plague ravage his village."

The lycan captive kept one eye on Kraven as he spoke, curious to observe the effect of his words on the double-dealing vampire regent. Kraven was figuratively sweating bullets, no doubt terrified that Singe would implicate him in the conspiracy. Singe caught the fearful vampire shooting a nervous look at the exit.

As well he should, the lycan thought.

"Corvinus alone survived the plague. His body was somehow able to mutate the disease, mold it to his benefit. He became the first true immortal." Singe grimaced in pain, acutely aware that his own prospects for eternal life were diminishing by the second. "And years later, he fathered at least two children who inherited the same trait."

Behind the transparent barrier, Viktor nodded impatiently. "The three sons of the Corvinus Clan," he observed with a tone of wry amusement. "One bitten by bat, one by wolf, one to walk the lonely road of mortality as an ordinary human." The Elder snorted scornfully. "A ridiculous legend, nothing more."

"That may be," Singe conceded, "but our two species unquestionably have a common ancestor . . . and the mutation of the original virus is directly linked to the bloodline of Alexander Corvinus."

Seated upon his throne, Viktor motioned toward the floor of the crypt, where a polished bronze hatch was emblazoned with an ornate letter *M*. "An heir to Corvinus lies there, not three feet from you."

Singe knew Viktor was referring to the undead Elder known as Marcus. "Yes," he replied, "but he is already a vampire. We need a pure source, untainted. An exact duplicate of the original mutated virus which we learned was hidden away in the genetic code of Alexander Corvinus's human descendants."

He remembered that glorious moment, when Michael's blood had tested positive back in his lab, before the jubilant eyes of both Singe and Lucian. He quickly had confirmed the results by placing a small sample of Michael's blood on a slide, then mixing it with an equal quantity of preserved vampire blood.

Through the microscope, he had watched intently as the vampiric blood cells swiftly bonded with Michael's mortal hemoglobin, producing unique two-celled platelets. The entire process had taken place in seconds, astonishing Singe with its speed.

But that was not the end of the experiment. Singe immediately had introduced a drop of lycan blood to the sample. Just as he had always envisioned, the double platelets bonded with the lycan cells, yielding the desired product: a singular-looking triple-celled platelet. Super blood, in other words, melding the best characteristics of all three species.

"The Corvinus strain allows for a perfect union," he explained to the attentive vampires.

Viktor's ancient face contorted in disgust. "There can be no such union," he declared emphatically, "and to speak so is heresy."

Singe lifted his head as much as his shackles allowed,

looking Viktor in the eye rebelliously. "We'll see about that," he chortled, "once Lucian has inject—"

"Lucian is dead," the Elder interrupted, cutting Singe off.

A crafty smirk crossed Singe's face. "According to whom?"

Selene's tormenting fingers withdrew from Singe's arm as she whirled around to confront Kraven. To her surprise, if not the lycan scientist's, the nefarious regent had vanished.

The female vampire clenched her fists in frustration, taking Kraven's escape as the ultimate admission of guilt.

"I knew it!"

Chapter Twenty-six

Kraven raced up the stairs from the crypt, fearful of Viktor's wrath. His face was drawn and slick with perspiration. Paranoid imaginings filled his brain. Once that loose-lipped lycan revealed that Lucian was still alive, that Kraven had not truly killed the illustrious lycan commander six centuries ago, there would be no safety for Kraven at Ordoghaz or beyond.

Once again, it was all Selene's fault. *God damn that ungrateful witch!* Kraven thought furiously. If only she had accepted his generous offer to rule at his side, none of these catastrophes would have occurred. *And all because she chose a mangy, flea-bitten lycan over me!*

He barged breathlessly into the grand salon. As usual, the opulent chamber was packed with stylish undead socialites. In anticipation of Amelia's overdue arrival, the languid sophisticates were wearing their finest evening attire. Expensively tasteful jewelry sparkled upon the throats and ears of the sleek vampire women, while their gentlemen companions sported medals and decorations acquired over centuries of faithful service to the coven and its Elders. The muted babel of numerous animated conversations was accompanied by the delicate melody of Bartok's String Quartet No. 1 playing softly in the background. Goblets of cloned blood were refilled dutifully by a discreet complement of serving girls bearing crystal pitchers of warm crimson plasma.

Ordinarily, Kraven would have been quite at home in this milieu, but now he eyed the chattering immortals with fear and suspicion. *Are they whispering about me?* he fretted. *Have I already fallen out of favor with my own kind, thanks to Selene and her perfidy?* Wringing his hands nervously, he noticed Amelia's envoy, Dmitri, standing vigilantly by the window that looked out upon the mansion's front yard. An impatient frown on his bony features, the ageless diplomat alternated between glancing at his gilded pocket watch and peering anxiously through the heavy velvet drapes at the driveway outside. No doubt, he was wondering what had become of his exalted mistress. How long would it be before he blamed Kraven for Amelia's nonarrival?

Kraven looked away, not wanting to make eye contact with the worried envoy. After all, he could hardly explain to Dmitri that Amelia had been met at the train station by a pack of ravening werewolves—especially since Kraven's original plans for a coup d'état were rapidly going down in flames. *This should have been my moment of glory,* he thought rancorously, *boldly taking charge of the vampire nation at the height of a historic crisis.*

Instead, it had become his Waterloo.

His eyes searched the crowded salon, looking for a minion he could rely on. Soren and his men, alas, had not returned from their mission in the city, leaving Kraven woefully short of allies. At first, he saw nothing but feckless libertines and voluptuaries, who would surely turn on him once his collusion with Lucian was exposed. Then, to his relief, he spotted Erika, serving drinks at the far end of the salon. The lissome servant girl, whom Kraven had last seen naked in his sumptuous boudoir, once again wore a sequined black maid's outfit. Her ivory skin was notably paler than usual, suggesting that she had not yet recovered from Kraven's voracious attentions.

Of course, he thought, recalling the girl's lovesick devotion. She was no Soren, to be sure, but then again, beggars couldn't be choosers.

Weaving hurriedly through the crush of undead bodies, he came up behind Erika and possessively grabbed her arm. The petite blond vampiress started, almost spilling a flagon of blood, then gazed up at Kraven with wide violet eyes.

He bent toward her, the better to whisper softly in her ear.

In the frigid atmosphere of the recovery chamber, Selene finished disconnecting the IV tubing from Viktor's arms, back, and chest. The Elder rose from his chair with obvious difficulty; it was clear that he had not yet regained his full strength. Fossilized bones creaked like rusty hinges.

"I can assure you, my child," he stated solemnly, "Kraven will pay with his life."

Selene was more concerned with Michael's life at the moment but shrewdly held her tongue. In the aftermath of Kraven's guilty flight from the crypt, Viktor appeared to have forgotten her own recent transgressions. She wisely judged that now was not the time to remind the Elder of her determined efforts to keep Michael out of the hands of the lycans. *Later, after Kraven and Lucian are dealt with, I can convince him that Michael is blameless in this affair.*

By contrast, her lycan prisoner—who apparently went by the name of Singe—felt free to speak his mind. Chained to the floor on the other side of the plexiglass divider, he grinned maliciously at his vampiric captors. "Soon this house will lie in ruins," he prophesied with a chuckle.

"Not before you," Selene stated darkly, as Viktor shot her a meaningful look. Alert to his wishes, she promptly exited the recovery chamber and seized Singe by the throat. Her face a mask of implacable hatred, she throttled the imprisoned lycan, fully prepared to choke the life from his worthless body.

"No, wait!" Singe croaked, barely able to speak. His bulging red eyes appealed frantically to Viktor. "You and you alone will know the truth of this!"

What truth? Selene wondered. She glanced back at Viktor, who raised his hand in reply. She obediently loosened her grip on the lycan's scrawny neck.

Singe coughed and gasped, sucking the cool air of the crypt into his famished lungs, before commencing to explain: "If Lucian is able to get his hands on the blood of an Elder, such as Amelia or yourself, Michael's blood will allow him to absorb the vampire blood without harm, joining it to his own lycanthropic hemoglobin."

Viktor reacted with horror and revulsion. "Abomination," he whispered hoarsely. The color drained from his already ashen features.

Selene felt lost. Viktor seemed to know what the lycan scientist was implying, but her own comprehension was lagging a few steps behind. *Dammit,* she thought. *I'm a warrior, not a biologist.*

"Lucian will become the first of a new order of being," Singe lectured, his Austrian accent torturing the Hungarian language. Despite his grievous injuries and the silver slowly poisoning his body, his eyes held a gleam of scientific enthusiasm as he warmed to his subject. "Half vampire, half lycan, but stronger than both." His gaze switched from Viktor to Selene. "The thing he's feared for centuries. A new breed." He nodded in Viktor's direction. "Look at him."

Selene turned her head toward Viktor. To her consternation, the kingly Elder looked just as worried as Singe foretold. Viktor's white vampiric eyes stared bleakly into space as though his very worst fears had been realized.

Is that what this is all about? she wondered, a chill running down her spine. *Lucian's desire to become some sort of hybrid monster?*

And Michael's blood was the key.

Flashlight beams raked the interior of the antique dining car, exposing a scene of ghastly carnage. Blood spattered the floor, walls, windows, and ceiling, while the ravaged bodies of Amelia and her entourage were strewn about like scraps from a cannibalistic feast. High-ranking members of the New World coven and Council had been torn apart and disemboweled, their mutilated remains testifying to the ferocity of their attackers' unleashed claws and teeth.

Mason, a veteran Death Dealer loyal to Kahn, had never seen anything like it. Although he had witnessed much violence during the long campaign against the lycans, the sheer ghastly enormity of the massacre shook him deeply. He glanced at the faces of the other two Death Dealers present and saw that they looked just as disturbed by what they had discovered aboard the violated train. The very air was thick with the smell of raw meat and blood. Vampire blood, spilled and wasted.

His appalled gaze turned reluctantly back to the ice-cold body at his feet. The Lady Amelia, oldest and most powerful of all female vampires, lay lifeless upon the floor of her private train, her bone-white body completely drained of blood. An expression of utter horror was etched upon her face.

Mason looked away. He decided that he had seen enough.

Extracting a cell phone from his long black trench coat, he speed-dialed the mansion.

"Mason here," he said curtly into the phone. "I need to speak with Kahn."

The heavy oak doors of the grand salon burst open. The booming noise silenced both conversation and Bartok, throwing a startled hush over the reception. The throng of elegantly tailored vampires parted like the Red Sea as Kahn marched into the chamber, flanked by a cadre of fully armed Death Dealers.

Cowering at the back of the crowded chamber, Kraven knew at once for whom Kahn had come. Judging from the smoldering fury in Kahn's dark eyes, Kraven knew he could expect no mercy at the hands of his former compatriots. *They know,* he thought with a certainty. His immortal heart pounded like the hooves of a runaway horse. *They know everything!*

He receded into the shadows as Kahn and his soldiers swept through the crowd, searching for the disgraced regent. Fortune favored Kraven as the venerable Dmitri demanded an immediate explanation for the Death Dealers' violent intrusion. The heated altercation gave Kraven the distraction he needed to slink surreptitiously through the crowd ahead of Kahn's advancing search party.

An open doorway presented itself enticingly, and Kraven scurried out of the salon with all deliberate speed. He bolted madly for the front door of the mansion, hoping with all his heart that the ride he had summoned would be there to meet him. *I can't let Kahn and his storm troopers catch up with me!* he thought cowardly, knowing that Viktor would have him tortured for all eternity for his crimes against the coven. *I must get away!*

No guards had been placed at the foyer, so Kraven ran unobstructed out of the mansion into the courtyard outside. His heart leaped in jubilation as a jet-black limousine came squealing to a stop right in front of the mansion's arched stone entrance. Soren sprang out of the limo and quickly opened the door, allowing Kraven to slide briskly into the backseat.

Thank the gods, Kraven thought. Sweaty and out of breath, he sank back against the charcoal leather cushions, exhausted by the strain of his narrow escape. Soren circled the limo and jumped in beside him, a loaded P7 pistol in his grip; the murderous janissary was ready to defend his master from whoever came after them.

Knowing that the sooner he put Ordoghaz behind him, the better, Kraven raised his hand to signal to the driver to depart. He was reaching for the door handle to pull it shut when a strident cry came from the front entrance of the mansion.

"My lord! Wait!"

Erika called out urgently to Kraven as she came dashing out the door toward the limo. A worn leather jacket had been thrown over her filmy black frock, but the chill of the evening still invaded her bones. There had been no time to dress more warmly, though, not if she wanted to join Kraven in his daring escape from Ordoghaz.

I'm coming, my love! she thought as her high heels clicked rapidly against the front steps. She didn't know the particulars of the scandal that had obviously overtaken Kraven, nor did she much care. It was enough that he had turned to her in his hour of greatest need. *He chose me . . . Erika!* She even forgave him for his abrupt departure from the boudoir earlier; it was clear now that nothing less than a crisis of the utmost magnitude had torn him from her fervent embrace. *This is my moment,* she exulted. At last, she had proven that she was the only vampiress who would always be there for him.

Her imagination soared ahead of her eager feet, picturing herself and Kraven winging away to some exotic foreign love nest where the exiled regent finally would reward her for her steadfast devotion, bestowing the plenteous bounty of his eternal affection upon her and her alone. She speculated excitedly about where their daring flight might take them. London? Paris? The Riviera?

Already halfway around the world in her Technicolor fantasies, she arrived breathlessly at the open door of the waiting limousine. Seated in the back, Kraven looked up at her expectantly. His probing brown eyes inquired whether she had done exactly as he had instructed.

Her triumphant face beaming in reply, Erika reached beneath her jacket and pulled out the weapon she had just stolen from Kahn's dojo in the loft. Exactly as Kraven had described it, the prototype gun with its silver nitrate cartridges was an extremely intimidating piece of ordnance. Erika felt like a Death Dealer just holding the massive gun.

Kraven smiled and snatched the pistol from her hand. Erika willingly relinquished the weapon, then moved to slide into the limo beside him. She saw, with a twinge of regret, that Soren was lodged in the back of the car as well. *Damn!* she thought. *Three's a crowd . . .*

Before she could enter the limo, however, Kraven slammed the door shut in her face. Erika stood frozen in shock, her jaw dropping toward the pavement as the deluxe limousine pulled away from her and took off toward the front gate. Kraven did not even give her so much as a backward glance before zooming away without her.

Erika watched the limo's taillights disappear into the night. She stood mutely at the edge of the driveway, stunned by the sheer enormity of Kraven's betrayal. *That's it!* she thought indignantly, fed up beyond all measure. She stamped her foot on the chiseled curb, nearly breaking the heel. *I'm through with Kraven forever.*

She wondered if Viktor liked blondes . . .

Selene unplugged the last of the IV tubing. A thin trickle of blood leaked from the end of its copper nozzle. She took Viktor by the arm, intending to help him rise from his chair, but he shrugged off her assistance. "I can manage," he said gravely.

For the first time since his resurrection, Viktor emerged from the claustrophobic confines of the recovery chamber. He stepped across the spacious crypt, pausing for a moment next to the bronze hatches that marked the individual tombs of the Elders. Selene wondered if he still planned to revive Marcus according to schedule, and it dawned on her that Amelia must be due at the mansion at any moment, if she had not arrived already.

Hurried footsteps approached the crypt by way of the security booth. For a moment, Selene thought that Kraven had returned, and she was both amazed and affronted by his audacity. *How dare he show his face before Viktor again,* she fumed, *after having deceived us all for years?* The slayer of Lucian, indeed!

But instead of the disgraced regent, it was Kahn who came rushing into the crypt. The veteran Death Dealer came to an abrupt halt as he laid eyes on Viktor. He bowed deeply before the Elder.

"My lord," he announced, "the Council members have been assassinated!"

Selene could not believe her ears. The entire Council? She glanced quickly at Viktor and saw that the all-powerful Elder was just as horrified as she. Freshly infused blood drained from his features.

"What of Amelia?" he asked somberly.

Kahn stared at the floor, unable to meet his master's eyes, but he did not shrink from delivering the awful truth. "They bled her dry."

Horror gave way to anger on Viktor's regal countenance. His hollow cheeks flushed darkly red. Selene had never seen him so incensed, not even when he had condemned her to judgment several hours ago.

For herself, Selene was rendered speechless by Kahn's catastrophic news. As much as she had despised Kraven, she had never thought him capable of conspiring in such a crime, yet she had no doubt that the vanished regent was deeply involved in the plot that had left Amelia and the Council dead. *This was a blatant attempt,* she realized, *to seize control of the entire vampire nation!*

Chained to the floor not far away, Singe smiled with malicious glee. "It has already begun," he crowed.

Viktor moved with lightning speed, so quickly that Selene barely realized he had lunged before the outraged Elder had crushed Singe's skull with a single blow. The prostrate lycan dropped lifelessly onto the cold stone floor, his wizened face pulped beyond recognition.

Selene was not even tempted by his blood.

Turning away from the ignoble carcass at his feet, Viktor approached Selene and gently lifted her chin. "I am sorry I doubted you, my child," he said gravely. "Fear not, absolution will be yours . . ."

Selene's heart lifted, grateful and relieved that her sire had not forsaken her. *I knew he would see the truth in time!*

". . . the moment you kill the descendant of Corvinus, this Michael."

Kill Michael? Selene stepped backward involuntarily, her rising spirits crashing downward. How could Viktor expect her to kill Michael in cold blood? It wasn't Michael's fault that his DNA was so dangerous. He was an innocent, albeit one contaminated by the lycan infection. *There must be some other way!*

Her face froze as she struggled to conceal her shocked reaction to Viktor's pronouncement. But Viktor had turned away from her. He briskly exited the crypt, followed closely by Kahn.

Selene lingered behind, wrestling with her turbulent emotions. A pool of bright red blood poured from Singe's shattered skull, spreading across the marble floor of the lonesome crypt. The scarlet tide lapped at the toes of Selene's boots, threatening to surround her.

Blood, she thought numbly. *Lycan blood.*

Just like Michael's.

Chapter Twenty-seven

Michael opened his bleary eyes, finding himself back in the converted subway station. *I must have dropped off again,* he realized, fighting to keep his heavy eyelids from descending once more. He tried to lift his head, only to have it fall backward against the hard steel examination table.

A voice spoke from the shadows of the ramshackle infirmary, just out of sight. "You were given an enzyme to stop the Change. It will take some time for the grogginess to dissipate."

Michael recognized the crisp British accent of the bearded stranger who had bitten him in the elevator two nights ago. *You!* Michael thought vengefully. *You're the one who did this to me, turned me into . . . whatever I'm becoming.*

If he were free, he would have leaped from the table and attacked the voice with his bare hands. But his wrists were still cuffed together behind the table, and heavy strips of nylon webbing immobilized the rest of his body, as though he were an Egyptian mummy being prepared for burial and not a nascent lycanthrope.

One of the two lycan cops, whose uniforms were probably as bogus as their human appearance, stepped forward. It was the long-haired one, Pierce, who had stabbed Michael with a hypo back in the squad car, when the young American's abortive transformation caused him to go berserk. Pierce flaunted an empty glass syringe, and his sadistic smirk made it clear he was looking forward to an encore.

He didn't bother to prep or disinfect the injection site; he just brutally jabbed the needle into Michael's arm. The captured American winced in pain, then lost his temper completely. *Screw this!* he thought furiously. *I'm tired of everybody treating me like an animal!*

He writhed helplessly against his bonds, but his frantic efforts snapped the needle off at its base. The syringe crashed to the floor, shattering into a hundred pieces. An impatient snarl came from the stranger in the shadows.

Pierce didn't like being embarrassed in front of the mysterious Brit. Growling with fury, he viciously backhanded Michael, hitting him so hard that he almost blacked out. Michael's head lolled to one side, and he blinked repeatedly, unable to focus. The inside of his skull was ringing like cathedral chimes.

"That's enough!" the unseen stranger barked. Even dazed, Michael heard the nameless Brit straining to contain his vexation. His voice was stern but firmly under control. "Just . . . go and see what's keeping Raze, will you?"

Pierce grudgingly backed away from Michael. His surly eyes shot Michael one last dirty look before he shuffled out of the infirmary. Michael groaned in misery as soon as the phony policeman appeared safely out of earshot. He shook his head, trying to clear the shock waves from his mind.

The enigmatic stranger stepped quietly from the shadows. "I really must apologize. Pierce is in desperate need of a lesson in manners."

As Michael's vision came back into focus, he saw that the

speaker was indeed the bearded stranger from the night of the subway massacre—when this whole craziness started. Michael recognized the man's deceptively genteel features, as well as the crest-shaped pendant dangling around his neck. The stranger seemed none the worse for being hit by Selene's speeding Jaguar. *Who the hell are you?* Michael thought, glaring at the soft-spoken Brit with a mixture of hate and dread. *And what do you want with me?*

"Speaking of manners," the man said casually, "where are mine?" He stepped nearer to the upraised examination table, close enough to bite Michael again if he felt so inclined. Instead, he bent down and removed Michael's gag. "Forgive me. I'm Lucian."

The name meant nothing to Michael.

"I need to go," he pleaded, struggling against his bonds. "I need to get back."

Lucian sighed and shook his head. "There is no going back, Michael. There's no going anywhere." He spoke slowly and carefully, as though instructing a slow-witted child. "The vampires will kill you on sight, just for being what you are. One of us."

He leaned even closer and looked Michael dead in the eye. "You *are* one of us."

No! Michael thought instinctively. *I'm a human being, not a monster!* But in his heart, he knew that Lucian was telling the truth, just as Selene had been. *I can feel myself changing inside.*

Jolted by Lucian's ominous statements, Michael failed to notice that the bearded lycan had produced a fresh syringe, until he suddenly felt the needle spearing his vein. He stared down in dismay as the cylindrical glass chamber filled with blood. "What are you doing?" he asked apprehensively.

Lucian kept his gaze on the syringe as he continued to

draw Michael's blood. "Bringing an end to this genocidal conflict."

"Your war has nothing to do with me," Michael insisted. He didn't even know which side to root for, the werewolves or the vampires. Lucian or Selene?

"My war?" Lucian asked harshly, and Michael sensed that he had hit a nerve. The bearded lycan tugged the syringe, now filled to capacity, from Michael's arm. Blood streamed freely where the needle had pierced his skin; a Band-Aid apparently was not on the agenda.

Lucian's free hand gravitated to the gleaming pendant upon his chest, drawing Michael's attention to the mysterious talisman. The sight of the pendant triggered a flood of bizarre, unaccountable memories. His eyes rolled upward, exposing their whites, as another round of hallucinatory sounds and images engulfed him.

His hand delicately swept along the edge of a gilded vanity table, tenderly exploring the combs, hairpins, and perfume bottles. Lifting his eyes, he gazed into the brass mirror above the vanity and found himself staring at his own reflection.

Lucian's reflection.

"Lucian?" Michael murmured weakly as he twitched spasmodically on the examination table. Now he understood, sort of. These had been *Lucian's* memories all along.

A.D. 1402. *Lucian and three of his lycan brothers made their way down a shadowy passage, on their way back to their den in the servants' quarters. Torches blazed from iron sconces mounted on the sooty stone walls. The sun had fallen outside, so they were no longer required to guard the castle from hostile humans. Their vampire masters once more could defend themselves.*

The clanking of heavy plate armor echoed down the corridor as a pair of Death Dealers advanced toward Lucian. The fear-

some vampire warriors marched in finely crafted suits of expensive Italian armor, quite unlike the antiquated leathers and chain mail worn by him and the other lycan sentries. Heraldic symbols were emblazoned on the vampires' steel breastplates, which easily could repel the wooden stakes or arrows of the superstitious mortals beyond the castle's walls.

Behind the armored Death Dealers, a procession of regal, pure-blooded nosferatu strode down the hall. Their elegant garb, much finer than Lucian's own simple garments, was trimmed with fur and embroidered with delicate gold thread. Gowns and cloaks of the choicest satins, silks, damasks, and brocades rustled as they approached, the hems of the vampire ladies' flowing gowns trailing behind them like silken shadows.

Stepping aside to let the lordly party pass, Lucian and his brothers lowered their gaze respectfully. Unlike his fellow servants, however, he could not resist sneaking a peek at the undead nobles as they glided past him.

And there she was! Sonja, the beauteous vampire princess of his most ardent desires. Her raven hair tumbled down onto her shoulders like the fall of night, and a gilt circlet rested gently on her head. Azure eyes gazed from a snow-white face of surpassing loveliness. A shining, crest-shaped pendant dangled from a chain around her swanlike throat. The priceless ornament rested securely on the ivory slopes of her bosom, above an embroidered burgundy gown.

She strolled beside Viktor, the undisputed master of the castle. A brocade cloak of a metallic golden hue rested on his imperious shoulders, its upright collar rising stiffly behind his neck. An intricate silver medallion, far more elaborate than Sonja's pendant, adorned his chest, while his dark satin breeches were girded at the waist by an ornate golden belt whose polished buckle bore a design similar to that of the medallion. Two matching silver daggers were tucked into the belt.

Lucian's face lit up at the very sight of the princess. He was riveted, unable to take his eyes off her. Conscious of his gaze, she turned and locked eyes with him. Caught! He felt a tremor of apprehension, until a playful grin appeared on her radiant features. Emboldened by her response, he smiled back at her, provoking an even wider grin. Her emerald eyes sparkled flirtatiously.

Alas, the buoyant exchange did not escape the notice of Viktor. A scowl turned his thin lips downward, and his expression darkened, yet he said nothing . . . for now.

Time jumped ahead suddenly, breaking the seamless flow of the ancient memories.

Lucian stared again into the gilded mirror, heedless of the silver beneath the polished glass. Sonja's reflection joind his as she slid up next to him, resting the soft curves of her body against his rougher form. They kissed, and she took his hand and gently pressed it to her belly. Beneath her satin gown, her belly swelled with the cherished life now quickening within her. Holding his breath in awe, Lucian could feel the baby stirring inside his adoring princess, the new and precious life their shared love had brought into being.

He smiled and kissed her again, feeling the passion rise once more. But before he could tell her again how much she meant to him, the door to her boudoir burst open. Viktor stormed into the bedchamber, his face a livid mask of rage—

Another break in the memories, as time took a jarring leap forward.

The medieval crypt was cold and damp. Sputtering torches threw writhing shadows upon the moldering stone walls. Rats scurried in the corners, alarmed by the sudden activity in the cavernous chamber. High above the floor, tucked away in a dark, umbrageous recess, a tinted black window admitted rays of filtered starlight into the fetid dungeon.

Viktor and his fellow Council members perched on craggy

stone pillars, like a flock of evil gargoyles looking down in judgment upon the floor of the crypt. Their luxurious velvet robes contrasted sharply with the dismal surroundings. They muttered darkly among themselves as a trio of armored Death Dealers dragged Lucian into the center of the crypt.

The scowling vampire warriors forced him to his knees. His body, already bruised and aching from the guards' rough treatment, was chained to the floor. The cold stones sent a chill through his bones, and he trembled despite himself. He was sore and hungry and thirsty, having been given neither food nor water since his capture. Despite this, he feared more for Sonja and her baby than for himself.

A horrified gasp caught his ears, and he looked up to see Sonja only a few feet away, suspended above him in some diabolical torture device. Her once-pristine gown hung in tatters on her slender frame. Iron and leather restraints held her fast, stretched cruelly against her flesh. Her snowy vampiric eyes were rimmed with red, and crimson tears ran in torrents down her smooth white cheeks. Lucian could not bear to see her mistreated so. Snarling like a mad dog, he tugged uselessly against his heavy chains.

Yet he and his princess were not the only prisoners in this forsaken place. To his dismay, he saw his fellow lycanthropes being herded into an iron cell by a superior force of sword-wielding Death Dealers. The confused servants yelped and whined piteously as the vampire soldiers locked them behind a swinging metal door. The iron bars of the cage were laced with silver alloy, the better to trap the distraught lycans inside.

Lucian's heart broke for his people. It was not just that they should be punished for his crime, if crime it was. His anger rose, supplanting any lingering fears for his own safety.

Soren, Viktor's brutal overseer, stepped forward, sporting a black beard he would eventually discard in the centuries to come.

He uncoiled a long silver whip, its gleaming links exquisitely crafted in the semblance of human vertebrae.

Lucian braced himself for the blow he knew was coming, yet no preparation could steel him against the searing pain as the silver whip viciously lashed his naked back again and again. The sculpted vertebrae made ribbons of his hide, burning his skin even as they sliced through his defenseless flesh, paring it to the bone. The pain was unendurable . . .

In her iron prison, Sonja flailed against her bonds and shouted desperately at Viktor and his ghoulish comrades. "Nooo! Leave him be!" she cried out on Lucian's behalf. "Stop it! Stop!"

But the lashes kept coming. Behind him, over the thunderous cracks of the whip, his lycan brothers and sisters went berserk, enraged to see one of their own kind tortured. Though caged, they threw themselves against the silver-tainted bars, growling like the untamed beasts within them. Without the moon's liberating glow, they could not shed their human guises, yet they raged like creatures of the wild, rending their crude woolen garments and gnashing their teeth. Angry curses gave way to lupine howls and roars as the pack voiced their primeval wrath against their one-time masters.

We will never forget this night, Lucian vowed, even as the merciless whip shredded his flesh anew . . .

In the lycan infirmary, Lucian looked on with concern as Michael Corvin spasmed in pain on the upright examination table. His head snapped from side to side, and anguished groans erupted from his cracked and bleeding lips, as though he were being flayed alive by some invisible tormentor.

Whatever can be wrong with him? Lucian wondered, not without a twinge of pity for the unlucky American. The enzyme he'd been injected with could not provoke this reaction. It was possible that these were the early throes of Michael's first full metamorphosis, yet he rather doubted it. Lucian had witnessed the rebirth of many a virgin werewolf, and these did not resemble the wrenching pangs of a lycanthropic transformation. Despite his obvious discomfort, Michael's skin and bones remained distinctly human.

I wish Singe were here, Lucian thought, wondering what had become of the old Austrian scientist, whom he had assigned to keep watch over the vampires' mansion. It had been several hours since he had heard from Singe and his contingent of lycan soldiers, and Michael looked in need of expert medical treatment. In theory, Lucian had extracted all the blood he needed from Michael, but he preferred to keep the young American alive. Michael was now a brother lycan after all.

The youth twisted and groaned on the table, lost in some hellish nightmare Lucian could not begin to envision.

Their vicarious blood lust satisfied at last, Viktor and the Council members exited silently from the crypt. They pounced effortlessly from their granite perches, then wound their way through an arched stone entrance. Their velvet robes rustled like cobwebs as they departed, and a heavy oaken door slammed shut, trapping Lucian inside the gloomy torture chamber.

Bloodied and exhausted, he collapsed onto the floor, which was now wet and sticky with his blood. Is this the end? he wondered, praying that the torment was finally over. Perhaps Viktor would be content with Lucian's destruction and spare Sonja and the others. He could not imagine that even the haughty Elder could condemn the beautiful princess forever, let alone her unborn child.

The scream of protesting metal reverberated nearby, echoing throughout the cavernous chamber. What? Lifting his head, Lucian spied two grim-faced Death Dealers wrestling with a heavy iron wheel mounted against the wall. The corroded wheel did not want to move at first, but the combined strength of the two vampires finally proved enough to crank the wheel in a clockwise direction.

As a result, timeworn metal gears began to squeak and grind against each other. Panic flooded Lucian's ashen face as he realized what the guards intended. Sonja also grasped what was transpiring. Her frightened eyes stared into his, terror-stricken.

Please, no, he begged silently, his parched throat too dry to speak, but the relentless gears kept on grinding. Directly above Sonja's head, a massive wooden hatch slowly creaked open. A fiery sun was carved into the underside of the oaken hatch, with a grinning death's head at its center.

Thunder boomed loudly outside the castle. Cold rain poured down through the open shaft, along with a deadly ray of misty sunlight.

No, not the sun! Not on her! Lucian lunged forward desperately, and the mighty chains snapped taut, holding him back. The iron shackles cut savagely into his flesh, yet he barely noticed the pain. He strained with all his might, working himself into a lather of blood and sweat, but there was not a damned thing he could do to save the woman he loved.

He could do nothing but watch as the first blood-red lesions appeared, popping and snapping across Sonja's delicate white skin. The unsparing sunlight shined down upon his princess's vulnerable flesh, which began to melt and liquefy as though she were being bathed in acid.

"Noooo!" he screamed hoarsely, his raspy cry of despair joining hers in one final, excruciating moment of communion . . .

Lucian watched in spellbound fascination as a single tear coursed down Michael's cheek. *Where is he now?* the lycan commander wondered. *What is he experiencing?* He felt an

300

unsettling and inexplicable kinship with the tortured American. *There is more here than mere bodily pain. He grieves as though his heart were breaking.*

His gaze remained fixed on Michael's unseeing eyes, as the American suffered beneath the illusory slings and arrows of whatever unseen demons haunted his mind.

Lucian shuddered uncontrollably on the floor of the medieval crypt, drained of tears and emotion. Several hours had passed, and the blood beneath him had long since dried. The killing sun had departed at last, and pallid starlight poured down through the open ceiling shaft.

Sonja was dead. All that remained of his beloved princess was a lifeless gray statue of charred bone and ash. Her powdery arms were raised above her in a futile effort to fend off the fatal daylight. A look of anguished sorrow, for both herself and her unborn child, was baked upon the statue's agonized features. Only a single metallic glint added a touch of color to the bleak gray figure: Sonja's crest-shaped pendant, still clasped around her carbonized throat.

The heavy wooden doors slammed open, admitting a howling wind into the desolate chamber. The furious gusts tore at Sonja's crumbling remains, causing her to disintegrate before Lucian's eyes. He sobbed violently as her ashes swirled past him like autumn leaves. Within seconds, not a trace of his beloved remained.

Two Death Dealers entered, the larger of the pair bearing a huge, two-handed axe. A ponderous stone chopping block was slid across the floor, and Lucian's head was forced ungently into the bloodstained grooves, which bore the doleful scent of many prior victims of the headman's axe. Sonja's death was not enough, he realized. Viktor demanded his life as well.

This came as no surprise.

The stately Elder entered behind the executioners, garbed in somber hues of mourning. Long-faced and solemn, he made his way across the chamber to the now-empty torture device that had recently held the departed princess. Of necessity, his polished boots crunched on the minute bits of charred bone that were all that was left of the beauteous and loving Sonja. If the dry, crackling noises troubled him, his dour face bore no evidence of it.

Ignoring Lucian completely, he bent low and gravely fished the shining pendant from the ashes. His eyes watered briefly, and a look of genuine grief flashed across his face, but it passed quickly as his aristocratic countenance reassumed a cold, distant expression. Rising from Sonja's ashes, he turned toward Lucian at last. Icy contempt and hatred smoldered in his eyes.

His callous inhumanity inflamed Lucian, and he matched Viktor's baleful gaze with a red-hot look of his own. Lucian's blood surged volcanically within his veins. "You bastard!"

He pounced at Viktor like the wolf he was, but unyielding chains jerked him back once more. The outraged Death Dealers fell upon him at once, bludgeoning his lacerated body with devastating kicks and blows. Fists and feet shod in forged metal plating crashed against him like a rain of meteors until his battered form dropped back onto the damp stone floor, panting and gasping.

But though his body lay defeated, his unquenchable fury still burned like the eternal fires of hell. "I'll kill you," he croaked through broken and swollen lips. "I'll kill you, you bloodsucking devil!"

Viktor stepped forward and grabbed his hair. He savagely yanked Lucian's head back so that he could stare into the lycan's pulped and bloody face. Viktor's regal face wrinkled in disgust.

"For you, death will come slowly. I can promise you that." A sadistic smile revealed his heinous intentions. "Forget the axe," he instructed his men. "Fetch me my knives."

At this moment, above the open ceiling shaft, the full moon slid into view from behind a bank of billowing storm clouds. The invigorating rays of the celestial lunar orb, god and goddess to Lu-

302

cian and his clan, shined down upon him, and he felt the Change begin. His blood-streaked eyes dilated dramatically as the color faded from his vision, giving way to the blurry, black-and-white perspective of a wolf. Renewed strength flooded his weary sinews as his body gained size and weight in the space of a heartbeat. Coarse black fur sprouted from his hide, hiding the ugly welt marks on his back. His hearing and sense of smell heightened immeasurably, so that he could practically taste the alarm in Viktor's blood as the Elder suddenly grasped his mistake.

You never should have let the moonlight find me, *Lucian thought vindictively. Now my power is at its peak!*

The transformation took place in an instant, and it was as a complete werewolf that he lunged once more at his persecutor. This time, the iron chains snapped before his inhuman strength, and he leaped at Viktor, his outstretched claws preceding him. With a single swipe of his shaggy arm, he snatched the gleaming pendant from Viktor's grasp.

Viktor recoiled from the werewolf's claws, stumbling backward across the crypt. He bumped into the iron bars of the adjacent cell, provoking a ferocious roar from within. The bestial noise alerted him to danger, and he threw himself away from the cell only seconds before a hairy arm clawed at him through the rigid metal bars.

He whirled around, stunned to discover that every one of the lycan prisoners had become a full-grown werewolf. The cramped cell was now packed with growling, snapping monsters, trying like hell to chew their way through the confining iron bars. The musky scent of a score of fur-covered werewolves filled the dank, unwholesome atmosphere of the torture chamber.

While Viktor blinked in surprise, the two Death Dealers charged at Lucian from across the room. Broken chains dangled from his wrists like decorative streamers, and he spun about with preternatural speed, sending the heavy chains slicing through the air at the oncoming warriors. The chains smacked loudly against his enemies' midsections, shattering their ribs.

An almost human smile distorted his wolfen snout. It felt good to be at the other end of the whip . . .

Heated shouts came from outside the crypt. Lucian moved to throw the heavy wooden doors shut, but he was too late. A squad of additional Death Dealers poured into the chamber, clutching silver-plated swords and pikes. "Get him!" Viktor shouted to his soldiers. "Kill that treacherous cur!"

There were too many of them. Even in wolfen form, Lucian could not stand against so many foes, not while his lupine allies still struggled to free themselves from their hateful cell. His eyes searched frantically for an escape route, coming to rest upon a tinted-glass window recessed in a dark alcove more than twenty feet above the floor. Eureka! he thought gratefully.

It was a long way up, but his powerful hind legs were sufficient to the task; exploding into motion, a single pounce landed him on the narrow stone ledge beneath the alcove. For a moment, he lingered on the limestone shelf, silhouetted against the darkly tinted glass. He looked back upon the ash-strewn site of Sonja's hideous demise, and he clutched her tiny pendant as if it was the most valuable treasure on earth.

Then he turned his murderous gaze upon Viktor himself, as the tyrannical Elder cowered behind his horde of vampire warriors. Someday, the werewolf's hate-filled eyes assured him, you will pay for what you have done to my princess and my people.

Crossbows laden with silver bolts aimed upward at Lucian, and he realized he could tarry no longer. Swiftly turning his back on the dungeon below, he dived headfirst through the blackened window. Shards of broken glass, flashing darkly in the moonlight, exploded outward as he fell through the air toward the ground below. Mercifully, he saw that the oppressive dungeon was located directly beneath the castle's outer wall. The open forest beckoned before his eyes.

Fragments of black glass rained down upon the rocky soil outside the fortress. Lucian hit the ground on all fours, then sprang up on two legs, standing as a man did despite the hairy pelt covering his body. He howled triumphantly at the savior moon even as angry cries and tumult erupted from behind the grim gray walls of the vampires' castle.

Behind him, the sinister fortress loomed ominously amidst the craggy Carpathian Mountains; before him, an impenetrable forest of dense mountain pines held out the promise of safety and freedom. He loped full tilt toward the sheltering woods.

The winter night was broken by the heated cries and pounding footsteps of a brigade of Death Dealers stampeding out through the castle's gate. The irate vampire warriors chased after the werewolf, hurling threats, curses, and unheeded commands at his fleeing back. Armor clanked loudly amid the towering pines, and silver crossbow bolts whistled through the air, coming to rest in the trunk of a bushy fir tree only inches from Lucian's head.

He ran from his determined pursuers as fast as aching hind legs could carry him. Clutching Sonja's precious pendant in his hairy paw, he escaped madly from his wretched past into the unglimpsed future . . .

Michael's eyes rolled back into place as the nightmarish visions let him loose at last. He blinked groggily and took several deep, ragged breaths before looking up into Lucian's watchful eyes. The bearded lycan regarded Michael with obvious curiosity and concern; he had no idea that Michael had just lived through the most harrowing hours of his life.

Michael felt sick to his stomach. *I understand now,* he realized numbly. "They forced you to watch her die. Sonja. That's what started this war."

Lucian's jaw dropped. He looked as if he'd just been hit by Selene's Jaguar all over again. The crest-shaped pendant—*Sonja's pendant*—glittered upon his chest. "How do you know this?" he asked in an awestruck whisper.

"I've seen it," Michael confessed. "Your memories. As if I were actually there." Obviously, Lucian's bite somehow had transferred more than just the virus that caused lycanthropy. "But why? How could he do that to her?"

Lucian's voice took on a bitter edge. "I was just a slave, of course, and she . . . she was Viktor's daughter."

His daughter? Michael's brain scrambled to make sense of all this new information. Selene had spoken highly of Viktor, claiming that he had saved her life after the werewolves killed her family. Could this possibly be the same vampire who had condemned his own daughter to death?

"They kept lycans as slaves?"

Lucian nodded. He slumped back against the edge of a rough-hewn lab counter, clearly shocked to be having this conversation. "We were their guardians during the daylight hours, the hellhounds of ancient lore. At one time, we had run wild, stalked by the vampires' relentless Death Dealers, who feared that we would incite the mortals' fury against both lycan and vampire alike, but by the fifteenth century, when Sonja and I dared to love each other, we had been thoroughly domesticated. We protected the vampires by day, and in return, they took us in, fed us, clothed us, and kept us under lock and key during the nights of full moon, when our unchecked depredations might have endangered us all."

He sighed, remembering. "It was an age of distrust and superstition. Suspected werewolves were being burned alive throughout Europe, while innocent corpses, and some not so innocent, were being staked and beheaded by fearful priests and peasants. We were forced to work together to survive, but they took advantage of the situation."

The venomous rancor returned to his voice, stoked by an undying fury that had survived the centuries. "It was forbidden, our union. Viktor feared a blending of the species. Feared it enough to kill his only daughter. Burned alive . . . for loving me."

To Michael's surprise, Lucian rolled up his own sleeve. He leaned back against the crumbling wall of the old subway station. "This is his war. Viktor's," Lucian said with simmering ire. "He's spent the last six hundred years exterminating our species."

He jabbed the needle into his arm, injecting Michael's blood into his own veins. "And your blood, Michael, is going to bring an end to it all."

My blood? Michael thought, baffled. He still didn't understand that part. *What's so special about me?*

Chapter Twenty-eight

$\mathcal{A}$ knock at the door of the infirmary interrupted Lucian's tense conversation with Michael. He turned away from the captive American as Pierce and Taylor entered the refitted subway station. The two lycans had discarded their ersatz police uniforms in favor of their usual brown leather attire. "We have company," Pierce announced.

Of course, Lucian thought. He did not need to ask who their guests were. Only Kraven and his minions knew of this hidden lair.

Nodding, he calmly extracted the needle from his arm. He placed a finger against the crook of his elbow, applying pressure to the site of the puncture. Michael's singular blood cells now flowed through his veins; he was one step closer to his long-sought apotheosis. All he needed now was the blood of an elder vampire to complete the process and bring him the victory he had craved for centuries.

This close to success, Kraven and his thugs were an unwelcome annoyance. Lucian could only assume that Kraven had bungled things at the manor if he was now seeking sanctuary in the lycans' subterranean lair. *The fool,* Lucian thought in contempt. Soon he would no longer require Kraven's deceitful cooperation.

He headed for the exit, anxious to complete the night's historic business. "Wait!" Michael called out as Lucian walked away deliberately. In truth, the lycan leader nearly had forgotten about the captured American. "What about Selene?" the young man asked anxiously.

That vampire bitch? Lucian recalled. *The one who shot me full of silver a few nights back?*

She would perish with the rest of her despicable breed.

Lucian's private quarters, located deep within the underworld, were distressingly unlike the luxurious settings Kraven was accustomed to. Dark and dismal in the extreme, the bleak compartment reflected the joyless and obsessive nature of its absent owner. Stark metal shelves, loaded with rolled-up maps and stores of UV ammunition, jutted from disintegrating brick walls, while an ugly steel desk occupied one corner of the claustrophobic chamber. A detailed map of Ordoghaz, its defenses and interior layout, was spread out atop the metal desktop, with the exact location of the Elders' crypt circled in red. A yellowing skull, with unmistakably vampiric fangs, rested atop a nearby shelf, and Kraven couldn't help wondering whose skull it was.

Grease-stained windows looked out onto the bunker's cavernous central chamber, the size of a jet hangar. Far too many lycans, at least for Kraven's taste, scurried about outside, coming and going on elevated catwalks and subway tracks like so many foul-smelling, subhuman worker ants. The noisome atmosphere of the lair stank of petroleum, animal droppings, and lycan piss.

Kraven held a silk handkerchief over his mouth and nose, but it did little to keep out the stench. *How have I sunk to this?* he thought bitterly. *I should be presiding over a palace, not hiding beneath the earth in a den of filthy animals!*

Lycan soldiers surrounded Kraven and his meager security force. The snarling beast-men held the vampires at gunpoint while they waited upon Lucian's pleasure. Kraven prayed there were no itchy fingers among the barbaric henchmen.

After several tense minutes, Lucian entered the chamber. He regarded Kraven and the others with ill-concealed annoyance.

"I thought we had a deal!" Kraven accused him. *How dare this presumptuous canine treat him like an unwanted intruder!*

"Patience, Kraven," Lucian replied. His seeming civility barely masked a mocking, dismissive tone. The lycan commander gestured at Kraven's men while addressing his own. "I would speak with Lord Kraven alone. Please escort the rest of our guests to the lounge."

Kraven found it hard to believe that anything as civilized as a visitors' lounge could be found in this foul, abysmal kennel. Nevertheless, he nodded at Soren, consenting to the arrangement. It was important, after all, to retain some semblance of authority, even as events rapidly spun out of control.

Six hundred years of planning, he reflected sourly, *and everything goes to hell in the last forty-eight hours!*

Reluctantly, Soren let himself and the other bodyguards be led away from Lucian's quarters. He glanced unhappily over his shoulder at Lord Kraven, until the master and his lycan counterpart disappeared from view. He didn't like leaving Kraven alone, not one bit.

A pack of lycan scum escorted them at gunpoint through a maze of winding, unmarked catacombs. Two of the subhuman savages were familiar to Soren. He identified the pair, from previous dealings with Lucian, as Pierce and Taylor. He regretted that Raze was not among them.

Vampire and lycanthrope marched in sullen silence, trading only hostile glares and sneers. Their uneasy trek ended at the rear of what appeared to be another abandoned bunker, where the long-haired lycan, Pierce, demanded that the vampires surrender their weapons.

Outnumbered and under the gun, Soren instructed his men to turn over their firearms. He glowered sullenly at both Taylor and Pierce as he handed over his own HK P7. An impertinent lycan frisked him for hidden weapons, but the vampire's baleful gaze and intimidating attitude ensured that the search was both short and perfunctory.

Satisfied, the lycan escorts stepped aside to let Soren and his men enter the indicated chamber.

The undead janissary arched a suspicious eyebrow at what he found within. The so-called lounge was surprisingly hospitable-looking. A plush red carpet covered the floor of the long, narrow chamber, while the original benches apparently had been ripped out and replaced with richly upholstered couches and easy chairs. Heavy damask curtains covered the windows, and frosted amber ceiling lamps cast a warm golden glow over the premises. There was even a decent maple coffee table, stacked with dog-eared reading material. Nature and hunting magazines, primarily, a trifle out of date.

If you squinted, you almost could pretend you were back in the mansion.

Almost.

I don't like this, Soren thought warily. Why would gutter-dwelling lycans need a place like this? How often could they expect honored guests?

He glanced back at the entrance. Pierce grinned evilly at Soren as he slammed the door shut. Soren heard the sound of heavy locks falling into place.

Hellfire! Growling, he ran to the nearest window and tore down the curtain. Beneath the heavy drapes, thick plexiglass windows were reinforced with gleaming titanium bars at least three centimeters across. He pounded angrily on the unyielding plastic, his worst fears confirmed.

This was no lounge. It was a trap.

"Son of a bitch!"

Back at Lucian's quarters, Kraven waited for the lycan leader to treat him with the respect he deserved. *I am your ally in this affair,* he thought testily, *not some pawn to be disposed of.*

Visibly impatient, Lucian took a calming breath before addressing Kraven in soothing tones: "The Council has been destroyed. Soon you will have it all. Both great covens and a historic peace treaty with the lycans." He flashed a conspiratorial smirk. "Who I trust will not be forgotten when the spoils of victory are tabulated."

Lucian's silky assurances were not enough to allay Kraven's concerns. "How do you expect me to assume control?" he demanded irritably. Their original plan—to take command of the covens in the confusion following the Elders' assassination—lay in ruins. "Now that Viktor's been awakened, there is no defeating him. He grows stronger even as we speak!"

That did not appear to worry Lucian. "And that is precisely why I needed Michael Corvin."

He gave Kraven a cryptic smile.

* * *

The armory.

A half dozen lycans went about their duties, loading ammo, cleaning weapons, and generally preparing for an all-out assault on the vampires' mansion. Bright-eyed men and women, wearing shabby brown clothing and military fatigues, beamed in anticipation, eager to carry their ancient war to the enemies' very doorstep.

The sharp report of gunfire immediately electrified the soldiers inside the old bunker. They snatched up their weapons instinctively. Had the cowardly bloods launched a preemptive strike?

The door burst open, and Pierce and Taylor stuck their heads through the entrance. High-caliber semiautomatic weapons were clutched tightly in their hands.

"Entrance shaft alpha!" Pierce shouted. "Move it!"

Lucian's quarters.

Kraven and Lucian shared a surprised look as the unmistakable roar of gunfire echoed through the meandering tunnels. For an instant, Kraven feared that Soren and his men had been summarily executed by Lucian's forces, but no, the gunshots seemed to be coming from a different direction— not that he could tell easily in this bewildering maze of rat holes!

Within seconds, an even more dismaying explanation hit him with the force of certainty. *Death Dealers!* he realized, his face going pale. *Kahn and Selene and the rest of their leather-clad assassins. Maybe even Viktor himself.*

His undead heart pounded within his chest.

They've come for me!

The rusted metal grate was just where Selene remembered it, but now the grate itself had been torn up and carelessly tossed to one side, leaving only a gaping black pit in the floor of the drainage tunnel. She recalled running for her life through this very tunnel, pursued by an enraged were-wolf.

Had that truly been only two nights ago? She felt as though her entire world had turned upside-down since then. *Before I knew what my purpose was, where my loyalties lay,* she lamented privately. *Now I'm not so sure.*

She and Kahn stepped over the lifeless bodies of a pair of lycan guards. Each corpse bore a single bloody bullet wound in its forehead. The dead lycans had defended the entrance to the werewolves' underground lair, but not for long. Selene had to assume, however, that the short-lived gun battle had been heard in the unexplored catacombs below.

So much for the element of surprise, she thought.

Kahn raised his hand, signaling the Death Dealers behind him. The assault team, consisting of six additional opera-tives, swept forward, staking out defensive positions in the newly secured stretch of tunnel. Oiled black leather helped the taciturn Death Dealers blend in with the inky shadows around them. AK-74 assault rifles, loaded with silver ammo and equipped with infrared night scopes, were prepped for action.

Selene chose to stick with her trusty Berettas. She kept her guns raised and ready as Kahn cautiously approached the open pit. Peering over his shoulder, she saw that the top of the shaft had been surrounded with chain-link fenc-ing and concertina wire. Apparently, the lycans didn't want visitors.

Tough, she thought coldly. One way or another, she was going to find Michael.

Kahn unhitched a silver-plated grenade from his belt and pulled the pin. He tossed it toward the pit, and Selene held her breath as the explosive device bounced noisily across the cement like a huge ball bearing. It clinked one more time before disappearing over the edge of the pit.

Selene thought she heard something moving below . . .

Chapter Twenty-nine

*S*een from the bottom, the yawning pit was revealed to be an old elevator shaft lined with steel ladders. Taylor and the other lycans scrambled up the ladders toward the unknown source of the echoing gunshots. In theory, two of their fellow lycans were posted at the top of the shaft, but Taylor wasn't holding out much hope for their chances. If they had been the ones doing the shooting, they already would have called for reinforcements.

Damn bloods! It was just like them to stage a sneak attack right before Lucian's master plan came to fruition. *We've got them running scared,* he decided, putting a positive spin on the situation. *They know their days are numbered.*

Then the grenade tumbled past him.

His beady eyes widened in alarm as the silver fragmentation device clanged against the concrete walls before splashing down into the deep puddles of murky water at the bottom of the shaft. "Oh, shit!" Pierce swore, only a few rungs beneath him.

Like every other lycan climbing the ladders, Taylor threw himself flat against the metal rungs, trying to present as narrow a target as possible.

A flash from below was followed instantly by an earth-shaking blast that sent a fountain of sludge rocketing up the shaft, along with a spray of white-hot silver shrapnel. The toxic fragments sliced through lycan flesh and clothing, shredding Taylor and the others to ribbons. His leather gear was instantly turned into bloody confetti. He screamed in agony as he lost hold of the ladder and fell backward down the shaft.

Taylor crashed to earth a split second after Pierce, but they were both dead before they hit the ground.

Lucian's quarters.

An explosive tremor rocked the cramped compartment. The heavy steel desk teetered like a wobbly stool, while the windows rattled and lightbulbs flickered and popped. The skull on the bookshelf, which had once belonged to a particularly formidable Death Dealer, toppled from its perch, crashing into bony fragments upon the hard concrete floor.

Sweat ran down Kraven's aristocratic features. "Viktor," he murmured fearfully, while Lucian sneered at the cowardly vampire quisling. The gunfire and explosion were alarming, true, but Lucian held onto his nerve without difficulty. He had been in far tighter pinches than this over the last six hundred years.

I hope Viktor is here, he thought. His fingers stroked the precious pendant upon his chest. *We have old scores to settle, he and I.* The dreaded Elder was powerful, but soon Lucian would be more than his match. *All I need is Amelia's blood.*

Another explosion shook the underworld. Lucian heard the strident wail of twisting metal coming from outside his private chamber, and he rushed to the window, pressing his face against the streaky glass.

The compartment looked out onto the enormous central cavity of the bunker itself. Catwalks, ladders, and tiers of forgotten subway tracks covered the towering walls of the massive excavation like rusty metallic ivy. Lucian's gray eyes narrowed in concern as, near the top of the gargantuan bunker, a huge steel pipe burst asunder, releasing a torrent of pressurized water high above the lower levels of his people's sanctuary. An artificial deluge poured down upon the underworld like a sudden storm.

Lucian bit his lip. *This complicates matters,* he fretted, praying that the flooding would not interfere with Raze's delivery of the final injection. *I need an Elder's blood within me to achieve the next level of immortal evolution.*

"Is there another way out?" Kraven asked him anxiously, like a rat already preparing to desert a sinking ship. The ousted regent wrung his hands as his shifty gaze darted about the room, hoping perhaps for a secret passageway out of the bunker altogether.

Lucian turned away from the window. He regarded his supposed ally with disgust. "I guess it never occurred to you that you might actually have to bleed a bit to pull off this little coup."

He tugged a UV pistol from his belt and racked a brightly glowing round into the chamber. The vampire winced at the sight of the luminous ammunition, and Lucian shot him a threatening look. "Don't even think about leaving."

The lycan commander whirled toward the door. The sooner he rendezvoused with Raze and received the final injection, the sooner he would be able to exact gory vengeance on Viktor and his bloodsucking parasites.

BLAM-BLAM-BLAM! A bone-shattering impact slammed repeatedly into his back. He collapsed face first onto the dusty concrete floor, feeling a burning sensation along his spine. *Silver,* he realized instantly, recognizing the excruciating heat at once. *I've been shot!*

With effort, he lifted his head from the floor and looked back over his shoulder. Kraven stared down at him, clutching a smoking pistol of unfamiliar design. The preening vampire smirked as he contemplated his perfidious handiwork.

You'll pay for this treachery, Lucian vowed, *once I expel these cursed bullets from my flesh.* He closed his eyes, and his lofty brow furrowed in concentration as he sought to rid his body of the deadly silver, just as he had done only a few nights before. Time was of the essence; he needed to squeeze out the bullets before the toxic metal poisoned him irrevocably.

To his distress, however, the fiery venom already seemed to be racing through his veins and arteries. Shocked and confused, he raised his hand before his eyes. The shallow veins running along the back of his hand grew swollen and discolored as he watched. The dark gray tracery extended from his wrist to his fingertips, pulsating beneath his skin.

What foul invention is this? he thought, eyes wide with horror. An agonized groan escaped his lips.

"Silver nitrate," Kraven explained breezily. He stepped forward and pried Lucian's own pistol from the lycan's palsied grip. "I wager you weren't expecting that."

The armory.

More lycans poured into the crowded bunker, snatching guns and ammunition from the mounted weapon racks. Other lycans, disdaining human modes of combat, ripped apart their garments, hastening the Change. Claws extended from splayed human fingers. Knife-sized fangs stretched open protruding muzzles. Bushy black fur clothed naked skin, which took on an inhuman bluish-gray hue beneath the thick, matted hair. Twitching snouts sniffed the air. Foam dripped from hungry jaws.

Gun-toting soldiers jostled shoulders with shaggy biped beasts. Heated profanities competed with canine growls as the pack rushed to defend its lair.

The final battle had begun.

The prison chamber.

Soren paced restlessly up and down the spurious "lounge." His fists were clenched at his sides, and he hissed through clenched fangs as he heard the unmistakable sounds of warfare without. To be locked away from the combat, trapped inside this sumptuously furnished cage, infuriated him.

More shouts and gunfire echoed outside. Frustrated, his men looked to him for a solution. His dark brown eyes scanned the interior of the camouflaged prison chamber, settling on a vertical chrome pipe about five centimeters in diameter. *That will have to do,* he decided.

He seized hold of the post with both hands and attempted to wrench it from its setting. It was sturdier than it looked, which boded well for his ultimate objective. Straining his muscles, he snapped the pipe off at its base. He twirled the liberated bar in his grip, then aimed it at the locked steel door like a battering ram.

Armed lycans stalked down a debris-littered access corridor leading to the violated entrance shaft. The gloppy floor was awash in the blood and mangled remains of their murdered comrades. Fragments of deadly silver shrapnel were still embedded in the flaking brick walls surrounding them.

More fully transformed werewolves joined their ranks, crawling up through open sewage grates from dens and whelping chambers one level down. Their monstrous, over-sized heads and pointed ears brushed against the soot-stained ceiling, and their enormous paws left Sasquatch-sized tracks in the rampant blood and gore. The beasts' furry hackles were raised in warning, and their rub-bery black lips were peeled back to expose their serrated yellow teeth. Cruel cobalt eyes glowed in the shadows.

The mixed lycans and werewolves crept closer to the arched stone doorway opening onto the entrance shaft. Grisly evidence of the devastating explosions was every-where, in the freshly gouged brickwork and in the splat-tered residue of their fallen pack mates. Smoke hung in the charnel-house atmosphere of the shaft, and the acrid odor of gunpowder and high explosives offended the sensitive nostrils of the werewolves on point, making it all the harder to scent their prey. A faint metallic click came from above, and the beasts' ears rotated toward the noise.

Too late! Gunfire erupted from the top of the blood-spattered elevator shaft, driving the wolves and lycans back before a blistering cascade of unleashed firepower.

Taunting gravity, Selene and the Death Dealers came swooping down through the veil of smoke like leather-clad angels of death. Bright white flashes blazed from the muzzles of their clattering weapons as they cut down the first wave of lycan defenders. The clamorous report of the guns drowned out the screams and yelps of lycans and werewolves alike. Bodies both human and otherwise dropped onto the floor of the tunnel, joining the ghastly agglomeration of mud, blood, and shredded carcasses clotting the corridor.

Although caught off guard, the surviving lycans hur-riedly regrouped and took the battle back to the enemy. All hell broke loose as the embattled defenders returned fire. Red-hot silver streaked past glowing UV rounds in the smoky air between the oncoming vampires and the besieged lycans.

Selene impatiently squeezed the triggers of her twin Berettas. She emptied one pistol completely, then discarded the spent weapon. This was taking too long; the lycans were putting up too much resistance. She didn't have time for this.

She needed to find Michael.

The prison chamber.

A metallic clang reverberated through the plush containment cell as Soren rammed the ruptured steel bar into the locked door at the end of the refitted bomb shelter. The door shuddered in its frame before bursting from its hinges. It landed with a heavy thud on the floor of the decaying brick tunnel outside.

Soren was the first one out the exit, quickly followed by the rest of his security team. His palm itched for his captured P7. He felt naked without a loaded firearm.

A burly lycan, his rumpled shirtfront bearing the greasy residue of an interrupted meal, came charging around the corner, no doubt attracted by the noisy demise of the prison door. He gripped a butcher knife in one hand and a wooden stake in the other.

Soren swung his metal staff like a baseball bat, catching the oncoming lycan in the midsection. Ribs shattered with a satisfying crunch, and the poleaxed barbarian dropped to the ground, where Soren gave his skull a few more whacks for good measure.

I'd rather be demolishing Raze, he admitted, frowning, *but this unwashed savage will do for now.*

Once he was convinced the pulverized lycan wasn't going to be getting up again, Soren stepped back from his victim and tossed the brute's knife and stake to two of his unarmed men. To his disappointment, the dead lycan didn't appear to be carrying anything with a bit more firepower.

Very well, he conceded, hefting his bloodied staff. He didn't need bullets to kill lycan scum.

His narrowed eyes searched the darksome tunnels, trying to remember the route back to Lucian's quarters where he had left Kraven with the treacherous lycan leader. Why did these loathsome animals have to live in such a tangled warren, anyway?

This way, he decided quickly. He nodded at the other vampires. "Move, come on!" Holding the captured steel rod like a club, he led his men away from the prison chamber.

It was time to teach their lycan allies a lesson.

Raze held on tightly to the large glass syringe, filled with the blood of the female Elder, as he hurried in search of Lucian. The lair was clearly under attack by their enemies, but the scarlet elixir in the syringe, combined with the mortal blood Lucian already had injected into his veins, surely would deliver victory to the pack, provided he got the blood to Lucian in time.

These arrogant bloods are in for a nasty surprise, he mused, grinning wolfishly in anticipation. Soon Lucian would be unstoppable.

He arrived within minutes at Lucian's private quarters. Barging into the room unannounced, he was shocked to find a familiar figure lying motionless in a puddle of blood upon the gritty concrete floor. A metallic pendant glittered around the casualty's neck.

"Lucian!" The lycan lieutenant could not believe his eyes. Their supreme commander was sprawled face first in the blood. Gory bullet wounds, leaking a peculiar metallic fluid, gaped from the back of Lucian's brown leather duster, making it abundantly clear how the legendary immortal had met his end.

Those stinking bloods have betrayed us! Raze raged inwardly. And by slaying Lucian, they had extinguished the pack's last, best hope for victory over the hated vampires. Despair vied with blood lust within the lycan's wild heart. *We should never have trusted those cold-blooded leeches!*

Rapid bootsteps approached from outside. Raze tore his homicidal gaze away from Lucian's martyred corpse to see Soren—*Soren!*—and his men rush through the bunker's main chamber, looking slightly lost. A cascade of water poured down from a broken pipe high overhead.

Raze shook with fury, unable to contain himself. For all he knew, Kraven's detestable bodyguard had fired the shots that had killed possibly the greatest lycanthrope of all time. The blood-filled syringe slipped from Raze's shaking fingers, to shatter upon the hard cement floor. He didn't even notice as he maniacally threw himself through the window at the vampires.

Glass exploded outward as Raze tackled Soren, knocking a bloodied steel truncheon from the janissary's grasp. Grunting and growling, they rolled across the drenched, uneven floor of the bunker before breaking apart and springing to their feet a few meters away from each other.

Soren's henchmen surged forward, but the vampire waved them back, a bloodthirsty smile on his face. He had been looking forward to this battle for as long as Raze had. He peeled off his leather jacket, revealing a pair of twin silver whips wrapped tightly around his torso. Sneering at his bald-headed lycan nemesis, he uncoiled both whips in two fluid movements.

The infirmary.

Growls, gunshots, screams, and explosions gnawed away at Michael's nerves as he frantically struggled to free himself from the angled examination table. He was alone in the dingy laboratory, while what sounded like an all-out war raged somewhere outside the walls of the converted subway station.

I've gotta get out of here! He panicked. His veins stood out like steel cords as he strained to break apart the cuffs trapping his arms behind the table. The cold steel edges of the cuffs dug into his wrists, threatening to cut off his circulation, but Michael kept tugging on the chain. Anything was better than being locked up inside a war zone, unable to defend himself.

At the back of his mind, an eerie howl was rising again. Whatever those "cops" dosed him with was apparently wearing off; even God knows how many feet beneath the ground, Michael somehow could sense the moon ascending in the distant sky, shining full and bright over the city above. Its celestial influence penetrated dense layers of stone and concrete to trigger something dark and primordial within Michael's soul. Goosebumps broke out on his skin, and every hair on his body seemed to stand up at attention. His heart rampaged wildly, flooding his veins with renewed strength and adrenaline. *One more try,* he thought stubbornly, straining his quivering muscles to the utmost.

SNAP! The chain linking the cuffs broke apart, freeing his arms. He had torn a solid metal chain in two.

"Holy shit," Michael whispered.

Chapter Thirty

*T*he silver whips felt at home in Soren's grip, just as in the old days when he had served as overseer on Viktor's sprawling estate in the Carpathians, before the damned lycans rose up in revolt. *Time to remind these insolent mongrels of their place,* he decided.

"Go!" he ordered his men gruffly. "Keep looking for Lord Kraven." Standing on the soaked floor of the bunker's main chamber, he faced off against that black barbarian, Raze. Water rained down from above, slowly flooding the vast excavation. "Don't worry," he assured the other vampires as they fanned out into the branching tunnels. "This won't take long."

One after another, the whips lashed out, claiming first blood. Twin lacerations opened on Raze's cheeks, and the snarling lycan raised a hand to his face, bringing away fingers stained brightly red.

Soren smiled, pleased that Lucian's guards had missed the coiled whips earlier. Next time, they would have to frisk him more carefully—if there was a next time.

Angry brown eyes glared back at Soren, then instantly changed color, turning a brilliant shade of blue. A low rumble began in Raze's broad chest, rapidly deepening in timbre. Bone and gristle crackled loudly as the lycan's shaved skull began to stretch and deform.

Despite his confidence and adamantine sense of certain superiority, Soren felt a tremor of apprehension as his lycan adversary transformed before his eyes.

Lucian's quarters.

More explosions rocked the underworld, rousing Lucian despite the silver nitrate that was surely killing him. His seemingly lifeless body twitched on the floor, and he slowly forced his eyes open.

Groaning in misery, he sat up and rested his back against a hard brick wall. His somber garments were soaked through with his own blood, and he could taste the deadly silver on his swollen tongue. He reached instinctively for Sonja's pendant, relieved to find it still dangling from his neck.

He was dying, he realized, but he was not done yet.

The lycans' sleeping quarters were just as revolting as Kraven had envisioned them. Filthy mattresses littered the floor, along with gnawed bones and half-empty bottles of wine and beer. Crumpled pornographic magazines of exceptional coarseness added to the squalor, along with heaps of unwashed clothing. The pungent stench of the place was unendurable.

The mattresses were unoccupied now, with every lycan gone to defend his sanctuary, so Kraven had the squalid chamber to himself. He looked about him in haste, trying to figure out the quickest way back to the surface—and out of the catastrophe his eternal life had become.

Footsteps sounded in the corridor outside, and Kraven froze in fear. He wasn't sure whom he dreaded most, the rapacious lycans or the invading Death Dealers. It might even be preferable to be devoured by a horde of carnivorous werewolves, rather than face Viktor and his unthinkable wrath.

At least I don't need to worry about Lucian anymore, he consoled himself, happy to have blasted the lycan leader full of silver nitrate. It was perversely amusing in a way: after years of falsely taking credit for Lucian's death, he finally had killed the legendary monster after all. *It's not a lie anymore but too late to do me any good!*

The footsteps turned out to belong to a squad of lycan soldiers rushing past the doorway. Kraven retreated into the shadows of the sordid den, hiding from sight.

There has to be some way out of this calamity, he thought. He held his breath as he listened to the snarling lycans. A cold sweat glued his silk tunic to his skin. *I've lived too long and too well to die in some godforsaken sewer!*

So far, lycan tenacity had proven no match for Death Dealer expertise. Their enemies either fallen or fleeing before them, Selene and Kahn had swept relentlessly down the cramped access corridor like an unstoppable killing machine. Selene fired her Beretta at will, shooting every hairy apparition that dared to show a flash of yellow fang or claw.

An unaccountable emptiness afflicted her. This was what she lived for, after all, so why did it now feel so hollow? Killing lycans by the score brought her no pleasure, not while Michael remained missing and in deadly jeopardy.

Viktor expects me to kill Michael, she recalled. *And Kahn and the others will be more than happy to help.*

The explosions had opened a sizable crack in the tunnel's poorly maintained brick wall. Pausing to peer through the gap, Selene spied a vast central chamber, the size of a football stadium. *Some leftover wartime bunker?* she speculated. The massive excavation looked large enough to house a small army of lycans.

Harsh fluorescent lights flickered from inside an abandoned Metro station, located on the perimeter of the central chamber. Her chestnut eyes widened as she spotted a slender brown-haired figure through the windows of the station, fighting to break free from some sort of restraints. She recognized the struggling prisoner instantly.

Michael!

Kahn led the assault team down the stygian corridor, past an apparently empty intersection. His expert eyes and ears were alert to danger. So far, the invasion was going smoothly, but he was taking no chances. The cramped and underlit nature of the lycans' underground lair made it the perfect venue for ambushes and booby traps. They were going have to be extremely careful—and lucky—to avoid losing any Death Dealers in this operation.

There had been no choice but to attack, though. The shocking assassination of Amelia and her entire Council demanded immediate retaliation, especially if the infamous Lucian was indeed still alive and plotting against the coven. Capturing Kraven, and bringing the fugitive regent to justice, was also a priority.

Kahn's cold blood seethed at the thought of Kraven's treachery. To think that Kraven once had been a Death Dealer himself. *Never in spirit,* Kahn admitted in retrospect, and now it appeared that Kraven's greatest accomplishment as a warrior—slaying Lucian—was nothing more than a self-serving hoax. *I should have known,* Kahn thought. He castigated himself for not seeing through Kraven's treasonous deceptions earlier. *Selene tried to warn me.*

At least the stubborn female Death Dealer had been exonerated after a fashion. Kahn had no doubt that Selene would prove herself by eliminating this Michael that Viktor was concerned about. Kahn had fought beside Selene in many a battle. Her commitment to the war could not be questioned.

Something rustled in the darkness behind him. He turned to make sure Selene was still watching his back. To his surprise, she wasn't.

"Selene?"

He whirled around in time to see the tail of her black trench coat snapping around a corner. The flapping garment swiftly disappeared down one of the branching corridors, heading toward only the Elders knew where.

"Selene!"

The crack in the wall was too narrow to squeeze through, so Selene was forced to find another route to Michael. She ran down a muddy tunnel, holding the Beretta in front of her. Brackish water trickled down the moldy walls. Spider webs impeded her progress, clinging to her like filmy fingertips.

Brick and mortar crashed behind her. She spun around and saw two rampaging werewolves explode from a collapsed archway. The gigantic beasts howled at the sight of her and immediately gave chase, pouncing from wall to wall as they charged toward her, fangs bared, eager to tear her to pieces. Froth flew from the corners of their snapping jaws.

Selene ran for her life, firing back over her shoulder. Gunshots echoed loudly in the dusky corridor, and the lead werewolf hit the mucky floor. His furry bulk tumbled end over end, splashing mud and clay everywhere. Smoke rose from the silver-tainted bullet holes in his pelt, filling the tunnel with the smell of burning flesh.

One down, Selene thought, not slowing down for a second. Her lungs sucked down the polluted air as she sprinted at full speed down the tunnel. For all she knew, every second counted. She prayed that Lucian had not already drained Michael of every last drop of his precious blood.

Not far behind her, the second werewolf lunged through the acrid smoke hissing from his dying partner. His powerful hind legs carried him forward by leaps and bounds.

Selene could practically feel the beast's hot breath upon the back of her neck. She tore around a corner, still heading roughly toward Michael, and risked a look over her shoulder. Shit! The werewolf was still in hot pursuit, splashing through the slimy puddles like a veritable hound of hell.

Her head snapped around to see where she was going—and another werewolf suddenly reared up in front of her. An inhuman roar assailed her ears as a monstrous claw swiped at her.

Decades of hardwon battle experience kicked in, and Selene sprang into the air, soaring just below the vaulted ceiling of the macabre tunnel. She arced over the looming werewolf, firing her gun as she smoothly tumbled head over heels.

Silver riddled the beast's skull, and he dropped to his death only a heartbeat before Selene's boots splashed down less than a meter past the exterminated creature. Landing squarely on the floor, she expertly ejected an empty magazine from her Beretta and slammed a fresh one into place.

Two down, one to go. She turned around with deadly speed and opened fire on the onrushing werewolf. White-hot death flared from the muzzle of the Beretta as she nailed the creature in the air above the second lupine fatality. Scarlet flowers blossomed across the monster's furry chest.

The werewolf crashed to earth, twitching spasmodically not twenty paces away from her. Jagged claws flailed wildly, and furious jaws snapped at empty air. The spewing foam around the beast's muzzle took on a crimson hue, but still the creature refused to die.

Selene stepped forward calmly and delivered two point-blank shots to his skull.

Three down.

Kraven nervously inched his way toward the entrance shaft leading back up into the city's Metro system. Judging from the butchered lycan and werewolf corpses strewn about the access corridor, Kahn and his Death Dealers already had blasted their way through this particular stretch of tunnel, making it unlikely that Kraven would run into them on his way out of the underworld.

Or so he hoped.

Bullet holes and fragmented silver shrapnel bore mute evidence to the fighting the corridor had seen. The welter of blood and body parts grew deeper the closer Kraven came to the abandoned elevator shaft, so that he found himself knee-deep in gore, wading through the gruesome leavings of the Death Dealers' passage.

Few would have recognized the once-dashing regent of Ordoghaz. Sweat, mud, and blood dripped from his designer clothes, while his flowing Byronic locks were disordered and plastered to his skull. Jewel-studded rings glittered ironically upon his trembling fingers, multifaceted reminders of just how far he had fallen. He gripped the stolen silver nitrate gun in his sweaty fist.

Selene will pay for this humiliation, he vowed, a truculent expression on his face as he arrived at the bottom of the elevator shaft. Lycan corpses, including two he recognized as Pierce and Taylor, lay in pieces beneath the rising ladders. The brutal deaths of so many vile lycans did little to appease Kraven's sense of righteous indignation. *They will all pay, Kahn and Viktor and the rest. Just as Lucian did.*

Tucking the gun into his belt, Kraven began to climb up the rusty metal ladder. This close to safety, his brain raced ahead, plotting his next move. From the Metro, he reasoned, he could reach the bus to Ferihegy Airport, where any number of escape options presented themselves. (Best to avoid the train station, where Kahn's agents still might be investigating Amelia's death.) As for final destinations, he was probably better off fleeing eastern Europe altogether, perhaps even the Continent. Asia maybe, or South America. *Once I'm safely barricaded in an impenetrable fortress somewhere,* he schemed, *I can begin to rebuild my power. Soren can assist me, if he survives tonight's bloodbath, or perhaps that idiot servant girl back at the mansion . . .*

Climbing hand over hand, he finally reached the top of the elevator shaft. He peeked warily over the edge of the shaft, and his face turned white as a ghost.

There, striding ominously toward the open pit, was Viktor himself. The mighty Elder, restored at last to his full strength, wore the garments and trappings of a medieval monarch, complete with a huge two-handed sword. A dark red robe, brocaded with an intricate design not unlike a spider's web, was draped upon Viktor's regal form. His sacred medallion rested on his exposed chest, and a pair of sharp silver daggers adorned his belt. He advanced from the shadows of the decrepit drainage tunnel as though emerging triumphantly out of the bygone reaches of history.

Three modern-day Death Dealers, clad in contemporary

leather attire, marched behind Viktor, but Kraven barely noticed the superfluous warriors. Viktor alone was enough to strike terror into his heart.

Biting down on his lip to keep from gasping out loud, Kraven let go of the ladder, plummeting more than six meters in the space of a second. He landed with a *splat* in the muck and gore below, his fall cushioned only by the putrefying heap of dead lycans at the foot of the shaft. Rising quickly, he made a move toward the exit, only to slip on the abundant blood and viscera. His feet careened out from beneath him, and he fell backward into the nauseating pool of carnage.

Only the night before, he had sipped cool, refreshing blood from the naked breast of a beautiful vampiress. Now he found himself sprawling gracelessly at the bottom of a stinking sewer, soaked in the unclean blood and filth of butchered, subhuman animals. Could anything be more unfair?

But there was no time to reflect on the gross ignominy of his downfall. Viktor was coming, sword in hand, and Kraven knew he had to get away. After scrabbling through the muck on his hands and knees, Kraven clumsily staggered to his feet. His drenched clothing, which was liberally bedecked with a revolting mixture of blood and sludge, weighed heavily on his shaking frame as he hastened away from the pit into the shattered wreckage of the adjacent corridor.

Selene will pay for this, he vowed once more, *and her lycan lover, too!*

Lucian's quarters.

Every muscle ached as Lucian climbed painfully to his feet. His head spun, and he slumped against the wall, waiting for the dizziness to subside. He could feel the liquid silver burning away at him from the inside out.

Steeling himself to face the worst, he raised his arm in front of his face. The distended veins bubbled and squirmed beneath his skin like wriggling worms. He winced in agony as his hand curled into an arthritic claw. In his heart, he knew it was too late for him; not even Amelia's blood could save him now.

Soon he would join his beloved Sonja in eternity.

"Not . . . yet," he grunted. Gritting his teeth against the pain, he lurched away from the wall. Darkness encroached on his vision, yet he refused to black out. Slowly, one halting step at a time, he staggered out of the dismal chamber.

The end was near, but he had something important to do first: kill Kraven.

The infirmary.

Snapping apart the handcuffs was not enough. Michael still had to break loose from the thick nylon straps binding him to the table. He strained with all his might, calling upon whatever atavistic potential the distant moon had awakened in him, until finally several overlapping strips gave way, freeing his right hand.

That's more like it! Michael thought, elated by his victory. *Maybe I'm actually going to get away from this madhouse.*

A rusty creak interrupted his moment of triumph. At the rear of the lab, beyond the translucent plastic curtain, the door slowly swung open. Heavy footprints, not unlike the ones he had heard on the roof of his apartment two nights ago, stomped on the floor of the dimly lit subway station. A monstrous shape entered the infirmary, its half-human silhouette obscured by the curtain.

Dread washed over Michael. Despite everything that had

happened to him over the past few nights, he had yet to lay eyes on a bona fide werewolf. Now, it seemed, his luck was about to run out.

The nightmarish intruder crept forward, audibly sniffing the faintly medicinal odor of the makeshift laboratory. Michael could hear the beast breathing. Its unseen claws scraped noisily at the floor. A musky animal smell filled Michael's nose and throat.

Overcoming his horrified paralysis, the terrified American desperately groped at the remaining nylon straps, trying to peel them away from his body before whatever was on the other side of the grungy curtain caught up with him.

He didn't stand a chance.

Emitting a fearsome roar, the werewolf reared up behind the curtain, raising claws like scalpels. Michael guessed that the monster had to be seven feet tall at least. *If a werewolf eats another werewolf,* he wondered irrationally, *does that count as cannibalism?*

The creature surged toward him. Michael flinched in anticipation of slashing claws and teeth, then stiffened in surprise as a deafening burst of gunfire splattered werewolf blood all over the dingy shower curtain. The bullet-stricken beast tore right through the plastic sheet and crashed to the floor only inches from Michael, who looked up to see Selene standing a few yards away, smoke issuing from the muzzle of her gun.

Talk about a sight for sore eyes!

Wasting no time, she ran forward and slammed her boot down on the werewolf's neck, cracking vertebrae. The downed creature convulsed reflexively, and Selene methodically fired three more shots into the monster's skull.

"I need to get you out of here," she said to Michael, before he could even lift his jaw from the floor. "Viktor is on his way, and he won't be satisfied until every lycan is dead."

Michael flinched at her terse declaration; it felt weird to be referred to as a lycan. His gaze shifted involuntarily to the monstrous carcass lying bleeding on the floor. *Please tell me I'm not one of those!*

Although he was still in over his head, he understood enough about this insane war to appreciate what Selene was doing for him. "They'll kill you, too," he whispered. "Just for helping me."

"I know," she said, tearing off the last of his restraints. The heavy nylon wrappings succumbed readily to her undead strength, and Michael was free at last. His feet slid from the examination table onto the floor, and he found himself standing in front of Selene, staring into her inscrutable brown eyes. He reached out to her and fell into her passionate embrace.

Her lips found his, and, for a precious instant, they escaped the bloodshed and madness surrounding them. She kissed him hungrily, and Michael was stirred in ways he hadn't felt since Samantha's death. It was almost worth being bitten by a werewolf, he thought rapturously, just to experience this kiss and this woman. *I don't care if she's a vampire . . .*

Gunfire blared outside the infirmary, and Selene reluctantly pulled away from him. They both knew the bloody conflict would not leave them alone much longer. An ancient conflict was barreling toward its genocidal conclusion, unless something could be done to stop it.

"I know why the war began," he told her.

Chapter Thirty-one

Viktor and his hand-picked team of Death Dealers paraded through the battle-scarred tunnels, encountering zero resistance. The bodies of exterminated lycan soldiers were strewn before his path like rose petals.

Kahn and Selene have done well, he noted approvingly. He had confidence that the advance squad of Death Dealers could clear out this rat's nest without his assistance, yet it felt good to go into battle again after fully a century spent interred beneath the earth. He hoped that Selene and the others had left him a few stragglers to dispose of, before he was called upon to exact final justice on both Lucian and the traitor, Kraven.

That, more than anything else, was what had lured him from the familiar comforts of Ordoghaz to this abominable, rat-infested breeding ground of lycan filth. In truth, he had been pleased to learn that Lucian still lived, because it meant that he might once more have Sonja's vile seducer in his power.

I have waited six hundred years, he reflected, *to punish Lucian for desecrating my daughter and inciting this damnable war, but tonight my vengeance will not be denied.*

He looked forward, too, to watching Selene restore herself to his good graces by eliminating the threat of this Michael Corvin. She had been like a daughter to him, ever since he had first granted her immortality, and he could not imagine that she would ever truly betray him for the sake of some meaningless infatuation.

I know her better than that, he mused. *In fact, I created her.*

Where the hell are you, Selene? Kahn wondered as he led the remainder of the assault team deeper into the enemy's lair. It wasn't like Selene to abandon her comrades in the middle of a mission. *There's something going on here I don't understand.*

His rifle ready, Kahn inched his way down yet another unmarked corridor. It had been several minutes since they had encountered any serious lycan resistance, yet Kahn was not about to let down his guard, not while a single werewolf was still breathing.

For perhaps the hundredth time since descending into the underworld, he regretted again that there hadn't been time to manufacture more silver nitrate cartridges before this raid. He and the others were stuck with the old-fashioned, slower-acting silver rounds while that thieving bastard Kraven apparently had pinched the only working prototype of the special silver nitrate gun.

One more reason to string him up like a side of beef when we catch him, Kahn thought vindictively. *Slow impalement on a wooden spike will be too good for him.*

A soft clattering noise caught his attention, and he flashed a hand signal to the commandos behind him. The alert Death Dealers came to an immediate halt while Kahn suspiciously scouted the desolate passage ahead.

Raising the muzzle of his weapon higher, he took a leery

step forward. Something small and insubstantial hit the floor just in front of the toe of his boot, and he glanced upward, searching for its point of origin. His probing eyes, now well adjusted to the murk of the tunnels, spotted bits of dust and powdered mortar sprinkling from the ceiling.

"Watch out!" he shouted. "We're not alone!"

But his warning came too late. With a tremendous roar, a homicidal werewolf came smashing through the exploding brick wall. Kahn spun toward the attacking beast, but before he could shoot, a second werewolf dropped through the crumbling ceiling in a shower of dust and debris.

Caught between the frenzied creatures, Kahn had less than a second to react before the werewolves' claws tore into him, rending leather and undead flesh like tissue paper. The other Death Dealers gaped in horror, watching their esteemed commander get ripped to shreds before their eyes, then opened fire on both victim and predators alike. The last thing Kahn heard, before his immortal life came to a violent end, was the roar of automatic weapons fire cutting down the two werewolves in a hail of unleashed silver.

It seemed a fitting eulogy.

Kraven scurried through the dark underground labyrinth like a frightened rat trapped in a maze. He didn't care where he was going, as long as it was away from Viktor. A blood-soaked parody of his usual elegant self, he held onto the silver nitrate gun for dear life, not that he expected it would do much good against the enraged Elder. Would even ultraviolet ammunition be enough to stop Viktor now that the all-powerful immortal had been restored to his accustomed prowess?

Kraven didn't feel like finding out.

Displaced entrails and ordure squished beneath Kraven's

boots as he treaded softly down a narrow catacomb that seemed to have witnessed its fair share of carnage. The disparate scents of blood, putrefaction, and gunpowder formed a malodorous medley in the smoky atmosphere, and Kraven wondered vaguely who might have won the battle, the Death Dealers or the lycans?

It doesn't matter, Kraven recognized bleakly. *Both sides want me dead.*

He glanced nervously back over his shoulder, watching warily for the silver glint of Viktor's mighty sword, then turned his eyes back toward the winding path ahead. His undead heart missed a beat as he suddenly spotted a crouching werewolf only a few centimeters in front of him.

Kraven swallowed hard. His mouth turned dry as chalk. By the gods, he was practically on top of the hellspawn.

The beast's back was to Kraven, and he appeared to be busily consuming the flesh of a fallen Death Dealer. The bodies of two other werewolves lay crumpled on the floor nearby, their shaggy carcasses bearing the bloody bootprints of a retreating force of vampires or lycans. Grotesque crunching and slurping sounds emanated from the slavering maw of the preoccupied monster as he enthusiastically feasted on the mangled remains of one of Kraven's fellow immortals.

Whom exactly was the beast devouring so voraciously? Kraven was not going to linger in hopes of catching a glimpse of the dead vampire's face. Holding his breath, he stepped backward as softly and silently as he could, retreating the way he had come. He prayed that the gluttonous beast was too immersed in his carnivorous repast to notice his arrival—and abrupt departure.

As quiet as the fleeing vampire was, some stray sound or scent attracted the werewolf's interest. He lifted his massive head from the ravaged torso of his meal and rotated his shaggy ears in Kraven's direction. A second later, he spun around on all fours and attentively sniffed the tunnel behind him.

Kraven was nowhere in sight. His entire brawny physique was squeezed into a dark alcove smaller than even the most minuscule closet back at the mansion. He pressed himself tightly against the slimy, mildewed walls, trying to make himself infinitely smaller and less noticeable. Alas, unlike the colorful vampires of fiction, he could not just turn into a bat and fly away.

He stood there, drenched in sweat and biting down on his own hand to keep from whimpering out loud, until the hungry animal turned back to his grisly feast. The sound of cracking bones and exploding organs followed Kraven away from the horrid scene of the slaughter.

The main chamber.

Soren backed up involuntarily as Raze completed his obscene metamorphosis. The muscular black lycan no longer looked remotely human; instead, an all-out werewolf faced Soren across the muddy floor of the forgotten bunker. Icy water rained down on them, and they splashed through greasy, iridescent puddles as they circled each other in a lethal dance of fangs, claws, and darting silver whips.

That's right, animal, Soren silently dared him. *Just try to get past my whips!* He felt like a lion tamer holding a rebellious carnivore at bay. Gripping a whip in each hand, he snapped the silver lashes in the air between him and the beast. Bright lycan blood stained the tips of the twin scourges. *Let's settle this once and for all.*

Livid red scars marked the werewolf's snout where Soren had slashed Raze's face with his whips. The lycan's clothing lay in a shredded heap at the creature's feet, replaced by a bristling coat of coarse black fur. Cobalt-blue eyes glared at Soren with predatory intent. A low, *basso* growl rumbled from the depths of the werewolf's ample chest.

Taking the offensive, Soren lashed out with his whips again. The silver cables whistled through the rain, but, instead of flinching away from the bite of the striking lashes, the scarred werewolf reached out and grabbed onto a whip with each gnarled claw. Smoke rose from the monster's hairy mitts, as the caustic silver burned the leathery pads of his paws, yet Raze held onto the captured lashes long enough to yank them both from Soren's grasp.

Hellfire! The dark-haired vampire suddenly found himself empty-handed. He reached automatically for his gun, only to remember that the suspicious lycans had confiscated it earlier.

I'm done for, he realized, *but I'll be damned if I'll let any slobbering cur see me afraid.*

"Come on, you motherfucker!" he challenged Raze.

Roaring like an entire pack of lycanthropes, the werewolf lunged at Soren with demonic speed. He slammed into the waiting vampire like a bullet train, knocking him backward into an ankle-deep puddle of turbid water. Soren fought back with everything he had as the two immortals thrashed violently in the sludge. The vampire sank his fingers into the beast's furry neck, trying to keep Raze's snapping maw away from his throat, but the werewolf's heavy forepaws pushed Soren's head and shoulders beneath the surface of the pooling water, causing the vampire to cough and sputter as he lost his hold on the monster's neck.

Raze's lupine snout darted into the shallow depths of the puddle, like a bird of prey diving for a fishy snack, and the turbulent water turned brightly incarnadine as powerful jaws crunched down on Soren's centuries-old skull.

The faithful janissary didn't even have time to wonder how Lord Kraven would survive without him.

Savoring the strength and speed of his wolfen body, Raze exulted as he tasted Soren's brains. The savage joy of the kill delighted the beast Raze had become, and he raised his blood-smeared muzzle from the crimson puddle as his eyes and nose and ears searched avidly for fresh prey.

His bestial prayers were answered by the sight, through a gap in a broken wall, of four more Death Dealers sweeping down the adjacent passageway, led by none other than Viktor himself. His aroused senses registered that the Elder was garbed in the archaic vestments and gilt adornments of a previous era, but the transformed shape-shifter was less interested in Viktor's antiquated apparel than in the savory meat and blood beneath the vampire's robes.

Soren was just an appetizer; Raze wanted more.

Fangs bared, he burst through the wall at the unsuspecting bloods. He pounced first at Viktor, eager to tear out the ancient blood's throat with his teeth. Then he would rip apart the other vampires, just as he had slaughtered Soren and that Death Dealer on the subway tracks two nights ago.

Life was good . . .

But, without so much as batting an eye, Viktor reached out and grabbed Raze by the throat. He effortlessly lifted the startled werewolf with one hand, holding him up and away from him as Raze flailed and twisted in the vampire's grip, snapping fruitlessly at the empty air. He clawed at the outstretched arm keeping him aloft, but his slashing talons had no effect on the impervious Elder. Cold, crystalline eyes regarded him with detached amusement.

What the hell are you? Raze's animalistic brain struggled to comprehend. This was impossible; he had never feared a vampire before.

Until now.

CRACK!

Viktor snapped the brute's neck in an instant, then dropped the lifeless animal to the floor and casually kicked the carcass to the side.

Interesting, he reflected calmly. It had been more than a century since he had killed a werewolf with his bare hands. He was pleased to discover that he still enjoyed the experience. *Some things never grow stale, it appears.*

A chorus of angry shouts disturbed his nostalgic musings. A quartet of bellowing lycans, clad in drab modern clothing, charged around the corner at Viktor and his cohorts. Their grimy faces were contorted with rage, and they brandished their guns and rifles in a berserk fury. "Throw down your weapons!" a particularly unkempt specimen shouted belligerently, aiming the muzzle of a futuristic firearm at Viktor. "We have you covered!"

They want to take me hostage, Viktor realized, grasping the lycans' intentions. A thin smile appeared on his lean, austere features. *How amusing.*

He moved with preternatural speed, so quickly that he appeared to be nothing but a blur of motion. Unsheathing his double-edged sword in a single fluid motion, he surged forward and cleaved the startled lycans into pieces before they could fire a single shot from their superfluously modern weapons. Within an instant, all four insurgents lay in fragments on the gritty concrete floor.

Viktor lowered his sword, his effortless task complete. The resurrected Elder was not even breathing hard, nor had his sluggish pulse quickened at all during the brief, uneven contest. He glanced back at his retinue of Death Dealers and found the younger vampires staring at him wide-eyed. They fumbled with their own firearms sheepishly, embarrassed to have been proven so thoroughly extraneous.

Clearly, it had been too long since these callow Death Dealers had last seen an Elder in action. Viktor hoped that standards had not become too lax during his century-long hibernation. *Yet another lapse to hold Kraven accountable for,* he decided, *once the traitor is cornered at last.*

Stepping over the diced remains of the four lycans, not to mention the dead werewolf to one side, he strode deeper into the enemy's lair. He had wasted too much time in these petty altercations. There were more pressing matters to deal with, now and for all time.

Chapter Thirty-two

*H*and in hand, Michael and Selene hustled through a chain of interlocking bunkers. Through the cracked and unwashed windows of the forgotten chambers, they glimpsed flashes of the brutal conflict being waged throughout the sprawling bunker by vampires, werewolves, and humanoid lycans. Gunshots punctuated the strident screams, curses, and growls coming from all around them. The air reeked of blood, death, and gunpowder.

I don't believe this, Michael thought, aghast at the appalling carnage. It was all he could do to keep his mind on their circuitous trek through the underworld, despite the frightful spectacle confronting him at every turn. *It's like some twisted Transylvanian version of D-Day!*

They emerged from the back of a derelict bomb shelter to find themselves at the foot of a winding metal staircase leading up into the higher reaches of the vast underground complex. A leather-clad vampire lay on the bottom step of the stairway, his blackened body carbonized by a barrage of UV shells. The charred remains were barely recognizable.

"One of Soren's men," Selene pronounced without sympathy. She bent down and plucked a semiautomatic handgun from the corpse's fingers. She tugged back the slide, and an enormous 50-caliber silver bullet racked into position. "Good. It's loaded."

She pressed the heavy weapon, weighing at least four pounds, into Michael's hands. He stared numbly, feeling the unaccustomed weight of it in his hand. Before a few days ago, he had barely ever handled a gun before, let alone been expected to fire it at another living being. *I'm a doctor,* his brain objected silently. *I should be playing medic, not soldier.*

But apparently there was no other choice, not if he and Selene wanted to get out of this freaky bloodbath alive. And Michael found that he very much wanted to keep living, lycanthropy and all, if only to explore this strange new love he had found with Selene.

They cautiously climbed the stairs, coming finally to an arched doorway maybe fifteen feet above the main floor of the bunker. Icy water continued to fall from the ceiling of the central excavation, and Michael hoped they wouldn't have to go out under the deluge.

Leading the way, Selene coolly entered the shadowy chamber beyond the doorway. A cacophonous roar greeted Michael's ears, and a werewolf exploded from the darkness. His razor-sharp claws sliced downward, right through Selene's shoulder and into her left thigh.

She shrieked in pain, dropping to one knee. Her gun went flying off down the stairs, rattling loudly against the descending steel steps. Reacting instinctively, Michael fired his own pistol at the attacking monster, who yelped sharply as the silver bullets struck him directly in the chest. Blood spouted from his furry coat, and the wounded werewolf jerked frenetically, the flash of the muzzle blasts creating a strobe effect as the beast went through its violent death throes.

By the time the werewolf thumped, lifeless, to the floor,

Michael felt as though he had been firing at the monster forever. Convinced the creature was really dead, he dropped down beside Selene and frantically checked her wounds. Her ivory skin pulled tightly over her graceful features, Selene sucked down the pain and tried to minimize her injuries.

"I'll be fine," she insisted.

The gaping red gashes would be enough to send an ordinary human being into shock. Michael prayed that Selene knew what she was talking about.

"I've heard that before," he said drily. As he recalled, she'd said pretty much the same thing before collapsing at the wheel of her Jaguar and driving them straight into the Danube. *Let's hope this turns out a little better,* he mused.

Selene smirked and took his hand. As gently as he could manage, Michael helped her to her feet, and they stumbled together past the deceased werewolf. Selene hobbled badly, despite her best efforts, but they pressed onward, lacking any better alternative. Michael wondered if he dared take the injured vampiress to an emergency room if and when they made it back to the surface.

I suppose an immediate transfusion would be the best prescription, he speculated, thinking like a doctor. How else did you treat a wounded vampire except with plenty of fresh blood? *Courtesy of her good friends at Ziodex, no doubt.*

"Come on," she murmured weakly. "This way."

A rusty iron door led to what appeared to be a working generator room. A blocky, diesel-powered generator, about four feet tall and ten feet long, chugged away at the other side of the bare, utilitarian compartment. Michael guessed that this was where the lycans got the power to run the underworld's meager lighting. The room's walls had seen better days; broken gaps in the brickwork offered unobstructed views of the bunker's main chamber, where the unchecked rain could be seen pouring past the open windows toward the ground floor fifteen feet below.

Ironically, the generator room itself was lit by a single naked light bulb dangling from the ceiling. Michael couldn't tell at first if they had hit a dead end or not. He peered into the unlit room, looking for another exit, only to find himself face-to-face with a vengeful-looking apparition covered from head to toe in dirt and blood.

Who? he wondered.

Kraven! Selene gasped.

The treacherous regent looked like hell, his once fine apparel literally caked with mud and gore. Selene's eyes widened in alarm as she spotted the stolen silver nitrate gun in his right hand.

She tried to lunge for the gun, but she was too weak. Before she could warn Michael, or even try to reason with Kraven, the experimental pistol whipped upward and fired point-blank into Michael's chest.

Blam-blam-blam! Michael fell backward onto the floor, three grisly bullet wounds showing through his punctured T-shirt. He began convulsing immediately, as the liquid silver raced through his veins. Volcanic tremors rocked his body, and an anguished grimace disfigured his face. Bloody foam bubbled up through his lips, signifying serious internal injuries as well as the corrosive silver poisoning.

Her moist brown eyes gleaming like gemstones, Selene collapsed next to Michael. Her own grievous injuries were forgotten as she stared in abject horror at the swollen silver veins creeping across his cheeks and forehead. He moaned piteously as Kraven's poison spread remorselessly through his body.

For one heartbreaking instant, he managed to meet her grief-stricken eyes, then his own bloodshot orbs rolled upward in their sockets, exposing their whites. His muscles sagged as he slipped into unconsciousness, looking only moments from death itself.

No! Selene thought in despair. *You can't die now. Not when I've finally found you!* She felt her only hope for love and happiness dying with Michael. *I never even knew what I was missing before!*

Who would have guessed that the imminent death of a lycan could affect her so? *Despite my so-called immortality,* she realized bitterly, *I haven't really been alive since my family died more than a century ago. I have been just what the mortals think we are, one of the living dead.*

Her unconcealed sorrow infuriated Kraven, who grabbed her roughly by her injured shoulder and tried to haul her to her feet. "That's enough!" He sneered in disgust. "You're coming with me!"

Selene couldn't believe that Kraven still thought she belonged to him. "Never!" she answered. Only the smoking gun in Kraven's hand, and the fact that her own gun had been lost on the stairs, kept her from killing him where he stood, despite her injuries. "I only hope I live long enough to watch Viktor slowly choke the life from you."

Hatred blazed in Kraven's eyes. "I'll bet you do, but let me tell you a little something about your beloved dark father. He's the one who killed your family, not the lycans."

What? Selene had thought her life and beliefs could not be overturned even further, but she had been wrong. Kraven's shocking declaration hit her like a blast of killing sunshine. Visions of her slaughtered family—her martyred mother, father, sister, and nieces—flashed through her memory like images from a never-ending nightmare. She

351

saw once again her father's skull broken open, exposing the bloody pulp inside.

Viktor? she thought unsteadily. *Viktor was responsible?*

"He never could follow his own rules," Kraven elaborated. He grinned broadly, enjoying her distress. "No cattle blood for him, not when he thirsted for something more stimulating." Kraven shrugged, taking Viktor's alleged atrocities in stride. "I cleaned up the messes for him, kept his secrets."

No! Selene thought desperately. *It can't be true.* She wanted to plug her ears, keep out Kraven's horrendous accusations, but somehow, deep down inside, she knew he was telling the truth. The awful realization washed over her like a tidal wave. *How could I have been so blind, so naive?*

"It was he who crept from room to room," Kraven said gleefully, "dispatching everyone close to your heart. But when he got to you, he just couldn't bear the thought of draining you dry like the others. You, who reminded him so much of his long-lost Sonja, the precious daughter he condemned to death."

Selene nodded, choking back a sob. *I thought of him as a second father,* she admitted, *and for these years, I never suspected him for a moment. I spent more than a century killing lycans for a crime they never committed.*

She felt utterly lost and defeated.

But Kraven was not done with her yet. He tugged once more on her wounded shoulder, trying to force her to her feet. "Now, come. Your place is at my side."

My place is with Michael, she resolved. She glared up at the loathsome, blood-caked regent. No words were needed to convey the full extent of her disgust.

"So be it," Kraven said, abandoning his obscene infatuation at last. He pressed the muzzle of the silver nitrate gun against her temple.

Do it! she dared him, her scornful gaze not faltering for a heartbeat. With Michael dying, she had nothing left to live for.

Kraven nodded grimly. He slowly squeezed the trigger.

A bloody hand grabbed his ankle, startling Selene and Kraven alike. He looked down in surprise to discover Lucian's withered hand clutching him.

The legendary lycan warrior looked much worse than Selene remembered him from their brief encounter at Michael's apartment building. His bearded face was ashen and streaked with throbbing, dull-gray veins—just as Michael's was. His breath rattled hoarsely in his chest as he crawled pathetically on his hands and knees, shaking with violent tremors. Selene guessed at once that Michael had not been the first victim of the stolen silver nitrate gun.

Kraven's smug laughter confirmed her suspicions. He sneered at Lucian's lamentable condition, taking pleasure in the lycan's dying moments. It appeared that he finally had vanquished the infamous lycanthrope after all.

But Lucian still had one more trick up his sleeve—literally. Biting down on his lip, he mustered his remaining strength and lifted his head to stare balefully into Kraven's eyes. Then a spring-loaded black blade shot out of the sleeve of his jacket and into Kraven's leg.

A phantom pain stabbed Selene in the shoulder as she remembered the same blade coming through the roof of the Jaguar. She hoped that the vicious blade hurt Kraven as much as it had hurt her.

Kraven collapsed to the ground, yelping in agony. As he fell, the blade twisted in his leg and snapped in half, sending another spasm of pain through the writhing vampire regent.

Looking across Kraven's fallen body, Selene and Lucian locked eyes uncertainly. The dying lycan's gaze shifted from Selene to Michael and back again. A strangely wistful expression came over the dreaded warrior's face, and Selene wondered just how much Lucian had seen and heard in the last few minutes.

Her own gaze was drawn inevitably to the gleaming pendant around Lucian's neck. *Sonja's pendant,* she now knew, recalling the story Michael had hurriedly told her back in the infirmary, about how this hellish war had begun. *Lucian and Sonja.* They had also defied Viktor's Draconian wrath to love each other despite the boundaries between their two species, and they had paid a terrible price for their passion, just as she and Michael were doing.

Did Lucian understand how history was repeating itself? Perhaps.

"Bite him," he croaked hoarsely.

At first, she didn't know what he meant. Then she remembered what that captured lycan scientist had explained before: "Half vampire, half lycan. But stronger than both."

Could it be true? Was there actually a chance? In theory, Michael's blood possessed the unique ability to absorb both lycan and vampiric attributes, but was she willing to risk poisoning Michael further, on the word of a lycanthropic mad scientist? Uncertainty flooded her face, and she stared anxiously at Lucian, who implored her urgently.

"Do it . . . it's the only way to save his life."

A bittersweet smile manifested itself on Lucian's stricken features as Selene nodded and turned back toward Michael. Only a few centimeters away, likewise sprawled on the gritty cement floor, Kraven winced mightily as he pried the broken blade out of his skewered leg. His pain-filled eyes blinked in surprise as he saw Selene dip her lips toward Michael's bare neck.

Surrendering to a profound longing she had not dared to acknowledge before, not even to herself, Selene opened her mouth wide and sank her fangs deeply into Michael's throat.

Yes! she thought ecstatically. *At last!*

"What the hell are you doing?" Kraven yelled at Selene. The horrified outrage in his voice was music to Lucian's ears.

"You may have murdered me, cousin," the lycan taunted Kraven with his dying breath, "but my will is done regardless."

If only Viktor could be here to share this moment as well, Lucian mused. His war finally over, he sagged limply upon the floor. He could feel the deadly silver nitrate completing its malignant work. His broken heart burned like a thing afire. Thin tendrils of yellow smoke rose from his lips and nostrils as his internal organs combusted volcanically.

The hour is come, my love, he thought, at peace despite the blazing pain consuming him. In his mind's eye, he could see the radiant face of the incandescent vampire princess who had won his heart so many centuries ago. *You need wait for me no longer. We will be together again.*

Not content to let Lucian die of silver poisoning, Kraven snatched up the silver nitrate gun from where it had fallen and leveled it at Lucian.

Blam!

Lucian, champion of the lycanthropes, was dead. This time for certain.

Michael's hot blood coursed down her throat. Even tainted with silver nitrate, which was entirely harmless to

355

her, the taste of him inflamed her senses. Her lips pressed tightly against his jugular while her tongue lapped at the crimson stream leaking from his neck. She sank her fangs into his flesh as deeply as she could, fighting the temptation to suck every last drop of his blood from his body.

By the Ancestors! she thrilled, finally understanding what it truly meant to be a vampire. *I never knew it could be like this!*

She had to remind herself that the idea was not to drain Michael but to infect him with the vampiric strain of the original mutation. Reluctantly, she withdrew her fangs and looked down at Michael anxiously. *Was that enough?* she worried. She had never tried to change a mortal before, let alone a lycan. *Have I saved him or ensured his death?*

Before she had a chance to find out, a powerful hand grabbed her by the collar and yanked her away from Michael. A second later, that same hand threw her forcefully into the nearby generator, so that she smashed into the bulky steel mechanism before tumbling to the floor. The steady thrum of the generator was joined by the sudden ringing in her ears.

"Where is he?" Viktor demanded. "Where is Kraven?"

The Elder stood over her, clad in the forbidding raiment of a medieval warlord. An enormous sword was sheathed at his side, while three undead bodyguards blocked the exit.

Conditioned to obey Viktor, despite everything she had just learned, Selene searched the chamber for Kraven, but the wily ex-regent was nowhere to be seen. Only a broken shard of Lucian's blade lay on the floor where Kraven had been moments before. *Damn him!* Selene fumed, realizing that Kraven must have slipped away while she was biting Michael. *That lying bastard's got more lives than a cat!*

Viktor's merciless eyes scanned the compartment as well. His saturnine expression darkened as he saw for himself that Kraven was missing. Scowling, he turned his attention to Michael instead. The moribund American was still lying helplessly on the floor, his eyes rolled up in their sockets. Silver nitrate leaked from the bullet wounds in his chest, and his limbs jerked spastically. The mark of Selene's crimson kiss glistened wetly on the young man's throat.

Viktor glared at the bite wound for a long moment. Then he turned and locked eyes with Selene. A look of extreme disappointment curled his patrician lips. His saddened gaze made it crystal clear that, to his mind, she had failed him again.

"Very well," he stated mournfully. "I'll do it myself."

He stepped toward Michael, reptilian eyes burning with lethal intent. Lost in his private battle against the toxic silver ravaging his system, Michael made no effort to save himself, was not even aware of the danger.

"No!" Selene cried out. She sprang forward to stop Viktor, but the mighty Elder knocked her aside with a Herculean blow that sent her flying across the generator room into the opposite wall. The chipped and flaking brickwork grazed her forehead, causing blood to trickle down her face. Dazed, she crumpled to the floor.

Hissing like a serpent, Viktor grabbed Michael by the throat and swiped him off the floor with a single hand. Fangs bared, the Elder savagely slammed Michael against the brick wall separating the generator room from the central chamber. Bones snapped and concrete crumbled as, with one smooth movement, Viktor shoved Michael all the way *through* the dilapidated wall, creating a jagged hole that looked out over the rain-filled bunker.

Selene watched in dismay as Michael, along with an avalanche of broken concrete, plummeted through the gap, falling five meters to the flooded floor below. She heard him land with a splash—and a sickening, bone-crunching thud.

Viktor smiled and wiped his hands together, as though finished with a mildly unpleasant chore. He turned back toward Selene, his eyes still vibrant with hatred. The shaken vampiress cringed as he stepped toward her. She glared at him, deeply hurt, like a blameless child who has been struck out of hand by a drunken parent. Viktor halted, taken aback by the betrayed expression on her face and the rivulets of blood coursing down her cheek. His own features softened and the fury slowly departed his gaze.

"Forgive me, child," he murmured. He held out his hand, intending to gently stroke her forehead, but she flinched from his touch.

Selene recalled everything she had learned down here in the underworld. She stared back at him defiantly.

"It wasn't the lycans!" she accused him. "It was you!"

Chapter Thirty-three

Although nearly comatose, Michael felt the tremendous jolt of his crash landing on the floor of the bunker. The jarring impact knocked the breath from his laboring lungs and sent shock waves racing through his entire body. He splashed down into an oily puddle, landing flat on his back. Half submerged in the greasy water, he vaguely registered his new surroundings, even as another wave of cataclysmic tremors shook his body.

His blood fizzed and fermented in his veins and arteries. Shattered bones shifted and warped as though possessed by demons. A peculiar throbbing sensation raced from the stinging bite marks on his neck to the inner depths of his broken body. The injured wolf inside his brain howled louder than the explosions and gunfire echoing through the endless artificial caverns. He felt the Change beginning.

Yet, over the din, he still could hear Selene's voice crying out somewhere high above him. "It wasn't the lycans!" she shouted angrily at an unknown foe, perhaps the same one who had just hurled Michael through the solid brick wall. "It was you!"

Despite the pain and trauma of his transformation, Michael's soul responded to the woman's voice. His beleaguered awareness, lost in the primal heart of darkness, crawled fitfully up toward the light.

Selene!

Fluttering eyelids peeled open. Inhuman eyes glowed cobalt blue.

"This is all because of you!" she accused Viktor.

For the first time in ages, a look of discomfort, perhaps even of guilt, passed over the Elder's face. He turned hastily toward his Death Dealer escorts. "Leave us!"

The obedient vampires promptly withdrew, closing the door behind them. Selene found herself alone with her immortal sire.

She climbed to her feet and faced him, unafraid. Michael was gone, thrown to his death before her very eyes, so what else did she have to fear? "What are you going to do?" she challenged him harshly. "Kill me, like you did my family?" Centuries of misplaced anger infused her voice with ringing fervor. "How could you bear my trust, knowing that you murdered my family?"

Viktor stepped forward, his eyes filled with sympathy. "Yes, I've taken from you," he confessed. "I've hurt you. But I've given so much more. Is it not a fair trade for the life I've granted you? The gift of immortality?"

The shock of his damning admission washed over Selene like a bitter tide. "And the life of your daughter?" she challenged him. "Your own flesh and blood?"

Her words struck Viktor with greater force than any werewolf's slashing claws. Pain deepened the somber lines of his face as he looked dolefully at Lucian's corpse, lying prostrate upon the floor. The Elder crouched down beside his ancient adversary and tugged the metallic pendant from Lucian's neck.

Selene *almost* felt sorry for him.

The Change gripped Michael again, just as it had in the back of the police car a few hours ago. His body writhed and contorted in a series of shock-inducing paroxysms that tore his soggy garments into ribbons. Fractured bones reknit themselves in new configurations. Protean skin and muscle expanded, gaining mass and density at superhuman speed. Glossy black hair sprouted from Michael's pulsating hide as fangs jutted sharply from his gums. Barbed claws extended from his fingertips, scratching senselessly at the rocky floor beneath the freezing water. His spine stretched and twisted, and he felt his entire body morphing into the primitive shape of an animal. The howl of his inner beast drowned out the world.

Viktor rose slowly from the dead lycan's side. He gazed down at the gleaming pendant resting in the palm of his hand. Ancient regrets, buried for centuries, surfaced in his pain-filled eyes and voice.

"I loved my daughter," he declared, "but the abomination growing in her womb was a betrayal to me and the entire coven." He glanced vengefully at Lucian's corpse, his scorching eyes all but incinerating the lifeless remains of his daughter's lover. "I had no choice."

Selene backed away from Viktor, suspecting that she might soon be joining Sonja and Lucian in the afterlife.

Michael Corvin was gone. In his place, a full-blooded werewolf lay sprawled on the floor of the bunker. The falling rain baptized the newborn monster, initiating him into a new and fundamentally altered existence.

But the transformation was not complete.

The lupine monster spasmed explosively, arching his back in agony. His hairy limbs splashed against the iridescent surface of the puddle, sending sprays of oily water flying in all directions. An anguished roar erupted from the creature's powerful jaws as the Change began to *regress*, taking Michael back through the singular genetic mutations behind the evolution of both vampires and werewolves.

The disembodied howl within his skull was joined by the flapping of invisible leather wings. Michael screamed through mutating vocal cords as he suffered the cataclysmic birth pangs of a brand new life form.

Viktor's eyes were moist, but his voice was cold.

"I did what I had to do to protect our species," he said without remorse. "As I am forced to do yet again."

He unsheathed his sword, which was stained with freshly spilled blood, and advanced toward Selene—until a blood-curdling wail came from the bunker outside. The eerie cry rose from the floor of the central chamber, many meters below the generator room.

Michael? Selene wondered, afraid to let herself hope that he was still alive. She listened to the bizarre wail in puzzlement. The tortured keening didn't sound human—or lycan.

Is that you?

Sword in hand, Viktor whirled toward the ragged crack in the wall. He peered through the gap at the inundated floor below. His brow wrinkled in confusion.

Michael Corvin was gone.

He turned back toward Selene, intending to extract from her the likely whereabouts of her lycan paramour. *Corvin will die by my hand before this night is through,* he vowed solemnly. It had taken six centuries for Viktor's vengeance to catch up with Lucian; he did not intend to wait that long again.

"Where—" He began his interrogation, only to be caught off guard by a roundhouse kick to his chin, delivered with extreme vigor by Selene herself. His head jerked sideways, and his bloody sword escaped from his fingers, flying out through the gap in the wall. He heard it land with a splash on the floor of the chamber below.

His temper flared murderously. *You dare strike your sire?* he railed silently at Selene. *So be it.* The treasonous slut had signed her own death warrant. He would not wait to capture her lover before consigning Selene to oblivion. *I should have killed you with the rest of your insipid family years ago!*

Turning his gaze ahead once more, he expected to see Selene putting up some futile show of resistance. Instead, he got the shock of his immortal existence as he found himself face-to-face with . . .

What? The uncanny creature standing before him, defending Selene from his approach, was like nothing Viktor had ever seen before. Not quite vampire, not quite werewolf, but something uniquely in between. Striking in appearance, the hybrid immortal looked more human than beast and more demon than human.

Jet-black eyes gleamed like quicksilver. An iridescent, metallic sheen added luster to his rippling flesh, giving him the look of a classical sculpture brought to life. His hairless chest gleamed beneath the flickering lights, while his soggy trousers preserved a modicum of decency. Although his handsome features were essentially human once more, sharpened teeth and nails betrayed his predatory nature.

"Michael?" Selene whispered in awe.

Viktor had only an instant to react to the unnerving sight of the hybrid creature and to marvel at the preternatural speed at which Corvin had returned to the generator room. Then Michael's clenched fist slammed into Viktor's chest with the force of a wrecking ball, driving the Elder's silver medallion into his chest and sending Viktor through what was left of the crumbling brick wall.

He fell fifteen feet before crashing into the muddy floor of the main chamber. His momentum sent him tumbling through the filthy muck until he smacked into a pair of unmoving, adamantine legs. He looked up in stunned amazement to see Michael Corvin staring down at him with his unearthly black eyes. *What?* he thought, flabbergasted. *How the devil did he get down here so quickly?*

He hurriedly rolled in the opposite direction and scrambled to his feet but once again found Michael standing directly in front of him. The hybrid's speed was astounding even by immortal standards. Viktor suddenly felt something he hadn't experienced in untold centuries: fear.

But he declined to let his fear undo him. *No mongrel freak will make me yield,* he resolved, girding himself for the battle to come. He faced off against Michael beneath the cascading rain. *My blood is pure. My will is supreme!*

They circled each other menacingly, searching for an opening, clawed hands poised to strike. Viktor's reptilian white eyes contrasted sharply with Michael's roiling black orbs. Two sets of pearly fangs gnashed in primal warning.

As if responding to some subliminal signal, they surged toward each other simultaneously. The past collided with the future as the Elder vampire and the newly created hybrid smashed together with stupendous force, sending seismic vibrations throughout the underworld. They traded colossal blows, hammering each other like warring gods.

The entire bunker trembled.

The earth-shaking jolts brought every other conflict to a halt. All around the vast subterranean complex, vampires, werewolves, and lycans stopped fighting as the epic clash commanded their rapt attention. Equally spellbound, they flocked to the catwalks and subway tracks overlooking the arenalike central chamber, jostling for a better view of the battle royal going on below. Even the dimmest and most bloodthirsty spectator realized that the history of his shadowy, secret world was being rewritten before his very eyes.

Michael had never felt so powerful, so unstoppable. Superhuman strength and energy throbbed in his transformed muscles and sinews, while his every sense was ten times keener than ever before. All his fear and confusion were things of the past. Michael didn't know exactly what it was that he had become, thanks to Selene's miraculous kiss, but he knew that he was now something infinitely more majestic than just a simple American medical student.

Bring on the vamps and wolves! He exulted, reveling in his new-found courage and vitality. *I'm not afraid anymore.*

He recognized Viktor from Lucian's memories, and his firsthand experience of Lucian and Sonja's tragic saga only heightened his desire to destroy the pitiless vampire tyrant, besides the fact that Viktor had tried to kill both him and Selene. He slashed at the Elder with his taloned hands and snarled at his enemy through clenched white fangs. In his heart, he knew that he was stronger than any mere vampire.

But Viktor had centuries of battle experience to draw upon. In a stealthy move, he caught Michael by surprise by dropping down and swiping Michael's legs out from under him. It took only a split second, and the next thing Michael knew, he was flat on his back with Viktor hammering him from above.

The vampire's naked fists fell like a meteor storm against Michael's face and stomach. His body shuddered before the blows, and his skull rang like the interior of an enormous cathedral bell. His vision dimmed as he felt himself blacking out.

Like every other soul in the underworld, Selene watched the fierce contest with both wonder and apprehension. She peered down through the shattered wall at the titanic battle between Viktor and Michael, knowing that her own immortal existence depended on the outcome.

Was it even possible for Viktor to be defeated?

Out of the corner of her eye, she caught a flurry of movement at the periphery of the scene. The instincts of a veteran Death Dealer fired up, and she turned quickly to see Viktor's three armed bodyguards drop from the top of the stairway to the floor of the bunker many feet below. They splashed to earth only a few paces away from Viktor and Michael and raised their automatic pistols ominously.

Selene didn't wait for them to get a clear shot at Michael. She sprang from the demolished generator room into the air above the bunker, landing nimbly right behind the three Death Dealers. Without even pausing to catch her breath, she snapped the neck of the first warrior, elbowed the second one in the throat, and snatched his gun from his hand.

Blam-blam-blam! Death blazed from the muzzle of the captured weapon, and three seconds later, a trio of corpses littered the ground. Vampire blood joined the rippling puddles of water flooding the floor of the bunker.

The massacre was over before Selene had a chance to re-alize that she had just killed three of her fellow Death Deal-ers. A gnawing sense of horror momentarily stopped her in her tracks. *Forgive me,* she thought. *I never wanted to slay my own kind.*

She would have no regrets, however, about executing Viktor for the murder of her mortal family. Gun in hand, she whirled around to blow Viktor away, but the indomitable Elder was still too fast for her. A jarring blow knocked the gun right out of her hand, and Selene gasped to see Viktor directly in front of her, less than a meter away.

"How sharper than a serpent's tooth," he whispered, quoting the Bard, "it is to have a thankless child!"

Before she had a chance to react, Viktor's open palm slammed into her like a battering ram, propelling her halfway through the nearest wall. Rock-hard chunks of con-crete tumbled down into the muddy water as Selene slid into the churning ooze. A fresh gout of blood streamed from beneath her hairline.

With Viktor briefly occupied with Selene, Michael seized the opportunity to haul himself to his feet. His ebony eyes widened as he spotted Selene's battered body slumping into the sludge, apparently out cold—or worse. He sloshed loudly through the ankle-deep water, rushing to her side.

"Selene!"

Even his voice had been transformed, becoming deeper and more resonant. His heartfelt cry echoed throughout the vast excavation, reaching the ears of werewolf and vampire alike.

"Selene!"

To his relief, her eyes slowly flickered open.

Thank God! he rejoiced, intent only on her. He wasn't

going to let her die, not like Lisa. This time, he had the strength to drive death away, just as Selene had brought him back from the abyss. *What's the good of all this incredible power if I can't save the only person who matters to me?*

In the rush of emotion, he forgot about Viktor, until the implacable Elder came swooping out of the rain and shadows, descending feet first like some ravenous bird of prey. Viktor's steel-toed boots smacked into Michael's head with breakneck force, spinning him around and sending him flipping head over heels.

He crashed facedown into the muck, stunned senseless.

Viktor moved in for the kill.

Selene saw Michael fall before Viktor's assault. Ice-cold blood dripped into her eyes, and she wiped it away with a frantic motion. She lurched forward, desperate to come to Michael's rescue, but the bunker spun around her vertiginously, and she dropped limply back into the mud, still too dazed and dizzy to get up. Her blurry eyes searched the flooded floor, looking for something she could throw at Viktor, just to distract him for a second or two.

Her anguished gaze fell on a swath of silver-plated steel glistening in the rain not three centimeters away.

Viktor's sword!

The abomination had to be destroyed.

Viktor waded determinedly up behind Michael. He grabbed the hybrid creature by the back of his neck and began to choke his obscene life from his body. Michael gasped for breath, and the veins on his throat bulged tautly beneath his skin.

"Time to die," Viktor decreed. "And then your traitorous consort will suffer the same fate."

A glint of light caught the Elder's eye, and he looked up to see a flash of gleaming metal in the rain. Selene appeared behind the metallic shimmer, landing behind him like a jaguar, with Viktor's own sword clutched within her grip.

Again she defies me? Is there no end to her perfidy? Dropping Michael into the muddy quagmire, Viktor turned to face Selene. His fiendish quartz eyes burned with fury, and he tugged the two silver daggers from his belt, gripping one in each hand. He opened his mouth to denounce her, but to his shock, bright arterial blood gushed forth instead of words.

What in the Ancestor's name? he wondered in confusion, staggered by the scarlet fountain cascading from his own lips. *How can this be?*

He stepped forward uncertainly, and Selene held up the sword. The edge of the silver blade was slick with newly liberated blood. Viktor's jaw dropped, spilling more blood into the murky waters below, and he realized that Selene had struck him already.

But I created you! his mind protested, overcome by the tragic irony. *I made you who you are . . .*

A thin red line materialized on Viktor's lordly countenance. The crimson streak ran from the Elder's left ear, right across his cheek, and all the way down to his collar.

The useless daggers dropped from his gloved fingers as he reached upward in a panicky attempt to hold his immortal head together. But it was a wasted effort. A frisson of razor-sharp pain flashed through his nervous system as fully half his skull slid off, splashing into the gloppy water.

The Elder's body stood erect for a moment more, then toppled backward to land with a crash amid the blood and muck. The Elder's lifeless remains were now merely part of the sewage flowing beneath the ancient city.

An era had ended.

That was for my family, Selene thought. Sword in hand, she stared grimly at the severed pieces of the fallen Elder. *And for all the other innocents lost to your evil and hypocrisy.*

Her heart leaped in joy as Michael rose from the ground. Her adoring eyes marveled at the wondrous being he had become. He had transcended his human origins and lycan curse, to evolve into something strange and beautiful to behold.

Who knew that the future held such remarkable possibilities?

He joined her, silently, inexpressible love and passion radiating from his transfigured face. Together they made a slow turn at the base of the massive bunker, surveying their surroundings for any possible threat.

But no attack was forthcoming. Stunned by the momentous victory they had just witnessed, the spectators on the catwalks and elsewhere appeared in no hurry to challenge either Selene or the manifestly dangerous hybrid. Vampires, werewolves, and lycans peered from the shadows, but none of them was brave enough to make a move.

Smart monsters, Selene thought.

Meekly and with little noise, the various creatures of the night scattered, receding into the sheltering darkness of the sprawling underworld. Within minutes, the bunker appeared as empty as the mortals above no doubt imagined the forgotten tunnels to be.

Selene was happy to see them go. There had been enough bloodshed tonight. She retrieved Lucian's pendant from Viktor's remains and pressed the talisman into

Michael's palm. After all, he was now the custodian of Lucian's memories and legacy. Hand in hand, she and Michael made their way across the flooded chamber and started the long trek back to the world above.

Wiping her blood-streaked hair away from her eyes, Selene smiled as she recalled that only two nights ago, she had regarded the possibility of peace with extreme apprehension. She had dreaded facing immortality without any enemies to destroy.

Michael shape-shifted back into his human guise. Selene squeezed his hand, feeling his warmth. He smiled back at her, and she laughed at her foolish fears.

The war was over, but she had found something new to live for.

Perhaps for all eternity.

Epilogue

*H*ours had passed in the silent crypt. The body of the lycan scientist Singe had gone stiff with rigor mortis, but his immortal blood continued to creep slowly across the marble floor of the underground chamber, threading its way through the intricate design containing the sacred tombs of the Elders.

The sanguinary tide passed by Viktor's empty niche, then Amelia's. Yet, with perverse inevitability, it came to rest atop the polished bronze plaque bearing the sculpted letter M.

For Marcus.

Rivulets of lycan blood seeped through the edges of the burnished hatch, slithering downward into the sepulchral cavity where Marcus, the last surviving Elder, hung upside-down inside his tomb, like a slumbering vampire bat. The energizing blood poured over Marcus's emaciated frame, streaming down his skeletal body until it reached the thin, withered lips of a skull-like face.

Minutes passed, until a dormant heart began to beat with growing strength. A sigh escaped the parched red lips, and a pair of hungry eyes awakened deep within the sunken recesses of their matching sockets.

Jet-black eyes, just like Michael Corvin's had become.

Hybrid eyes.

About the Author

GREG COX is the *New York Times* bestselling author of numerous *Star Trek* novels, including *The Eugenics Wars, The Q Continuum, The Black Shore,* and *Assignment: Eternity.* He recently wrote the official movie novelization of *Daredevil* and has also authored novels and short stories based on such popular series as *Roswell, Farscape, Xena, Iron Man,* and *X-Men.* Recent short fiction can be found in anthologies such as *Star Trek: The Amazing Stories; Star Trek: Enterprise Logs;* and *Buffy the Vampire Slayer: Tales of the Slayer, Volume 2.*

Cox also has co-edited two volumes of futuristic vampire and werewolf stories: *Tomorrow Sucks* and *Tomorrow Bites.*

He lives in Oxford, Pennsylvania.

Visit
❖ **Pocket Books** ❖
online at

www.SimonSays.com

Keep up on the latest new
releases from your favorite
authors, as well as author
appearances, news, chats,
special offers and more.

SIMON & SCHUSTER
A VIACOM COMPANY
www.SimonSays.com

Pocket
Books

2381-01

Before *Underworld,*
the war raged on....

UNDERWORLD
BLOOD ENEMY

A Novel by Greg Cox
Based on the characters created by
Kevin Grevioux and Len Wiseman &
Danny McBride

Throughout history, the clandestine conflict
between the vampires and the werewolves has been
fought in the shadows of the mortal world. But as
the nocturnal combat escalates, the bloody carnage
threatens to spill over into the daylight—and now,
no one is safe....

**An all-new prequel novel to the major motion
picture—coming in December 2004**

Available wherever paperback books are sold.